CRIME AND FAMILY

CRIME AND FAMILY

JOSEPH MONTGOMERY

Library of Congress Control Number: 2011961270
ISBN: Hardcover 978-1-4653-0928-0
Softcover 978-1-4653-0927-3
Ebook 978-1-4653-0929-7

This book was printed in the United States of America.

To order additional copies of this book, contact:
Xlibris Corporation
1-888-795-4274
www.Xlibris.com
Orders@Xlibris.com
107072

CONTENTS

AMICUCCI CRIME FAMILY 2010

Boss: Nick Amicucci (imprisoned)
Underboss: Danny Serafini (imprisoned)
Consigliere: Vacant
Acting Boss: Dominic Amicucci

Captains/Lieutenants

Angelo Rea	Fabian Bosca*	Eugene Modica	Mario Marconi	Benny Mancini	Jack Mattea
Frank Noutten	Paul Viccaro	Billy DeStefano	Mickey Taza	Matt Mancini	Frank Zocola
Mike Urnstein	Frank Jagge	Anthony Inserro	Norm Rupolo	Tony Iannetti	Angelo Tomassi
Bobby Rubelli	Alex Harris	George Zito	Rocco DiNapoli	Henry Agosto	Rocco Gurino
Greg Rizzo	Ralph Verilla	Mario Zangarra	Earl Oswald	Moshe Levin	Donnie Vallero
Frank Luisi		Tom Caruso	Jason Paul	George Pirelli	

*Bosca is acting captain for Vinny Jagge, imprisoned.

Character backgrounds available at www.crimeandfamily.com

AMICUCCI FAMILY TREE

sb= see below *= in prison *d*= deceased

Nicodemo Amicucci *d*

Wife: Rosemary *d*

Dominic *d*
Wife: Helen
Nicodemo**sb*
Marie *sb*
William
Daniel
Salvatore
Alberto

Giacomo *d*
Wife: Carmela *d*
Dominic
Nicodemo
Lucia

Raymond*
Wife: Victoria *d*
No Children

James (Ziggy)
Wife: Hillary
Charles *sb*
Timothy
Isabella

Nicodemo Amicucci (Boss)* sister
1st Wife: Laura (died)
Dominic (Acting Boss)
2nd Wife: Helena
Valentina
Salvatore

Marie Amicucci cousin
Husband: George Rea*
Angelo (Captain)

Charles Amicucci
Wife: Lonna
James (crew member)
Patricia
Alexis
Dominic
Benjamin

Character backgrounds available at www.crimeandfamily.com

CHAPTER 1

SUNDAY GATHERINGS

"EIGHT BALL SIDE pocket," called Dominic Amicucci for the winning shot. Dominic nonchalantly drew his cue stick back and sank the eight ball in the side for the win. "Double or nothing?" Dominic asked his cousin.

Angelo Rea pulled a hundred-dollar bill from his pocket and dropped it on the pool table. "No, no thanks. Listen, Dom, I need to talk to you," Angelo answered.

Finally! Dominic had sensed all day that there was something on his younger cousin's mind. "Not here, out by the horseshoe pit," he said, fearful of speaking indoors, due to possible wiretaps.

It was Sunday at the Amicucci household in Emery Beach, and it was never a small event. Every Sunday, Dominic's family gathered at his father and stepmother's house for dinner. The dinners were always massive, even on the tiniest of gatherings. The smell of marinara filled the air as Dominic and Angelo went up the stairs from the basement and into his stepmother's oversized kitchen, heading for the outdoors. Dominic's Aunt Marie, Angelo's mother, spotted the two and called them over. "Where are you two off looking so suspicious?" Both boys' fathers were away doing long prison terms, and she was fully aware that they had followed in their fathers' footsteps.

"Just playing some horseshoes, Mom," Angelo replied, while Dominic reached for a cannoli in front of his aunt. She slapped his hand away.

"What the hell's wrong with you?" she demanded.

"What? I wanted a cannoli."

"After dinner," she told him. Dominic was thirty-seven years old and knew it would always be this way. He'd always be a child to his Aunt Marie. His mother died when he was three, and his father, Nick Amicucci, was now serving twenty years. Nick was a member of the local crime family, and he tended to business with his crime family, but paid little mind to his other family. In essence, Dominic was raised by his Aunt Marie and her husband, George Rea, who was sentenced to life in prison sixteen years ago for murder. "Why don't you go barbecue with your uncles? You could never get your fathers away from those grills, let me tell you." Her younger brothers, Billy and Daniel, were not involved in "the life," and she still hoped Dominic and Angelo would follow their example, but in her heart, she knew it was far too late.

"Maybe later," they said in unison and left, walking through the door wall to the back patio, past their barbecuing uncles and toward the horseshoe pits for a private conversation. The fact that Angelo had waited until Sunday, when the family would be plentiful, to tell Dominic what he needed to tell him hinted to a serious problem, and Dominic was anxious to find out.

The 1990s was filled with government indictments, dismantling the Michigan crime family in which Dominic was raised. For ten years, the government arrested the entire hierarchy of the crime family from top to bottom. By the time the government eased off, the family was so crippled there wasn't even a boss. The end result was a bookie and breadmaker named Nick Amicucci, who rose to a captain after all of the indictments and, simultaneously, killed off any competition, thus taking over the family. Nick's reign lasted only three years on the streets before the feds took him down and gave him twenty years. But during his short reign, he was able to make his crime family strong again. It was strong enough, and when he placed his thirty-two-year-old son, Dominic, in charge, things ran smoothly and no one protested, at least not for a few years, enabling him to still run his crime family from his Michigan prison cell.

The cousins passed the pool and were flagged down by Dominic's half sister, Valentina, who was lying in the sun with her friends, Sabrina, whose father was also in jail, and Angela, Angelo's fiancée. "Dominic, Tom just called me. He said he's on his way here and that he needs a minute with you." Tom was her father-in-law, whom Nick had made a lieutenant, much to Dominic's irritation. Tom was always coming to Dominic, for one thing or another, breaking the crime family's protocol and skipping his own captain.

"He called you, to come see me? Here? On a Sunday?"

Valentina looked toward the horseshoe pits and then back to Dominic. "Why? You're too busy? And besides, Tom's a part of this family and he can have dinner here if he wants."

"Yeah, except he's not coming for dinner," Dominic answered.

"You think he'd come here just to see you? Well, if you can spare a minute for my husband's father, Dom, I'd be personally indebted to you," she said, walking back to her lounger.

"Why aren't you girls in the kitchen cooking with everyone else?" Dominic yelled to the trio.

Only Angelo's fiancée, Angela, responded, lifting her hands in the air, "Just got the nails done. Sorry, guys." And she blew a kiss to Angelo. Their wedding date was less than two months away.

"Let's go," Dominic said, nudging his cousin, and started back to the pits. "What are they going to do? Eat dinner in their bikinis?" Dominic said, causing Angelo to smile at the thought.

When Dominic and Angelo finally reached the horseshoe pit, of course it was occupied. Dominic's half brother, Sal, and their cousin,

Jimmy, were playing. Sal and Jimmy went to high school together and were both aspiring gangsters. Jimmy, twenty-one, and Sal, twenty, felt they were the next generation of the mob. Dominic was under strict orders from his imprisoned father not to allow Salvatore to be involved in the crime family, and Dominic tried his best to mentor his young brother, but all Dominic really knew was "the life." "How can I teach him something else, when I don't know nothing else?" was a constant question to his father. Dominic felt his half siblings, Valentina and Salvatore, were spoiled brats, but what probably irked him the most was the fact that he felt his father had been a good dad to them, a side Dominic didn't see until he was almost a teenager.

But Dominic's third cousin, Little Jimmy Amicucci, was another story. Jimmy had a hard life, and Dominic felt a certain bond with him. Both were raised by the people around them. Jimmy's parents, Charley and Lonna, had been heroin addicts and were a constant embarrassment for the Amicuccis. After years of drug abuse, Charley and Lonna stayed clean long enough to start raising a family and had four children in a five-year span, Jimmy being the first

It was after that five year span when it went bad for them again. Charley's father, Ziggy, went to jail for seven years and Jimmy's parents, perhaps without Ziggy's supervision, went back to using. Ziggy's older Ray turned a blind eye to the problem after Ziggy was away and it became Nick's problem when Ray caught a life sentence.

Nick had been promoted to captain, and he was not going to have any junkies endangering his reputation. His cousin, Charley, and his wife had on several occasions embarrassed the family with their drug use and were once again full blown junkies by the time Nick was in charge. This time around, though, Charley and Lonna had four children, ages five to one.

One day, Nick had his son, Dominic, drive him to check up on Ziggy's family.Dominic drove his father the few miles from Nick's house to thier Uncle Ziggy's house, stopping to pick up pastries at Pasquale's, the local Italian bakery, for their Aunt Hillary. They opened the unlocked door after no one answered the doorbell, and the sight was horrifying. The house was a disaster—tables thrown and broken, TV smashed, nothing looked undamaged. Lying on the couch, with no cushions, was his cousin, Charley, with a needle sticking out of his arm. Dominic ran upstairs and found Lonna naked, curled up by the toilet, laying in her own vomit, but no children or Aunt Hillary.

Charley awoke to what appeared to be his cousin, Nick, with his knee in Charley's chest holding a needle to his eye, slapping him. "Where are your fucking kids, Charley?" he kept repeating as he slapped Charley awake.

"They're gone, they're gone," was all Charley could muster.

The slapping stopped, and Charley was lifted in the air and slammed to the floor. Nick placed one thumb on Charley's throat and pressed; he poised his other hand to stab him in the eye with the needle. "So help me, God. Charley, I will inject your fuckin' eye with this shit if you don't tell me where your kids are." Charley's first reaction was to defecate himself.

Nick raised the needle to stab, and Charley yelled out, "I sold them! They're gone! I sold them for some H. Mom's gone too." And he started sobbing. Nick slowly stood up and dropped the needle on the floor. He turned his back to Dominic and rested his hands on his head. Dominic didn't know if he was holding back his anger or his tears, for he'd never seen his father really cry. His eyes sometimes misted up when it came to Dominic's mother, but that was it. He'd seen his father's rage, but this was odd. He felt something bad was going to happen.

"Dominic, call Mario and Fat Kenny from a pay phone. Tell them to come here and bring shovels and guns. Call Danny, tell him what happened, and tell him to find the dealers. I want them alive," he ordered.

Nick took a whiff of the air and looked at Charley. "You shit yourself, you nasty fuck."

The first thing Danny Serafini did when Dominic gave him the news of the missing family was to send an emissary to inform the crime family's leadership that a made man was in need. Wiseguys flooded the streets, rousting any dealer they knew, desperate to help their brother. Violence and crime was one thing, but when it came to innocent women and children, honor still prevailed.

Mario Marconi and Fat Kenny Infelice, friends of Dominic and associates at their bookmaking operation in Clemency, about twenty minutes from Ziggy's house in Emery Beach, and were ordered to clean up Charley and his wife once they arrived. Neither Nick nor Dominic had even considered cleaning the couple themselves. Once they were coherent, Nick hoped to a get better lead on what happened there that day. After showering, the couple still had no recollection of the events other than Charley remembering his mother yelling a lot. Lonna remembered someone throwing money at them, and her driving and maybe hitting something. Sure enough, an inspection of her car showed the front left fender had hit something.

Nick called the last number on the caller ID, but no one answered—same with the redial button. He was out of options. "Charley, you gotta call your dealers, retrace your steps."

"I owe them all a lot of money. I haven't the foggiest idea who I would've called."

"Who do you owe? They could be holding them ransom," was Nick's logical thinking.

"No, I don't think that's it. I think this has something to do with Dad," he said, meaning his imprisoned father, Ziggy.

Nick yelled, "That's enough," and he knocked Charley down with a right cross to his jaw. Lonna screamed and ran to his side.

"I don't think you see the severity of the situation, Charley. Maybe you don't care about your mother and your kids, but that's my aunt, and those are my cousins, and this just got very bad for you, paisan. Tie them up," Nick ordered. Mario and Kenny bound Charley and

Lonna to chairs that had to be brought down from upstairs because none could be found intact downstairs.

"Your lives depend on the safe return of my aunt and those kids. Anything happens to them, you two get buried up north. Now, when do you two remember buying your last score?" Before anyone could answer, Nick's cell phone rang. It was his wife. "You hear anything?" he asked without saying hello.

"They're okay. Hillary called, looking for you."

Nick visibly sighed in relief, "Where are they?"

"They're at a hotel. She said Charley went crazy because Hillary wouldn't give him any money, so he slapped and kicked Little Jimmy because Jimmy told him to stop yelling at his grandma. He threatened to beat all the kids, Nick, one by one." Nick could tell his wife was holding back tears at the thought of what those poor kids just went through. "She threw some money at him, grabbed the kids, and left. Who does this?"

"The worst kind of junkie, that's who," Nick answered his wife through clenched teeth, glaring at Charley the whole time. Charley felt another defecation coming on now. "Why didn't she call anyone?"

"She said Ziggy luckily called during all of this and heard Charlie yelling and breaking things. He told her to get out and that he'd call you. But he never called here. I've checked the caller ID." Later they'd learn that Ziggy immediately lost his phone privileges when he started slamming the phone into the receiver. After hearing his son's tirade for drug money, the fact that he couldn't do anything about it was enough to make Ziggy decide to retire when he got out in two years and make sure something like this never happens in his family again.

Nick hung up with his wife and ordered the couple untied. "You sold them to your mom, you stupid, drug-using motherfucker, and they're fine, if that matters to you." Nick just stared at Charley, clenching and unclenching his fist.

"Do you remember kicking your son, because he told you to stop yelling at your mother?" Nick asked, inching his way toward Charley until he was right in his face. "Do you?"

"No, of course not, I would never—" And he collapsed to the floor after Nick punched him in the stomach. "It's the drugs, Nick. I need help. Please, it's not my fault."

Nick kicked him the stomach. "What? You need what, Charley?"

"Help, I need help! Please Nick, stop! I'm sorry," he said sobbing.

Nick kicked him again. "Is that what your five-year-old son said, Charley? Help? Did you help him, Charley?" Nick leaned in to hear Charley over his sobs. Lonna could only watch in horror as to what had become of their lives.

"No, I didn't help him. I'm sorry. I'm so, so sorry." Charley continued to sob, curled up in a ball, trying to protect himself.

"No, no, you didn't help him, you worthless fuck. You just kicked him." Nick kicked him again, and everyone in the room cringed at the severity of that kick. Charley started to spit up blood. Lonna started to protest, but Nick pointed his finger at her and told her to "shut up," and she did. Nick kicked him again. "You're not very good at this when they can fight back, are you, Charley? You just kind of curl up and cry, don't you, Charley? Is that what Jimmy did? What did your mother say when you were swearing and breaking her furniture? Not your furniture, Charley, because you don't have a job or any money, Charley, your mother's and your father's furniture, that you feel free to just break. You're not going to pay for this fucking mess, you asshole, I got to. Charley, what the fuck is your purpose?" Nick waited for an answer, but only got sobs in return. "Charley, you gotta give me a purpose, paisan, because I'm not seeing a reason to keep you two around."

Charley suddenly seemed to understand the position he was in. He stopped sobbing and sat up, wiping the blood from his mouth. "I'm still family, Nick, and I'm sorry."

"My family doesn't act that way, Charley. And this is my watch now," Nick said, pumping his chest. "You want to keep blaming the drugs?

You know what my father and grandfather always said, what your uncle and grandfather always said about heroin, Charley? They said, 'You can't cure it, it's like a dog with rabies, you got to put it down.'"

"Nick, please, we'll get clean, we've done it before."

Nick got down on one knee and looked his cousin in the eye. "You're a junkie, Charley. I'm sorry. I love you, paisan, but you're a junkie, like a dog with rabies. Next time will be worse than this, guaranteed." He stood up to walk away.

"No, there won't be a next time, Nick. Please, I swear, I swear on my parents' life," he pleaded, clinging to Nick's leg.

Nick knocked Charley back to the ground with a bitch slap. "Your parents' lives? You mean your mother who you terrified out of here and broke all her shit? And your father who you blamed for the whole thing? You mean them, Charlie? See, even when your life depends on it, you're still just a junkie. You're right about one thing, though, there will no next time." Nick motioned to Mario and Kenny. "Take them up north. Dominic, give them directions to the cabin." It was an isolated cabin, about a four-hour drive away, owned by Danny Serafini's elderly parents. They had used the cabin for hunting years ago, but it had long been deserted since.

Charley and Lonna had to be dragged out, begging and pleading, and thrown in the backseat of a car. Mario and Kenny drove off after a brief discussion with Dominic. Charley and Lonna thought they were being driven to their deaths, but Nick was not planning on killing his uncle's son, just letting him think so for a few hours. Dominic's instructions to his two friends were to take them to the cabin and keep them there until they dried out. Nick would decide when they would come home. Nick disagreed with all arguments to send them to rehab. "It doesn't work," he argued, "relapse, after relapse, after relapse. What's the point? I don't want them kids to ever see that again. My way will work." Nick's way was to leave them there until he felt they could come home, with the understanding that if they use again, they die. The threat of death had worked in every aspect of Nick's life, so why not here, he reasoned.

Nick called Danny Serafini's cell phone from his own cell, which meant they couldn't speak openly but had to speak in code because it was assumed their conversations were being listened to by the FBI. "Danny, let's shoot eighteen holes tomorrow instead of nine." The golf reference was Nick and Danny's code for "all clear."

"Great, that's great to hear. You feel better, huh?"

"Much." There wasn't much for the feds to gather with a conversation like that. And with that, Danny called off the search for the missing family.

Sal hit a ringer at the horseshoe pit and was doing his usual, "take that, bitch."

Dominic called out to his younger brother, "Sal, let me and Ange get a game in."

"Fuck that, Bro, I'm whipping some ass here."

Dominic looked at Angelo in disbelief. "You believe this kid? Little fucking punk . . ." Dominic started walking toward Sal.

Jimmy ended the problem when he interceded, "Let them play, Sal, you win. Here's your $5." Sal took his winnings.

"Five fucking dollars?" Dominic asked.

"And it's all mine," Sal said with a big grin.

"I'll tell you what, big shooter, you guys go shoot some pool, get some practice, and me and Ange will come down and give that five of yours four to one odds."

"Twenty bucks if we win?"

"Good math, Sal. Yeah, twenty against your whole five."

"You're on, sucker. Come on, Jimmy."

Jimmy and Dominic shared a smile. But Dominic's smile had a little more meaning behind it than just Sal's excitement over $5. Dominic knew Jimmy was involved in a crew. Jimmy and the Gurino cousins were working for a bookie, and Jimmy thought Dominic had no idea. After everything Jimmy had been through with his parents' drug addictions, they did stay clean after Nick's intervention, though. The kicker came when Charley was diagnosed with cancer. Treatment was hopeless, and Charley was now at home, waiting to die. Dominic wasn't going to bother the kid about collecting some bets. He believed Jimmy was perfect for their world and told Jimmy's captain, Fabian Bosca, to keep an eye on him.

Once the boys were far enough away, Dominic sought to find out what was bothering his cousin and his capo regime. Angelo Rea became the youngest captain in the crime family's history at twenty-five years old.

"Okay, Ange, what happened?" Dominic asked, expecting the worst.

"Carlo lost the book." The book was the cash that a bookmaking operation keeps on hand to pay off its bettors. In this case, the book was $250,000.

"What do you mean 'lost the book'?" Dominic asked.

"We lost $275 grand last week." Angelo couldn't look Dominic in his eyes.

Dominic took a moment to think, then asked, "$275 grand? It's fucking baseball season!"

"All-star game" was Angelo's answer.

"You're shitting me, right?"

"I wish. Everyone took the under, Kenny and Carlo thought it was a joke and kept all the action." The over/under is a bet on whether a total score will go over the total points, supplied by Las Vegas, or go under the total. All-star games are normally a high-scoring event, and Carlo DeMini and Fat Kenny, neither of whom were actually running the bookmaking operation, decided all the bettors taking the under were suckers and kept all the action. Bets of that size are normally laid off to other bookmakers, some of whom are out of state and with other Mafia families. Carlo and Kenny thought it would be an easy score. The all-star game final was three to one, four runs total and a loss to everyone that took the over.

"So they bet the over. They bet money that wasn't theirs to bet with, and bet the over."

"Not intentionally, Dom, they . . ."

Dominic continued speaking, totally ignoring Angelo's words, "The book was $250,000, that's what you owe. They're on the hook for the other twenty-five grand. And get Jackie Beans off his ass. I want to see him tomorrow. He's supposed to be watching them assholes." Jackie Beans was Jack Pinto, an old friend to Dominic's father, who was officially in charge of running the bookmaking operation. Now semiretired, he only showed up in football season.

"I'm sure Jackie knew."

"You haven't even talked to Jackie yet?" Dominic asked his cousin, incredulously. "$275,000? What the fuck? You waited a week to tell me, for what? Not to talk to Jackie obviously, for what then? Scared? You know what's really scary, Ange? Getting married in two months and going in hock for a quarter mil." Angelo's wedding date was less than eight weeks away, and he had spent about everything he had on it and the new home he had purchased.

"Dom, you know I don't have that kind of money right now."

"I should pay? I could put my little brother in charge of it. At least we'll make money off the juice. You know, Ange, my father always said, 'Show me a bookie that bets, and I'll show you a bookie owned by the sharks.'"

"But I didn't bet it, they should do the borrowing."

"Well, now that sounds like a boss-like decision there, to tell them they owe you the $250. Way to hold them accountable. Either way, though, it's just not my problem." Dominic patted him on the shoulder and turned to leave before saying one more thing over his shoulder. "Oh, and Ange, I better not hear of any bettors not getting paid, capische?"

"Of course not, Dom," and Dominic left him at the horseshoe pit.

Dominic started walking toward the house to play some pool when he saw Tom Caruso, his sister's father-in-law, cutting him off. "Tom, if this is something stupid, I'm not in the mood," and he tried to keep walking.

Tom kept pace. "It'll just take a minute, Dom, please."

Dominic kept walking. "You talked to Eugene first?" Eugene was Eugene Modica, Tom's captain.

"No, I was hoping to avoid that."

Dominic finally stopped. "Dammit. Just because your son married my sister, doesn't mean you skip protocol and come right to me, Tom. What, you wearing a wire?"

"Come on, that's why you won't talk to me? Frisk away then." Tom raised his arms and turned around. "Just need a minute, Dom."

"Knock it off, I'm not frisking you. You got your fucking minute, go."

"I need money."

Dominic got right in Tom's face. "How the fuck do you need money?"

Tom started to talk, then stopped, started, then stopped again. Dominic couldn't take it any longer. "For fuck's sake, Tom, spit it out. Pretend we did the little 'I dragged it out of you' routine, and spit it the fuck out."

"My book got crushed, $400,000. Dom, I don't know what to do," he said, almost crying.

"$400,000? How? And you better not say all-star game."

Tom perked up. "How'd you know?"

"Because I'm the only one with a half a fucking brain around here, that's how. You got played. Find out who the bettors were, or who they bet for. And you gotta fucking suck it up and go see Eugene tomorrow. You should have done that day one. And get the fuck out of here. You're not staying for dinner, you fucking dummy." Dominic, now realizing several crews may have taken the same big hits, thought, *Now may be the perfect time to question Little Jimmy about who he's been collecting bets for.*

Dominic made it to the basement, ignoring anyone who tried to talk to him, and took his cousin, Jimmy, to the horseshoe pits. "Look, let's cut the bullshit. I know you're working for Angie Jars (Dominic had no idea where Angelo Morabito's nickname came from). I told Fabian to keep an eye on you. I'm not busting your balls. I just need to know something."

Jimmy didn't know what to say and blurted out, "Sal's not involved, I swear."

"Well, that's good, because you know I'll break your legs, right?"

Jimmy slowly nodded his head, never taking his eyes off his cousin, not sure where this was going and said, "I'm aware."

"What I wanted to ask you was, does your crew settle up on Tuesdays, or Fridays?" Settling up is the day the bookies pay off their winning bettors and collect from the losers. The old-time books mostly still settled up on Tuesdays, most modern books will settle on Fridays. Books that settled up on Fridays probably already got paid, and there was no chance of getting that money back.

"We settle on Tuesdays, why?"

"Listen, Jimmy, I want you to tell me if there're some unusually large payouts, and where they go. You can do that for me?"

Jimmy, happy to be involved with Dominic but not sure if what he was doing would get him trouble, took a moment to see if he could even get something else out of it. "What's in it for me?"

Dominic laughed. "Good kid. I'll give you three thousand dollars." He wanted his cousin to feel like he was really earning something, and besides, his father was dying.

"You serious? Shit, Dom, I'd have done it just because you asked. But okay, I'm in." Jimmy was really excited.

Dominic put his arm around Jimmy and started walking back to the house. "Let's go eat." Tomorrow Dominic would meet with Jackie Beans and find out what was going on at the book. If Jackie had been there, or been aware, a veteran like himself would have noticed instantly that that was unusual betting and something must be amiss. Jackie, though, will still be able to track the bettors down, and Dominic would send word to his captains to look into any unusual all-star game betting and report back. Dominic wanted some answers before he consulted with his father on Thursday, plus Danny Serafini, the crime family's underboss, would be coming home after his five year prison stint in just two weeks, and Dominic sure didn't want this to be his first impression of how he handled the crime family.

CHAPTER II

BETRAYAL

DOMINIC ARRIVED AT Amicucci Bread Distribution in Clemency, Michigan, at a quarter to five in the morning. It was one of two of the crew's headquarters, the other being Dominic's father's bar, Cooch's Corner, just three blocks away. Both the bar and the bakery have been headquarters to the Amicuccis since the 1960s, when Nicodemo Amicucci, Dominic's great-grandfather took over the Lissoni crews. The bakery, as they call Amicucci Bread Distribution, was a full-scale bakery at one point, but scaled down to bake only breads for distribution to the local grocery stores.

When Dominic turned sixteen and got his driver's license, he started delivering bread, as did his father, Nick, when he got his license. It was everyone's first job in the crew, because in addition to delivering bread, the Amicuccis used the deliveries to pick up and deliver betting money from their book. Nowadays, Dominic or Angelo opens up every morning, ever since Nick, Danny, and Denny Greco went away in 2005.

This early morning, Dominic had planned on meeting with all the crime family's captains, one by one. He brought with him the

Amicucci crew's top enforcer, Eugene "Scary" Scarelli. Scary, at six foot five and a solid three hundred pounds, was a very intimidating individual, not much in the brains department, but that wasn't his purpose. Today, he just needed Scary to look scary.

At five o'clock, the bakers arrived to start baking, and by 6:00 a.m., Gary Nussman arrived to start the trucks rolling out to distribute the breads to local grocery stores. Gary, for the most part, ran the bakery and set up Dominic's appointments while functioning as another enforcer for the Amicucci crew.

Most mornings, Dominic would take a nap on the couch in his father's back office, which was more like an apartment. Complete with a kitchen, shower, couch, and even closets, Dominic would spend days living in bakery without going home, which was only six miles away. There was nothing at home for the thirty-seven-year-old Dominic. His wife of eleven years was shot dead during a mugging gone wrong in 2006, and the couple had no children due to his wife's infertility. Despite the emotional toll of losing his wife, Dominic also had to contend with the pressure from the FBI, who was blaming him for the murder at the time.

This morning, after a shower and a nap, Dominic was eating breakfast with the hulking Scary Scarelli, when Jackie Beans arrived. Dominic took one look at Jackie and could see he had fallen off the wagon. Jackie was a recovering alcoholic who'd lost his wife and son to his alcoholism. Jackie entered the crime family at the same time as Nick, Danny, and George Rea, delivering bread at the same time, and even helped teach Dominic the gambling business. Jackie pulled himself together, got himself made, and ensured his ex-wife and son wanted for nothing. Jackie lived in a small apartment, while he bought his ex-wife and son a nice house away from this life. He was even able to put his son through college. "Jackie, you look like hell. Have some breakfast."

"Nah, I already ate, Dominic."

"Sit down, eat. Obviously, you need it," Dominic said, pointing to a chair. Jackie pulled the chair out and had a seat. "No bullshit, how long you been drinking?"

"Dominic, if I was drinking, I'd tell you 'it's none of your fucking business,' but, I'm not. You want to smell my breath?"

"No, I don't want to smell your breath. Who the hell knows what's been in there!"

"No booze, Dominic, I just haven't been feeling good lately."

"You been to a doctor?"

"Here and there, no big deal."

The two had known each other since the first day Dominic's father took him to the club, and from that day to today, Jackie Beans had been there. "So what the fuck happened with the All-Star game?" Dominic asked.

"I don't know, Dominic, these fucking kids, they're idiots. I gave them too much room. It's my fault, and I'll take care of it."

"We're not paying them," Dominic answered.

"We're not?" Jackie was completely surprised. "No offense, Dominic, but that's not gonna be good for business." Once word gets out that a bookie doesn't pay, bettors will most often find a new bookie.

"Tom Caruso's book got hit, too—$400 grand. I'm going to find out how many others, but we got to track these bettors."

"Well, that's no problem, but if this is what you're thinking, the biggest bets are gonna be dead ends. And shit, Dominic, most of them probably already got paid."

"Yeah, I know. Who do you think would have the fucking balls to try this?"

"Well, if it's just these two books, it could be just a coincidence. But there's probably more. The question is: who would know which books would be dumb enough to keep that kind of action? That's some excellent inside information."

Dominic paused a moment to think, then dropped his head at the recognition. "One of us," he said, meaning a crime family member.

"Smart like your old man, but yeah, if this was New York, there'd be all kinds of groups that could pull this off, but not here. It's gotta be somebody that deals with a lot of our books, another bookie maybe."

It wasn't the best of news for Dominic. He'd just squashed a civil war last year, when a captain, Jerry Lissoni, and, Lenny Silesi, both old Amicucci family friends, went to war to dethrone Dominic.

Dominic leaned in close to Jackie; he had the room electronically swept for listening devices every week, and despite the state-of-the-art alarm system for the building, Dominic paid someone to watch the recordings from the high-tech camera system, looking for intruders. He also used a jamming device that scrambles the area's airwaves, even a cell phone is unusable, so he felt free to speak freely over the small, old wooden table they sat at. "Maybe not just another bookie."

"Think someone's testing you?"

"It hasn't even been a year yet, maybe someone's taking Jerry Lissoni's place, and this is still going," Dominic said, referring to the war.

"I'll start on my end. Guess I better hang around a bit more, eh?"

"Would you mind?" Dominic asked sarcastically. ***This whole thing shouldn't have gotten this far,*** he thought. "Send Fat Kenny over here when you see him, tell him he's done at the book, fat fucker."

"You want me to have Angelo tell him?" ***Angelo is the captain,*** Jackie figured.

"I don't give a fuck, just tell my cousin to stay out of my sight for a few days. Let's you and me meet later tonight, tell me what you've found, okay?"

Jackie hated having to work around his captain just because the boss was mad at him. "Just let me know where and when." Jackie Beans left to go meet up with Angelo at Cooch's Corner.

Gary Nussman returned from his rounds and gave Dominic his itinerary for the day, Dominic and Scary Scarelli, then left for his next meeting; it was 10:30 a.m.

They arrived at the Golden Dream, an eatery in Greektown and the headquarters to Jeff Parkos, who ran a huge bookmaking operation out of the Greektown area. A little over a year ago, it was headquarters to Jerry Lissoni, the mutinous captain. Dominic and Scary took a seat in a corner booth and ordered lunch. Twenty minutes later, Jeff Parkos arrived after getting a call by his staff. As Jeff walked toward the table, he felt a chill that Dominic might just pull a gun and shoot him right here, or the ogre next to him might tear him limb from limb. "Hey, Dominic, what brings you here?"

Dominic's thought was to gauge Parkos's first reaction. "All-Star Game," he said and waited.

Jeff stared blankly at Dominic. "All-Star Game?" he asked him back.

Dominic, in an instant, decided Jeff Parkos was not involved in the plot. "I lost my ass, how'd you do?" he said, changing to a friendlier demeanor.

"Actually, it's the first year we're not paying out. Didn't win much, but it's better than losing on that fucking game, like usual. Pitching duel, who'd have thought?"

"We got a lot of action on the under this year."

"The under? Shit, I laid off action on the over, just like every year. You watch, next year it'll be half and half, over and under."

Parkos hadn't heard of anyone losing on the under apparently, thought Dominic. His cell phone rang, and Jeff left to give Dominic his privacy. "Kenny, where the fuck are you?" Dominic answered Fat Kenny Infelice.

"Where am I? I'm at the bakery, where Jackie told me to go see you at."

"I'm in Greektown, Golden Dream," he answered and hung up.

"Greektown? You know the fucking traffic at this hour out there, let alone here? Dom, I'll be on the road for two fucking hours, and you ain't gonna even be there. Hello? Hello?" Kenny looked down to see the "call ended" message on his phone.

Jack Mattea arrived at the Golden Dream for his meeting with Dominic. He spotted Dominic and his big goon in a back corner and approached the table. “Gentlemen,” Jack and Dominic embraced each other and kissed each other on both cheeks, both showing respect to one another. At eighty-four years old, if you didn’t know his age, you wouldn’t guess him to be even seventy.

Jack sat down and asked Dominic, “How’s Charley?” not forgetting the incident with Charlie’s family a dozen years ago.

The question took Dominic completely off guard. “He’s, umm, he’s dying.” Dominic forgot that Jack Mattea was the acting boss when the incident happened. It was Jackie Matts that sent the wiseguys to the streets in search of Ziggy’s grandchildren; he had also stopped over at Ziggy’s house to drop off a nice envelope to Ziggy’s wife, Hillary. He even offered to split Charley’s rehab bill with Nick; of course, Nick refused. He never sent Charley to rehab, but Jackie’s respect as a boss had grown. Two months later, Jackie Matts went to prison for ten years. When he got out, Jackie had some problems with Dominic for whacking his great nephew, but eventually a sixth captain’s position was created for Jackie Matts, and crews were taken from other captains and given to him to placate the former acting boss.

Jack’s shoulders slumped, and he was visibly affected by the news. “Dying? How?”

“Cancer, forty-five years old, a fucking shame after all that other shit too, a real kick in the balls.”

“I just can’t believe it, Dominic. How’s Ziggy taking it?”

“He’s flying in today, staying until Friday. He flies back to Florida Friday morning. He does this every week.” Ziggy was able to retire upon his release from prison, but his timing couldn’t have been worse. Immediately upon his release, his nephew Nick Amicucci told him of his plans to take over the crime family and wanted Ziggy to be part of his administration and help with the older guys. Ziggy knew he had no chance of staying in Michigan and being retired with a war going on, so instead of taking care of Charley and his family, like he planned, he relocated to Florida and helped his son from afar.

“Your father did well with Charley, though. So what’s on your mind?”

Dominic nodded to Scary, who got up and took his beer to the next table over and let the two talk alone. Dominic wasn't completely sold on Jack's concern for his family. While Dominic was handling the revolt by Jerry Lissoni, Jack Mattea was on parole. In Dominic's mind, if Jackie Matts wasn't on parole, he would've opposed the Amicuccis. Especially, when after he did make parole he arranged for a late-night meeting in some woods with Dominic, where Jackie expressed his unhappiness with Dominic ordering the murder of Jack's great nephew, Vic Mattea Jr.

One theory Dominic had was the entitlement that Jack Mattea must feel for the title of boss. Jack's first cousin was Peter Mattea, and his uncle was Carmine Mattea, the crime family's only two bosses before Peter went to prison in 1996. Jack's son was doing fifty years in a state maximum security prison. His brother, Richie, did his ten years and was kicked out of the mob when his son became a witness for the feds in 1998. The Mattea family being royalty in the crime family, Dominic wanted to ensure he wasn't behind any of this betting scheme.

"Jack, the reason I asked you here, did you get any odd action for the All-Star Game?" Dominic asked.

"Odd? Not that I know."

"Ask around, would you?"

"Why, what happened?"

"A lot of action on the under, I mean a lot of action. Took it in the ass, so did Tom Caruso," Dominic told him.

"I don't know him."

"Almost half a million," Dominic said.

"On the under, what the fuck?"

"Tell me about it, I'm trying to piece it together. Someone's a dead man, that's for sure," Dominic said.

They talked for about ten more minutes until Dominic saw Norm Rupolo come in the front door. Norm was Jeff Parkos's lieutenant and former Lissoni associate. Norm was promoted for not going with Jerry Lissoni; he just quit until there was a resolution to the uprising. He received a call from Parkos telling him the boss was at the restaurant. "Goddammit, it's turning into a fucking social event." Dominic had no time for this today. "We're done here. Jack, take care, and if you hear anything, let me know."

Dominic stood and shook hands with Jack and kissed each other on both cheeks again, then walked to greet Norm, who waited so as to not interrupt the boss' meeting. After a brief hello, Scary walked out the front door in front of Dominic to survey the area for any feds or bad guys. Once Scary gave him the okay, Dominic followed him out the door.

Scary was driving on I-96, when Dominic pointed to the next exit on the freeway and told Scary to take it, and then had him make a right. After three miles of driving, Dominic pointed to a small bar at random and told him to pull in. Dominic pulled out his cell phone and called the next captain to meet with seventy-seven-year-old Eugene Modica, giving him the location to meet him at. Eugene told him it would take an hour to get there, so Dominic and Scary grabbed two seats at the bar and ordered two beers.

Eugene Modica was a union guy, and one of the few men who were made without killing. Eugene was instrumental in so many crime family members' pensions and insurances that he became a made man. In the late 1990s, the government also went after the unions and was able to get dozens of mob members out of union offices, including Eugene Modica.

Eugene would show his violent side in pursuit of his ambition to rise in the crime family and after being assigned to a bookmaking operation after his banishment from the unions, killed his way to the spot of captain. Today, Eugene was driven by his right-hand man, Mario Zangarra, who was the proliferate killer Eugene used to attain his position and was considered a sociopath by almost everyone. They entered the bar, and Dominic and Eugene Modica sat at a back table while Mario Zangarra watched the car and Scary Scarelli continued sitting at the bar, drinking a beer. "I already talked to Tom this morning. I'm fully aware," said Modica. Tom Caruso was one of Eugene Modica's lieutenants. "I'm not going to whack him over $400,000."

"I'd whack him over $400,000. But did Tom tell you other books lost big on the under as well?"

"No, he did not. How many books?"

"Not sure yet. I know of two books, including fucking mine, $700,000 so far."

"Holy shit!" Eugene exclaimed.

Then Dominic's phone rang; it was Fat Kenny. Dominic forgot all about him; if he wasn't so mad at him for screwing up his book, this would be pretty funny. "Where're you at, Kenny."

"Golden Dream, guess I just missed you, huh?"

"Stay there, have some lunch, and call me back in an hour," he said and hung up.

"Dominic, you're not saying you want to care of Tom, are you?" Eugene asked leaning in and made the sign of a gun with his fingers.

Dominic, just hanging up the phone, stared a second at Eugene. "That's what you got out of this? You do what you want with Tom, but check with your bookies. They might not even know they've been taken."

"I'll get Mario on it, but I have another problem," Eugene said.

"What?"

"I got to lodge a complaint against Fabian, Fabian Bosca, Dominic's boyhood best friend and another captain."

"What'd he do?"

"My insurance racket in Emery Beach, he took a company for ninety grand."

"Mike Sodano's racket? $90,000?"

"Yeah, Mike's racket. Well, not one of our companies, it was one of our marks. He robbed someone we rob, and I want the $90,000."

"Fabian doesn't have an insurance racket."

"What do you mean? He's got that thing with those Mexicans and the staged fender benders."

"What Mexicans? What the fuck are you talking about, Eugene?" Dominic said it loud enough for his bodyguard to keep an eye to see if he was needed.

"I guess you don't know about it then, but I'm still registering my complaint."

"I'll get back to you," Dominic said in pure amazement at what just transpired. "Check on those under bets, and I'll check on this. Doesn't Mike Sodano work for Tom?"

Eugene nodded his head. "Kind of odd to mention one, but not the other, ain't it?"

Yes it was, Dominic thought. "This whole fucking day is getting odd, Eugene."

Scary and Dominic were driving to their next meeting at a gym with best friends and captains, Fabian Bosca and Mario Marconi, where they could talk and get a work out in, when Scary noticed they had caught a tail. "We got a tail, two cars back, your side."

Dominic saw it in his side mirror. "How long's he been behind us?"

"Second time I noticed him," Scary answered.

"All right, doesn't mean he's a fed. Hang a left up there." Scary turned left at the next mile road, crossing three lanes to do so. Dominic turned to watch the car go by, which it did without even hitting its brakes. Nothing else seemed amiss. Dominic figured it was possible that the feds had been tailing all day and they didn't even know it. When the FBI doesn't want to be seen, they won't be seen; they use multiple cars with radios, cars that can turn off one headlight at night, helicopters, even satellites.

Fat Kenny called again as they were approaching the gym, "Kenny, come to the Bally's by my dad's house."

"Bally's?" Kenny was not a fan of gyms.

"Yeah, get some exercise, maybe it'll save your life," Dominic told him.

"I'm in a suit, Dom. Besides, I'm fucking tired of just driving."

"Try jogging then, you fat fucker. Be there," Dominic said and hung up. Kenny looked for a store he could buy some workout clothes at and head back to Emery Beach. In his suit, in this ninety degree July heat, Fat Kenny was not a happy man.

Dominic grabbed his duffel bag from the trunk and signed in at the desk. Scary stayed at the car. The pretty brunette at the desk told Dominic that Mario was upstairs waiting for him, and after a few flirtatious minutes, Dominic went to the locker room to change. He met Mario upstairs, and they started walking the track together. It wasn't beneath the feds to send in an agent to work out and spy on them. They talked in whispers as they walked and changed subjects when someone was near.

"You know anything about Fabian running some insurance racket?" Dominic asked.

"Fabian's got a lot of things going on, but I don't know about no insurance. Why, what's up?"

"I just heard he did, that's all. No big deal."

"Is that why you were at the Golden Dream today?" Mario had replaced Jerry Lissoni as captain just last January, a move not appreciated by the other crews. Mario wasn't considered to be very bright; most people thought of him as an errand boy, but he had what Dominic needed most, Dominic's trust. Although not very respected as their captain, Mario was notified by Norm Rupolo and Jeff Parkos that Dominic had been to their Greektown restaurant today.

Dominic smiled at his lifelong friend. "At least they're talking to you now. I just needed to look in Parkos's eyes for a reaction to something."

"Reaction to what?"

"Someone hit our book for $275 large on the under of the All-Star game, Tom Caruso's book too, and apparently others."

"How would you lose $275, it goes against to whole setup of the book?" Mario asked in disbelief.

"Kenny and Carlo kept the action, thought they had a lock."

"When did Kenny and Carlo take over?"

"That's the problem, they didn't. They never told Jackie, they just ran wild. I just got to figure out who knew these two were stupid enough to do that and who knew the other bookies were that stupid too."

"A lot's changed in six months since I left the crew. Maybe it's Kenny and Carlo themselves," he suggested.

"Not smart enough. And I don't doubt Kenny's loyalty. We've known him our whole lives. He wouldn't burn our book."

"For 275 grand? You sure?"

"No, there's someone behind this. And it ain't about the money for him either. I don't think." Scary Scarelli came from behind, holding Dominic's other phone, his throwaway phone that Scary carried for Dominic, and only a select few had the number.

"Dom, it's your dad." Dominic's father's guards allowed him use of a cell phone privately, in exchange for money, a lot of money. Dominic took the phone and walked back outside and to the back of the parking lot where he could be alone.

"Hey, Dad, what's up?"

"Where are you at?" his father asked him.

"Working out with Mario, why?"

"I hear you're meeting all the captains today, what happened?" Nick's bribed privileges also extended to another Michigan gangster, Eddie Turco. Eddie was the first to receive a large sentence, sixty-five years and had been locked up since 1990. His oldest son, Eddie Jr., was destined to replace Eddie; instead, he forced his son into retirement at the age of thirty-seven. Even though retired from the life, Eddie Jr. kept his ears to the ground and talked to his father daily, giving Nick another set of eyes and ears on the streets.

Dominic shut his eyes in disbelief; he thought he had until Thursday, fucking Eddie Turco. "I'll tell you about it Thursday, when I see you."

"Why? You're on a clean phone, right?"

"Yeah, it's just . . ."

"Are you not alone?"

"No, I'm alone."

"No other excuses not to talk to me then, what happened?"

"I just wanted more info before I talked to you, that's all."

"Okay, I won't judge. Maybe I can help. Lay it on me."

Dominic didn't buy one ounce of that "I won't judge" crap, for his first words will be, "you shoulda' done this and you shoulda' done that." "We lost a ton on the All-Star game last week."

"How much is a ton?"

"Our book lost 275 grand, Tom Caruso lost 400, and I'm finding out how many others."

There was silence for about thirty seconds before Nick spoke, "I'm not judging, but tell me how we lost so much, and especially on the fucking All-Star game."

"Jackie let Kenny and Carlo run the baseball season, and they thought they'd make a quick buck."

"Fat Kenny?" Nick asked, his voice starting to rise.

"Yeah," Dominic answered, bracing himself.

"How about my daughter's father-in-law, Tom?"

"Oh, Tom lost his himself. He didn't have any assholes to blame, he's his own asshole." Dominic didn't really care for Tom Caruso. Nick forced Dominic to make him a lieutenant and take crews from others and give them to Tom after his son proposed to Nick's daughter. Tom was a collector for Eddie Klein, a Jewish gangster with ties all the way back to the Purple Gang. After Eddie Klein went to jail, the Italians took it over. Tom Caruso took over the book once Eugene Modica became captain; Eugene had killed Tom's boss.

"Doesn't appear to be any random winning streak or coincidence?" Nick asked.

"No, it's an inside job. One of our own hit us, and I'm guessing it's going to go over a million dollars."

"Sounds like you got a good handle on it. Uncle Ziggy's having dinner at our house tonight, and you should be there. Sal's picking up your grandma."

"I'll try. I got a lot to do here. I might even have a date tonight." ***Maybe with the brunette at the desk,*** Dominic thought. Fabian Bosca pulled into the parking lot, late for the meeting. Scary flagged him down and told him to wait outside while Dominic finished his phone call.

"Okay, good luck with that, I'll let you go. I got a chess game in twenty minutes against some hick. A hick playing chess?" he joked. "We're betting twenty-five candy bars. Should be a big draw." ***That explains Nick's good mood,*** Dominic thought. "I'll see you Thursday, let me know what you find out, and be careful."

"Speaking of careful, where's Doug?" Dominic inquired about his good friend Doug Sullivan, who was locked up with Dominic's father doing ten years, until his trial in Miami earlier that year.

Doug Sullivan ran the Westside crew. The Westside crew was the enforcement for the Amicuccis and became the crime family's biggest earning crew, all non-Italians. While the Westside's boss was incarcerated, Doug's best friend, Tommy Herrick, ran the crew.

"In Miami," Nick answered.

"I don't think he is, and why would he be? He was not guilty. He should be back with you by now."

"I don't know, ask Tommy," he said, meaning Doug Sullivan's stand-in.

"I do. He gets all weird, like you do, and tells me to ask you. If it wasn't you two, I'd think he'd gone rat."

"You just take care of your little betting problem there. Oh, and you got to throw Danny a big party for him and Vinny Jag." Vinny Jagge had the same release date and was supposed to take over as captain for Fabian, a discussion Dominic was not in a hurry to have.

"Speaking of Vinny Jag, you really going to make me demote Fabian? He's made us so much money and been loyal to me, Dad," Dominic said, campaigning for his friend.

"What part of 'acting' captain is so hard to understand? His job was for five years. Five years is up, and Vinny's coming home. Fabian's job is over. I love the kid, but rules are rules, Dominic. Be sure to throw a nice party."

"I will. I'll get some strippers and . . ."

"No strippers, you dumb fuck, you ever see Danny with a stripper?"

"I've seen Danny with other women. And after five years . . ."

"You better be fucking with me. A family party, and if you're going to have one at my club, just have the crew. No women, Dominic. Okay?"

"Sure, but I want to go on the record that if I do five years, I want two strippers for every year I'm in," Dominic said, amusing himself.

"Whatever," said Nick and hung up the phone.

"Him and his fucking high horse," Dominic said to himself, putting his phone away, walking over to Fabian. "You got some fucking insurance scam running with your Mexicans that I don't know of?" Dominic asked as soon as he was in distance.

Fabian could see his friend's anger. "What do you mean?"

"Mike Sodano says you scammed one his companies for ninety grand. Is that true?"

Fabian thought for a second. "Ninety grand? You mean T&B Enterprises?"

Dominic lost his composure and started to yell; his bodyguard inched his way closer. "I don't fucking know, Fabian. That's why I'm asking you."

"I didn't know they were connected. I'll talk to Mike."

"You'll talk to Mike? You'll give Mike the ninety grand," Dominic told him.

"For what? He didn't do anything. I'll give 25 percent, as an apology, but that's it."

"What the fuck are you doing, Fabian?"

It was Fabian whose voice was raised now, "I'm fucking earning. Ain't that what I'm supposed to be doing?"

"Yeah, but not out of the mouths of other made men," Dominic answered.

"Oh really? You took six crews out of my family's mouths and gave them to Jackie fucking Matts. You're godfather to both of my daughters, the one that's dead and the one's that's alive. And you put Jackie Matts over my family?" Fabian's first daughter died when she was ten.

And there it was. "You did this, didn't you?" Dominic asked after a sudden realization.

"Did what?" Fabian asked with disdain.

"You pulled the under scam, you motherfucker," he said, grabbing Fabian by his shirt.

"What under scam?" Fabian asked, shoving Dominic away. He stumbled back and looked at something behind Fabian. Fabian turned his head to see what Dominic had glanced at, and was dropped to the ground by an overhand right by Scary.

Dominic just looked at Scary, as Fabian lay motionless in the parking lot. "That wasn't necessary."

"I'm supposed to let him just push you around?"

"He didn't push me around," Dominic said, trying to keep some pride.

"Well, he's not supposed to put his hands on the boss, and that he did."

Dominic couldn't deny the logic. "He did do that, didn't he? A little tact though, eh? Maybe a headlock, a choke hold?"

Scary just shrugged, and they both stared at Fabian on the ground, who was starting to get up now. "What do want to do with him?"

"Get him up, take him to his car."

Fabian pushed Scary away when he tried to help him up. "Keep your fucking hands off me, I'm a fucking captain," he said and turned to Dominic. "What the fuck, Dominic? I want him dead."

Scary threw his huge shoulders back and started walking back toward Fabian. "Come on and kill me then."

"Hey! Knock it the fuck off." Both men stopped in their tracks and turned to look at Dominic. "Fabian, swear to me on your dead daughter that you didn't take down our book—the same book you grew up in, that *we* grew up in. Swear to me you didn't." His eyes met Fabian's, and he had his answer. Dominic dropped his head and told Scary to "let him have it."

Scary was on him in a second. "You mean a headlock like this, Dom?" When Fabian was able to land an elbow in Scary's gut, Scary figured play time was over. He lifted his knee and drove Fabian's head right into it, splitting his forehead open and dropping him back to the concrete, belly up. He let Fabian stagger to his feet and hunched over, with one hand covering his cut forehead; his other hand took a lazy swing, which Scary slapped away and countered with an uppercut to Fabian's jaw, dropping him to his knees. Scary looked back at Dominic and with no response, he shrugged his shoulders and landed a right cross, opening a gash above Fabian's left eye, rendering him unconscious.

After ensuring no one was still around, Dominic called Mario, who was still in the gym, to tell him it was time to go and called Fat Kenny to tell him to hurry up. He looked down at his best friend's beaten and bloody body on the ground and turned to Scary. "Put him in the trunk."

CHAPTER III

OLD FRIENDS

December, 1989

FABIAN BOSCA DROVE the Amicucci Breads' truck through the worst snowstorm of the winter; in the passenger seat next to him was his friend and boss' son, Dominic Amicucci. Three years his junior, Dominic, was only working weekends while he was still in high school. His father, Nick Amicucci, was the boss of the area and owner of the bread company and spent every night at Nino's Bar, later to become Cooch's Corner, one block from Fabian's house. Fabian's father was gunned down in a small bar when he was only two years old, a victim of a mob rubout. Larry Bosca worked for the Agosto brothers, and it was always assumed that the brothers had Fabian's father whacked. Fabian started hanging around Nino's Bar at a young age. Nick's father, Dominic, and Nick's uncle, Giacomo, who ran the book, took Fabian in and would always send him home to his mother with money. As a teenager, Fabian was taught the ropes by none other than Scary Scarelli, who would split Fabian's forehead open in the Bally's parking lot over twenty years later. When Dominic started delivering bread, it was Fabian, at nineteen years old, teaching Dominic the ropes.

"The snow's too bad, I can't see shit," said Fabian, trying to drive through the early morning snowstorm.

"Where are we anyway?" asked Dominic, who'd just gotten his driver's license and had not ever driven in the snow.

"Right now? I got no fucking idea, but we have to get to Cicirelli's Market and pick up thirty grand."

"Why are you going this way? My dad takes a totally different way there."

"Scary always takes this way. It's the only way I know."

"There's no lights or nothing out here, can't even see the road ahead. It's like we're not even in Michigan anymore," young Dominic complained.

Fabian turned to look at Dominic for a second. "Will you shut the fuck up for a minute and let me drive?"

At that moment, a car came from around a bend that Fabian wasn't aware was even a bend. "Look out!" Dominic yelled as Fabian turned back to look at the road. Fabian slammed on the brakes, and the old bread truck started to slide. It seemed to slide forever, and after becoming perpendicular to itself prior to the slide, the bread truck seemed to be coming to a stop. But just as Fabian turned to Dominic, they both realized they had run out of road, and the truck started to tip on to its side and slide down a hill.

"Get out, Dom!" cried Fabian as he tried to reach the passenger door handle and push his charge out of the tilting truck, but he wasn't quick enough.

The truck landed on the driver's side, throwing Fabian violently back and breaking the driver's side window with the back of his head, and the truck started sliding down the hill. Gravity threw Dominic to the driver's side also, pinning Fabian between the steering wheel and the driver's door. "Dom, kick the windshield! Kick the windshield!" Fabian yelled, hoping for an escape route before a tragic finish to the ride down the hill.

The truck had picked up too much momentum, and Dominic couldn't move a muscle. "I can't!"

After what seemed like an eternity, the truck leveled off and came to a stop. Dominic lay on top of Fabian, and they both didn't move for a good thirty seconds before Dominic noticed the blood. "Fabian, you're bleeding, you okay?"

Still reeling from the near-death encounter, Fabian had to think before he answered, and then he heard the cracking. He quickly surveyed their surroundings. "We're on a lake! Get the fuck up!"

Dominic had to stand on Fabian in order to reach the passenger door, which was facing the sky. He pushed the door open and pulled himself up. While hanging with one hand, he offered his other hand to Fabian. "Get the fuck up there, my life ain't worth shit if you die. Go!" Dominic showed reluctance to leave his friend, but he knew time was of the essence. He pulled himself out of the truck so that his friend would follow. "I'm coming, go ahead and climb down," said Fabian and started freeing himself.

When Fabian got to the top, there was no sign of Dominic, just a hole in the ice. "He wouldn't have jumped from here onto the ice, would he?" Fabian asked himself. The ice under the truck finally gave way, and Fabian jumped on an angle and rolled onto the ice to soften his landing and avoid Dominic's fate. With no truck, and no Dominic, Fabian did the only thing he felt he could. He crawled to the hole that Dominic plummeted through and without hesitation, jumped in. He instantly saw Dominic a few yards off, frantically trying to break the ice. Fabian grabbed a hold of Dominic's ankle and pulled him to the hole, then he took them both to the surface.

Once they recovered, Fabian tried reassuring Dominic, "We're okay, we're okay."

Dominic, still on all fours and coughing up what water was left in his system, panted, "Holy shit, holy shit. That was intense."

They took a moment to gain their composures and started back up the hill, snow still coming down heavily.

"We got to get to a pay phone," Dominic said, trudging slowly behind Fabian.

Fabian was keeping a quicker pace. "There're no pay phones out here. Obviously, we're not where we thought we were."

"Where *you* thought we were? I knew we were lost."

"You never fucking said lost. Besides, I know enough not to jump from ten feet in the air onto cracking ice, you stupid shit. Come on, keep moving," Fabian called back as Dominic, started to fall way behind.

Dominic dropped to his knees. "I can't Fabian. Go, go on without me."

Fabian ran back to Dominic. "Save the fucking drama, get up, let's go. We got to keep moving."

"I can't. My legs are all tingly. I can't feel my feet."

Fabian, even at age nineteen, was not unaware of the symptoms of hypothermia and frostbite. "Hang on, I'll piggyback you." He dropped to all fours and turned around so Dominic could cling to his back. Once on, Fabian rose to his feet using the muscles acquired from all the heavy leg squats in the weight room during his high school years as the star running back on the football team. He ran as hard and as far as he could until he'd have to stop and put Dominic down to regain enough strength for another dash. After finally reaching the road, Fabian slung Dominic's arm around his shoulder to support him. "Move the legs, Dom. Move the legs," he urged, each word coming in between gasps for air.

Headlights appeared in the distance, and the boys raised their arms to flag it down. Just as Fabian had hit his brakes, so did this driver, and the car slid into the guardrail on the other side of the road opposite the hill. The car, still running, came to a stop, and a woman got out. "Are you okay?" Fabian called out to her.

The woman, of course, bewildered at the sight of two teenagers in the middle of the road during a snowstorm answered back, "Yes, what happened?"

Fabian, basically carrying Dominic, approached the woman. "Ma'am, please, our truck ran off the road and into that lake," he said, pointing toward the hill and at the tiny lake, "and my friend's getting hypothermia. Please, let him sit in the heat of your car while I flag someone down to help us all. Someone will see your headlights and stop to help."

The woman opened her backseat door, and Fabian laid Dominic down in it. "His father's a very important person. He'll buy you a whole new car for this. Thank you," he said and shut the door, then started to wait for another car.

"They'll see the headlights, wait in the car. You'll get hypothermia too, and you're bleeding," she reasoned.

Fabian had forgotten about the back of his head. "No, I have to make sure, thank you ma'am." Fabian, despite the physical toll it took to carry Dominic back to the road, while dripping wet and a head wound, stood by the headlights waiting for another car to stop.

After finally being rescued by another car, which didn't slide off the road, both boys shivered in the backseat, while the woman sat in the front. "We'll get you to a hospital," she told them.

"Just drop us off at a pay phone, I'll call an ambulance. No need to cause any more accidents today," Fabian replied through chattering teeth.

The woman turned to look at them. "It'll be fine. We'll go right to the hospital."

"I need a pay phone. I have to call his father."

"Just call him from the hospital, you don't know what kind of damage may have been already been done to you two."

"It's not my decision to make, so please, I need to use the next pay phone." The driver complied and pulled over at the next gas station. Fabian braved the cold again to call the bakery. Danny Serafini answered the phone, "Danny, it's Fabian, I gotta talk to Nick."

"Fabian, what's up?"

"It's Dominic, you gotta get Nick, please." Danny immediately dropped the phone to go get Nick.

Nick and Denny Greco were watching the morning news, and George Rea was counting stacks of money at a table, when Danny burst in from the kitchen. Everyone followed Nick to the phone, waiting to get the news as to what happened to his son. "Fabian?"

"Nick, we had an accident. The truck slid into a lake. Dominic's sick, I think he's got hypothermia. We're at a gas station with two strangers that helped us, and I promised one you'd buy her a new car if she helped us."

"What the hell?"

"Nick, he needs a doctor. Do I take him to the hospital?"

"The truck's gone?"

"Yeah, right in a fucking lake," Fabian answered, still amazed at the events that had transpired that morning.

"Everything okay to talk with authorities?"

"Got nothing to even lie about, no wrongdoings here, Nick."

"Okay, take him to the hospital. Which one are you going to?"

"No idea. I'll call you when we get there and let you know." Fabian then ran back to the car.

George Rea was right next to Nick trying to hear the conversation. George had practically raised Dominic after his mother died, and Nick showed total disregard for his responsibility. Dominic was as much a son to George as his own son, Angelo, was. "Well? What happened? Dominic all right?" he asked immediately after Nick hung the phone up.

"Fabian says he's got hypothermia. Their fucking truck slid off the road and into a lake. After that, I don't have a fucking clue. Fabian will call from the hospital. Denny, get the ovens back on. All the stores on Fabian's route didn't get their deliveries. Call them, tell them what happened, and tell them we're on our way. Can't believe no one's called complaining." As ordered, Denny departed to take care of business.

"We're staying here?" George asked incredously.

"I don't know where to go," Nick answered back, annoyed.

"Let's at least get on the road. Danny can beep us when Fabian calls."

"What? Go the wrong way and turn around? It's a waste of time and energy. Wait until we know where to go. Don't panic."

Danny asked, "Why don't you just take Dominic to our guy?" Nick knew a doctor who did side work for his men without having to make a police report.

"For one, he's only done gunshots and stitches for us. And two, we need the police report for the truck."

George was thoroughly disgusted with his best friend and brother-in-law. "Good fucking thing we needed the police report, eh?"

Nick was accustomed to George's overprotectiveness. Dominic was ten before George and Marie had Angelo, and for those ten years, Dominic was their son. Sometimes Nick felt angry when George felt he knew better for Dominic than Nick, but for the most part, Nick was thankful for the good upbringing of his son.

About a half hour later, Fabian called and told them what hospital they were at, and Nick and George headed out. "You want me to call Helena?" Danny asked Nick as he was leaving.

"She's fucking pregnant. Do not upset my wife." She was pregnant with their second child, Salvatore, at the time.

With the snowy conditions, what would normally have been a twenty-minute ride took over an hour. When they arrived, they were taken to Dominic's room where the doctor informed them that Dominic would be fine and actually could probably go home later that night. Dominic told them both all about Fabian's heroism in saving young Dominic's life. Nick sought to find Fabian, who was being treated for his head wound and hypothermia. The doctor told him where to find him, and Nick entered the room.

Fabian looked bad, his color had not yet returned, and he looked almost dead. Nick sat down in the chair next to the bed and watched Fabian, who had just dozed off. He awoke immediately when he heard the chair scuffle. "Hey, how's Dominic?" he muttered. Despite the hypothermia, Fabian was completely exhausted. The man's body was almost drained of all fluids.

"He's fine. He's better than you are, so just rest, Son. Listen, Fabian, I don't know what to say to you. Words can't come near expressing my thanks. Without a thought I'd give my life for my son, happily. I give that same offer to you. You're one of mine now. You, your new wife, and your mother will want for nothing, as long as I've got breath in these lungs. I swear." Fabian had married his high school sweetheart over the summer and moved her into his mother's apartment.

Fabian had to whisper due to his weakened condition and the lump in his throat. Nick had to lean in to hear him. "I can't hear you, Fabian."

"I was doing my job."

"I'll be the luckiest man in the world if my son turns out like you. Did you call your family?" Fabian shook his head.

"Why not?" Nick asked.

Fabian was expecting to be released shortly. "Not staying here," he whispered.

"Hey, you gave more than your body was able to give today, Fabian. You did something special. You are truly a hero. You stay here and heal your body. I'll take care of everything, won't cost you a penny. I'm going to have someone pick up your wife and mother and bring them here, just rest."

Fabian watched Nick walk out the door and thought to himself, *Is that what it's like to have a father? To be cared for like a son?* What Fabian didn't know was that the man that just walked out the door was the same man that had shot his father seventeen years ago.

Fabian awoke in a dimly lit room; he could make out only a silhouette sitting in a chair. He grabbed his throbbing head in pain from the beating he took from Scary Scarelli. "Dominic? Is that you?"

"Yeah, it's me."

"Oh, my head." The pain dropped Fabian to his knee. He then noticed he was on a plastic tarp. "Where are we?"

"We're in my basement," he said, still not exposing himself to the dim light.

"Is this plastic?"

"It is so that blood doesn't get on the carpet."

Fabian understood the world he lived in and knew what it meant to lay down the plastic. "You really gonna whack me, brother?"

"It's what our life says to do in this situation, page one."

"No one got hurt, Dom," said Fabian as he couldn't even stand, "no one, but me at least. You can have the money back."

"Can I really? Gee, thanks, buddy. What do you want to do, go catch a Tiger game now? Or maybe you should tell me I can have only 25 percent as an apology. After all, you did do all the work."

"Come on, Dom. I'm sorry, what do I gotta do here?"

"Start with why, tell me why. You need money? You got to be bringing in ten million a year from Mexico alone."

"Until Vinny gets out," Fabian complained.

"Grow the fuck up. You can't live on five mil a year?"

"Can you, Dominic?"

Dominic finally came into the light, and Fabian could see they were alone, but Scary was probably right up the stairs. "What is your fucking problem with me all of a sudden, huh?"

"My problem with you? You've had a hard-on for me ever since your father put me in charge of the Lodulli crews. What? Did you want it?" Fabian told of his promotion to lieutenant after Nick became a captain.

"You're talking ten years ago. I was never going anywhere but my father's side. He'd never send me off, like he did you. And when did I ever give you a hard time?"

"Always busting my balls over money, all the fucking time," Fabian answered.

"You mean when you were late all the fucking time? You really went off and got yourself killed because your feelings were hurt?"

"You treat me like we've never known each other our whole lives. When was the last time we went for beer, huh?"

"Just last week after we worked out. What the fuck?" Dominic asked in disbelief and anger.

"Yeah, but that was work. I'm just a captain to you, so fuck it."

"This is pretty fucking dumb if you ask me."

"And what about Angela?" Fabian asked.

"Angela who?"

"Your wife."

Dominic was totally confused. "What about her?"

"That wasn't no mugging, you whacked her. Why? Because she couldn't have kids, you fucking animal! We all grew up together, remember? My wife still asks about that mugger. You were Angela's whole world—you were everything to her. How could you? A woman? That's how much you've changed."

"You think I killed Angela?"

"Everyone does," he replied, finally able to get to his feet. "Everyone does."

Dominic tossed his gun to Fabian, who sidestepped the gun as a natural reaction, and it tumbled to the floor. "It's not loaded. Just like I could never kill you, I could never kill her. She was my life too, you know. I'll never marry again. I'd never disrespect her like that. No, I didn't kill her, but I died with her. And that's all I've got to say about that. None of it gives you the right to get one over on the family, nothing does."

"There's a lot of people getting over on you, Dom, card games with secret books you don't know nothing about, books selling coke . . . there's a lot of shit you don't know, all because you treat people like shit."

"I'm not talking about that shit. We're talking about you fucking me in the ass because I didn't treat you as a 'friend.' I still don't see how I treated you like shit. You were the first person I promoted when my dad went away."

"To an acting capo, Dominic, a temp. How about Mario? He's a full captain. Now you give everything I made to fucking Vinny Jagge. What happens to me? I gave my crews to his fucking kid, and he's going to give them back now?"

"I've argued with my father to do something else with Vinny and leave you the fuck alone. What am I going to do? He's fucking adamant. He made Vinny a capo when he went to jail, and that's that. His words, not mine."

"I'll be honest with you. I bought a house down there last year, a real nice villa, overlooking the ocean. My wife and daughter are down there right now. I just can't lose Mexico. My wife, she's been through so much, Dom," and tears started to flow. "I'm the man down there, Dom. There they treat me like people treat you here."

"Like a fucking jerk-off, apparently."

"I'm sorry, Dom. I don't know. Sometimes, man, I feel like everyone's against me. Ever since my baby girl died, I'm just not right. Even my wife tells me I should talk to someone."

"Someone who? Like a shrink? For what, pills? That ain't going to do nothing for you, just turn you into a fucking zombie."

"No, to talk to someone about what I'm feeling inside and why I don't think right. Not for no pills. And can I get the fuck off this plastic now, please?"

"Yeah, come on," said Dominic and led his friend to a table and chairs and finally turned on the lights. "Look, Fabian, we've both lived some pretty hard lives. Your father was whacked when you were two, my mother died when I was three, you buried a daughter, and my wife was murdered. Look me in the eyes, Fabian, I didn't kill her."

"I'm sorry, brother. Forgive me, please."

"Yeah, fine. But listen, you can't be this way, you got to move on, be strong. Life's not done kicking you down, Fabian, any of us—you just get up every time it does. It's all a test—every minute is, to live the right way, by the code, no matter what. There's not one minute in a day when you can break down, and if you do, you do, move the fuck on. You can't be running around, pulling shit like this. Now my life is on the line with you, you fucking jerk-off."

Fabian, finally able to muster a laugh through his mangled face, said, "Now it feels like old times. So how do I make this right? Just take my demotion and shut up?"

"Yes, shut the fuck up about your fucking demotion. Be happy to be alive right now. But how do we keep you alive?"

"Take all the money."

"How much was it anyway?"

"$1.8 million, I'm good for every penny of it, too."

"Oh my god, it's that much? How'd you do it?"

"You would've only accounted for probably about a million of it. The rest would come through other losses, mostly card games. Like I said, there's a lot you don't know. But let's clean it up, since I'll probably be your driver now."

"I could not listen to this bitching and moaning, every single fucking day if you were driving me. Go ahead, move to fucking Mexico. You want to raise my Goddaughterto be a Mexicano, who am I to give a fuck? My dad already agreed with me that you should keep everything you got, outside the state."

"No shit?" Fabian tried to smile, but that wasn't happening. "Did somebody stitch my head?" he asked as he rubbed his fingers along the cut of his forehead.

"Don't worry about that right now. You keep the drug operation in Mexico and whatever else you got there and in Miami. But you understand, Vinny's your capo, you kick up to Vinny." Fabian didn't respond; he just kept feeling the cuts on his face. "Can't you even be happy about this? This is good fucking news for you here."

"I am happy, and I'm indebted to you. I get it, but I think I'm fucked up here. Did you guys drug and stitch me or something? I don't feel good, not like a 'I just got my ass kicked' not feel good, which I don't really feel, which is odd. I mean, I hurt when I move, but that's it. I just feel like the nausea's bad, you know what I mean?"

"You're fucking rambling. Lay down on the couch over there. Take a nap. Kenny'll drive you home later."

"I need a mirror. And who stitched me up, Dom?"

"Use the bathroom behind you," said Dominic, retrieved his gun from the plastic tarp, and started up the steps. "Fat Kenny stitched you." As Fabian tried to run to the mirror, Dominic ejected the one bullet that was left in the gun's chamber and continued up the stairs and outside to a waiting Scary and Fat Kenny.

"Dom, how's he like his forehead?" Kenny asked.

"You're gonna poke fucking fun now?"

"What? I think I did a really nice job on his forehead. He just needs to keep applying Neosporin and aloe vera. He'll barely have a scar."

"What the fuck is wrong with you?" Dominic asked Kenny.

"Why's it so wrong to have some empathy for a fellow human being?"

Dominic lost his temper with Kenny and started slapping him. "All the fucking grief you've caused me today, and you want to talk about fucking empathy?"

Kenny could only put his arms up in defense, as he knew retaliating could cost him his life. "Dom, please."

Finally, Dominic stopped slapping Kenny. He gave him a push and exhausted from throwing fifteen slaps said, "And don't you start crying now. Those weren't even punches. You ain't going to feel a fucking thing anyway you're so fucking fat."

Scary just stood and watched, thoroughly enjoying himself with all the fun he was having today. "Boss, want me to get involved?" he asked, inching his way for another melee.

Dominic turned to Scary and pointed, "Shut the fuck up!"

Scary stopped dead in his tracks. "Damn, what did I do?" he asked himself.

Dominic took his finger and pointed it at Kenny now. "Angelo talk to you today?"

"Yeah," Kenny answered, nodding his head.

"You owe a lot of money."

"Yeah," Kenny answered, nodding his head again.

"$137,500, to be exact. How much is Angelo charging you?"

Kenny thought about it for a second. "2 points, $2,750 a week."

"I'm going to pay your marker with Ange."

"Wow, thanks, Dom. I don't know what to say."

"I'm charging you the fucking degenerate rate, 3 points, $4,125 a week. You're going to drive me around, and I've always paid my drivers a grand a week, but I'm paying you five hundred a week, for being such an asshole. I'll take it out of what you owe every week."

Kenny was speechless. "No offense, Dom, but if I'm out driving you all day, how am I going to earn to pay you every week?"

"You fucking figure it out. Use that brain of yours for something other than fucking recipes. Or why don't you go borrow the money from someone else, find yourself a nice ball game, and put *your* money on the fucking over, you fat fucking cocksucker you."

"I don't know what to say about that, Dom. I'm sorry. I'm just an idiot, I guess."

"Yes, you are, and an asshole too. And Angelo was clear on the book? That you don't go nowhere near it, right?"

"He was clear."

"Even if you drive me there, you stay the fuck in the car, capiche?"

"Capiche," Kenny answered.

"Good, I'll see you bright and early, tomorrow morning. Bring coffee. Take Fabian home when he feels better. He's sick from the anesthetic you gave him. Oh, and Kenny, be sure to give him a lot of empathy, okay?" Dominic and Scary left, and Kenny went downstairs to check on his patient.

CHAPTER IV

Prison Visit

DOMINIC TOOK ANOTHER swig from his fifth of Jack Daniels while watching *SportsCenter*; it had been a rough day, and Dominic planned on drinking himself to sleep. He'd met with Benny Mancini, the last captain to meet with, and learned that Benny had three books that were hit with Fabian's under scam; his losses were just shy of $600,000. Another book under Angelo was found to have been taken, making a total of almost one and a half million dollars. More losses from card games should be coming up soon. Fabian's scam would most likely exceed two million. Even his sister, Valentina, gave him a hard time at dinner about not helping her father-in-law, Tom Caruso, with his debt.

After another swig, Dominic headed upstairs to his bedroom. He walked past the bed he and his late wife had slept in; he hadn't touched it since the day she was murdered. He pulled out the bottom drawer of his dresser, reached into a secret compartment, and pulled out his .32 caliber Beretta, loaded it, and put it in his waistband. Dominic grabbed his car keys, and with bottle in hand, he drove off in his black F-350.

Angelo Rea awoke to a figure sitting next to his bed; his first reaction was to reach for the gun in the nightstand, but Dominic caught his wrist and announced it was him.

"Dominic? What the fuck?"

"Ange, get up. Let's go for a walk, and don't wake your mom."

Angelo did as ordered: threw on some clothes and headed for the lakeside backyard. Dominic stood looking out at the lake smoking a cigarette; he had grown up here, and it still felt like home. He still knew the alarm codes and could walk through the house in the dark. "Okay, Dom, what's up?"

"Couldn't sleep," Dominic said, still looking at the lake.

"Well, I was sleeping fine," Angelo told him.

"Fat Kenny," Dominic said.

"What about him?"

"You know, he's really not such an idiot."

"I never thought so. You're the one that treats him that way."

Dominic finally looked at Angelo. "I know. I always have. When we were little, we'd kick the ball over the neighbor's fence and make Kenny go and get it. Let me tell you, even when we were young, it was never easy for Kenny to climb a fence. When he'd finally make it over the fence, we ran—we always ran."

"Yeah, that's pretty mean, Dom."

"But you know what, Ange? No matter how far we ran, he always caught up to us—every single time, and believe me, there was a lot of times."

"He always has been loyal to you, Dom, like a dog. He's always looked out for me because you told him to."

"That's my point. Who's he trying to burn here, you or me?"

"Dom, he didn't try to burn nobody. He thought he was making us some money."

"Is that what he was thinking?"

"How the fuck should I know what he was thinking?"

"Well, you're with him more than anybody else is. I mean, you are at the book every night."

Angelo suddenly had a bad feeling in his stomach. "You saying something, Dominic?"

"Yeah, funny thing I remembered. Last week, night of the All-Star game, your fiancée was with my sister. We were here, and your mother cooked dinner." Angelo looked away from his cousin and into the sky. "You were at the Corner, watching the game."

"Yeah, I was."

"How could you not know the action on the game?"

Angelo was silent for a moment before he sighed and then spoke, "I did. I told them guys to take the action. Nobody wanted to do it. I made them. I did it, Dom."

Remaining calm, Dominic looked into his cousin's eyes. "And you let Kenny take that kind of abuse?"

"Yeah, I told him I'd pay everything. I'm sorry, Dom."

"That's all I ever get anymore, sorrys. How could you lie? How could you let them guys take the rap for you?"

"I didn't want to let you down."

"Let me down? It ain't about that shit, Ange. I'm going to jail, sooner or later. Could be today, you never fucking know. Are you ready to run this family?"

"I'm not even sure I'm able to be a captain."

"No, you're not, obviously. You got to be better than this. You've got to take my place when I get my twenty years. Not if, but when, I go to jail, someone's going to kill you and that can't happen. You got to be smarter. You're not a kid no more, Ange."

"I know, Dom . . ."

"You don't know. You say you know, but look at how you act. A fucking liar? Your father is like a father to me, and you weren't raised to be no liar."

"I'm sorry."

"Stop with the fucking 'I'm sorrys.'"

"What else can I say?"

"Swear to me this won't happen again."

"I swear."

"If you fuck up, and you will fuck up, you'll tell me, and we'll deal with it. I can't not trust you, Angelo. We clear?"

"I swear."

"After all this bullshit, Fat 'fucking' Kenny is the most stand-up motherfucker around. How about that?"

"What happens to me now? You going to demote me?" Angelo asked.

"I wouldn't embarrass myself like that. No. What happens to you is you're going to open the bakery every morning, starting today."

"I had something to do today, Dom," Angelo protested.

"You see? I feel like you're already learning. That's right, you *had* plans. But now you'll spend every day with me. I'm going to finish my bottle, and I'll see you sometime later." Dominic started staggering toward his truck.

"Dom, stay here awhile. Sleep off the whiskey."

Dominic turned back to his cousin. "Ange, I thought you were smarter than you are. Me and Jackie gave you too much room. I'll be there to teach you, I have to. But personally, between you and me, you can go fuck yourself, you fucking liar. I don't even want to beat on you, I'm so disgusted." Dominic drove back home and finished his bottle.

Thursday morning

The lights went on in the bakery's back office, waking Dominic up after sleeping the night on the couch. He covered his eyes through the blinding light and was able to make out his cousin, Angelo. "What time is it?"

Angelo jumped, for he hadn't noticed Dominic. "You scared the shit out of me. It's ten to five. You know, if you were going to sleep here, you could've called me. I could have slept in."

"Ten to five?" Dominic asked, ignoring Angelo's gripe. "You sure about that or is it more bullshit?"

"Come on, Dominic, how long you going to call me a liar?"

"Where's Kenny?"

"In the kitchen, probably eating the bread dough," Angelo answered, frustrated with his cousin's avoidance.

"Tell him I've got breakfast with Fabian at six and then I'm off to see my dad. He's driving." Dominic locked the door behind Angelo and took a shower.

Kenny was in the car when Dominic came outside. "Kenny, get out of the truck," Dominic ordered.

Kenny climbed down. "Sorry, Dom, Angelo said you wanted me to drive you today."

"Come here, walk with me." The two walked to the back alley. "Why the fuck did you cover for fucking Angelo?"

Kenny shrugged his shoulders. "He told me to. What can I do?"

"I'd like to strangle the stupid fuck."

"He looks up to you, Dom. He's young. He didn't want to disappoint you."

"You've done enough for him, and you don't need to stick up for him too." Dominic stuck out his hand to Kenny. "I apologize for the bullshit I put you through." Kenny shook his hand. Dominic smiled and told him, "And for all the bullshit I put you through in the future."

They started walking back to the truck when Dominic stopped one more time. "One more thing, Kenny. When I promoted Ange to captain, I never replaced his lieutenant position. Consider it yours, Lieutenant." Kenny was overjoyed and picked up Dominic in a big bear hug. "No, no, no. We don't do this, Kenny." Then the big man put his boss back on the ground.

Once in truck, Dominic told Kenny of his next plan. "While I'm in with my dad, go find a mall and buy some clothes and shoes for the gym."

"Oh, come on, Dominic."

"Every day, you and me are going to walk that track at Bally's. You've got to get in some better shape."

"That's just it, Dom, I'm happy. I don't want to diet or exercise. I like myself the way I am."

"Didn't you hear what I said back in the parking lot?"

"What's that got to do with this?" he asked, careful of revealing information of Kenny's promotion inside the truck in case the feds were listening.

"Everything. It doesn't matter what you want anymore. I want you healthier, and you have to listen, it's an order. You'll be Not-So-Fat Kenny when I'm done with you." Dominic pulled out a wad of cash. "Here, that's about four grand. Buy some other clothes while you're at it. All you ever wear are those suits, you're like Matlock."

"Who's Matlock?"

Dominic turned his head quickly at Kenny. "No fucking way. You don't know who Matlock is? Lawyer, never lost a case, always wore the same suit? It was my dad's favorite show."

"I never watched much TV. I was always too busy with sports."

Dominic just laughed. "Fuck you. You never did a physical thing in your life other than beat people up."

The first truck at Amicucci Breads was being loaded when Tommy Herrick pulled up and entered the bakery through its loading dock. Gary Nussman, surprised to see Tommy, stopped him before he reached the office. "Tommy. What's up?" Gary was six foot two and taller than Tommy, but he was still reluctant to cause any trouble with the Westsider. Everyone knew it was Tommy that ordered the RPG to be fired at that house last year.

"I want to see Dominic."

"He's not here. It's Angelo today. You want to see him?"

"Fine."

"I'll let him know." Gary waited for Tommy to nod his okay before he left to enter the office. "Ange, Tommy H is here."

Angelo was online, looking at the day's baseball spreads and probable pitchers. "What the hell does he want?"

"I have no idea."

"Okay, let him in." Angelo got up and greeted Tommy with a handshake. "Kind of early, no?"

"Been on the freeways for an hour making sure I was clean. Fucking feds are all over me. Where can we talk?"

"Sit at the table. You can leave your cell phone out there," Angelo said, pointing to the kitchen. It had become popular for the feds to place recording devices in the phones themselves and have an informant pass them out free of charge. It had become a family rule to never take a free cell phone from anyone. Angelo flipped a switch on the airwave scrambler and sat down with Tommy. "So what brings you out so early?"

"My guy says your guy won't pay him his twenty-five grand."

"Did your guy take the under on the All-Star game?"

"I don't fucking know. What's the matter?"

"We got scammed on the under. Dominic said not to pay anyone."

"I'm not just 'anyone.' All the fucking money we send your way and you think we're going to scam twenty-five grand from you?"

"I can't do nothing about it. You got to talk to Dom."

"What's his new number? His other one is disconnected."

"I can't tell you if he hasn't. Call his regular cell."

"I'm trying not to be found right now, so how smart would that be? You're really not going to give me his number?"

"Come on. Don't do that. I lose either way here. I can only tell him you came by, I'm sorry."

"This was a waste of my fucking time." Tommy got up and walked out the door.

Angelo looked at Gary. "Man, he makes me nervous."

Tommy left and drove the four blocks to Cooch's Corner, just in case Dominic was there. He passed the bar once, looking for surveillance, but not seeing any cars in the lot either, Tommy chose to just keep going. Just before he reached the end of the street, he noticed headlights turn on in his rearview mirror and a car pulling out behind him. Tommy turned right and punched it, so did the car behind him. He wasn't so sure it was a fed behind him now and wished he had brought a gun.

Tommy slammed on his brakes after three blocks and skidded to a stop after a car cut him off from the street ahead and stopped in the middle of the intersection. Three men with guns exited a parked windowless van to Tommy's left. "A fucking hit," he said to himself as he prepared to run his car into the three shooters. Thankfully, one of the shooters pulled a badge, and Tommy killed his engine. Within minutes, four more undercover cars were on the scene. Tommy realized the feds had the whole area wired to follow the coming and goings of the Amicucci hangout, and jeopardized it all just to bring him in. That wasn't a good sign for Tommy, in his opinion.

After Tommy's acquittal in Miami, he stayed off the radar. The FBI of course wanted to know where he was at all times. They had "lost" Tommy's voice analysis results and issued a warrant to attain new ones, giving authorities probable cause to arrest him upon sight.

"Tommy, where have you have been? We haven't seen you since your acquittal in Florida," Special Agent Todd Weddler asked Tommy in the interrogation room.

"I've been home."

"That's one place you haven't been. What are you doing at Cooch's Corner?"

"Needed a drink."

"Funny. You know what's really funny? The fact that it places you in a criminal conspiracy with Dominic Amicucci makes me laugh."

Tommy was able to call his wife before he was arrested, so he knew his lawyer was on his way. He thought he'd have a little fun in the meantime. "It does? You guys used that same theory in Miami. How'd it work out down there for you?"

"When *we* bring you to trial, rest assured, you're going to jail."

"Well, let's just review your case here. You've got one predicate act of me getting an early-morning drink. It is a bad habit of mine. What else?" Most organized criminals in today's times were very familiar on the RICO laws and the predicate acts that were required for an indictment.

"Where were you last Christmas Eve?"

"I've been through this a hundred times with you guys."

"But you've never answered the question. Were you one of the two that got away from that RPG attack? If not, give me an alibi."

"I've answered your question before."

"No, you haven't."

"Yes, I have. It's the same fucking answer every time."

"Then what is it?"

"Lawyer."

"Yeah, you wait for your fancy expensive lawyer. But guess what? You know those fingerprints we just took of you? I think they just got damaged. We'll probably need new ones next week. Keep that expensive lawyer on standby, as you're going to need him."

Tommy just sighed, "Why do you guys always keep talking? I've asked for my lawyer. I could confess now, and you can't keep the confession. That makes no sense to me. You take this way too personal. It's very unprofessional."

Tommy's lawyer joined him twenty minutes later. "They want you to read something so that they can compare it to a recording. They've got a subpoena, and if you don't, they'll lock you up."

"What is it? Some confession?" asked a skeptical Tommy.

"No, it's nothing incriminating at all. You won't like it, and it's immature, but they're adamant it's what they've got to compare it to," he answered, handing an index card to Tommy.

"I'm not doing this. There's no recording with anyone saying this."

"I know, it's for their laughs. But they will put you in jail. You're a marked man."

"Make them play the fucking tape then."

"It'll be ninety days before we get a hearing, and we both know it's going to be a recording of a child. But they're going to put you through the whole process and keep you locked up the whole time. So just give them their fun."

"I'm not doing it. Fuck them."

"Tommy, once you're in, it's going to be one thing after another. You'll never get out, at least not with any money. Just read the fucking card and do what you do best," he said, leaning in to whisper in Tommy's ear, "Disappear."

Tommy took the card and faced the two-way mirror. "I'm so pretty."

"Louder," was ordered through the intercom.

Tommy begrudgingly recited the index card and could hear the laughter on the other side of the mirror throughout. The laughter reached a high when the electronics expert entered the room with the equipment to record Tommy's voice. "Okay, read the card," the expert ordered, handing Tommy a microphone.

After enduring the FBI's humiliation, Tommy retrieved his property and entered an elevator with his lawyer to go home. Two agents followed them onto the elevator, and Tommy knew they were going anywhere he was going.

Tommy, not known to let things go, was still fuming and decided, as usual, not to let matters rest. He took out his cell phone and pressed a button. "I want to know the daily activities of one FBI agent Todd Weddler. I want to know his every move," was as far as Tommy got before he was facedown on the elevator floor. Tommy never called anyone; he just pressed a button and pretended to start the groundwork of a hit. Nonetheless, the agents still were charging Tommy with threatening a federal officer. The judge would see it for what it was and he'd be out in the morning, but the feds didn't mind sticking it to Tommy for anything they could.

"At least it's one night off the streets, and it'll keep your lawyer on the clock," one agent said to Tommy on the way back up.

Tommy's lawyer, after being in awe at the stupidity he had just witnessed, said, "Tommy, I'll you get in front of a judge in an hour. You'll be right out of here." It was still only 9:00 a.m.

"Don't bet on it. I'm sure these guys will find eight hours' worth of work to do before getting to me." Tommy knew the feds would keep him as long as they could.

"Too bad it's not Friday," said one agent, hoping to keep Tommy locked up all weekend.

The elevator door opened and the agents led Tommy out in handcuffs. "You know, I'm very impressed with your guys' sophisticated harassment. It's amazing how you're all on the same page. This is all so very thourough," Tommy said, complimenting the agents.

"You haven't seen nothing yet."

"No, I didn't think so."

Fat Kenny Infelice and Dominic Amicucci left breakfast with Fabian Bosca and drove to see Dominic's father in prison. Dominic and Fabian came up with the story that the whole loss on the All-Star game was actually pure bad luck and dumb bookies, not a scam. He was aware of Tommy's arrest, and the whole neighborhood was abuzz. And now it was a two-hour ride to his father's prison with his new big buddy.

"You see how good his forehead's looking after only two days?" Kenny asked.

"I hate to say it, but yeah, you did a real nice job."

"Experience? That was the sixth person I stitched up."

"Who the hell else have you stitched up?" Dominic asked, not believing one word.

"Scary, your Uncle George, and Denny Greco, twice," Kenny answered. "They all turned out good except for one. Only Denny's turned out bad—his back got infected. But he didn't take care of it. You should remember that, it was a big ordeal."

"So Fabian won't be a Frankenstein after all, eh?"

"Nope, he's still going to be a good-looking guy."

Dominic shot him a quizzical look. "You think he's a good-looking guy?"

"Fabian's always been a good-looking guy, why?"

"You don't think that makes you sound kind of gay? Especially, not being married?"

Kenny turned his head from the road to look at Dominic. "You've known me my whole life—you think I'm gay?"

"Not at all, well, not until now," Dominic answered jokingly, and Kenny chuckled and looked back at the road.

"When you see some dirty-looking guy, you never hesitate to call him a scumbag. But someone that looks like Fabian you don't say a word, because he's a good-looking guy. Not in any gay way."

"It doesn't mean you go around saying it. What do you think of me?" Dominic asked, looking at Kenny.

Kenny looked back at him. "It is kind of gay to care what I think, though."

"Should have driven myself—put on fucking sports radio."

By 10:00 a.m., Dominic was sitting at a table in the prison's visiting area, waiting for his father. The guards, always happy to see Dominic, assured him the table was not bugged and took a wad of $5,000 as payment. After almost ten minutes, Nick was finally let in, and he already seemed irritated.

"That fucking brother of yours, when's he going to grow up?"

"You're asking for miracles from me if you think I can fix him. He acts like he's twelve."

Nick agreed, "He does, doesn't he? I told him this morning, 'I got twelve years until my parole, and you better pray to God I don't get it, because I'm going to kick the holy living shit out of you when I do get out if you don't change your ways.' He didn't know what to say. I mean, I don't even want to talk to him lately."

"What's he got you so bothered about anyway? What'd he do?"

Nick thought for a moment. "It's not just one thing, it's everything about him. His demeanor, he's lazy, whiny, he's just weak."

"That's not fair. Don't get me wrong, I think he's pretty fucking spoiled myself, but you call him weak, like it's a fault."

"How is weakness not a fault, Dominic?"

"He's weak because he's never had to face nothing. You always protected him, I protect him now, what's he supposed to be like? It's not like he's a bad kid."

"The kid's a pussy and it's my fault?"

"You tell him to grow up, but you don't let him. Cut the strings, I'll make sure he's okay."

"I don't want him in this life, capiche? That's that. Now, what else you got?"

"Tommy Herrick was arrested this morning, about six thirty."

"What? Why?"

"No idea. He stopped by the bakery asking Angelo why they weren't paid their twenty-five grand. Then he drove by the Corner and the feds had the whole fucking area under surveillance. One fed saw him and they all pounced, six cars in three blocks, probably more."

"I thought you said the feds were gone."

"Well, they weren't visible. I just figured indictments were coming."

"You got to find out about Tommy. And why wasn't he paid his twenty-five?"

"Because everyone around me is fucking ignorant. I withheld payment on the under winners, and our guys figured it included the Westside guys too." The Westside was Doug Sullivan's crews.

Nick just stared at his son, wondering what in the world was going on in the Amicucci book. "I'm getting some real fucking concerns here, Dominic. Take care of Tommy and his money, first fucking thing. Don't fuck with this guy, Dominic. His fucking army keeps the sharks away from you. Give him thirty grand and get one of his guys in our book to tighten things up."

"You're kidding me, right? I got Jackie off his ass, it'll be fine."

"You see me laughing? The fact that Jackie was even on his ass means it's too loose. Fucking morons don't even know what to do with a quarter of a million dollars in bets. What is this, the minor fucking leagues? Training camp? It's a fucking means to an end, and you're the skipper, Dominic. So what about the All-Star game? Go ahead, tell me you have no fucking idea and it's all just a coincidence."

"No coincidence at all, it was your beloved Fabian."

CHAPTER V

Old Habits Die Hard

"WHAT DO YOU mean it was Fabian?" Nick asked after Dominic delivered his bombshell.

"It was Fabian that hired bettors to take the under with a list of certain bookies, over two million dollars."

"You're wrong. What's your source?"

"What's my source? Fabian."

"He told you himself?"

"He did. He did it because you're demoting him."

"Why would he tell you?"

"Because I was going to whack him in my basement and he told me there's all sorts of secret rackets not kicking money up. He's got his own little rackets too, and he's going around ripping off others in the family."

"I'm lost here, Dominic. Fill me in."

"He stole ninety grand from Mike Sodano's racket, and I confronted him about it. He went nuts about taking crews from him for Jackie Matts and him being demoted. The asshole even bought a villa down in Mexico. He pushed me, Scary leveled him, and we took him to my basement. I'm going to get a handle on everything he knows and get our own people down in Mexico, and then I'm going to whack him.

"You gone crazy? Fabian's like family."

"Not at all, in fact, I'm quite inspired. Fabian's a jealous fuck—you give him a pass and he's going to put a bullet in the back of my head and take my job. It's not just the under scam, he's got too much ambition. He can't let this 'captain thing' go. And a villa? Come on. He thinks he's a fucking king."

"I have practically raised this kid. You're his fucking daughter's godfather."

"Yeah, yeah, yeah, how about I give him two million dollars and his own rule book for only him to follow? Oh, wait. That's what's already happening."

"You better knock this fucking chip off your shoulder you've got or I will."

"Go ahead. I don't give a fuck anymore, this stupid fucking life of ours. Fabian was like my brother, and look what it's turned into. Even my own blood, Angelo, lies to my face."

"You know why all this is happening? Because of you, because you have no control—you don't even know what's going on at our book and you live fucking six miles away. Blame yourself before you blame the life."

"Fuck this," said Dominic and got up to leave.

"So help me, God. Dominic, you turn your back on me and I will break your fucking neck and spend the rest of my life right here."

Dominic sat back down.

"You're so fucking temperamental," Nick told him.

"Who threatened to break whose neck?"

"I don't care if I'm a hundred years old, if you ever disrespect me, I will break your neck."

"I'll remember the fatherly advice."

"You do that. When Danny gets back, he'll tell me the condition of your fuck ups. I'll decide what happens to Fabian. I got fucking zero confidenceyou got any idea what the fuck's going on, so I'm not going to whack someone based on information from someone who don't know nothing about fucking nothing."

"I'm just one big fuckup, right?"

"Worse. You're like the Grim fucking Reaper. Ever notice how everyone seems to die around you, Dominic?" Before getting up to leave, Nick whispered one last parting shot at Dominic, "I killed because I had to. You kill because you enjoy it. And that's just fucking sick."

Dominic watched his father disappear into the prison and just sat there for several minutes before a guard asked him if he was okay. Dominic ignored the guard and silently made his way back to Fat Kenny and his truck.

"How'd it go?" Kenny asked as Dominic climbed in.

"Ball of fucking joy. You know, I get it. I'm going to die in jail or get whacked in the streets. But I wish it would hurry the fuck up, because this interim bullshit is for the birds. I found something out today, Kenny. Words can really hurt sometimes."

Kenny, sensing his friend's visit didn't go so well, tried cheering him up. "You think that's bad? Try waiting to eat yourself to death. How many bowls of spaghetti do I got to fucking eat, huh?"

That got a smile out of Dominic. "I got to get away. Let's get the fuck out of here for the weekend. Where do you want to go, Florida or Vegas?"

"You serious?"

"Serious as the heart attack you're bound to have."

"Let's go to Vegas, I got some new clothes."

"Deal. You got until Monday to pig the fuck out. I won't even make you walk the track today. Just drop me off at Bally's. I want to hit the weights hard. You can go to fucking Dairy Queen if you want, just make the plane reservations. Make it first class. Oh, and sorry about the heart attack comment, Kenny. Old habits die hard."

"Fly out tomorrow? What hotel?"

"I'll take care of the hotel. Get a flight for tonight, and we'll come back Monday morning. And the week after, Danny comes home."

Dominic strolled to the front desk of Bally's, happy to take a time-out and get away for a few days and put his father's words behind him. Things were looking up, and even the pretty brunette was working today. "Hey, Marsha, what are you doing this weekend?"

"Working," she answered with surprise.

"Get someone to take your shifts and grab a friend and come to Vegas with me and my buddy, Kenny."

"You serious?"

"Tonight to Monday, let's go."

"Let me see what I can do."

"Good. You've got until the end of my workout," he said and headed for the locker room.

"Dominic," she called. Dominic turned around. "My name's Michelle, not Marsha."

"Huh?"

"Yeah, right here," she said, pointing to her name tag. "Michelle."

Dominic got a big smile. "My bad."

The two locked eyes and she smiled back. "You're forgiven. Go do your thing," she suggested, nodding to the locker room.

Dominic worked out for an extra hour today trying to blow off some steam. He took his shower and approached Michelle for her answer. "Well?" he asked.

"Count me in, me and my friend, Rachel."

Dominic gave her his address to meet at later and opened the passenger seat of his truck. "Kenny, I got some broads coming . . ." his seat was covered with fast-food wrappers and bags. "This isn't going to work for me."

Kenny looked at Dominic innocently. "What?"

"It's only been two fucking hours."

"You said I got until Monday, and I'm taking full advantage."

"You got shit from Taco Bell, McDonald's, and Burger King." Kenny was eating a banana split from Dairy Queen when Dominic came out. "Get it all the fuck out of here, right fucking now, Kenny."

Kenny got the truck cleaned out and the two hit the road, heading to Dominic's father's house. "First off, Kenny, I love this truck more than most people. So when you throw garbage on my truck, you're throwing garbage on me."

"I'm sorry, Dom. I didn't know."

Dominic held his hand up toward Kenny. "I'm not done. Secondly, there're two girls coming with us, so shit like that can't happen."

"Who are the girls?"

"Michelle and her friend."

"The girl from Bally's?" Kenny asked.

"Doesn't fucking matter, just don't be a fucking slob." Dominic's throwaway phone rang, and Kenny went to answer it. "Don't answer it. No more business until Monday. Just drop me at my dad's, go pack, and then we'll wait for the girls at my house."

It took ten minutes to get to the house, and Dominic walked into a yelling match between his stepmother and his brother, Sal. His Aunt Marie was in the kitchen cooking, and his Uncle Ziggy was on the couch drinking a beer and watching TV, both paying no mind to the yelling. Just another day!

"Oh great, now it's the top mobster," Helena Amicucci said when her stepson walked in the front door. She accepted what her husband and his son were in this world, but she made Nick promise her that if she bore him a son, he could not be a part of that life.

Dominic was hoping to grab a bite to eat, use the phone to make some calls, and grab some suits out of the room he still kept here. He had no intention of inquiring of Sal's wrongdoing and chose to forego the bite to eat. "Just grabbing some things, I'll be gone before you know it."

"Will you please tell your brother of his one condition to be in this world?"

"Yes, Sal. That was their agreement to let you be born," Dominic answered, trying to hurry to the stairs.

"That's not my problem," Sal said.

"It's not mine either," said Dominic, finally reaching the foot of the staircase before his Uncle Ziggy called him.

"Hey Dom, I need a moment before you leave." Dominic realized he wasn't getting out of this house now without having to take care of these problems, but he gave it one last try.

"Everyone, I'm going to Las Vegas in the next four hours. Is this anything that can wait until Monday?"

All three adults answered in unison, "No."

As much as Dominic was hoping to start some relaxation, this was family. Despite his father's hurtful spews, there wasn't any situation conceivable to Dominic that would have him turn his back on his family. "Okay, Sal, what did you do?"

Helena answered, "He has bullets."

"He has bullets?" Dominic asked in disbelief.

Uncle Ziggy piped in next, still watching TV. "The kid has bullets, so what?"

"I don't want him to have any bullets," Helena said.

Dominic felt another betrayal coming on. "I don't want him to have any bullets either." Dominic grabbed his brother by the arm. "Let's go out back and have a little word."

"Do you have a gun, Sal?" Dominic asked once they were in the backyard.

"They're fucking bullets."

"I asked you a question. Do you have a gun?"

"So what the fuck if I do?"

Slap! "I will break your fucking neck and spend the rest of my life with Dad than let your punk ass disrespect me again. Who gave you a gun?"

"I ain't no snitch, you motherfucker. You ever touch me again and I'll . . ."

As much as Dominic tried to work out all his built-up aggression at the gym, it wasn't enough, and the rest of it was about to come out. Dominic cut his brother's sentence off with a big punch to his gut, and Sal bent over in pain. Then blood spattered the patio from Sal's lip popping from a backhand right. Everyone came running out the house, yelling for Dominic to stop; they had been watching through the windows. "This is long overdue," Dominic yelled back. He grabbed Sal by his leg and dragged him across the yard. Once they reached the pool, Dominic spun himself and Sal until Sal was off the ground. Dominic let him go, right into the pool.

Dominic started throwing everything in sight at Sal in the pool. "You motherfucker! Where's your fucking gun? I'll fucking drown you!"

Sal, now terrified, yelled out, "In my car, under the driver's seat."

Helena gasped; she was still hoping Sal really only had bullets. Dominic ran past everyone to Sal's car. He opened the unlocked door and pulled out the gun from under the seat. Sal was out of the pool when he saw Dominic walking back toward him with his gun, and all four just stood and watched him approach.

"Sal, you do understand what I'm going to do to you next time, don't you?"

"I'm over eighteen. I should be able to do what I want."

"None of us can, Sal. None of us can. We all do what Dad wants, and you're no different. Go get cleaned up. We good?"

"I guess so, Dom. It's not fair, but okay."

Dominic turned to look at his stepmother. "He'll be fine. There's no need to tell Dad—he's mad enough at Sal right now as it is."

"Promise me, Dominic, you'll keep him out if it."

"I promise to do everything I can. And I promise I'll let everyone know that if they get this kid involved, they'll pay a heavy price."

"I hope so, for your father's sake." Helena left to tend to her son.

"Okay, Uncle Zig, what's on your mind?"

"My grandson Jimmy. You gotta talk to him."

"Talk to him about what?"

"Talk to him about his father, Charley. He don't spend no time with him. He's going to regret it the rest of his life."

"I'll talk to him. You're absolutely right, he should be home more."

"Tonight, I need him home tonight."

"Come on. They said Charley's got months. I'll talk to Jimmy next week."

"What, are you shittin' me? Doctors don't know shit. I've got Charley's brother and sister coming over tonight. I'm having all my family over for a nice night with a dying man. Fucking Jimmy has to be at his club with his little cronies and can't come home. I need you to get him home. Please, Dominic."

Dominic now planned another stop before he got home. "Fine. I just got to make some calls, and I'll go get him."

"You think the phones are safe here? As much time as you spend here?"

"They've been safe for years. How many hours do you think the feds could listen to Valentina gab with friends?"

"At least Danny will be home in case they're not safe and you go away for twenty years."

"Good one." Dominic said and went upstairs to his room.

Dominic's first phone call was to Doug Sullivan's lawyer, Carl Voight, to inquire about Tommy Herrick's situation after his arrest that morning. "Carl, it's Dominic."

"Are you on a safe line?" the lawyer asked.

"Yes." Carl Voight gave Dominic another number to call, a clean phone for the lawyer who was not so clean. Carl Voight had gone from defending drunk drivers to having one of the state's largest law firms and hobnobbing with politicians both in Lansing and Washington DC. "What's the story with Tommy?" Dominic asked after calling the other phone number.

"They'll drop the charges after seventy-two hours. But he is super pissed at you."

"At me? For what?"

"He says if he wasn't chasing you down, he wouldn't have been over there. And you are aware that whole neighborhood is under watch, right?"

"I am now. Did he really pretend to order a hit on an agent, in front of an agent?"

"Unfortunately, yes. And he wants you to call his brother, Billy. Here's a good number for you." Dominic took the number and hung up with the lawyer. He'd call Billy in a minute, but first, he wanted to get his reservations in Vegas together. Their man in Sin City was Stevie Turner, another top Sullivan crew member and best friends with Doug Sullivan and the Herrick brothers.

"Stevie, it's Dominic, I'm heading out there tonight, four of us."

"Dominic, we're all booked up over here. No room for you," replied Turner.

"You fucking kidding me? What do you mean you're all booked up?" Dominic had called Turner's cell phone, so this couldn't be an open conversation.

"Talk to Billy."

Dominic hung up and called the number he had for Billy Herrick. "What the fuck? You really think you can stop me from going Vegas? You guys fucking represent *me* out there."

"Wrong, Dominic. I represent my brother, everywhere. I got everything locked down until Tommy gets out of jail. Doug's been trying to call you, wanting to know what kind of shit you're trying to pull here."

"No one's trying to pull anything. This is all over twenty-five grand?"

"It could be ten fucking dollars, it's the principle. Why the fuck wouldn't you pay us?"

"I never said not to pay you guys. I told my men not to pay the under winners on the All-Star game, and they took it to mean you."

"Sounds like you run a pretty loose camp. Both Doug and Tommy said you changed your number and didn't tell them."

"Believe me. No one's more pissed about my camp than I am. Come on by, I'll give you a fucking hundred grand right now, just to show you there's no bad intentions here. And I just never got around to calling Tommy with my new number, with all the bullshit on that All-Star game I've been dealing with."

"Then why not answer when Doug called? Then you turned your phone off?"

"I thought it was my dad calling. I turned it off because I was trying to just go to Vegas with a couple of broads and forget about everything else. I wasn't ducking Doug, who I have no idea as to where he's at. And how did he get my number?"

"Your father called him. They're arranging a court date to get him home."

"My dad called him? They're arranging a court date? What the fuck is going on?"

"Obviously, Dominic, you'll be the last to know. Keep your hundred grand, just send our twenty-five over and have a good time in Vegas. Later."

After Kenny picked Dominic up, they headed to Little Jimmy's hangout, and Dominic ordered him home as per his Uncle Ziggy's request. He then had Angelo send the twenty-five grand to the Westside and was finally en route to Metro Airport with the girls when Dominic's secret phone rang; he had turned it back on. Kenny answered it and handed to Dominic. "It's Angelo."

"Angelo, there better not be no fucking problem with getting them guys their money."

"That's done. Vito called." Vito Paganini is a captain in New York's Grazzitti Family, the largest of New York's five Mafia families. Dominic's great grandmother was Vito's aunt, making Vito, Dominic's third cousin. He was nicknamed Wall Street due to his college education and the stock racket he handled for the family. "He just flew in and wants to meet you now. I told him to wait at the airport, as you were already on your way there."

"He flew in? That ain't a good sign." Vito always drove. The reason was, he hated giving a paper trail to the feds of his coming and goings. The fact that he sacrificed a paper trail that diligently avoided to get herein a quicker manner was troubling. "Give him my flight number. Tell him to meet me at my terminal. And Ange, don't ever tell anyone where I'm heading unless I tell you to. You're going to send me right into an ambush someday." Vito was family, so Dominic wasn't so concerned about Angelo giving him his whereabouts. But then again, the world was different in New York.

"Sorry, Dominic."

"As usual," Dominic said hanging up the phone.

"What do you mean ambush?" Michelle asked Dominic. Michelle was driving her Honda Civic and heard Dominic's conversation from the passenger seat.

"Not a real ambush, don't worry about it."

The foursome cleared the security checkpoints and checked in their luggage, heading to the flight terminal. Dominic was walking with Michelle, enjoying the day after working through everything he did today to get to this point. Now just one more quick meet and they were off. But his first glimpse of his distant cousin from New York put all of his senses into alert mode and brought him right back to the world he was trying to escape from for a few days. Blocking his entrance was Vito and his right-hand man, Nino Valenti. To their left were two of his guys Dominic recognized from New York, and a quick survey of the area had another guy sitting in a chair to their right, reading the paper. Problem was that his eyes never hit the newspaper. Dominic quickly recognized the danger of a hit, and if he had planned it himself, there should be someone coming from behind.

Dominic stopped in his tracks and immediately turned around, bumping into Kenny and Michelle's friend, Rachel. He grabbed

Michelle by the wrist to ensure her attention. "You girls get right on that plane, don't fucking stop for nothing. Just get on the plane."

"What's going on?" Michelle asked, starting to panic.

"I need you to get on that plane. We'll be on in a minute. I recognize some old friends, that's all. Just go."

Dominic released his grip on Michelle, and the girls marched toward their plane, and toward Vito and Nino. "Watch the two on the left and make sure the girls get on the plane," Dominic ordered Kenny. Dominic made eye contact with Vito, and they nodded to each other. Then Vito starting walking toward Dominic. Once the girls got past Vito and Nino, Dominic made a quick right and was quickly by the rows of chairs, which, Dominic believed, contained a shooter.

"Dominic? Where the fuck are you going?" Vito yelled out and started walking after Dominic.

Vito's two bodyguards to the left moved to follow their boss, as Kenny tried to cut them off. "Get out of the way, fat boy," one of them said, paying no other mind to him.

Kenny swallowed the insult and did his job—he watched the girls enter the tunnel before he turned to follow the duo. He noticed the authorities reacting to the situation but was approached by a man with a newspaper, who got up from a chair and showed them a badge, identifying himself as a federal agent. The authorities backed off.

Dominic, after looking back and seeing the quizzical look on Vito's face, stopped to finally talk to him, "What's with the fucking goons? You never bring no muscle."

"You thought you were going to get whacked?"

"It would be a fitting end to this fucking day," Dominic replied, adrenaline coming down. "What was with the guy in the chair?"

"He's a fucking fed, you moron." Vito almost broke into tears, he started laughing so hard. "Nino, did you see the look in his face? How about that Romeo? Giving himself up for the women." It went on for a few minutes before Vito could get on with the business that brought him there in the first place.

"Okay, seriously now. A rumor's around about you, and I got sent to ask you about it," Vito said, whispering to avoid the prying ears.

"What kind of rumor?" Dominic asked.

"We lost a lot of money on that All-Star game, and people are saying it came from your family, all the action that is. You know me, I told everyone to go fuck themselves. But I can't tell my boss that. So how about it? Heard anything odd?"

Dominic's heart dropped to his stomach. ***Fabian had to fuck with New York,*** Dominic thought. This just got very bad. He knew he couldn't even keep a poker face, so he just didn't deny it. "Yeah, I'm hearing some things," was all he could muster.

"What the fuck does that mean, Dominic? Every fucking family is griping here. What the fuck happened?"

"My dad's handling it."

"Not good enough. My boss is bigger than your boss. We're talking almost three million dollars here."

"Why didn't your bookies lay off the action?" Dominic asked.

Vito gave a small chuckle, "We're New York, kid—the country lays its bets off to us. We're where the buck stops. I need some answers to take home. Like a dumbass, I've been sticking up for you."

Why the fuck didn't I put a bullet in Fabian's fucking head when I had the chance? Dominic asked himself. "Something bad happened. We're still investigating. I'll pay the money if I have to."

"That's a start. But you know the bosses aren't going to let this go until someone's in a fucking trunk, right? Don't let it be you." Vito walked off, leaving Dominic to ponder his thoughts.

"Kenny! Take the girls to Vegas. I'll take the next flight."

"Where the hell are you going?" Kenny asked.

"I gotta take care of something. And Kenny, watch your back."

A common sight in airports is people running to catch their flights. Dominic was running the opposite way through the airport. He stopped at the car rentals and rented a car for the night. He then hit the highway and raced home. *Fucking Fabian* was the only thought permeating through Dominic's brain.

Once in his room, Dominic stopped at the bed he hadn't touched in over four years. Dominic could hear Fabian accusing him of killing his wife; he could hear his father call him the Grim Reaper. He heard Billy Herrick treating him like a punk, and he could hear his own distant blood, Vito Paganini, threatening his life, all because of Fabian. Dominic flew into a rage. He flipped the mattress across the room. Next came the box spring, Dominic sent it airborne. He eventually tired himself out and collapsed to the floor, and his own words came back to him, *I'm either going to die in jail or in the streets.* Dominic got back to his feet and went to his secret compartment in the dresser. He pulled out his Beretta, loaded it, and grabbed a silencer. Dominic tore open the bottom of the box spring and retrieved a duffel bag he had hidden there years ago. The bag contained a half million dollars, passports with IDs for two different identities, and two more guns with ammunition—a lam bag he called it. He put the gun in the bag, grabbed a bottle of Jack Daniels, and drove off into the night in his rented car.

CHAPTER VI

Surprise

DOMINIC PARKED DOWN the block from Fabian's house and enjoyed his whiskey for a few minutes before exiting the car. He walked the block of the secluded street and into Fabian's backyard. All the lights were off, except one in an upstairs room. The door wall was open, as Fabian rarely ran his air-conditioning. Dominic drew his gun, with silencer attached, and entered the house. What the moonlight revealed calmed Dominic's rage. The house was bare. Fabian had cleaned it out and probably gone to Mexico. He must not have believed for a second that Dominic wasn't going to tell his father.

Dominic kept his gun ready as he climbed the stairs to the only light in the house. In the room, Dominic found four suitcases, each with one and a half million dollars. He took a seat on the floor and had a few more swigs before carrying the bags to his car. Dominic's whole plan was to string Fabian along and retrieve enough information to fix his family. Fabian's plan was to string Dominic along long enough to make a safe getaway. Lifelong friends. Dominic could only muster a laugh, the anger was gone. Dominic felt outsmarted, but he was okay with it. He had always looked up to Fabian when they were young, and for some odd reason, this just felt right.

Fabian would hole up in Mexico for a while, Dominic figured. Eventually he'd have to make contact, as he couldn't hide forever. He drove the money to Aunt Marie's house and left it with Angelo to count. Dominic didn't know how much was in the suitcases yet, but he was sure it was enough to cover New York's losses and put that terror to an end. He told Angelo to have someone drive the money there in the morning. After a meal from his aunt, Dominic finally started heading back to the airport and called Kenny in Las Vegas. Kenny was on top of the world.

"Dom, how much did these girls cost? Christ, they got loaded on the plane, and they're all over me. They dragged me to the dance floor and started freaking me. This is a great fucking time already, Dom. When are you coming out?"

"They're all over you?"

"Dom, they're the meat and I'm the sandwich. No wait, I'm the meat, they're the sandwich."

Sounds like the girls weren't the only ones getting loaded on the plane. "Kenny, I get the dancing, but what do you mean they're all over you?"

"Can't you get the picture? You like one of these hookers or something, Dom?"

Dominic actually thought he did like Michelle. "What? Are you kidding me? I was calling to let you know I wasn't coming out there. I don't know what I was thinking. I can't get away for no weekend. But, hey, have a fucking blast Big Daddy. I'll see you Monday." Dominic turned his car around and headed to his sister's, just a few blocks away. He pulled in the driveway and grabbed his lam bag. He put a hundred thousand dollars in his waistband and rang the bell on the front door at the late hour.

Valentina answered the door after knowing it was Dominic. "Dominic, what happened?" she asked, assuming it was an emergency.

Dominic, after taking everything out of the bag except for four hundred thousand dollars, handed it to Valentina. "Here, give this to your deadbeat father-in-law. Tell him it's a family loan, and I won't even charge him interest."

Valentina was floored. "Thank you, Dominic."

Dominic, with his bottle in one hand, reached into his waistband with his other and pulled out the ten stacks of ten thousand dollars in one hundred bills bundled together. "Put this aside for when you got some kids, which should be soon. You've been married two years already."

"You can be a good man sometimes, Big Brother. I don't know what to say."

"Just make sure you hang on to that money. Don't be dumb with it. I'll see you, sis."

"You shouldn't drive. Come on in, stay the night. I'll have some drinks with you."

Dominic held up his bottle of Jack. "Since when the hell did you start drinking whiskey?"

"I didn't say I'll be drinking whiskey."

Dominic spent the night at his sister's and in the morning met his cousin, Angelo, at the bakery and went back to business as usual.

A week went by and there was no word from Fabian. Even his villa in Mexico had been abandoned. Dominic had been able to make amends with the families in New York by covering their losses, with interest. The day finally came for the crime family's underboss, Danny Serafini, to come home, and Dominic had a little surprise for his father's boyhood friend.

Danny was being driven back to town by his son, Danny Jr., a sophomore at the University of Michigan, majoring in law. Danny Jr. was driving his father to Cooch's Cucina, Nick Amicucci's restaurant, under orders from Dominic.

"He said I have to absolutely bring you here before you go home. What do you want me to do?" Danny's son told him.

"Is it a party?"

"No. Mom and everyone's at home with our party."

"Fuck him. Take me home."

"I'm not getting in the middle. Mom knows you'll be a little later."

They pulled into the lot and it was vacant, except for Dominic's truck parked in the handicap spot up front. "Odd for a Tuesday at lunchtime, huh?" Danny asked more to himself than to his kid.

"I'll go in with you, Dad."

"You'll stay in the car. Get the fuck out of here if something bad happens," said Danny. He walked to the front door and entered the restaurant.

It was dark except for one table with a lit table lamp on it. Dominic met Danny at the door and gave him a quick embrace. "We gotta talk," he said, motioning Danny to the table.

"I haven't even seen my fucking wife and daughter yet."

"You will. But I need to speak with you first."

Danny followed Dominic to the table. "I don't know if this is supposed to be romance or a hit," Danny said, keeping his senses on full alert.

"You've been gone a long time, Danny," Dominic said after they took their seats.

"Not too long."

"Well, things have changed in five years."

"Yeah, like manners. I should be home with my family, not listening to you tell me you're the fucking man. Okay. I got it. Can I go now?"

"Not yet. I've got something for you."

"My fifty grand I hope." The crime family paid its made members ten thousand dollars a year for every year of incarceration upon their release.

"No, it's more of a surprise," he said and quickly stood, signaling the people in the kitchen to come out.

Danny stood up in alarm as the kitchen doors threw open and the lights came on.

"Surprise!" shouted the family members as they piled out of the kitchen, led by Danny's wife, Bianca, who ran right into his arms. His son, Danny Jr., had parked the car and come in the back way. Danny's daughter, Sabrina, and her husband were there, and Danny's brothers and sisters wheeled out his parents, both in their nineties. Dominic's family was there with the Jagges, of which Vinny Jagge had gotten home hours earlier from his five-year stint.

Waiters and waitresses passed out glasses of champagne and brought out a smorgasbord of dishes; the room filled with hugs and cheer. Danny finally got back to Dominic after getting some time with his immediate family. "You really had me going, Dom," and they gave each other a real embrace this time.

Dominic handed Danny an envelope. "Here's your fifty grand." Dominic handed him a second, thicker envelope. "And here's a little something extra."

Danny got a big smile. "How much extra?"

"Like, enough to finish putting your fucking kid through law school, so say thank you."

Danny gave him another hug, and then they went to eat. Nick called on Dominic's phone and got to talk to his old friend, still with another fifteen years left on his sentence. Danny spent the rest of the day eating and drinking, enjoying his freedom. He would spend the evening at home and be right back at work in the morning after a five-year absence.

It was 9:00 a.m. and Dominic and Angelo were in the back of the bakery when Danny strolled in. Dominic looked at the watch he wasn't wearing. "Wow. Prison's changed you. I remember you with your '6:03 ain't 6:00' bullshit. And you come empty handed as well? Never would've happened five years ago."

Danny was one for punctuality. "Are you kidding me? Finally sleeping on a fucking mattress, pure discipline alone got me out of bed. So where do we talk at nowadays?

Dominic flipped the switch on the scrambler and took a seat at the old wooden table. "No safer place than right here," he said, slapping the top of the table. "Ange, give us a moment," said Angelo and left the room.

Danny sat down. "Are you sure it's safe here? Feds got all kinds of shit these days. I didn't exactly enjoy my five years, you know."

"No? I heard you were the life of the party in Arkansas, heard they called you Teeny Weeny Fini."

Danny Serafini had to laugh at that. "Did you wait five years for that one?"

Dominic nodded his head and smiled. "Yeah, I did. But I got a guy who handles changing all the settings on the scrambler to stay current with the feds, worked so far."

"Humor me. Let's talk out back." Once alone in the back parking lot, Danny turned to Dominic. "What the hell happened with Angela? And are you okay?"

Dominic hadn't expected that. Angela's murder had happened during Nick's trial, but Danny had already pled guilty and was off serving his time. "Just fucked up, that's all. Random mugging gone bad, what are the fucking chances?"

"Well, I'm real sorry, Dominic. I know how you cared for her."

"Anyway, what else?" Dominic said, changing the subject.

"I can understand you whacking Vic Jr.—I never heard a good thing about him. But how could you whack Nino?" Nino Kalko had been an Amicucci family friend since the 1960s.

"I didn't have a choice."

"You didn't have a choice?" Danny asked skeptically.

"You read about the shooting with Joey LaFilia?"

"I remember Joey. And I know you whacked him from the fallout from Vic."

"Yeah, he started giving Fabian a real hard time. He was caught meeting with what was believed to be agents. I okayed the hit and gave it to Doug to make him disappear. Well, Nino had a problem with that. It was Doug's guy that took out Vic and got caught, then another one of Doug's guys went down for a different hit. Nino wanted to use his guy, this Ronny Chimney kid he wanted to get made. He kept arguing not to use Doug's guys anymore. I told him to leave it alone. It had nothing to fucking to do with him anyway. He still sends his kid, and he shoots and kills Joey in broad daylight, and Joey's got two fucking agents following him around. The agents shoot back, Ronny kills one and hits the other in the stomach, and he gets away."

"So I get hitting this Ronny Chimney fuck, but Nino's like family."

"I left Ronny dead in the streets, but that wasn't enough. The feds wanted more than just the shooter—they wanted who ordered it. So the feds completely shut us down. They raided the Corner three days in a row—once for guns, once for drugs, and the third time, just looking for evidence. Now how does that get signed off by a judge, looking for evidence? They brought me in, told me they wanted me to rat on my dad, saying he ordered the shooting. After a while, I just flat out old them, we did not order the hit."

"You talked about it with the fucking feds? Why not just get your lawyer?"

"Believe me, Danny, I asked for my lawyer a hundred fucking times. A fed got killed, my rights weren't their priority, revenge was. I told them it was an unsanctioned hit. This top fed comes in, takes me out of the interrogation room and into the men's room, and wants to know who did it. He told me it was off the record and that there wasn't a chance in hell that anyone was going to jail here. They were going to die. I asked him if I was getting the green light to take this guy out. He tells me, not just the green light, but my life's going to be not worth living if I don't."

"You should have blackmailed him, get it on paper."

"Even my old man agreed with me, Nino had to go. Those feds were just doing their jobs—killing civilians is just plain murder. The hit wasn't even supposed to happen that way. So we give the hit to Angelo and Nino's not been seen since."

"And you make Angelo a captain?"

"That's been a mistake. But it had to stay in our crew—we couldn't just give all that power away. Who else than Ange? Jackie Beans don't want to do shit and that's everyone that's halfway competent. Maybe Fat Kenny, but that would go over worse than naming Angelo did. It really pissed a lot of people off."

"You've been through a lot in five years, that's for sure. Your father told me you'd done great and he's very proud."

Dominic scoffed, "My father? You don't have to do that, Danny. I know that man hates me."

"You don't really think that, do you?"

"Think that? I know that. He blames me for my mother's death. I get it."

"That was never the case."

"It's fine. What can you do?"

"You have no idea how much Nick loves you."

"Danny, my whole youth that man avoided me like the fucking plague. I remember his face when we looked at each other—he always looked away. We never were like a real father and son. He got better after he met Helena, but I was always baggage, something he was stuck with. I just wanted to live with Uncle George and Aunt Marie, but that would've hurt his image. I'm not crying about it. I think I turned out okay."

"You'll never know how different your father was before your mother died. He'd do nice things for her in front of people—he was a romantic."

"You're so full of shit, Danny."

"Ask your Uncle George. Your mother was his absolute world—he was such a different man back then. He acted like a teenager sometimes with her. Your grandfather always would bitch at him for it."

Dominic was hanging onto Danny's every word, not sure if they were talking about the same person. "And then when you were born, Dominic, he was the happiest man in the world."

"That's why he hates me. My mother was sick until she died. I ruined his happy little world by being born."

"No, Dominic. I look at you and I still see your mother. Do you have any idea how hard that was for him when you were only three? It was too painful for him. He'd break down with just a look at you. When you would stay at George and Marie's, he'd always come by late, after you'd gone to bed. He'd be drunk like always back then and sit and watch you sleep. George and I could hear him through the door—he'd just sit there and cry. He never blamed you once, Dominic. He just couldn't handle the pain for a long, long time."

Dominic just looked off, scared to say a word; it was taking all of his efforts to not shed a tear. "And you've gone through hell, and you've kept the family intact and strong. Nick's very proud of that. He told me about Fabian and what he said to you. He can be a fucking dick, and he knows it. He was hurt by Fabian—we've all watched him grow up. You got duped by your best friend—your father sees that now. I'm sure he won't apologize to you, but you gotta know, he didn't mean that shit. Don't you?"

"He did apologize, somewhat. Let's head in, and I'll finish bringing you back up to speed over lunch. Got any plans tonight?"

"You got to take me to a Tiger game."

Dammit! If there was one thing in the world Dominic hated, it was going to a Tiger game with his father and Danny. There was no getting up, never until the seventh inning stretch. They never sat in the suites, which Dominic much more enjoyed, and there were always confrontations with the people in front of them. Nick expected his orders to be obeyed, even of other spectators when told to sit down. It was mandatory for the beer and hot dog vendors to plant themselves by their seats, but Nick at least made it worth their while. It was just too much of an ordeal for Dominic to enjoy, and after being gone for five years, he knew Danny was itching for it.

"Big game, White Sox tonight. I'll get us a suite, bring the crew," Dominic said, hoping Danny might agree.

"Fuck those suites. I got to be in the action. Come on, Dom, same area as always, as close as you can you get to the White Sox dugout."

"You want to be on TV or something? Believe me, I saw you five years ago on TV, walking into the courthouse. You ain't something to write home about."

"You do know your jokes are going to get old, don't you? I'm gone five years, and you're the class fucking clown," Danny said, entering the bakery. "And I don't want to be on TV, I want to heckle Ozzie Guiilen, the White Sox manager."

"Yeah, this sounds like fun," Dominic said sarcastically.

Angelo was waiting for them to come in. "Sammy Regina died this morning. And apparently, Jimmy Torta died yesterday."

Sammy Regina was in the twelfth year of a twenty-year sentence; he was seventy-eight years old. He was the captain that Nick replaced. Jimmy Torta was eighty-five years and doing life. He was a well-respected family advisor in his day. These were respected men who deserved a respectful send-off, and Dominic and Danny knew they'd have to attend. Mob funerals are magnets for the FBI—they photograph everyone coming and going.

Dominic slapped Danny on the back. "Nice. You can give the feds a current photo for their wall."

Two funerals in two days, both pretty much the same. Dominic and Danny went together and gave each grieving family an envelope full of cash. All six captains attended, which included Angelo, who came with Fat Kenny. Other than that, the only active gangsters present were any old-timers who knew them personally. The FBI showed up, and as always, with full disrespect for the dead, recorded everything they could. Dominic and Danny knew it was just giving ammunition for the feds, but they believed in their world. It would be the beginning of the end, in their opinion, for bosses to stop showing respect for their men in their deaths. Once the code starts breaking, it would be like New York, where every other person you talk to is wearing a wire.

Summer ended and fall began, and life was beginning to return to normal, whatever normal was. Danny settled into his freedom at a quick rate, and he and Dominic had started the task of cleaning up Fabian's mess. There still was no word from Fabian, but with Angelo's wedding finally here, Dominic believed Fabian might finally show his face.

Vinny Jagge also adapted quickly to life on the outside with his new captain position. He was not happy about the money he found out he wasn't getting a piece of in his absence from Fabian. Nonetheless, Vinny made it an easy transition and already had the respect of his men. Dominic and Danny would now be able to really groom their young protégé, Angelo. Even Fat Kenny was starting to become a respected lieutenant.

The priest called for the ring, and Angelo turned to his best man, Dominic. Dominic reached into his jacket pocket and came up empty. He started looking frantically, as Angelo looked on despairingly. "Wait a minute. This ain't my jacket," he said, looking back at the row of groomsman. "Who's got my jacket?"

"Come on, guys," Angelo growled in a whisper heard throughout the church.

Everyone started looking; even Fat Kenny checked to make sure he wasn't wearing Dominic's tuxedo jacket. Finally, Mario Marconi called out that he had it and handed Dominic the ring while taking off the jacket. Dominic took the ring and started taking off his jacket.

"Just give me the ring! Swap jackets later for crying out loud," Angelo pleaded, as the audience broke out in laughter.

The ceremony went off without any other hitches, and everyone left for the reception. As the best man, Dominic was required to give a speech. He was handed a microphone and raised his glass in a toast. "As always in our weddings, the first drink is to those who couldn't be here today—to Angelo's father, George, to my father, to Uncle Ray and to your father's mentor Angelo, and all our mentors, for that matter, to Denny Greco. We drink. Salud."

Everyone took a drink from their glasses and raised them again. "I remember my wedding day. I got married at twenty-two, and everyone pretty much told me I was too young. Well, at my wedding, Angelo comes up to me in his little mini-tux. He was an usher, and he kept seating people on the wrong sides. He wasn't very bright back then."

The huge reception gave some chuckles. "Hey, Dom," Danny called out from his table, "it's supposed to be a toast, not a roast," thus drawing more laughter.

"Danny, please. I've got the floor," said Dominic and Danny threw up his hands in mock surrender. "Anyway, little Angelo comes up to me before the ceremony and says 'everyone says you're too young, why are doing this?' I tell him 'Ange, you just know, someday you'll understand.' That someday came after his first date with Angela. That night Angelo comes to me and says, 'I understand why you got married. I found my Angela.' Angela, I've known this kid since the moment he was born. You're his soul. I know he'll devote the rest of his life to making you happy. My wife's name was Angela, and that alone makes you a wonderful person in my book. My family opens its arms to you and yours." Dominic turned back to the guests. "A toast—to Mr. and Mrs. Angelo and Angela Rea, may God bless them both. Salud."

Danny took his drink and turned to his wife, Bianca. "Dominic seems so grown up now, huh?"

"He did take care of us while you were gone. He helped make sure Danny Jr. stayed on the right path. He's a good kid, Danny."

"He's always been such a follower. I never envisioned him a leader. He reminds me of his father up there. Hard to believe it's only been five years."

"Only? It's been five very long years, Danny—which I don't ever want to go through again."

Here we go again, Danny thought. "You think I do? I'm getting a drink."

"Sure, go ahead. I'm talking to you so you have to get your own drink. Any other time, there're five people fighting to replace your drink before it's even empty."

"Little overemphasized, don't you think?" Danny looked over her shoulder and waved to someone. "Wow, you look great."

Bianca turned to see who Danny saw, and when she did, there was no one there. Danny took off in the other direction. "Such an asshole," she said to herself, shaking her head.

After dinner, Danny, Dominic, and Vito Paganini, the captain from New York, sat at a back table and talked business. It was the first time since Danny got out that Vito had been in town. "So who's in charge?" Vito asked the two leaders of the crime family.

It was Danny that spoke, "All titles stay the same. Dom's the boss, I'm the underboss."

"What are you doing with Mexico?" Years ago, Dominic's father set up drug trade routes into the country from Mexico and in Miami. Fabian sent some guys down there and turned it into a small empire.

Dominic answered this question, "We're giving it to Doug Sullivan. He's coming home around Thanksgiving time."

"What's that? Two years on a ten-year stretch? Not bad. What was the over/under on that one?" Vito asked. Danny laughed along with Vito on the ballbusting. "Just fucking around, kid. But what is the word on that Fabian fella?"

"He'll turn up," Dominic said. "Speaking of turning up, where've you been lately? I used to beg you to go back to New York."

"The old man's been sick." The "old man" was the Grazzitti Crime Family boss, Eddie Battaglia. He'd been the boss since the late 1990s. "And get this. My name's been mentioned as a possible replacement, or at least in the top administration. Can you believe that?"

Both Danny and Dominic were stunned by the news. "No. I can't," blurted out Danny.

The Grazzitti Family was the biggest family in New York and therefore the country. Danny was a year older than Vito and had a hard time ever of thinking of him as a captain for the legendary crime family, let alone a boss. When Nick and Danny had done their hits, Vito was in college in New York. Vito graduated with a bachelor's degree in finance and went to work swindling millions of dollars for the Grazzittis in stock rackets. In 2001, Nick Amicucci contacted his cousin Vito in New York and told him of his plans to take control of his crime family, which had no boss at the time. Nick was acknowledged as the boss and as his power grew, so did Vito's. Vito became a twenty-five-percent partner with Nick in most of the action, and he turned half of that over to his bosses in New York. With the millions rolling in through the stocks and the Detroit rackets, Vito soon became a captain, leading the Sicilian faction of the family. In Danny's mind, Vito owed all it to all to Nick and his family. "You'd be a hell of an asset for us," Danny reminded Vito.

"You'd be a hell of an asset for me," Vito answered. "We'll rule the world." They already were international, just by their families alone. Both the Paganinis and the Amicuccis hail from the same town in Sicily. Dominic's great-grandfather, Nicodemo, married Rosemary Paganini, Vito's aunt, before settling in New York. Nicodemo couldn't stand the city, far too crowded for the young man who had to live in the mountains to avoid the Fascist oppression of the 1930s. Nicodemo took Rosemary and their two boys and moved to Cleveland, going to work for the Cleveland mob. Nicodemo soon struck a friendship with the Lissoni brothers of Michigan and went to work for them. The Paganinis stayed in New York and joined the Grazzitti Family.

Dominic's father, Nick, set up a drug trafficking partnership with Vito and the boss of their hometown in Sicily, Nino Amicucci. Nick handed the Sicilian connection to his young protégé, Doug Sullivan, who established even more connections in the Middle East and in Colombia, with a cartel. Doug worked with Fabian on bringing the drugs into the country through Mexico and Miami. He set up a base in North Carolina where the drugs get distributed from.

"It might not be such a peaceful transition when Eddie dies", said Danny.

"Depends on how it goes down. Word is he's stepping down and naming a successor."

"Well, if you ever need any help, we're always here for you," Danny reminded him.

"You're already in my plans."

"With all that money you'll have rolling in as boss, a nice act of friendship would be to drop your twenty-five percent with us. Cut us loose."

Dominic sat in awe. His father's biggest complaint was the deal he made with New York. Vito had wiggled himself into twenty-five percent of all Nick's action. Vito had even bought a house in Michigan and kept his bosses back home aware of all Detroit's activities. Danny saw an opportunity to get out from under their thumb and pounced on it.

"Time will tell," Vito said.

"I'm just saying, when it does, remember who got you where you're at. And it wasn't that diploma you got either."

"Yes, Danny, I got the message. All business with you, huh? All right, I'm going to find someone a little more funnier than you two."

Vito left and Dominic stared at Danny. "That was fucking amazing."

"Feels good to be back in the game. You know how much more we could do if he's the boss over there?"

Just then, Vinny Jagge walked over to the table and took a seat. "Gary Piazza's in the parking lot, waiting for you," he said, nodding to Dominic. "He says he has a gift for Angelo." Gary Piazza was Fabian's second in command. He disappeared when Fabian did.

Danny was irritated with the idea of leaving him in the parking lot. "Feds are snapping pictures of everything outside. Why leave him out there? Bring him in, put him in a back room."

Vinny left to have him brought in, and Danny and Dominic walked to find a back room. "Who's this Piazza guy?" Danny asked Dominic.

"He was a collector for the Lodullis. Fabian took a liking to him when you guys sent him over there. They call him Gary Pizza."

"Obviously. What is he, young, old? Married, not married? Kids, no kids?"

"He's got a daughter I think. He's my age, thirtysomething. I know he lives in Sterling Heights."

"His family is still here or did they lam it with him?"

"I don't know," Dominic answered.

They found a suitable room and waited for Gary Pizza to be brought in. When he was, he handed a wrapped present to Dominic.

"I'm supposed to give this to Angelo," Gary told them.

Dominic shook the box. "It's money."

"Good thing it wasn't a bomb, eh, Dom?" Danny asked.

Dominic put the box down. "Okay, where's Fabian?"

"He told me to be totally honest with you. We were in Miami, I don't know where he's at now. He told me he'd contact me here in Michigan."

"When?" Dominic asked.

"That's all I know. He put the box in my car, and I drove all the way here."

"Where's your family?" Danny asked.

"My family? They're here," answered Gary with a weary feeling.

"Not at your Sterling Heights' home," said Danny, implying they'd paid his house a visit.

Gary's family really was at home, but the innuendo was enough. "Any message for Fabian when he contacts me? I'll tell you when he does and where he's at."

Dominic answered, "Tell him to come home. He paid the money back. My father gave him a pass."

Danny spoke next, "Let him know he's family to us. I was really hoping to see him when I came home. Tell him this ain't no permanent damage."

"I'll tell him. That should make him happy." Gary left the box in the room and left the wedding.

Danny looked at Dominic. "Think we laid it on too strong?"

The wedding went on until early in the morning hours. Dominic was sitting at a table with his stepmother, Helena, when the groom and bride came to say good-bye. Angela was supporting a very drunk Angelo so he wouldn't fall. "I'm taking him home," Angela said.

Angelo perked up. "Yes! Hey, Dom, I'm going to have sex now."

Dominic and Helena laughed, while the bride showed her disgust. "Oh, I doubt that."

"At least, there's no early flight in the morning," Dominic reminded Angela. They decided to have their honeymoon on Mackinac Island.

"You want to try driving his corpse around tomorrow?" Angela asked Dominic.

"Just say the word. I'll have someone drive you."

"It's supposed to be our honeymoon."

"Well, have fun driving."

"Sex," reminded Angelo, unable to lift his head.

"You want someone to at least carry him out? He might start humping your leg." Dominic joked.

"Better mine than Kenny's I guess." And they left to try and finish their good-byes.

The night tailed off, and Dominic went home with his stepmother and younger brother, Sal.

CHAPTER VII

Another Comes Home

"CASE DISMISSED," THE judge said banging his gavel and giving Doug Sullivan his freedom. He turned and hugged his wife and six-year-old son, Graham. Within two hours, Doug would be home, a two-story mini-mansion he had built in Birmingham. He also had a fourteen-month-old son, Robert, at home with his in-laws, who lived with him.

A welcome home party took place at Doug's house, under the full scrutiny of the FBI. The party included the Herrick brothers, Doug's lifelong friends, and Danny and Dominic and their families. Long before they had children, Doug and his wife, Grace, had been guests at the Amicucci Sunday gatherings.

Toward the evening, the men built a fire in Doug's fire pit and gathered in lawn chairs out back. Only Tommy knew the real circumstances of Doug's release, and, of course, everyone else was anxious to learn how as well. "Okay, Doug, we've given you slack all day, let's hear it. A court session closed to the press and a gag order from the judge. How are you here? National security, really?" Danny asked.

"I can't talk about it, gag order."

"If it wasn't you, I'd think you're working for the government," Dominic told him.

Danny asked, "You're just kidding about the gag order, right?"

"Yeah, I'm just kidding. And I am working with government, just not the FBI."

Everyone gave Doug a puzzled look until Danny finally understood. "Your Middle East rackets?"

"Yeah, some people approached Sami for some weapons. I'm going to introduce Homeland Security and the CIA to them." Sami Nasser was born in Iraq and moved to the United States at an early age. He and his brothers went to high school with Doug and the Herricks and moved back to Iraq years after graduation.

Everyone sat in stunned silence. "You know they're going to make a movie on you someday, don't you?" Dominic asked.

"Think it'll be a happy ending?" Doug asked him back.

Danny wanted to know what kind of weapons these people wanted to buy and where Doug had access to them. "RPGs, surface-to-air missiles, and assault rifles. I met some arms buyers through some army contacts I met in Baghdad years ago. I've sold rifles in New York and in Sicily, but never in Iraq. We've got several caches throughout the state right here."

"International arms dealing gets you more time than drug trafficking," Danny reminded Doug.

"But now, I'm doing it legally. And hopefully, these are some real terrorists, and this will do some good. Besides, I've got bigger plans. I'm going to France after Christmas to meet some people. I'm going to slip away and work on opening some new routes in Europe."

"How long have you had this planned?" Dominic asked him.

"Since Tommy came up with the idea of launching that RPG last year. I knew we were going to trial on some kind of charge, so what better time? I told your dad my plan and had Carl Voight make the call. When I was locked up in Miami, they put an agent undercover as a prisoner, and they confirmed my information."

"What if you were found guilty at your trial down there?"

"Didn't matter, the acquittal just made it easier. They only got me over fifty thousand dollars on a stock purchase in the first place. I couldn't explain it. They wanted to take everything I ever made since then—over fifty-six fucking grand. Feds went through every dollar I ever made, all three of us." Doug pointed at Tommy and Billy. "They offered me five years and wanted to clean me out. I told them to double the time, leave my money alone, and drop the charges on Tommy and Billy."

"I still couldn't believe they did it," Dominic remembered the time vividly. Doug was making money hand over fist. He copied Vito's stock market rackets in New York and started buying up stocks at will. Once Doug bought into one of the Big Three auto makers, the feds had had enough. They arrested Doug and the Herrick brothers, right at the time the uprising was beginning in Dominic's family.

Doug knew Dominic was vulnerable with all of them off the streets, so he made the best deal he thought he could in the quickest amount of time possible. Doug threw some big money around, got himself imprisoned with Dominic's father, and Tommy led Doug's troops to stop the revolt on the Amicuccis. "With the acquittal and the shady plea, it just made it easier for them to spring me. Made a good case of harassment by the FBI."

"Too bad you couldn't do anything to help Nick get out," Danny said.

"Not yet."

"You really are a piece of work, kid. Hey, who are the Pistons playing tonight?" Danny asked.

"Nope. I'm not going to any sporting events with you, Danny. Once was enough," Doug answered, remembering the one Tiger game he went to with Nick and Danny. Too many beers and too much sun, they were worse than teenagers, in Doug's opinion.

Thanksgiving Day, Doug spent with his family, watching the Lions lose. In the evening, he and his wife, Grace, went to the Amicucci household. The atmosphere was fun. Times were looking up with people coming home from jail, even with the terminally ill, Charley, present for what was expected to be his last Thanksgiving. It was always a big moment when Nick called from prison and spoke on speakerphone, the same with Dominic's Uncle George.

Later on, the cards and the dice came out, and the money was flying. Members from the crew started straggling in, and the men turned the basement into a casino, while the women turned the upstairs into a gossip session.

"You kids and your Texas hold 'em. Why can't anyone play just seven-card stud anymore?" Ziggy complained as he pulled out his wad to buy more chips.

"You're just no good at reading bluffs, Grandpa," said Little Jimmy, who just took the rest of his grandfather's chips.

"Horse shit! You kids play stupid hands and call it skill when you get lucky. And bluffing? You always look like you're full of shit to me."

Angelo looked at the money Ziggy dropped down for his chips. "You're paying in tens and twenties?"

"I'm on a fucking pension," Ziggy answered.

Dominic let out a laugh. "I pay your pension. And I know I never paid you in tens and twenties."

"Fucking ballbusters, just give me my chips. I should've played craps."

At the craps table, Kenny's girth was becoming a problem. "Come on, Kenny, just stand in the back," said Carlo DeMini, an associate at the book.

"I got money at the table, I'm not fucking moving."

"We all got money at the table," said Jackie Beans.

"Fuck you, Jackie. I'm your boss now, and I'm not moving."

Danny, with the dice in his hand, put a stop to it. "And I'm your boss, step the fuck back. Who's rolling?"

Mario Marconi just crapped out, and Sal was up next. Everyone threw their money and bet with Sal or against Sal. Danny made up the difference for the "againsts," and Doug Sullivan made up the difference for the "withs." Most everyone went against Dominic's younger brother.

"I got to cover six hundred? Roll a fucking seven, Sal," Doug said.

Sal rolled a three, and everyone that bet against him cheered. "That's bad, right?" he asked.

Doug was not happy with losing six hundred dollars. "Is that bad? How the fuck you don't know how to play craps at your age?"

Sal started to walk away, but Danny stopped him. "Where you going? You lost, but you keep rolling."

"Let him go, Danny," Doug said hopefully.

"Not a chance in hell. Here's the dice."

No one bet with Sal this time, much to Doug's dissatisfaction. "Come on, guys. Eighteen hundred? How much you got, Sal?"

"I just bet my last fifty."

"The kid can't even bet on himself."

Danny wasn't having any of it. "Let's go, Doug. Put the money down." Danny had bet five hundred dollars himself.

Doug placed the money on the table. "Okay, Sal. This is called the come-out roll. You need a seven or eleven to win. You roll a two, three, or twelve, you lose but you roll again. But I'll shoot you dead before you do, so don't roll a two, three, or a twelve." The crowd loved the craps 101 lesson.

"What about the other numbers?" Sal asked.

"They're okay. But do me a favor and roll a seven or eleven. Make me feel better, please."

"I'll try." Sal shook the dice and let them fly: twelve. Big cheers from everyone but Doug.

"Goddammit! I'm done." And Doug bought some chips at the poker table.

"Your fucking brother just cost me two grand," Doug informed Dominic.

"That's what he does. I was just telling these guys about how you paid for everyone's groceries yesterday."

"They don't need to know that. It's not to brag or boast."

"What? You're like some Robin Hood or something?" asked Ziggy.

"I prefer to call it, taking care of your own. If you must know, I have this store owner not charge his customers the day before Thanksgiving and give me the bill. I do the same thing the day before Christmas Eve too."

"How much does that run you?" Angelo asked.

"Doesn't matter. I can spare it, so I do it."

"Mother Teresa ain't got nothing on you, kid," Ziggy said.

The following Monday, Dominic, Angelo, and Kenny drove to a movie theatre on the west side city of Veeling to meet Doug Sullivan. The lot was empty except for one car, which they assumed was Doug's. The building was obviously vacant. "What'd he do? Buy this dump?" asked Angelo, as they opened the unlocked front door.

"What'd you think?" asked Doug, standing in middle of the lobby.

Everyone looked around, not impressed. Dominic shrugged his shoulders. "You've done better."

Doug's smile fell from his face. "No imagination. You a hundred percent sure you weren't followed? I don't want the feds getting a whiff of this yet."

"No, we're sure. When you reminded me to make sure I didn't have a tail, we were extra careful," chided Dominic.

"Anyway, check it out." Doug led them to a hallway that adjoined four theatres. "I'm going to make this a club." The trio perked up. "Each theatre's going to be a different bar. I'm going to pull the chairs out, level some areas off, and have a dance floor at the bottom."

Doug walked them back to the step-down lobby at the entrance. "This will be another dance floor. Over there." Doug pointed to the vast concession stand. "It'll be a bar. Upstairs there's a lounge area with a bar, I'm keeping that, just fixing it up. There're three more theatres upstairs. One I'll make a real nice restaurant. One is going to be a banquet hall, for a very expensive price. And the other, I'll make it into a kitchen and offices. So now, what do you think?"

"I love it. Not bad, for being out of jail a week," Dominic answered.

"The best part is that there's nothing like it around here. Everyone around here goes away to go to a nice club. Let people come here. I'm working out a deal with a local hotel and a cab company to buy package deals. I'll pay cabs to wait outside—that should win the city over. And it's going to be one hundred percent legit. No bullshit here."

"You really going to keep it legit?" Dominic asked.

"I'm fully aware the feds are gunning for me, they'll probably have undercovers all over the place. No, this I want to hang on to. This is going to be nice, going to call it the Four Seasons. The four bars will be four different themes."

"If you're keeping really legit, can you give Sal a job?"

"Yeah, I'll give that shit a job. Let him work off that two grand he cost me on Thanksgiving."

"How much did all this cost?" Angelo asked.

"Why are you always asking how much things fucking cost?" Doug asked.

"I don't know, probably because I don't have any money," Angelo answered, shrugging his shoulders.

"Well, get some, and stop asking about others peoples'," Doug told Angelo.

"All right, I'm sorry. My wedding set me back quite a bit, that's all."

Dominic intervened, "No one fucking cares. Just stop being so damn nosy."

Doug showed them the upstairs, and everyone loved the whole idea. "You own it now?" Dominic asked.

"No. Two or three weeks. Still have to finish crunching the numbers, be sure it's even worth it. Than deal with the city, and they're no fan of me."

The next day, Dominic had lunch with his cousin, Jimmy, at Cooch's Cucina. "Jimmy, I told my dad you were running around with the Gurinos, collecting bets for Angie Jars."

"Oh man. How mad was he?"

"Not mad at all. I told him you belong here, with us and our crew."

"And he listened?" Jimmy asked suspiciously.

"Well, Danny told him too. So tomorrow, be at the bakery at 6:00 a.m. And be early, Danny's a little nuts about being on time."

Mario Marconi entered the restaurant and took a seat. Dominic told his cousin to leave so he and Mario could talk alone. "I got some news last night," Mario told him.

"Okay."

"You know how John Lissoni's been missing?" He was a younger cousin to the Jerry Lissoni killed in the RPG blast and had been missing since. Four others of his crew were still unaccounted for, as well, leading Dominic to still believe he had one more loose end to clear up from the Lissoni revolt.

"Any chance you might just tell me?"

"He was spotted in Greektown last night, playing blackjack. I also found out that two of his buddies have been hanging around there as well."

"Who hides for a year and then walks into a casino, sits down, and just starts playing blackjack?"

"You've known the Lissonis all your life. Can't you give them a call?"

"Fucking for real? Hi, sorry about killing Nino and Jerry and ruining all your lives. But can you tell me where John is? I gotta whack him too. Moron."

"I wasn't thinking. I forgot, you got a lot of baggage."

Dominic laughed. "Whatever. You have any idea where he's been or how long he's been back?"

"Dom, if I did, I would've told you, and I wouldn't have suggested you call the Lissonis."

"Fucking smart ass today. Than what do you think? Is this fucking kid getting ready to make a move or something?"

"Can you afford to take a chance? Your father always said, 'hindsight ain't worth shit when you're dead.'"

"Well, Mario, you're in charge of Greektown. Get me some answers, and quickly."

"I'm on it."

Dominic left and went to the bakery to fill Danny in on the new development. Angelo and Vinny Jagge were at the bakery too. Vinny had been hanging out there a lot since he got out. Danny still had no faith in the scrambler, and he and Dominic convened in the back parking lot, even in the cold of late November.

The thought of whacking the thirty-year-old grandson of Pete Lissoni troubled Danny. "John Lissoni was the apple of his grandfather's eye. He never wanted him involved in this shit."

"Blame Jerry, he's the fucker that brought him in. But this kid's gotta go."

"Jesus Dominic, you're like the fucking antichrist for that family. Poor Nino was Pete's son-in-law. Jerry was his nephew. Jerry's brother, Tommy, is doing life. You better hope he never gets parole."

"At that point it's a no-brainer. I'll just whack him too," which they both found funny.

"Take it to your father on Thursday. In the meantime, let's all watch our backs," Danny said.

Later that evening, Dominic stopped over at Aunt Marie's for dinner with her and Angelo. Marie and Angelo were already eating when he opened the door and sat at the dinner table. "Are you hungry?" his aunt asked him.

"That's why I'm here. Ange, where's your wife. She leave you already?"

"Shopping with your sister."

"Spending all your money, huh?"

"Christmas shopping."

Marie asked, "Which reminds me, you boys will both be donating to the church this Christmas, right?"

"Yes, Aunt Marie. I will donate to the church I don't go to," answered Dominic.

"That's your fault you don't go, not God's. And you'll send some guys to help work in the soup kitchens?"

"Sure. I'll even give some a bell and a red bucket and have them stand out front of department stores."

"You will? You're wonderful, Dominic."

"No. I was kidding. I'm not sending my men to work in a soup kitchen. The fucking courts do that."

Marie put her utensils down and scolded the crime family's boss, "Don't you swear at this table. I don't care who you think you are."

"I'm sorry. It slipped."

"It better not slip again. It would do you a world of good to show your face in God's house."

"I'll give God's house money, that's going to have to do for now. You're so involved in charities at Christmas time, what about the rest of the year? No one's needy any other time?"

"The holidays bring out the best in people, Dominic. Try and have some joy."

Angelo finally butted in. "Yeah, Dom. Try and have some joy," he said, smiling.

"You know, Aunt Marie, you should talk to Doug Sullivan, charity giver number one. He'll give you people to help."

"You'd let the Irish help your paisanos before yourself?"

Dominic knew she had him. "No. How about I go to Christmas mass with you and we'll call it even?"

"You'll still give a nice donation?"

"Of course, now if you two don't mind, I would like to have some joy in my life and enjoy this dinner."

After dessert, the threesome played some Rummy and had some drinks. Dominic was walked to the door by his aunt and cousin. It was a quarter to midnight. "Ange, how come your wife never called you?"

"I got to open the bakery in five hours. She knows I'm sleeping here."

"Do you know where she's sleeping?"

"Knock it off, Dominic. You said you've got a driver, right?" Marie asked, concerned because of the drinking.

Dominic opened the door and said good night. The driver in the car waved to the porch. "Is that Jimmy?" Marie asked. And with a realization, she continued, "It is Jimmy. Dominic, how could you?"

"What? He's my driver tonight."

Marie pushed her nephew aside and went to the driver side to see Jimmy. "Jimmy, you've been out here all night?"

"Yes, and he doesn't let me eat either."

Marie scowled back at Dominic, who just rolled his eyes. "Come on in and eat something, you poor thing," she said, opening the car door and walking Jimmy past Dominic and into the house.

"He has to be at work in five hours," Dominic called after them. "He was going to sleep on my couch."

Marie stopped and turned around. "Well, then Jimmy will sleep in your room here, and you can take this couch."

"No. I'm putting my foot down, Aunt Marie. He's driving me home."

"You can put your foot down in dog shit for all I care," she said and walked into the house. Totally powerless, Dominic slumped his shoulders and did the same.

The next morning, Jimmy found Dominic waiting in the car outside. Dominic was in the driver's seat with the car running. "Don't you want me to drive, Dom?" Little Jimmy asked.

Dominic put the car in reverse and backed it out the driveway. "No, I got it Jimmy. The car's all nice and warm for you. Where do you want to go today?"

Jimmy wasn't sure if this was sarcasm or anger about to erupt. "You know last night's not my fault, right? I just waved."

"You just waved and said I never feed you to woman who never 'not feeds' anyone."

"It was a joke, I'm sorry."

"Next time, you say 'no.' Say 'you've already eaten' or say 'you need sleep,' but don't ever stick me like that again."

"Okay. Can I drive now?"

"No. You're the boss today. Where to?"

Jimmy was still puzzled. Dominic had no traces of anger, yet Jimmy readied himself for an explosion. "Wherever you want to go?"

"Wherever I want to go? Okay, there is something I'd like to do today."

Dominic drove the few miles to Jimmy's house. Inside was Ziggy, his wife, Hillary, and Jimmy's parents, Charley and Lonna. "Dominic? What brings you here?" Ziggy asked when he opened the door.

"We've come for Charley," Dominic told him as they entered the living room.

"What do you mean?"

"We're taking him out for the day."

Everyone protested, "He can't leave here."

Dominic didn't stop once, but walked to Charley's room. "Let's just ask Charley," he said over his shoulder. Charley was reading a magazine in a chair by the window when Dominic entered. "Charley, you want to get the hell out of here and spend the day with your son?"

Charley just looked at him. "Of course, I do. Will he spend it with me?" Charley's other children were spending a lot of time with him, but Jimmy had alienated himself from all of them.

"We'll spend it together," Dominic answered.

Lonna was having none of it. "Dominic, it's cold out there. What the hell are you doing? Where are you taking him?"

"To get some fresh air," Dominic answered, irritated to be questioned.

"It's too cold out there for him."

"What? He's going to get pneumonia?"

Only Charley laughed. He got up out of his chair. "I want to go."

Ziggy patted Dominic on the back. "Let them go," he told the women.

Dominic went into the living room, where Jimmy was waiting while the women bundled up Charley. "Jimmy, I want you to hear what I'm going to tell you. Not listen, but hear. Every single person in this world, since time began, has lost someone and not had a chance to say good-bye or right their wrongs. To me, the opportunity is almost a miracle. You have that opportunity. You can tell your father how much he's hurt you. You can tell him how unfair it's been. And you can do the best thing ever and let that man die with your forgiveness, knowing you love him. Knowing you'll be okay and not all fucked up from his mistakes. Give your father that peace, Jimmy."

Dominic dropped the father and son off on a bench in a remote park and left to see his accountant, which was nearby. He had an appointment with his lawyer today as well. Something in Dominic's stomach had him thinking indictments were near.

After being gone a little over an hour, Dominic pulled up to a heart-wrenching scene of father and son crying in each other's arms. He wiped the tear from his eye and lit a cigarette, giving them all the time they wanted.

Dominic finished his good deed and went to see his lawyer, who assured him there were no grand juries convened against him. He had some time to kill after his appointment, so he went to Bally's earlier than usual, arriving before Kenny.

Michelle was working the desk when Dominic approached, handing her his membership card. "Hello to you to," she said after Dominic failed to greet her.

"Hey."

"Where's Kenny?"

"Figured you could tell me."

She gave him a curious look. "Why would I know? I only see him when you come here."

"Please. He tells me all the time of you two. Can I have my card back now?"

"Tells you what all the time?" she asked, her voice starting to rise.

Dominic was not so sure now that Kenny had told him the truth about Las Vegas. "About Vegas. And booty calls." She threw her pen at the desk. "I'll kill him. The only thing we did in Vegas was dance and drink a lot. I think he got a hooker one night. Wait until he gets here."

"Settle down. Maybe I got the story mixed up between you and the hooker."

That didn't make things any better. "Did he call me a hooker?"

"No. Let's just drop this whole thing. Please, for me."

"For you? Why? You stand me up in Las Vegas, dumping me and Rachel on your fat friend, who by the way, got himself pretty wound up on the dance floor with us, if you know what I mean. And you think I'd sleep with that pig?"

"Well, not just you, your friend Robin as well."

"Rachel. Her name is Rachel, I just said it. What is your problem with names? And no, she didn't sleep with him either."

"Okay, Rachel. I'm sorry. Feisty thing, aren't you? Listen, we can have some fun with this Kenny thing. Don't let him know you know anything. Okay?"

"What's in it for me, to not defend my honor?"

"A hell of a good joke. And it'll be a lot easier for me to get away to Vegas now than it was then. You did like the suite, right?"

"Never seen anything like it in my life. But I'm not a girl who really flies off to Vegas with strange men. I just got caught in the moment I think. I've always wished you'd ask me out, and you break out with Vegas. What's a girl to do?"

"You should go back to Vegas. We'll leave Kenny at home, no strange men."

"I'd settle for dinner and a movie."

"A simple girl, huh?"

"Take me or leave me."

"I'll take you. How about tonight?"

"Not a chance. Not until I see this hell of a joke to redeem my honor."

"You keep talking about honor. Does that mean something?"

"Does honor mean something? I don't know, but I surely don't want that animal going and telling everyone he banged me and my friend. To me, that's my honor, and it means a lot to me."

"I just thought you meant something else. In my world, honor is everything. And I mean everything."

"Your world? Your world isn't the only one that has honor you know, Mr. Amicucci," she said, hinting to her knowledge of Dominic's profession.

"Kenny said he was the meat in your sandwich," Dominic said, smiling.

"Better be a good joke."

"I'm good at jokes, trust me."

"I trusted you in taking me to Las Vegas, so you're not doing very well in that category. But it was still a blast, and Kenny was fun, until now. So there's hope for you. Make Kenny eat his words, and we'll see. At least, I now know why you stopped talking to me. I had no idea what happened."

"Kenny happened. It's typical that someone else is always messing something up for me. I was heading to the airport for the next flight, sleep in my car if I had to."

"Well, that was sweet. So what happened at the airport? Who were those guys?"

"That's all for another day. For now, let me plot your revenge on Kenny and restore your honor so I can take you out."

She smiled back at him. "Okay, I'll be waiting. But not forever you know." Dominic did his workout and left to hang out with his crew at Cooch's Corner.

The next day, Dominic and Kenny parked their car in the Bally's lot and walked toward the front door. Kenny stopped dead in his tracks when he saw Michelle walking out the gym, arm-in-arm with Tommy Herrick. Dominic whispered in Kenny's ear, "Why is Tommy with your girl?"

Kenny couldn't answer; his thought process was that Tommy was the one responsible for the Christmas Eve Massacre with the RPG. "Hey, guys," greeted Tommy, waving to Dominic and Kenny, looking a little embarrassed to be caught with a girl other than his wife.

"You know these guys? They're the ones that stood me up in Vegas that I was telling you about."

"What about Vegas?" Tommy asked, looking at Michelle and then to Dominic and Kenny.

Dominic nudged Kenny. "You better do something. She's your piece of ass, not mine."

Tommy got in Dominic's face. "What's she talking about with Las Vegas? I've been with her two years, Dominic. What the fuck?"

Dominic shoved Tommy back, and Kenny finally overcame his fear and admitted to his falsehoods. "Stop! It was me, Tommy. I told Dominic I slept with her in Las Vegas. But she didn't do nothing wrong. She's a sweetheart, Tommy. I'm sorry." Kenny's voice rose in a panic.

Dominic and Tommy broke out in laughter as Michelle let Kenny have it. "Aha! You fucking, lying pig! I was nothing but nice to you, and you do that. You're disgusting." Michelle stomped back into the gym.

"Oh, Kenny, that was too fucking funny," Dominic said, wiping tears from his eyes.

"I thought she was going to murder him right here," Tommy said, also regaining his composure.

Kenny just stood dumbfounded. "I really liked her," he said, and Dominic and Tommy lost it again.

CHAPTER VIII

Washing Money

DOMINIC WALKED DOWN the flight of steps and could hear laughter. "Hey, Dom, here, catch," he heard when he reached the bottom. He caught the cigar Tommy Herrick threw to him and looked it over. "Cuban. Nice. What's the occasion?"

Doug Sullivan answered him, "Tommy's having a baby. Come here, have a drink."

Dominic joined them at the bar in Doug's basement. "Congrats, Tommy. Ooh, Crown Royal, make mine big."

They had a few drinks, and the cigars were lit, when Doug asked Dominic, "So what was so important you came all the way here to talk about?"

"I got a line on that Sony TV." In code, he meant he knew where John Lissoni was hiding.

"Can we get it right now?"

"No."

"Let's worry about it tomorrow then. Have another drink."

"I drove myself here. Take it easy on me."

Tommy gave him the shot glass. "Don't be rude."

"Dominic, stay the night here. Danny says you're only at the bakery half the time anyway."

"Do you know what half the time is to Danny? I'm taking two days off now instead of none. He's such a miserable bastard about that shit. And I talk to you almost every day. When do you get the time to deal with Danny?"

"I'm very active. Here, have another drink."

"Okay. I'm here for the night. Better not be any kids screaming."

Hours later, after Tommy had gone home, Doug and Dominic had moved on to a bottle of Jim Beam. "Doug, there's something I never told anyone about Angela."

This is not an area Doug wanted to get into. "No offense, Dom. But keep it yourself."

"Everyone says I killed her because she couldn't have kids. That's not the case."

Doug dropped his head. He knew Dominic wasn't going to stop.

"I'm the one who couldn't have kids."

"You serious?" Doug asked, shocked.

"Yup. She said she couldn't, so I could look like a man. She did that for me."

"Wow. You know they have doctors for shit like that."

"We went to doctors. You ever jack off in a cup? It's horrible."

Doug thought about it and shrugged his shoulders. "Doesn't sound so bad. Maybe dress the cup up a bit."

"You can joke because you can have kids."

"You're right. Let's do another shot and call it a night."

The next morning, after breakfast, Doug and Dominic met with Danny to formulate a plan on finding John Lissoni. Danny was able to attain some photographs of their target. He gave them to Doug to give to his guys who would start spending some time hanging around Greektown, looking for the young man in the photos. The trio parted ways with Danny, returning to the bakery, Dominic going home and going back to bed, and Doug getting a hotel room in Toledo.

Once in his hotel room, Doug set down his two empty suitcases he checked in with and called Tommy Herrick to tell him where he was. Tommy arrived with two more suitcases and a duffel bag. The bag contained two bill counters and bags of money bands. The suitcases contained several million dollars, the money Tommy had collected for Doug in his absence. Their bagman, Joe Armstrong, had always taken care of this end of counting and splitting up the loot, but he was convicted in Miami earlier this year and got seven years. They now had to do it themselves until they found a new system.

Doug picked up a suitcase and opened it on the bed. "What's this?" he asked, eyeing a lot of green.

"It should be 4.9 million, from Plato." Plato was a young rapper Doug had helped when he was homeless. He had put him in touch with the right people, and Plato became a star. He had paid a yearly commission to Doug ever since, but this was his final payment he proclaimed.

"I thought it was seven million? The producer took his two, where's the other hundred grand?"

"I didn't know what it was supposed to be. That producer gave me the suitcase and said it was 4.9. I hid the bag, and here it is. Maybe he felt it was his."

"And that's that. Plato says he's done?"

"How many years can he just keep taking millions of dollars out the bank in cash? You been good to him, he's been good to you. Why make a fuss?"

Doug looked at Tommy in question. "Since when do you not make a fuss? You couldn't even make it out of the fed station without being dragged back upstairs."

"Not all good things last forever, do they? Eventually, it's going to get traced back to you or the kids going to go broke. One way, you got another scandal and probably more jail time. The other way, if the kid goes broke, you didn't help him at all, you just lined your pockets. We're supposed to help, remember?"

"Such a diplomat in just two years, I still say we decide when he's done, not him."

"Well, if that 'we' includes me, I say, let the kid off the hook and let him enjoy his life."

"I'm speechless. Okay, Tommy, let him enjoy his life. Fuck it."

"Let's count it up. Who gets what?"

"I get three million, Vito in New York gets one, and Dom gets one. Someone's got to lose a hundred grand now."

"Take it from Dominic, he'll never know." The Herrick brothers had little, if any, respect for Dominic or his position as a Mafia boss. Ever since Dominic's father had gone to jail, Tommy had seen the inner workings of Dominic's rule, and he wasn't impressed. Whenever Doug was either out of the state, out of the country, or in jail, Tommy had to work with Dominic. Tommy always had led his and Doug's crews while Doug dealt with the bigger picture goals and the mob. But he knew the importance of Dominic's connections and the importance of keeping him alive. When Dominic's family rebelled against him last year and attacked Tommy first, Tommy told Dominic to stay out of it, that he would handle the traitors. He didn't want Dominic anywhere near where he could mess it up for Tommy—that's how little of an opinion he held for Dominic Amicucci.

"I hate to say it, but you're right. Make his end nine hundred grand."

After verifying the amount in the suitcase and dividing it up, Doug and Tommy moved onto the second suitcase. "Now, this one's all yours," Tommy announced, opening it up. "Five million, one hundred fifty-seven thousand, six hundred and forty dollars."

"Down to very dollar, huh?" Doug joked.

"Absolutely." Tommy did not joke.

"All right, let's count it."

The money was right to the dollar, and now they waited. Tommy's driver sat in the parking lot and watched for any surveillance. After a while Doug left to get some fast food, watching to see if he had a tail. Tommy watched the hallway to see if any feds were going to check out Doug's room after he left, and Tommy's driver watched the parking lot and the front door. When Doug returned, it was clear the FBI did not know they were here. With the hotel being picked at random, the feds could have no prior knowledge of where to stake out and record. Doug now felt confident the feds could not take the ten million dollars away.

They called to have their money launderers meet them, men who would take this money and get it to an overseas bank account. They had perfected their system over the years, to the point that Doug would receive his bank account number and verify the funds before the money even left the room. Tommy's driver would be extra vigilant when they pulled into the lot for any signs of a tail, and the whole process of counting the money would be repeated in the room. Doug had a rule: You rat, you die. You rat one word about overseas money and your whole family will be stalked and slaughtered—a threat Doug had never had to carry out.

After Doug received his account numbers and the account numbers for Dominic and Vito as well, he and Tommy waited a bit before heading back to Michigan in their separate cars.

Dominic arrived at the prison for his visit with his father. Today's visit would be different than other visits. Today he brought with him Danny Serafini, who signed in as Nick's brother, Daniel Amicucci, and Doug Sullivan, who signed in as Sal Amicucci. They brought with them twenty-five grand for the guards to allow the mob meeting. It was the first time Nick had seen his boyhood chum Danny in over five years. Doug had spent nine months incarcerated with Nick before going to Miami to beat more federal charges there. It had been close to a year since they had last seen each other.

After pleasantries, Nick got right to business. "What's the story on Fabian?"

Danny answered, “Still no sign.”

“And nothing from his guy here? That Gary Pizza guy you told me about Dominic.”

“No, Dad. No sign of him anywhere.”

Doug had his Miami crews looking for Fabian as well. “There’s some small villages in Mexico he used for storing drug shipments. I’ve got some people checking them out. Virgil Boyle, in Miami, says he thinks Fabian was hiding in one them for a while.”

“He’d probably have the protection of any local police,” Danny added.

“Aren’t the drugs still coming in?” Nick asked.

“Nothing’s missed a beat,” Dominic answered.

Nick looked at Danny. “Well, someone’s got to be giving the orders down there, right? Is his end still going to his Swiss account?”

Doug answered, “Fabian always moved his money to his own accounts after he got his cut. His money isn’t under our umbrella. His cut now goes to an account I made for Vinny Jag.”

“Okay then, how about John Lissoni?”

“Last seen in Greektown. We know where one of his buddies is staying, but he hasn’t led him to us yet,” Dominic said.

Danny still didn’t like clipping the grandson of a mob legend. “We’re not even sure if he’s planning any sort of a move.”

“If he’s not making contact with anyone, it’s got to be assumed he’s up to no good. At the least, he’s breaking our fucking rules. You’ve still got a problem, Dominic. There’s no way he sets foot in a Greektown casino and Jeff Parkos don’t know about it. Jeff’s a Lissoni ally, you got to assume he’s on it too,” Nick said.

Danny still wasn’t convinced. “We’ve all known John all his life—he wasn’t even supposed to be in this life. Maybe his uncle being blown to bits has changed his mind and he just wants out and he’s scared. Why go to the worst-case scenario?”

Doug spoke up, “Because the risk is too great not to. You guys aren’t safe until we do know what his plans are. When his uncle went to war against Dominic, he attacked Tommy Herrick first. My guys aren't safe until I know what his plans are. And that's unacceptable to me."

"His fucking grandfather is the only reason the Amicuccis are even around. But I'm not willing to risk a bullet to Dominic's head that John Lissoni isn't planning to avenge his uncle's death, not any of your heads. Doug, snatch up his friend that you guys are watching and find where the fuck John is and put an end to this."

"Will do. Should I pick up this Gary Pizza guy as well? You should consider that Fabian also might not be sitting around waiting to get caught. He's no dummy. Worst-case scenario, there is Fabian teamed up with Lissoni and plotting a move."

"Good point," Danny observed.

"Yeah, good point. But don't act on Pizza boy yet. I think Fabian's coming back hat in hand," Nick said.

"And if he does? What then?" Dominic asked.

"You've got to find out if there's any other dissention in the family before anything. How's Jimmy coming along?"

"He's at square one, delivering bread, picking up payments," Dominic said.

"He's a natural." Danny had been impressed with how Jimmy had matured in the five years Danny had been away.

"Just remember, you're all accountable for his safety. My Uncle Ziggy's not going to bury his son and his grandson, capiche?" Nick turned to Doug. "You brought numbers?"

Doug pulled a folded piece of paper from his pocket and handed it to the imprisoned crime boss. Nick opened it up and raised his eyebrows. "Almost fifty million? More than double from last year." The profit from their drug trafficking business was two hundred million. Nick's family always took half, and Doug's family took the other half. Nick split his with Dominic. Doug split his with Tommy and Billy Herrick.

"Let's be honest here. Fabian is due some props. He's got Mexico running like a machine, it seems like it doubled on its own," acknowledged Doug.

"So we're importing more? There's a bigger demand? How does anything double on its own? If that's the case, I want everything doubled."

"The demand is not bigger, we're just filling it faster. Logistically speaking, it's a model for success. The cartel in Colombia ships it to Fabian in Mexico, where he has to get it on the right boats at the right time to my guy in Miami. What's increased is the amount of boats he's able to send and the amount of protection he's got with the Mexican local governments and the customs department of our own country. Anyone can send a boat full of coke, but Fabian's sending dozens without any getting caught. Like I said, it's a model for success."

"He *was* sending dozens of boats," reminded Dominic. "Obviously, it runs fine without him."

"That's called efficiency," said Doug.

Danny interjected, "It doesn't sound like you think we should whack Fabian, Doug."

"Honestly? I think you only whack him if he's a threat, not for pulling that under joke. Nick you said you think he's going to come back hat in hand. If he does, I'd smack his hand and let him keep earning."

Dominic was floored. "It wasn't a joke. He fucking ripped us off."

"What if the All-Star game had gone over? Would the money have been paid?" Doug asked.

Danny responded, "Common sense says he would have paid it to cover his tracks. Lesson learned."

"If that's the case, he didn't rip anyone off. He just simply bet it. Where's the robbery? And it is a joke, Dominic. It's a very common joke around here."

Dominic was now pissed. "I had to fucking answer to New York. Why did he have to fuck with them? Where's the joke in dealing with those animals?"

"He didn't fuck with them. The money they lost was your bookies doing their jobs and laying off the action. Instead of running from Vito at the airport, you should have told him his bookies took that action and deal with it. I wouldn't have given a penny—nobody ripped them off, either."

"You're saying it's my fault?" asked Dominic.

"Yeah. Where's the discipline? How could Fabian even know to pull something like this? Because he knew nobody was watching. I don't think that warrants a death sentence. You just want to whack him because he embarrassed you."

Nick butted in, "Doug, we've already been down this road. It's not Dominic's decision, it's mine. And I believe if he saw a weakness, he should have brought it to Dominic's attention, not taken advantage of it. Giving him a pass opens the door to anyone else to do the same. Just pay back the money and let bygones be bygones? Not the message to send to the troops. That's the feds way, just tell on someone else and you can go free. There's always got to be consequences to the actions we choose. Whack a guy because he embarrassed me? Don't whack him because he makes a lot of money? I choose honor over money, every time. Plus the fact that he won't come home implies a danger I won't tolerate. I won't second guess the safety of anyone in my family. And you don't either, Doug. You're mad at the twenty-five grand your buddy Tommy was collecting when he got arrested."

"That wasn't my fault," said Dominic.

"Yes, it is. Your people don't know who to pay and who not to pay, and those are the people closest to you."

"That's enough, Doug," ordered Nick.

"I'm just saying. Nick, you're locked up, and I've done everything in my power to protect and look after your people. I don't deserve the same when I'm away? I can't have Tommy being hassled over twenty-five grand. He never would have come out from hiding other than the fact he thought he was getting fucked. My friends have been put in harm's way, and that's a risk I can't take. My point with

Fabian was he was only doing what probably a lot of others were doing—taking advantage of a lack of discipline."

"You've made your point, Doug. I let things get too free. Danny's out now and everything's already coming back together. And thanks for calling me out in front of my dad. I really appreciate that."

"It ain't personal, Dom. But he's the boss, and he's got to know everything. He's the one responsible for everything. I need to know my guys are in good hands when I'm away. Tommy's a fucking maniac around the feds. I can't have him anywhere near them."

"Okay, I think it's good, Doug. What's next with your CIA endeavor?" Nick asked.

"I'm leaving for France right before New Years'. I'm meeting with some people who want to buy weapons. They've approached my guy over there in Iraq, and I'm going to meet them in Paris. Then I'm unofficially going to Germany to see if we can weasel into anymore drug routes in that area. So your fifty million dollars I'm betting will be more than twice that again next year."

"Who do you know in Germany?" Nick asked.

"No one yet, but give me a couple of days there and I'll have all the answers I'll need."

"Make sure you take care of that Lissoni thing before you go. Is there anything else?" Nick was trying to conclude the meeting.

Everyone shook their heads, and they spent the rest of their time together playing cards.

CHAPTER IX

Back from the Dead

THE LAST THING Chris Fullaria remembered was opening his car door after leaving his apartment. He tried to rub the back of his head, which was causing him pain, but realized his hands were chained to something. His senses starting to come back to him, he tried to adjust his eyes and realized the lighting was fine, but he was disoriented from a blow to the back of his head.

With his vision coming back to him, Chris could now see his hands were chained to iron stakes that were welded to the forks of aforklift. He stood and tried tugging on the chains; the tugging only hurt his wrists. Panic started to set in; Chris now realized the Amicuccis had finally caught up to him and were going to want to know where John Lissoni was hiding. He sat back down on the ground to relieve the pressure on his wrists and waited for the men he knew would come.

After what seemed an eternity, he heard a door open and chairs shuffling. Two men, who apparently were in the warehouse the whole time, appeared from out of Chris's line of sight and stood in front of him. Then Chris's heart stopped when he saw the other two men come from the other side. It was the Amicuccis's heaviest hitter, Doug Sullivan, who Chris thought was doing ten years, and his partner, Tommy Herrick, the madman who ordered the Christmas Eve Massacre. "Raise the forks so he can stand," Doug yelled to the operator. Chris was now able to stand with his hands resting on the forks.

"Got the big dogs out for me, eh?" Chris asked.

Doug paid no attention to the question. "You see those stakes are welded on those forks for a reason, right? You're not the first person to be chained to them. Believe me when I say, I've done this a few times."

"You don't have to convince me, I'll take your word for it."

"My point being, Chris, is that I need information you have. Trust me when I say I speak from experience. At first, you're going to be a tough guy and you're going to deny knowing anything and maybe even tell me to go fuck myself. Then I'm going to beat you up a little and give you another chance, and more than likely, you're still not going to answer my questions. That's the point of no return in my opinion. Then I turn Tommy loose on you." One of the men handed Tommy a blowtorch, and Tommy gave Chris a sly smile. "So instead of walking out of here with your life, you'll probably end up like everyone else, begging Tommy for death. I'm hoping you'll be the first. Where is John Lissoni? Right now, all you got is a bump on the head. Answer my question and you'll be back at the casino in hours."

"As God is my witness, if I knew I'd tell you."

"Okay then, what information can you tell me?"

"I don't know anything. I didn't even know John's in town," Chris pleaded.

"Who said anything about him being in town? Where is he when he's not in town, Chris?"

"I know he skipped town after his uncle was killed in that explosion. I don't know where. And I thought you thought he was in town. I haven't been hiding. I've been here all along. So picking me up now, I just thought something happened with John."

Doug looked at Tommy, who then stepped toward Chris with the blowtorch. "Raise the forks!" Doug yelled. Once Chris's hands were extended to their maximum, with his feet still on the ground, did Doug order the forkliftoperator to stop.

"Why? I've told you all I know," Chris said.

"That can't be all you know. I know more than that. I know that when you say you weren't hiding, you also weren't checking in. Did you retire?" Doug asked.

"Come on, you blew a house up. Yeah, I guess I figured I became retired."

"So you haven't seen nor heard from John Lissoni since he skipped town Christmas morning a year ago?"

"Well, no, I've talked to him."

"You see, Tommy? You were right. He's just like all the dumb motherfuckers before him. Raise him up!" The forks were raised until Chris's legs were at eye level for Doug and Tommy. Doug yelled up to Chris, "I tried. Now, let's see how long you last with Tommy."

Tommy lit the blowtorch and applied it to Chris's right knee. Chris tried to kick Tommy in defense, but Tommy grabbed that leg and burned that knee to. Chris yelled in agonizing pain, let alone the pain the chains were causing his wrists, trying to keep him suspended in midair.

"I'll talk, I'll talk." He was set to the ground, but his knees would not support him, and the pain was unrelenting.

Doug grabbed a hammer and whacked Chris on one of his burned knees with it. He drew the hammer back and whacked Chris's extended left elbow with it, as hard as he could. They set Chris down and unchained his wrists, letting him lie on the ground in his pain.

Doug lit a cigarette, and Tommy unzipped his pants to take a leak on Chris. "Tommy, come on. That'll leave your DNA on him, in case he decides to talk now and goes to a hospital."

Tommy zipped his pants and kicked Chris's broken elbow instead. "Don't forget to burn those shoes now," Doug chided.

"Enough already. Where the fuck is he, Chris?" Tommy asked, towering over Chris's pain-riddled body.

"California," Chris answered.

"I know people in California. Where in California?" Tommy asked.

"I don't know. I just have an emergency number."

Doug scoffed, "Well, I'd say this was an emergency. Wouldn't you, Chris?"

"What's the number, asshole?" Tommy asked.

"I don't know it from memory. It's on a piece of paper at my apartment."

Tommy turned to Doug. "You believing any of this shit, Doug?"

"Not at all, chain him back up."

"No, please. He's got a loft downtown, too. I'm not sure where, but I know he has one."

The two men that were going to chain Chris back to the spikes on the forks of the forklift, stopped and looked at Doug, waiting for instructions. "Who told you to fucking stop? Chain him the fuck up. You see, Chris? Twice now you've added to your story after saying you don't know anything else. Now you're not leaving here. You've got for more info, and we all know that, except now, instead of the reward being you going home, now your reward will be death—once you finally tell us all you know. So dumb, you could have gone home with just a bump on the head. Tommy, if you still got to take that leak, go ahead, ain't nobody finding his body now."

The next morning, Dominic arrived at the bakery with his younger cousin, Jimmy, at six thirty in the morning. Danny, Angelo, and Vinny Jagge were already there. Dominic walked in the back room, grabbed a danish, and took a seat on the couch next to Angelo. Danny got up from the table and started putting on his coat. "Where're you going? Is it me?" Dominic joked.

"Outside, we got to talk. Don't we?" Danny asked.

"It's fucking nine degrees out there, not counting the wind. How about we just write notes and burn the paper?"

"Come on. It's still better than getting twenty years," Danny said, turning to the door.

Once in the parking lot, Danny asked Dominic, "What did Doug find out from that Fullaria kid?"

Dominic, bracing himself from the winds, said, "We got a location of a hideout in Detroit and a couple numbers."

"Doug's going to follow up?"

"Yes."

"What about the kid?"

"He's gone, Doug and Tommy took care of him," Dominic answered.

"Okay. Let's get the fuck back inside."

"Good talk, Danny. Well worth it," Dominic said, following behind.

A little after lunch, Gary Nussman, who ran the bakery, knocked on the door to the back room in an urgent manner. Angelo opened it. "What the fuck, Gary?"

"You're going to want to get Danny and Dom out here right away," Gary answered.

Angelo tried looking past Gary to see what the problem was. "What's so wrong?"

"Fabian's here."

Angelo stopped looking and without saying a word turned to tell his bosses of the news. The foursome was playing cards, and the others were waiting for Angelo to return. When he did return, he walked over to his cousin and whispered in his ear.

Danny watched the look on Dominic's face change. "What is it?" he asked.

Dominic stood and gestured Danny to follow. "Come on, you're not going to believe this one." Dominic walked to the front of the bakery with Danny behind him. *Sure as shit,* Dominic thought to himself as he saw Fabian Bosca standing at the counter like a customer. Jimmy and Gary were standing behind Fabian, ensuring he didn't leave. "Well, well, well, look who's back from the dead."

"At least you can't call me a deadbeat," Fabian said, forcing a smile.

"Maybe just the dead part," Danny interjected, walking past Dominic. "You got some fucking balls," Danny said loud enough that all the workers stopped working to watch. Danny, realizing everyone's eyes were on him, leaned in to Fabian's ear and snarled, "You fucking show up here, knowing the feds could be watching? This is how I get to see you for the first time after five years? Since you were a child, we looked after you, you and your mother. And this is how you come back? You think showing up in front of the feds is going to keep you safe? You were safe, you stupid fuck, until you pulled this shit."

Dominic got in the middle, "Not here." He waved at Jimmy and Gary. "Take him in back." And Dominic turned the open sign on the door to closed, and he sent the employees home. He next picked up the store phone and dialed Fat Kenny. "Kenny, are you close to the bakery?"

"Yeah, I'm here at the Corner."

"Good, grab Carlo and get over here."

"Be there in five minutes."

Dominic hung up and followed Danny in back. Danny walked right by Fabian and into the bathroom, turning on the shower. Dominic grabbed Fabian's arm and led him into the bathroom, closing the door behind them.

Gary handed Jimmy his gun and told him to stand outside the door. "I still got drivers on the road. I'll be gone not even five minutes. If you hear anything wrong, like Danny or Dominic yell in any bad way, break the door down and shoot Fabian. You got it?"

"You mean if they yell in distress?" Jimmy asked, taking the gun and checking the safety.

"What?"

"You said if they yell in any bad way, you should say 'yell in distress.'"

"I'm going to make a few calls, and then I'm going to slap the shit out of you when I get back."

"Too bad I got the gun now, though, Gary," Jimmy said, waving the gun.

Gary just looked at him. "Five minutes. Get the fuck on the door," he said, then turned and left.

In the bathroom, the shower was used to make noise to interfere with any wiretaps. Danny, Dominic, and Fabian huddled near the water stream, trying to keep their animated voices low. "Tell me how else to come back. I'm not going to meet you down a dark alley," Fabian told the two. "So yeah, at least if the feds see me come in, they got to see me go out."

"If this place is even under surveillance," Dominic reminded.

"Please. You know the Corner is, and that's only blocks away. How can you not assume it is?" Danny asked.

"Okay, well, I'm here now. What do you guys want to do with me? I'm here to apologize, and I hope I can still run the Mexican operations. I can work for Vinny Jag," Fabian said.

Dominic answered him, "What happens the next time, if you feel like you're not being treated appropriately?"

"Just between us, I'm taking medication. I saw a shrink to help with the self-doubt."

This was too much for Danny. "You what? A shrink?"

"I've had some problems, Danny. Ever since Melissa died, I don't think right." Melissa was Fabian's ten-year-old daughter that died. She died just three months after her younger sister, Tracy, was born. "I just want to do the right thing and raise Tracy."

"Fabian, I'll be honest with you. I don't remember you acting any differently when your daughter died, other than grief," Danny said. "Even when I went away, you didn't pull no bullshit. It was only after

Dominic was placed in charge, and more specifically, Fabian, after the war with Jerry Lissoni. Can you believe I asked Dominic if you were involved in helping Jerry? That's where we're at now. And you want to keep Mexico?"

"You saying I'm using my daughter's death as an excuse, Danny?" Fabian asked with a menacing tone.

Danny held up his index finger. "Because you're like family to me, Fabian, I'm going answer your question. If you're telling me that Melissa's death hit you late, okay, but if you're telling me that you've been fucked up since she died, I'd say you're wrong. I'd say you think you've been fucked up the whole time, but let me tell you, you weren't. I was fucking there. With that being said, don't you ever question me again. I tell you it's snowing out, and it's fucking June, you better get out your fucking winter coat." Danny's finger was right in Fabian's face now, and he was no longer whispering. "Dead mother, dead wife, dead daughter, don't fucking matter. You do your goddamn job. Your daughter dies and that gives you the right to fuck over Dominic? What'd he do? He gave you a captain position, and you fucked him over. That wasn't you five years ago. And your daughter died nine years ago, do the fucking math. It ain't Melissa—it's that you're a jealous fucking asshole." Danny's temper took over, and he hit Fabian in the eye the butt of his hand, causing Fabian to fall into the running shower. He hit the other side of his head on the tiled wall and sprained his knee from the awkward fall into the tub.

Jimmy was banging on the door. "Everything okay?"

Dominic pulled Danny away from Fabian and Jimmy kicked open the door when no one answered him, with his gun drawn.

The door hit both Danny and Dominic, knocking Danny into the wall and onto the floor, pulling down the towel bar with him. Dominic crashed into the étagère above the toilet. Gary heard the commotion and charged into the bathroom and took the gun from Jimmy. He saw Danny and Dominic thrown about and, unaware it was from the door that he kicked in, grabbed Fabian, who was showing great restraint and still lying in the shower. Gary put his gun in Fabian's face, and Fabian's instincts took over. In one swift move, Fabian grabbed Gary's wrist and slammed his hand into the shower wall. The blow forced Gary to drop his gun in the shower and before he could use his other hand that had gripped Fabian's drenched shirt, he was lifted into the bathtub.

Angelo and Jimmy now squared up to take Fabian down, if they could. "Stop! He didn't do nothing," Dominic ordered.

Fabian was out of the bathtub now and talking to Angelo, "Listen to him, Ange. I don't want to go through you, but I sure the fuck will."

It was Fabian's turn to go flying when Dominic pushed him. "Enough! Start showing some sort of humbleness. You say sorry, but look at you, you act like a fucking asshole. You really want to walk out of here? If you really want to live, Fabian, the time is now to show it. The game's over. Knock it the fuck off or die."

Everyone stood still, and Danny finally got out from behind the door, with a bloody nose. "Just come back and be a part of the crew, then we'll see about Mexico," Danny said, grabbing a tissue for his nose in the overcrowded bathroom.

"I'm sorry. The God's honest truth, I was trying to get every penny I could before you guys got out of jail, Danny. I knew I'd get the short end of the stick when Vinny got home. That's the truth, and it's pretty fucking humbling to hear it out loud," Fabian confessed.

"And the shit about the shrink?" Danny asked.

"True. You're right about Melissa, her death hit me late. These pills are supposed to help not feel so bad."

"What do you talk about at the shrink's? Us?" Danny asked.

Fabian's face contorted to a look of horror. "No, why the fuck would I? Me and my wife talk about our daughter, not nothing else. I wouldn't go if I had to talk about something else. I'm that fucking low on your totem pole?"

"You're not back on the totem pole yet. Pill popping ain't the answer, either."

"Just temporary, Danny. I don't want to be an asshole no more."

"Where are you staying?" Dominic asked.

"I sold my house, and I just got back in town this very minute. I got my bags in my car, probably a hotel."

Dominic hugged his old friend. "Fuck that, you stay at my home until you find a place."

Once the tension had depleted, and only Danny, Dominic, and Fabian were left in the bathroom, Vinny Jagge came in. "I got a beef."

"Now? It can wait, Vinny," Dominic said.

"It can wait? It's waited for years, and you don't know if this guy's skipping town tonight or what," Vinny complained.

"What's your beef?" Danny asked, still with the shower running.

Dominic didn't let him answer. "He's not skipping town, he's staying with me."

"Be careful he doesn't slit your throat while you sleep," Vinny said.

"Whoa, that's not right, Vinny," Danny said.

"What did I do, Vinny? The under bet? I fucked up, I've made it right the best way I can. I took care of your family. I gave my crews to your kid, Frankie, and made sure you got every penny," Fabian answered in defense of himself.

"I am grateful for what you did for my family, don't think I'm not. Honestly though, it was your job. But I didn't get every penny, did I? Where's my cut of Mexico?" Vinny asked.

"Mexico? That's what this is all about? There was no Mexico before you went to jail. I never figured you should get a cut."

"You did it under my umbrella, didn't you? Everything you did, I'm entitled to my end."

"He's right, Fabian," Danny said.

"Of course he's right, Danny." Fabian turned back to Vinny. "How much do you want? Give me a number."

"You give me a number. I just want what's mine."

Dominic intervened, "All right, we'll take care of this later. We'll agree to a fair number, and Fabian will pay it. The past is the past, this beef is settled."

Everyone shook hands and hugged, and they left the bathroom. Kenny and Carlo came walking in. "You're just getting here now?" Dominic asked.

"Kenny got his Jeep stuck in the snow," Carlo said.

Dominic looked pissed. "Kenny, a word in the kitchen," he said and walked out.

Kenny caught up with Dominic. "Dom, I'm sorry, it's a sheet of ice out there."

"You got four-wheel drive, how the fuck do you get stuck ? But seriously, what if I really needed you here? Next time, leave the Jeep and walk the few blocks. I've got to be able to count on you."

"I'm sorry, Dom. I won't let you down."

"Listen, Fabian's back now and you have to let the guys know, he's okay. He's good with us now. He'll be staying with me until he gets a place. Between you and me, keep your ears open as to what people are saying about him. He can be a sneaky fuck."

"How's his forehead look?" Kenny asked.

Dominic couldn't help but laugh. "You can hardly tell his head was ever split open. Good job stitching him, Kenny." Kenny beamed with pride.

The next night Danny walked into Doug Sullivan's new unopened club, The Four Seasons, and met him in the lobby. "Holy shit, when's the heat going to be turned on?" Danny asked, giving Doug a quick embrace.

"Two days ago," Doug answered.

"Why's it so fucking cold then?"

"Because it ain't on, them motherfuckers."

Danny found it funny. "With all your clout and all that money, you can't even get the heat in your own club turned on. What a shame. You want me to make a call? I'll get it right on."

"Hey, if you can, by all fucking means, I'd thank you. The construction is supposed to start back up next week, and I don't know if they will in this cold."

"You mean the construction that you own?"

"Used to own, Danny," Doug reminded him. "Dominic said Fabian was back. You guys letting him off the hook?"

"Not at all, but we'll need your help getting a handle in Mexico."

"Yeah, no problem. I'm going to Europe tomorrow, and Tommy will be in charge of everything here for me."

"Going someplace warm, huh?"

Doug gave Danny a quizzical look. "Where do you think Europe is?"

"Don't start, it's too fucking cold. I saw a Coney Island down the street, let's go there."

"Danny, I don't mean to be rude, but I got a few things to do here, and I want to stay up with my kids tonight," Doug pleaded.

Danny gave Doug the same quizzical look that Doug gave him about Europe. "Where do you think you are? Let's go, we can drive separate cars to save you some time."

Doug stomped off ahead of Danny. "Doesn't save me any time."

The two met at a corner booth, and Danny ignored Doug's irritation at being away from his family. "So your wife's not going with you?" Danny asked, starting in on his Greek salad.

Doug just stared at Danny. "No."

"I'll tell ya, if I ever even thought about going to Europe without Bianca, my balls would never leave the States."

Doug just nodded. "That's great, Danny."

"Okay, okay, I see you're bothered, there are a few things we got to talk about."

Both men stopped talking when the waitress brought them their coneys and chili cheese fries, and then Danny continued after she left, "Are you stopping in Italy when you're away?"

"I wasn't planning it."

"Nick wants you to go to Sicily, see Nino." Nino Amicucci, a very distant relative to Nick and Dominic, was the boss of the Sicilian town that Nicodemo Amicucci immigrated from. Doug had been there plenty of times in his organizing of their drug trafficking routes.

"Any particular reason?" Doug asked, now curious.

"He wants you to offer Nino ten percent more of the split in exchange for men?"

"For men? And his ten percent, right?"

"Five percent each. And he wants a dozen men, a secret crew. You're supposed to get them jobs and make them legal, so they don't get deported after a week."

Doug was shocked at this one. "Who's going to be in charge of them? Where are they going to live?"

"They're all yours," Danny answered.

"You want me to be in charge of Sicilian hit men, instead of you,? They'll fucking kill me. Than Tommy's going to try to kill them, it'll be a whole international incident."

Danny said after finishing his drink, "Doug, I know you done a lot in the five years I was gone, but don't think this is a conversation. Nick gave me an order and I gave it to you. I don't know if a bunch of Sicilians will listen to you. I don't know if you can do what Nick asks, but it's my job to tell you to do it. So do it."

"Okay, consider it done. I'll take care of it, but, not as an order."

Danny asked for the bill. "Whatever. How long will you be gone?"

"Well, it was about six weeks, but stopping in Sicily now, who knows."

Danny took the bill, looked it over, and handed it to Doug. "You got this, right? I'll see you when you come home." Danny walked to the door but stopped to turn around. "I forgot to tell you, your club's a great idea. Nice job."

Doug just nodded and got up to pay the check. "Didn't even want to be here in the first place," he mumbled to himself.

When Doug got to his car, he noticed another car pulled out behind Danny. Doug started his and followed in the same direction. He called Danny on his cell. "Did you bring a second car?"

"What are you talking about?" Danny asked him back.

"Someone just pulled out right behind you."

Danny had seen the car as well. "Think it's a fed?"

"I don't know, but I'm right on his ass."

"Stop flashing your high beams, Doug," Danny ordered.

"Fuck him."

"You remember that little old lady you waited behind in line to pay?"

"Yeah, why?"

"Because that's who's behind me, I can see her now with you flashing your lights. You're terrorizing her, asshole."

Doug quit the high beams and slowed down to turn around. "All right, Danny, I'll see you when I get back," Doug said, feeling pretty low.

"Good night, Doug. Good looking out, though." Danny said, smiling to himself.

Doug returned home a little after midnight, and everyone had already gone to bed. He could hear the TV still on in his in-laws' room on the first floor; his stepfather must have fallen asleep with it on again. He crept up the stairs to his one-year-old son's room. Doug didn't open it, he just listened. Even the tiniest of noises woke little Bobby up, Doug found that out quickly once he was home. He crept further down the hall to his oldest boy's room. Doug had no problem waking up his six-year-old, Graham.

Graham gave a big smile once he was awake. "You're home. Mom wouldn't let me stay up and wait."

"I know, she's mean like that," and they shared a laugh. "Your Uncle Tommy's going to come by and put in these webcams. We'll be able to talk to each other on the computer and watch each other at the same time. It's the neatest thing."

"Dad, we've already got that."

"We do? Since when?"

Graham just giggled at what he thought was his father's silliness. "Okay, Graham, did you throw the ball today?" Doug had Graham throw a tennis ball against a wall in the basement a hundred times a day. He believed it would grow his arm faster than the other boys and give him a huge leg up in little league baseball and football. He had been teaching him both sports since Graham was able to learn.

"Yes. Grandpa played catch with me too."

"Good. You be good for Mom while I'm good, don't cause her no trouble."

"I won't, Daddy."

"Throw the ball every day."

"I will."

"Okay, give me a kiss. We'll talk every day, I promise. I'll be back before you know it." Doug tucked his boy in and was able to get into bed without waking his wife. In five hours, Doug was to be on his way to the airport, en route to Paris.

CHAPTER X

THE KAJINO

New Year's Day 2011

DOMINIC AMICUCCI PULLED into the restaurant in Brighton to meet Danny Serafini and Vinny Jagge. He couldn't understand why he had to drive way out here to meet two people he was going to be watching college football with when they were done. Why couldn't they just walk into the backyard like usual? He spotted them in the back of the restaurant and took a seat.

"You look like shit," Danny greeted Dominic with.

"Rough night. Then the fucking drive here, 2011 looks like a piece of shit already."

"Wow. You should do some time in the can, it'll make you appreciate life a little more," Vinny told him.

"Whatever, Vinny. Let me ask you guys something. What are you going to do after this meeting?" Dominic inquired.

"What do you mean? We're all meeting at the Corner for the games, you are too," Danny said.

"That's my fucking point. Why drive all the way out here?"

"We've got something very important to talk about, very important. I don't want to take any chances, as it affects your father too," Danny said.

"Can't whisper in the backyard?"

"Fucking knock it off. Can you get serious for a few minutes?"

"Okay, what's going on?"

"We got to have a plan for Fabian," Vinny told him.

"What kind of plan?"

"To whack him, and be able to keep his rackets," Vinny answered.

Dominic looked to Danny and pointed to Vinny. "Does he need to fucking be here?"

"What kind of talk is that?" Vinny asked.

"He's here because he's doing the hit, your father's orders," Danny said.

Dominic glared at Vinny. "I'll tell you what kind of talk this is, any kind I fucking want."

Danny just put his head down, and Vinny swallowed his pride. "My apologies, Dom. I didn't mean any disrespect."

Dominic just looked back to Danny. "So what's my father's plan?"

"It was Vinny that got shortchanged in Mexico, so it's only right he gets the hit," Danny explained.

"Yeah, I understand that part. What's the plan? I assume that's why you two brought me all the way out here, to tell me what I got to do," Dominic said in irritation.

"We'll take some time and make sure his guard is down, which you'll take care of, with him staying with you. Once we can take over his rackets, Vinny'll make him disappear," Danny explained.

"What about his top guys?" Dominic asked.

"We'll take his guys out first, and you'll have to keep a close eye on Fabian to make sure he don't run."

"What else?"

Danny answered him, "Mexico's not going to be so easy. He must have some solid connections there, connections that have no alliance to us."

"Doug's moving some guys down there. They'll find them and kill them."

"Nick has Doug going to Sicily and recruiting a dozen men, they'll be the ones doing the killing in Mexico."

"What about Fabian's top guys, like Gary Pizza, let the Sicilians whack them too?" Dominic asked.

"That's the plan," Danny said.

Dominic thought it was a good idea. "Less chance for our guys to get a murder pinch."

Vinny finally spoke again, "And I get Fabian."

"You really got some hard-on for the guy, eh?" Dominic asked.

"Besides the money, I got my two boys in this life to worry about. I don't know if Fabian will try to move on them, to weaken me," Vinny said.

"The decision's been made, but I've known this guy my whole life, and I'd appreciate it if you didn't enjoy whacking him so much in front of me," Dominic said.

"He won't," Danny answered.

"Are we done?" Dominic asked.

"No, we're not," Danny said, now getting irritated with Dominic. "We need to decide who's close to Fabian, who might have to be whacked."

"Obviously, Gary Pizza's got to go. But isn't that why we're waiting to whack Fabian? To find out everything we need to know? It's too early to decide who lives and who dies, other than Fabian and the fucking Pizza guy," Dominic said.

Vinny raised his eyebrows and looked at Danny. "He's right."

"Vinny, I don't need you to tell Danny I'm right. Did you get some promotion I don't know about?"

"Dom, I can't just talk? I don't mean nothing," Vinny defended himself.

Dominic didn't answer him; he just talked to Danny. "So we'll plan the whacking session for when we know who to whack. I'll keep Fabian under my thumb, Doug will have Mexico ready when it's time, and Vinny, here, will handle the final piece, killing Fabian. We're all clear?"

Danny nodded, but Vinny wanted to ask a question. "Can I ask something?"

Dominic nodded, and Vinny asked, "Who's getting the information? I'm in charge of Mexico now. His men are now mine. I'd like to be kept in the loop. I've got my boys to worry about."

"I agree," Dominic answered. "Your men will have to work with Doug's men. That's where our info will come, I suppose."

Danny chimed in, "You'll also have to watch his crews here—that's the closest danger to home. That's your priority, let Doug take care of Mexico and whatever he's got in Miami."

"I've heard nothing but good things about the crew in Miami, they're already adjusted to life without Fabian," Vinny said.

"Doug's men have Miami locked down solid. Fabian couldn't pull any bullshit there," Danny said, noticing Dominic's face. "No offense, Dominic."

"None taken, I admit it, I trusted the fucker."

Vinny sided with Dominic. "It's easy to believe those closest to you. You never had a red flag, how would anyone know?"

"Doug would know," Danny said, taunting Dominic.

"Oh, fuck this," Dominic complained.

"I'm just fucking with you, settle down."

"Who do you plan pulling the trigger?" Dominic asked Vinny.

"My youngest, Mikey. I'd like to get him his button, but I'll be there with Frankie." Frank Jagge was Vinny's oldest son; he was promoted to a lieutenant when Vinny went to jail.

"A real family affair, huh?" Dominic asked.

Stevie Turner kicked off his shoes and sat back to finally watch what was left of the New Year's Day bowl games, Connecticut and Oklahoma in the Fiesta Bowl. It had been a busy day in Las Vegas, and he just wanted to have a beer and enjoy some football.

His cell phone rang. ***It never ends,*** Stevie thought to himself. "Yeah," Stevie answered.

It was Noah Brooks, his top guy. "Got a pen?"

"No," the irritated Stevie Turner answered.

"You're going to want to call me back from a pay phone."

"I just got fucking comfortable."

"I wouldn't bother you if this wasn't important."

Stevie got up and drove to a pay phone, one not close to his house. "Okay, what's so fucking urgent?"

"I got a call from 'The Kajino.'" The Kajino was a Japanese themed hotel/casino that Stevie was responsible for. The casino made a killing from all the Asian gamblers that flocked there. "John Lissoni's name came up, he's here right now."

"He's there right now?"

"He's even checked in under his name. Using a player card at the tables, Stevie, this kid ain't hiding."

"You have him under surveillance, right?" Stevie asked.

"Yeah. He's playing blackjack. If he leaves, we're on him."

"I'll call you back at that number." Stevie hung up and called Doug's satellite phone, one that had been given to him by the CIA. "How's Paris?"

"Not for me. What's up?" Doug asked.

Still being cautious with his words and speaking in code, Stevie answered, "I found that old style Sony TV you wanted for your wife."

"No shit, where?" Doug asked, knowing he meant John Lissoni.

"Here," which Doug knew meant Vegas.

"She don't want it no more, fucking destroy it."

With that, Stevie called Noah Brooks back, "Take him out, quietly."

Noah hung up the pay phone and got in his car to drive to the casino. Stevie had had him use their contacts at some of the casinos to flag John Lissoni's name if he ever used his player card or checked into a hotel. No one ever expected Lissoni to turn up in Vegas, and so blatantly at that. There was no plan for executing him, and Noah was using the drive time into the city to formulate one. He called his man at the Kajino, which literally means casino in Japanese, to meet him at the delivery dock where he could enter the casino discreetly. His plan so far was to gain entrance to Lissoni's hotel room, but there was the possibility that he wasn't alone. Noah also wanted to talk to the man that had his eyes on Lissoni, to establish if there was anyone with him.

He parked his car, grabbed his revolver that he kept hidden in the trunk, and met his man who led him in. Phil Zodol was employed as the beverage inventory manager, but his real function at the casino was to be Stevie Turner's eyes and ears.

The days of the Las Vegas skim are long gone, and the mob's role in the Vegas casinos has greatly diminished. In prison, Nick Amicucci had met a Chicago gangster who owned a hidden percentage in a popular topless bar in Vegas. When the man who ran it for the imprisoned gangster was arrested and sent to prison, Nick saw an opportunity. The Chicagoan, who had been away for a long time and didn't have anyone reliable to run it for him now, accepted Nick's offer to send one of his guys. Nick had his son, Dominic, give the assignment to Doug Sullivan, who sent his boyhood buddy, Stevie Turner.

Soon, Stevie was running all the Chicago action in Vegas, the bookmaking, loan-sharking, and prostitution rackets. Eventually, through Vito Paganini, Stevie was handed the Grazzitti Family's rackets there too. From prison, Doug had Stevie expand into construction and followed New York's methods of corrupting of the unions. Stevie's biggest asset was his anonymity; the FBI had no idea who he was. He left Henderson before Doug became headline news and stayed out of the limelight in Sin City. He had never been arrested and wasn't even listed as an associate by the feds. Being able to operate free of surveillance, a bankroll well into the millions, and the muscle of the crime families from three states allowed Stevie to bribe and intimidate himself to a top power in the city.

The Kajino had been open for less than a year, and Asians just flocked to it with the oriental theme. Half the unions involved with the casino already had been corrupted and the owners paid a stiff fee to Stevie who passed it along to Chicago, Michigan, and the Grazzitti Family of New York. The power also enabled Stevie to give jobs at will, as long they had no records or known criminal affiliations.

He picked Phil Zodol to watch his interests and got him a job that gave him room to roam the casino. It was Phil that it was reported to when John Lissoni's name came up.

"Is he still playing blackjack?" Noah asked Phil.

"No. Right now, he's at the sushi bar. He dropped ten grand."

"Cash?"

"Yeah, apparently, he's got a huge wad on him," Phil reported.

They walked out of the employee areas and into the casino. "Where's the sushi bar?"

"Second floor, you can see it right off the escalator."

"I want to see the man that's watching him, get him replaced and down here," Noah ordered.

In the meantime, Doug had called Tommy from Paris and told him of what was going down. Tommy called Dominic to set up an impromptu meeting, and Dominic told him to come to his father's house. Tommy pulled into the driveway and into the garage.

Tommy entered the house through the kitchen and was met by Dominic. Sal was at the kitchen counter eating a sandwich. "Ain't that your little brother?" Tommy asked, nodding at Sal.

"Yeah, that's the one."

Tommy walked to the counter. "Doug wants his four grand back from Thanksgiving."

"I know. He's supposed to be giving me a job at his new bar," Sal said.

"That won't last long," Dominic joked.

"He told me, you're working for free until that money's paid back," Tommy told him.

"No, he didn't. You're just fucking with me."

"Don't say I didn't warn you when you're washing dishes for free," Tommy said as he and Dominic walked outside to the horseshoe pit.

"So what's up, Tommy?" Dominic asked.

"We got John Lissoni under surveillance in Vegas. We're taking him out, right?"

Dominic raised his eyebrows at Tommy. "In Vegas?"

"He's staying at the Kajino, of all places, under his own name and using his own player card," Tommy reported. He knew Doug had already given the order to whack him, so Tommy was being sure the correct order was given. "We're moving on him, unless you say no. Time is of the essence, Dom."

"Why isn't he hiding? His fucking buddy just disappeared?" Dominic thought out loud.

"I don't know, but we're working on your standing orders to whack him. Now's the time to call it off if you want. If you want my opinion, something's wrong here. No one's this stupid."

"Stay on him, but don't whack him yet. Do not lose him."

"Call me and say you thought you were calling someone else if you decide to whack him. Until then, we'll stay on him." Tommy left to call Doug and Stevie.

Noah was playing a slot machine, watching John Lissoni drink his saki after finishing his sushi. By now they had ascertained that John was alone, and Noah had sent someone to check out his room. A waitress brought Noah a drink and told him Phil Zodol wanted to meet him by the men's room.

He passed the table games and found Phil. "What was in the room?"

"Stevie called it off, just follow him."

"I already got guys digging a hole in the desert," Noah complained.

"What do want from me?"

"What about his room?"

"I don't know yet, should be soon. Wait, here he comes now."

The man Phil sent to check his room was reporting in, "It ain't him. There's about eighty grand in cash in a bag, and buried in a suitcase is a wallet with a different name, from Michigan. I'm running the name now, we should know soon."

"Stay on this clown, I'm going to call Stevie," said Noah Brooks and left the casino.

Tommy Herrick was pacing around his living room when his safe phone rang; it was Stevie Turner. "Tommy, it ain't him."

"What do you mean, it ain't him?"

"He sent someone with his ID. We think the guy is someone in his crew."

"He's there, he's there," Tommy said, excitedly. "He's watching your men watch his man. He wants to see who your men are out there, Stevie. Put the plan back in action, whack this fucker before he whacks one of us. You got a green light."

Tommy ended his call, and called Dominic. "We got to get some coffee. I'll meet you halfway."

Dominic understood there was a problem and called Danny and told him he was coming by to pick him up, and then they drove to meet Tommy for some coffee.

Phil Zodol sat at a bar on the first floor of the Kajino, receiving updates from the men who were watching who they thought was John Lissoni. Now, they had no idea why they were still watching this guy. One of his security guards walked up to him and handed him a phone; it was the guard's personal cell phone. "It's a Mr. Brooks."

Phil took the phone. "How did you get this guy's number, Noah?"

"You serious? I've got everyone's phone number. But listen, there's been a change of plans again."

"Noah, why can't these guys out east make up their minds? Whack him, don't whack him, what the fuck?"

"You don't like your job, I'll find someone else. As for now, we're going to whack this guy you're watching. He's one of John Lissoni's last four crew members," Noah explained.

"What about this Lissoni fuck?"

"This is the kicker. Stevie says he's there, watching you and your men."

Phil stayed silent. He started spanning the room around him, looking for any faces that might be watching him.

"Phil, you there?" Noah asked.

"Yeah, talk about a fucking creepy feeling. You telling me he sent one of his guys, with his ID and checked into our casino, knowing we'd flag him and put a tail on him?"

"Sounds like it."

"And now is watching us?"

"That's why you got to find him and not lose the other guy."

"I don't want to fuck with a guy like this. We obviously walked right into his trap," complained Phil.

"Stay fucking calm. I'll be there in fifteen minutes."

Phil ended his call and handed the guard back his phone, who had stayed out of earshot. Phil continued to scan the faces around him, paranoia starting to set in. "Call your supervisor, tell him to put all the guards on high alert," Phil ordered the guard.

"Sir?"

"Do it now. I can't give a reason, just tell him to order the guards to keep their eyes open for any trouble."

"Yes, sir," said the guard and hurried off.

Phil called three of the four men who were watching the Lissoni imposter to stay at his side and stood with his back to a wall, still scanning the area.

Tommy Herrick drove to Ann Arbor and got a room at a Holiday Inn and waited for Danny and Dominic. He knew they knew where to go by the code he had given them: getting coffee meant a hotel and meeting halfway meant driving all the way to Ann Arbor. When they went to Ann Arbor, they used the same Holiday Inn. He went to the counter and checked in under David Johnson with a fake ID.

He got into his room and prepared for what he believed to be a long night. He unpacked four phones: a satellite phone for his conversations with Doug Sullivan in Paris, his secret phone for his illegal businesses, a second secret phone which he just had activated for this occasion and only Stevie Turner had the number, and his regular cell phone. He used his first secret phone and called Dominic and said only the room number he was in and hung up. He picked up his new secret phone and got an update from Vegas, giving that update to Doug through the satellite phone. Then he called his pregnant wife and told her not to expect him home tonight, since he had left the house without letting her know.

Danny and Dominic arrived twenty minutes later, at the same time that Noah Brooks arrived back at the Kajino to aid the panic-stricken Phil Zodol. Tommy let them in, and they gathered to hear what was transpiring in Las Vegas.

"It wasn't John Lissoni that checked in—it was one of his crew members. We found his wallet stashed away in his suitcase," Tommy explained.

"I gave Doug photographs to distribute, why wasn't it compared to it?" Danny wanted to know.

"It was, it's just a slow process. We didn't give the fucking guys watching the cameras a photograph of a guy and then they see him dead on the news. It's on a need-to-know basis, just for basic security. By the way, there is a good similarity in appearance."

"Okay, let's not get stuck here," Dominic said. "Fact is, it's not him. Where the fuck is he? And what's his angle?"

"We think he's there, watching the surveillance on his buddy, looking to see the main guys, possibly making a hit list, but definitely checking the security. That's the only thing that makes sense here."

"Why Las Vegas?" Danny wondered.

"Well, Doug said he was first spotted in Greektown, just playing blackjack. Of course here, he's known, so that had to be him at the tables. But he had to know his appearance would be reported and men would start looking there. We got a tip on a loft he has in Detroit and been staking it out. Mine and Doug's theory is that he was probably staking out the car that was staking out the loft, same plan as in the casino."

"So he's just collecting information?" Dominic asked.

"For now, hopefully. It is possible, though, that he's not in Vegas at all and using this decoy to strike here, now. Could be going after the men that were staking him out or he could be going after any of us—one reason I wanted to come out here."

"You think this fuck is coming after us?" Danny asked incredulously.

"It would put that possibility to rest if someone could physically spot him at the casino, but until then, we have to assume the worst-case scenario. And let me tell you, Jerry Lissoni and Lenny Silesi were very worthy opponents. This kid's a chip off his uncle's block. He's no joke, this is a brilliant strategy. We're the ones on the defensive now."

"So what's your plan?" Danny asked.

"Right now, my plan is take a leak. I'll be right back." Tommy left to use the restroom.

Danny looked to Dominic. "Good fucking thing this guy's on our side. You sure he ain't Sicilian?"

Noah Brooks stopped one of Phil Zodol's men in the casino. "Hey, what's with the fucking security? They got the metal detectors out at the door and everything."

"Something with Mr. Zodol, he's spooked about something," the man answered.

"Motherfucker," Noah sneered to himself and took off to find Phil whose phone was going right to voice mail.

On the first floor Noah spotted the man that had searched the room talking to two other men. "Where's Phil," Noah asked him.

"He's in his room."

"He's in his room?" Noah asked him back.

"Yeah, with two guards stationed at his door."

"Come with me," said Noah and took off for the escalator. "Please tell me someone's still watching the guy that checked in here," Noah said once they were away from the other two men.

"Still the original man."

"Get someone else on him and get your guy on a vacation out of Vegas, he's a marked man. Where is this guy now?"

"Betting big in the Samurai Room at a Texas Hold'em cash game, third floor," the man answered.

"Okay, go switch your men and send me two more, I'll take it from here. And be sure to get that guy out of town, now. Nice job here, you've got Phil's job now. Send a doctor in there and get him sedated before he hops on the phone or something stupid."

"Will do, thank you, Mr. Brooks."

Noah just nodded back, not too shabby for someone with no legal affiliation to the casino at all.

"Stevie, did you check the registry for other guests from Michigan? Could be three or four of them, could be one room for the other three," Tommy explained on the new secret phone.

"Done that, gone back a whole week now. I'm getting nothing, no one's seen this guy. I've got my best guy with his eyes on the imposter right now, though." Stevie was on a pay phone in Vegas.

"Dammit. If he ain't there, then he's fucking here. Dammit."

"Give me an hour—my guy will know one way or the other."

"Fine, but in one hour, I'm taking everyone off the fucking streets and locking everything down. That means Vegas too. I'm not taking no fucking chances with this kid."

"Okay, one hour."

Tommy turned to Danny and Dominic. "I suggest you do the same. We don't know for sure this kid won't move against you too."

"One hour," Danny agreed.

Noah sat at a slot machine outside the Samurai Room, trying to survey everything. To his dismay, he saw one of the owners of the casino walking toward him. Noah stood up to greet him. "Mr. Yamamoto, what brings you here?"

"More importantly, Mr. Brooks, is to why are you here? Is there some problem?" Noah was Yamamoto's connection to Stevie Turner and the key to keeping his union help alive. Noah Brooks just doesn't stop by to play a slot machine.

"No problem at all. Just playing some slots," Noah said, also realizing his conversation probably had been noticed if anyone was watching him.

"You take me for a fool. Please, Mr. Brooks, enlighten me as to what is taking place in my casino."

Just then, Noah noticed an old man, in very good shape, get up and leave his slot machine. He was playing in one section over from Noah, and he had discounted him as some old man. But now, watching him get up and walk, it wasn't the movement of an old man. But he sure did look like one. The old man looked back and the two made eye contact. "Got him!" Noah screamed in his head.

"Are you listening to me, Mr. Brooks?" Mr. Yamamoto asked.

"Mr. Yamamoto, please forgive me, but I've got to go," said Noah and caught the attention of one of the men given to him. Noah nodded at the old man and noticed his man didn't believe him. He took one look at the old man, looked back to Noah, and shook his head, but still followed. The other two stationed there stayed, watching the Lissoni imposter play cards. Yamamoto could only watch as Mr. Brooks disappeared from his view; he knew there was nothing he could do, not if he wanted to keep his casino running.

"They're in hot pursuit of someone in a disguise, can't be sure it's John Lissoni himself, though," Tommy reported after getting the play-by-play from Stevie, who kept driving from pay phone to pay phone with each update from Noah.

"What kind of disguise?" Dominic asked.

"Don't know. But the fucking casino owner had a chat with Stevie's guy, so we can't pull nothing in there now."

"So what now?" Danny asked. "You can't just wait for them to check out and leave town."

"No, I was just hoping we could clip these guys in their fucking room and take them out with the laundry. Now there's a witness, he's an unknown. We have to figure he'd tell anyone that asked that Stevie's guy was in the hotel that night. Nothing can happen there now."

"Plus, we fucking answer to too many people with that casino to bring that kind of attention. You want to tell them guys in Chicago that you lost them all those millions? I don't," said Danny.

"That's my point. You guys got to tell them to come home. You got to bring John Lissoni in to negotiate. We got to keep them at that hotel until you get the message to them," Tommy explained.

"Sure you don't want to just blow up the casino, Tommy?" Dominic joked about the RPG attack Tommy had once ordered.

"Very fucking funny, fight your own battles next time, asshole," Tommy responded.

"Not now," Danny said. "Any other options, Tommy?"

Tommy's phone for Stevie rang. "Maybe there will be now," Tommy said and answered the phone.

"We tailed the old man to a hotel room. The room's registered to a Henry Crawford from Pennsylvania. We think we've got eyes on a third one now, a perfectly disguised woman. Her movements and shoulders give her away—they think she's a man. These guys are fucking good, Tommy," Stevie reported.

"Seems to be the case, find that fourth person, Stevie. He could be in that room."

"I know, we're on it. You got to admit, Tommy, the danger is here. I wouldn't put no stock in the notion anything's going to happen there."

"Find me that fourth person," said Tommy and hung up, checking the time. It had been fifty-five minutes, and Stevie's guy inside the casino was obviously proving his worth, so he decided to give them another hour. He just didn't bother to tell that to Stevie.

Desperate and out of time, Noah stood in a central point staring down anyone by themselves, throwing discretion to the wind. He heard a glass break and looked to see that a waiter had dropped his tray onto some gamblers, causing a big distraction. The first thing Steve Turner had ever told him, when he hired Noah to handle his security at a popular topless bar, was "when there's a distraction, look the other way, someone's always trying to pull something with a distraction."

Noah quickly looked to his right, noticing an employee door close. He grabbed one of the two men with him and told him to take the waiter who dropped the tray to a back room and keep him there, then Noah and the other man, who had an electronic key, followed through the employee door.

CHAPTER XI

Disguises

NOAH BROOKS RAN into two casino workers on the staircase a floor below. "Did you two ladies see anyone come down before me?" Noah asked, as his man that was with him went the other way and up the stairs.

"Are you even supposed to be back here?" one of the workers asked Noah.

"I'm a cop, undercover, did you see anyone?"

"Where's your badge?"

Noah reached into his pocket, pulled out a hundred-dollar bill, and tossed to them."Did you see anyone?"

"Just some brother, tall and lanky," one finally answered.

"A black guy? In a casino outfit, right?"

"Yeah, sugar."

Noah continued down the stairs and called the man that went the other direction to tell him to turn around and come down the staircase. At the first floor, Noah knew he lost his target. He entered the casino floor and took a survey for any tall and lanky black casino workers. He didn't see any. He did see Hector Martinez, though, the man he had promoted to replace the incapacitated Phil Zodol, heading toward him.

"Hector, tall, lanky black casino worker, we need to find him," Noah told him.

"Tall, lanky black casino worker? No one came out that Mr. Brooks."

"What do you mean no one came out that door? There's nowhere else he could've gone." Noah had a realization. "Them bitches, they lied."

"Mr. Turner's here, that's what I was coming to tell you. He's in suite 3410."

"Stevie Turner's here? I just talked to him not too long ago."

"Well, he's here. He wants you to go to his suite."

Back in Michigan, Tommy, Danny, and Dominic remained in their hotel room, converted into a mini headquarters for the action in play in Las Vegas. Tommy's phone for Stevie Turner rang. "Is he there?" Tommy asked him.

"Yeah, he's here, Tommy." Stevie was ordered to call Tommy once Noah had arrived in the suite.

"Ask him this: he has seen the guy that checked in as John Lissoni, right?"

Stevie asked him, "Yeah, he saw him. Point blank."

"Ask if he's seen the photograph?"

"Yeah, he's seen it, Tommy."

"Then why didn't he know it wasn't him?"

"I thought it was him to, Stevie," Noah answered.

"Even after all the time you watched him?" Stevie asked him.

"Never in a million years would I have thought it wasn't him if you guys didn't say it wasn't," said Noah defending himself.

"Stevie, ask what he thought the second time he watched him, after we said it wasn't him."

"I got this Tommy, quit. What about the second time, at the Samurai Room? You didn't think it was him anymore?"

"There seemed to be some differences, nose seemed smaller, eyes more sunken, after reviewing the picture. But I was mostly watching around me, content with the other men to watch the fake."

"Tommy, he said . . ."

"I heard. Stevie, I think that's him. Plastic surgery maybe? Throws a dummy wallet in his suitcase, knowing we're going to search it, to put the idea in our heads. Dresses his crew up to watch our movements, probably just like in Greektown. Got us chasing ghosts, while he watches the whole thing, again."

"This is what we have, Tommy. Someone dressed up like an old man runs into a room registered to a Henry Crawford of Pennsylvania. We got a plane ticket from there to Vegas in that name, age sixty-eight. We got a woman we think is a man still playing slots and a waiter locked down in a room. The waiter dropped a tray at the same time an employee opened and closed, an employee door that needs an employee key to open. We don't know who went through the door or if it even matters, but we're going to talk to the waiter about it. And you think the ringleader is sitting dead center, out in the open, the only one without a disguise?"

Despite not being talked to, Noah spoke up, "I think it is. These disguises, the wallet, this whole plan is masterful."

"I agree with him, Stevie. Someone's just got to walk to up to this guy and shoot him in the fucking head, end this madness," Tommy joked.

"If it's him, what's his exit plan? Obviously, we're not going to let him go," Stevie said.

"Something tells me he has a plan. Get inside that room and keep a good watch on Lissoni. If it's him, he's the priority," Tommy ordered.

"No one's left that room, someone's still in there," Stevie said.

"That's why you got to get in there. The one room is obviously the decoy. They got to be operating out of somewhere."

"Maybe this old man is just an old man and not some conspirator," Stevie said.

Noah answered that one, "That was no old man, I'm one hundred percent positive."

"Get in the room, Stevie."

"Okay, we'll go in the room," Stevie conceded.

"Why don't we just go to the cameras?" Danny asked once Tommy was off the phone.

"Because then we can't control it anymore. That's just too many hands in kitty. A phone even rings up in that room, and everyone knows something's going on. We're only missing one crew member, and it's got to be the guy that went in the stairwell."

"So all is well," Dominic said.

"Not out of control is the wording I'd go with. And we seem to know where our enemy is. We're all right," Tommy said.

Noah assembled three men and stood outside the room the old man had entered. He used the key given to him to open the door and they all ran in, with the last man closing the door behind him.

Inside they found Henry Crawford sitting on the bed, watching TV. "What's, what's going on?" the obviously sixty-eight-year-old man asked, slowly getting off the bed.

"You're not the same person I saw playing the slot machines. You're not the same man I followed in here," Noah said.

Henry Crawford looked at Noah. "I remember you. Yeah, I was playing some slots over by you. I saw you with that Japanese guy."

"No. That wasn't you."

"Sonny, I don't what else to tell you. I got up and came here, been here ever since."

Noah stood speechless. The man was so fit he had followed into this room, but the man in front of him now looked like he could be carried away by a gust of wind. "Check out the room," Noah ordered the other men. "Where're you from, Henry?" Noah asked while the men looked around.

"Small town outside of Philly."

"You come here alone?"

"Every year, my wife died years ago. Feel free to go through my bags if you like, I got nothing to hide. Just please don't throw everything around, as I won't be able to fold everything as well as my daughter-in-law did packing my clothes," Henry offered.

Noah walked to the window and looked for a ledge or anywhere a person could've exited the room from, but he saw nothing. "No, we're leaving," Noah announced once his men also came up empty. He kept the same man posted in the hallway to watch the room and returned to Stevie Turner's suite.

"I don't have a fucking clue what's going on, Stevie. I hate to say it, but we might have to go to the cameras if we're going to catch this whole crew," Noah reported.

"What's the word with the waiter?" Stevie asked.

"Martinez questioned him, but he came up empty." Noah's phone rang, and it was reported to him that the woman they believed was a man was on the move and heading for the exits. "Follow her out, go where she goes. You cannot lose her, or him." After getting off the phone, Noah headed back to the casino floor, wanting to lay his eyes on the man they believed, for the second time now, was John Lissoni.

Eight hours of playing this game was getting on Tommy's nerves as he talked to Doug Sullivan, who was just hitting lunchtime in Paris. "The fucking sun's coming up, and we're still running around like fucking morons. I don't know what to do. We can't whack Lissoni in the casino. He could sit there for days, this motherfucker. I feel certain there's no danger here at home, though that's the only positive I can think of right now. Still not even a hundred percent that's even Lissoni playing cards, this is so fucked up, Doug."

"What happened to the woman?"

"Last I heard, they were trailing her walking down the fucking strip. She's probably going to walk all the way to Canada just to keep fucking with us."

Danny Serafini was listening to Tommy's conversation when he asked him a question. "Didn't you say the owner was there? Could he be helping them somehow? You said he gave your man a hard time."

Tommy asked Doug, "Danny asked if there's some chance Yamamoto could be involved. For some odd reason, that doesn't sound so out of reach."

"Stevie did say this guy's a prick. He was a hard one to shake down," Stevie said. "Maybe he cuts a deal with Lissoni for less money if Lissoni can take power away from Dom and Danny?" Doug thought out loud.

"Doug," Tommy said, having a breakthrough. "Remember last year, when Stevie thought someone had taken a few shots at him? Maybe John's uncle cut a deal with Yamamoto last year, and that's when they took a shot at Stevie. Maybe the plan was to take a power base like Vegas away, like they're trying now. Obviously, this Noah Brooks has to be on the top of their hit list by now. Yamamoto could've told him the names of everyone over here, and today they put a face with the name, even knowing the whole layout of the casino."

"But this all is just theory," Dominic reminded Tommy.

Tommy looked back to him. "Well, yeah, for now. But you got to start somewhere."

"Tommy, I'm still waiting on the background check on Henry Crawford. I'll call when I get it. Run the Yamamoto theory by Stevie, he knows him better than any of us. And why don't you just take a picture of the guy playing cards and send it to Dom and Danny, they've known John Lissoni since he was born?" Doug pointed out.

"Not the best picture to send over the airwaves, considering what's going to happen to him, eventually."

"Tommy, I'm sure you can find a safe way. They're the only ones involved who've seen this guy, that's the certainty we need. Later."

Noah sat down at the card game in the Samurai Room, directly across from his subject. The man had been sitting there almost five hours now and showed no signs of tiring. Noah got his chips and looked across the table. "John, how you doing?"

"Good, Noah. Thanks for asking. Yourself? How's the wife and kids?"

Noah was stunned; that wasn't the reaction he was looking for. "Fold," Noah said, tossing in his cards. "So what brings you out here?"

"A lot of people go to Vegas, Noah. I'm just one of the many. Besides, I thought I'd get a look around."

"Ah, Mr. Turner, so good of you to call me and have breakfast. Please, have seat," Yamamoto greeted Stevie at a booth at the breakfast buffet.

"It's not the breakfast I had in mind, but okay. I have some questions for you."

"You have some questions for me? Oh, Mr. Turner, you so flatter yourself."

"If I remember right, you started construction here, spring of 2009, right?" Stevie asked.

"That is no secret, Mr. Turner."

"If I also remember this right, when you and I were negotiating a price, you took a vacation to Philadelphia, right?"

"That also was no secret, Mr. Turner."

"But what was a secret is that that's where Jerry Lissoni was hiding when Tommy couldn't find him. Isn't that right, Mr. Yamamoto?"

"Mr. Turner, I do not . . ."

"You know Henry Crawford too, don't you?" Stevie asked, getting a little animated.

"There is nothing you can do to me, Mr. Turner," Mr. Yamamoto said, defiantly.

"Because of John Lissoni? Are you fucking mad?"

"You will not shut down my casino with your union, Mr. Turner. I call your bluff."

"I'll shut your casino down in a fucking minute, you dumbass."

"And you will let the young man playing cards walk out front door."

"We're just going to let John Lissoni walk right out the door, eh?" Stevie asked.

"If that's John Lissoni," Yamamoto said, showing his hand finally.

"You have no idea what you're fucking with here, do you? I've already gotten the fingerprint results off his beer bottle back from the county cops. Your stupid little game was just that, a stupid little game," Stevie bluffed.

"So be it then. Even your crooked policemen won't look other way with a murder right in the casino. Or are your plans grander, Mr. Turner? Headline news: casino owner go missing. You will have no more casino to play *your* stupid little games in, Mr. Turner."

Stevie could think of only one thing to say. "You're such a dead man." He then got up and walked away.

Tommy was speculating with Danny and Dominic when Doug called Tommy with Henry Crawford's background. "Get this, Tommy. This fucker's career was a costume-makeup artist for Broadway or some bullshit like that."

"You saying the old man decorated Lissoni's crew in the hotel? There were no signs in the room. And the woman has a room at another hotel, you think they operated out of there? All this just to identify a few faces?"

"Pretty much, they're telling us to go fuck ourselves, that they ain't scared. Where's Lissoni now?"

"Eating breakfast with Stevie's guy two tables behind."

"Tommy, brace yourself for this: he is going to walk right out of that casino. And we're going to let him," Doug told Tommy.

"No, we're not. That would be the dumbest move ever."

"Yamamoto's right, we can't do anything at the casino and we can't do anything to him. We'll muscle him out, but it's going to take some time. But we can't whack him, it'll ruin everything we have going out there."

"So would letting these fuckers get away with this," Tommy said.

"Only get away today, not for good. No chance in hell. We can't fight in Vegas, though. We have to get Lissoni somewhere else."

"Doug, I'm having a serious problem with letting these guys treat us like fucking scumbags," Tommy said.

"Tommy, the feds leave us alone with Vegas, it is possible they don't even know we're there. Why bring them into it? Vegas has been good for us—this will only fuck it up. They all got to walk, Tommy. We'll get Lissoni, we'll chase that Jap fuck, Yamamoto, out of Vegas, and everyone will still know not to fuck with us. Let's not make the news on this one, okay?"

"Fine, but I'm personally in charge of the manhunt on this asshole. This one I'd like to look in the eyes when I pull the trigger."

"That's where you earn the psycho rep."

"Anyway, Stevie said he mentioned Jerry Lissoni hiding in Philly to Yamamoto, just made it up, and he thinks he hit it on the head. Is it possible the Philly mob was backing the Lissoni side during the war? Then sends this costume fuck out there with John?" Tommy asked.

"Maybe Yamamoto promised a piece of his casino if they could unseat Dominic. Ask Danny and Dom if they know of any Lissoni connections to Philly. If Philly was involved, they were probably backed by a family in New York. This could be really fucked up."

Tommy ended his call and discussed the Philadelphia situation with Danny and Dominic. They all agreed it was a matter to be brought immediately to Dominic's father in prison.

Stevie Turner paced around his suite in a rage. He had just gotten off the phone with Tommy and got his order to let everyone walk. He got up the nerve to make his call. "Noah, it's official. The man in front of you is John Lissoni."

"I know it is. We're drinking coffee staring at each other. He's got the stupidest fucking grin, Stevie. Give me the nod," Noah said, wanting the okay for the hit.

"You got to let him go."

"Say again."

"Let him go, it's our order." Noah didn't answer. "Noah, tell me you understand. You're letting him go, say the words."

"I'm letting him go. We're still tailing him out of the casino, right?"

"Negative. You're walking away."

Noah hung up the phone, and John Lissoni got up walked toward him, extending his hand. "No hard feelings, eh, Noah?" Noah just stared at him. "Well, I thought you should know you're first on my list. I'll be seeing you around." John Lissoni turned around and walked right out of the Kajino.

Noah had called one of his own men to watch Henry Crawford's room, one not employed by the Kajino as directed by Stevie. He called Noah immediately when Henry finally came out of the room with his bags, and Noah came running. Just before Noah arrived, his man watched the doors of three hotel rooms open and a lone man come out of each with their bags.

The casino guard, who was watching Henry's room, approached Noah's man. "Tell Mr. Turner I'm sorry. Mr. Yamamoto gave me a hundred grand cash and threatened to fire me if I didn't play along. There was nothing I could do." The guard ran off, and Noah was left with just his own man when he arrived.

After leaving the hotel room, Dominic dropped Danny off at the bakery, and Dominic raced to see his father. Nick advised his son to visit their Uncle Ziggy, who would have the most information, if any, of a Lissoni-Philadelphia connection. Nick also urged him to inform Vito Paganini of New York of the situation, just in case it does involve another family from New York.

Dominic headed to his Uncle Ziggy's house; he was in town this weekend for New Year's, and Danny was going to drive to New York to speak with Vito. It was Sunday and Ziggy would be at Dominic's father's house in a few hours, but neither him nor Danny were waiting around. On the way there, Michelle called Dominic's cell. "Are we still on for tonight?" she asked him.

"Actually, I've got to cancel, something's come up."

"Three out of four times, nice. I guess you're really not that interested."

"It's something I can't put off. Besides, didn't you have a nice time New Year's Eve? At least the one out of four that I did make was top notch."

"I did have a great time," Michelle admitted.

"My twenty-five percent is better than anyone's one hundred percent, trust me. I'll make this one up to you."

"How about we really take that trip to Las Vegas?"

Dominic cringed. "You know, I'm a little over Vegas right now. Pick somewhere else and I'll make it happen."

"I'll think about it, let you know. Call me later?"

"If I can."

Dominic arrived at his Uncle Ziggy's house and spent some time visiting with his dying cousin, Charlie, and his wife, Lonna. Once he and Ziggy were alone in the yard, Dominic started filling Ziggy in on the Lissoni situation.

Ziggy threw his hands in the air. "Look, when I came out of prison, your father came to me and told me what he was planning and asked me to be his consigliere. I told him I was giving Charlie my house, taking my wife to Florida, and retiring, so leave me the fuck out of it. Now I'm telling you: leave me the fuck out of it."

"You can't just tell me if you know of any connection between the Lissonis and Philadelphia? How the fuck does that make you involved and unretired?"

"Because it does. Last time I'm going to tell you: leave me the fuck alone."

"Whatever, but the next you need your grandson to come spend time with his father, don't fucking even think of asking me. You can go fuck yourself, you miserable fucking prick." Dominic turned to leave.

Ziggy gave a sigh. "You're right, I'm sorry. Philadelphia, eh?" Ziggy took a moment to think. "I can't say I can think of any. But we would've had a connection there. Our family, here in Michigan, would've had a representative there. I can't remember who ours was, but if it was the Lissonis, I'm sure I'd remember it. More than likely it would've been through the bosses, probably through the Matteas." The Matteas had held the throne of boss until the 1990s when Peter Mattea went to prison.

"That would put Jack Mattea in the mix now if you're right." Jack was a captain, appointed by Dominic after Jack's ten-year prison stint and parole and was the former boss' cousin.

"I'm not saying anyone's in the mix. But you did whack his brother's grandson, Dominic," Ziggy said.

"There is the chance that Philly got involved from another family in New York, got to consider every possibility, right?" Dominic asked.

"Dominic, I answered your question about what I knew of Philly, I'm not here to bounce theories around with. I will give you a suggestion, though. Go see my brother, Ray. He was in the know. I've always been the happy-go-lucky one. Plus, you haven't seen your Uncle Ray in prison for almost ten years now."

"Happy-go-lucky? Not the way I remember it. Uncle Ray's in Tennessee, right?"

"Yeah, you've been there."

"It seems like decades. There was a lot of shit to do there. I remember it was pretty nice," Dominic said.

"Not much to do there for my brother, but yeah, I have a good time when I stay there."

"Thanks, I'll see you at dinner." A few days in Tennessee with Michelle didn't sound too bad, Dominic thought as he turned to leave.

"Dominic, don't forget our family history."

"Dominic turned back to his uncle. What do you mean?"

"You know I'm the only one of my father's sons to be born here in Michigan, right? Your grandfather and Uncle Jack were born in Sicily, and your uncle Ray was born in Ohio."

"So?"

"So when my father, your great-grandfather, lived in Ohio, it was Paul and Pete Lissoni that brought him here to work for the Club. That means our family and the Lissonis have been united since before I was even born."

"What's your point, Uncle Zig?" Dominic asked.

"My point is, you're fighting some good blood."

"John is hardly like his uncle, Jerry."

"You don't even really know who you're fighting. John isn't even Jerry's nephew, they're cousins. You should know this."

"Well, after John, it's seems to me there's no more Lissonis in our world. So the past don't seem to make a difference. You think the Amicuccis are supposed to always work for the Lissonis, don't you?"

"I believe that what the boss says is the rule. Pete Mattea, from prison, just like your father is now, said there was to be no boss until he decided otherwise. Your father disregarded that order and named himself boss after a killing spree. I believe we wouldn't have the fortunate lives we have now if it wasn't for the Lissonis. And I believe you are too young and lack the respect to run this family, that's why you have problems like these."

"Okay, don't hold back now. What the fuck else you got an opinion on all of a sudden?"

"If you don't like my opinions, do not ask for them. When I told your father not to involve me, it wasn't just because I wanted to be with my family more, I also told him no because he was wrong. He broke the rules. Since day one of our Club, there has never been an attack on a boss, that's why it's stayed so strong for so long. Our family here has kept our rules and our honor intact, until your father did what he did."

"You speak about something you don't understand, old man," Dominic said, his blood starting to boil. "Benny Cellini was making a move for boss—he fucking tried to kill me. You didn't get out until a few months later. My father didn't have a fucking choice."

"You don't know he was trying to kill you," Ziggy said.

"Two motorcycle gang members beat me in an alley and threw me in my trunk, to me that sounds like I was going to my death. And since Benny Cellini handled the motorcycle gangs, it all seems pretty obvious."

"But the only person that knew you'd be there was that Irish kid Doug Sullivan."

"He shot them both dead and took me to my wife. I'd say he didn't set me up," Dominic said.

"Two dead assassins can't tell who sent them. And he's been 'in like Flynn' with you and your father ever since."

"I'm done here. You're locked in the past, I come to you for help and advice and you tell me I'm getting what I deserve. Well, if it works out for John Lissoni, don't forget to say 'I told you so' to my fucking casket," he said and left.

Tommy Herrick drove to his brother's house after leaving Danny and Dominic to start formulating a plan for finding John Lissoni. "This kid ain't no punk, Billy. This was fucking bold. I'm really leaning to shutting everything until we find this guy."

"He hasn't done nothing but be a bother so far," Billy replied.

"So far. But his fucking uncle came out of nowhere and tried to kill me, shooting at me on the road. I don't want to wait until he makes a move."

"You're telling me? I had to shoot one on my lawn, while covering up my own wife. But why shut everything down? Even with the war with his uncle, he never attacked any rackets, just us."

"These fuckers have allied themselves with our casino in Vegas. Maybe has an alliance with the family in Philly. And this is just a four-man crew? I want this fucker dead, now."

"And he will be dead, but for now, you should get some sleep. You've been up almost two days now," Billy told his elder brother.

"How can I sleep while this asshole's still alive?"

"Go see your wife and daughter, put your head on a pillow, and watch what happens."

"This year's looking like a pain in the ass."

Just as Tommy started dozing off, his satellite phone rang. "Hey, Doug," he answered.

"I got some info on that Henry Crawford. He ain't mobbed up, he's a family member to that guy that disappeared last week," Doug told him. The guy that disappeared last week was Chris Fullaria, the fifth member of the Lissoni crew, who Doug and Tommy tortured then killed. "Apparently, they're distant cousins on Fullaria's mother's side, who came from Philly."

"No shit, so no Philly problem?" Tommy asked.

"Don't see one now. What are you sleeping?"

"Trying to."

"Get this shit, Wednesday I'm meeting with a terrorist to talk about buying weapons. Ain't that something?"

"Doug, I just can't handle what you got going right now. I need sleep, and I got to kill John Lissoni."

"You have to admit, it is kind of cool, though. I'm like a James Bond."

"Very cool, Doug. Good night."

"Hey, before you go, you do have someone going to Philly to watch Crawford's house, right?"

"Of course. Good fucking night." Tommy laid his phone on the dresser and stared at the ceiling for a moment before kicking the covers off and getting up to send someone to Philadelphia to watch Henry Crawford's house.

CHAPTER XII

Business as Usual

DOMINIC AWOKE TO the smell of bacon permeating from his kitchen. Through the pain in his head from the amount of alcohol he had consumed the night before, he lifted his head to check his alarm clock. Shit, it was already 9:00 a.m., and he had planned on being on the road to see his father today by eight. Dominic climbed out of bed and headed for the smell in the kitchen. He came down the stairs and peeked into the kitchen. Michelle was cooking breakfast in just a T-shirt, and his cousin, Jimmy, was seated at the kitchen table, enjoying his view.

Jimmy was there to drive Dominic to the prison, and to Dominic's dismay, he couldn't remember Michelle being at his house, or how he even got home, for that matter. Dominic tiptoed into the kitchen and slapped Jimmy on the back of the head. "Ouch. What the hell?" Jimmy exclaimed, turning to see his cousin and knowing he was caught eyeing Dominic's girl.

Dominic shared a grin with Jimmy and asked, "Why didn't you wake me?"

"I told him not to," Michelle said, pouring Dominic a cup of coffee.

"Don't tell him not to wake me, it's his job," Dominic said, taking the coffee and nodding his thanks.

"Someone's a little grumpy. You sure were a character last night," Michelle said, starting to serve breakfast.

"What was he doing?" Jimmy asked.

"Don't worry about it," Dominic told him.

"After I picked him up on the freeway, we went to his father's restaurant and he was singing and dancing on the bar like in some movie."

"He what?" Jimmy burst out.

"I what?" Dominic asked in disbelief.

"You don't remember?" Michelle asked.

"I'll be honest, I don't even remember you."

"You called me to pick you up, your car broke down on 696. But it wasn't your truck, you wouldn't say whose car it was. We went to the restaurant and your brother Sal was there with some guy," Michelle explained.

Dominic looked to Jimmy, who was enjoying every minute of this. "Any idea?"

"I was home. I haven't talked to Sal in a couple days."

Michelle asked, "You don't remember smoking pot with them?"

"Awesome," exclaimed Jimmy.

"Oh my god," Dominic said, putting his head in his hands.

"You really tied one on, huh?" Jimmy laughed.

"I don't have time for this, let's go, Jimmy." Dominic got up and said bye to Michelle, leaving her at his house.

"Dom, that is nice. She's got some body," Jimmy said, once they were on the road.

Dominic turned to Jimmy. "She's works in a gym. And shut the fuck up, would you, Jimmy?"

It was business as usual as crime family underboss, Danny Serafini, stood in the back parking lot of the bakery with captain, Angelo Rea, and their lieutenant, Fat Kenny Infelice. As they did once a month, Kenny met with his bosses and turned in the money he had collected. One by one Kenny gave an envelope to Angelo and explained where it was from, how much the take was, and how much was already split up before it got to Kenny. He also announced the twenty-five percent of each one that he took.

"This one's from the Graphic's Union—one hundred grand. John took his twenty and I took mine. There's fifty grand in the envelope." John was the made man that extorted union members that operate in Ohio. Dominic's grandfather had the foresight to get involved in it in the early eighties. It also provided legitimate jobs to friends and family members of the Amicucci crew.

"Here's San Diego's, it's a good one. Four hundred grand—one hundred to Dontae out there and a hundred grand to me. There's two hundred k in the envelope." Dontae Marino ran the family's interests in California.

"Fifty grand from the Warren book. Twelve thousand five hundred apiece for Eugene and myself, there's twenty-five grand in the envelope." Eugene Mudd ran the decent-sized Warren book.

"This one has the book and card game in Rochester. Fifteen grand total, minus seventy-five hundred, there's seventy-five in the envelope. Bad month for them."

Danny took the last envelope and realized there was one missing. "I talked with Jackie Beans on New Year's Day. He said we were having our best month in a long time. Where's the envelope?"

"We were having a good month, until the end of those bowl games," Kenny explained.

Danny was at the Corner during most of the games; they were making a killing. But he was wrapped up with the Las Vegas affair, and he really didn't catch up on the other games. "What happened?"

Angelo answered, "We went from a having good month to having a great month. The fucking money won't fit in an envelope, Danny," Angelo beamed.

"After getting paid our money from what we laid off, we cleared a million. Four hundred grand on the BCS games alone. There's five hundred and fifty grand in a bag in my trunk for you guys," Kenny explained.

"Very fucking nice," Danny said.

Danny and Angelo would count up the money given to them by Kenny. Angelo would take twenty-five percent of the just over eight hundred thousand-dollar pot. Danny and Dominic would split the rest, after putting twenty-five percent aside for made member pensions and imprisoned gangsters and their families. The NFL playoffs and college bowl games proved to be very lucrative for the newly promoted Kenny; his take for the month was 420 grand.

Angelo's take was just over two hundred grand, and he had five more lieutenants to collect from. Dominic and Danny would take over two hundred grand apiece and placing another two hundred grand aside for the crime family. This was just from the Amicucci crews. There were still five other captains to collect from, not counting the money from Doug Sullivan's crew and the drug trafficking business. Despite the distractions from John Lissoni and Fabian Bosca, business was good and 2011 was looking profitable to Danny, especially, with the super bowl right around the corner and then college basketball's March Madness, then hockey playoffs and then basketball playoffs. *Freedom is a wonderful thing,* thought Danny.

Hiyoshi Yamamoto had just sat down for his breakfast when his phone rang; it was his casino manager at the Kajino. There was a problem: their linen company wasn't delivering to them anymore. "Why not?" Yamamoto asked him.

"All they tell me is to call the union. I call the union and they tell me they want to talk to you. Bottom line is we're not going to have any clean linen by tomorrow."

"I will call the union then."

Three hours later, Yamamoto was greeted by Noah Brooks at a hotel room in his own casino. He was taken into the bathroom and strip-searched by two men before being brought before Stevie Turner. "I do not appreciate this treatment in my own hotel, Mr. Turner. And I will not be shaken down by your unions either."

"How much did they ask for?" Stevie asked him.

"Two hundred and fifty thousand dollars or no more laundry, I will not stand for it," Yamamoto said defiantly.

"That's a steep price. Next week your bartenders and waitstaffs are not going to show up for work. The next week will be your janitors. The list goes on and on, and it's going to get real expensive," Stevie explained how their squeeze was going to work.

"I will not pay."

"Suit yourself. You won't be operational in a month."

"I will go to FBI."

"Then what? You haven't been no innocent bystander, you'll lose the casino. I'll go to jail, you can go into the witness protection or back to fucking Japan. But I told you before, you have no idea who you're fucking with. You will be killed, someday, somewhere."

"I will not be intimidated."

"Shut the fuck up. I've already talked to someone about buying you out, it'll be more than a fair price. You can take that, or you can run to the feds and get nothing and wind up dead. Or you can pay or not pay the unions, but how long can that really last? Tell me where John Lissoni is and we can work out a deal for you to keep your casino. Those are your only options now," Stevie said and sat back to await an answer.

The defiance was now gone and Yamamoto's shoulders slumped. "I think I make mistake."

"A fucking big one," Noah said from behind him.

Stevie held up his hand to silence Noah. "How'd the Lissoni thing come about? It's time to come clean."

"I can keep my casino?"

Stevie was hesitant. "You can remain a partner. There's other people involved who just want you clipped, take the lower percentage. Tell me how this started?"

"Your friends have bad apples around them."

"What the hell does that mean?" Stevie asked.

"I was introduced to Lenny Silesi. He introduced me to Jerry Lissoni. They told me you weren't long as boss out here. They told me Jerry will be boss, that he would cut my payment in half. So I said I would help."

That's when it hit Stevie. "You're the reason I got shot at? It wasn't even a good attempt, you oriental motherfucker."

Yamamoto bowed his head. "I am at your mercy."

Stevie took a deep breath; he still needed more information. "How did John Lissoni come into the picture?

"Him and Lenny's son, Lenny Jr., were my connections. Even after his uncle died, he never stopped contacting me."

"The million-dollar question: Where is he?"

"That, I do not know. But I will contact him and set him up for you."

"That'll work."

Noah chirped in with a question, "You said you were introduced to Lenny Silesi. Who introduced you to him?"

Yamamoto paused. "I was introduced to him by the bad apple, that Fabian person."

"Fabian Bosca?" Stevie asked, amazed.

"That is him. He came to me when I was taking construction bids. He has a connection in one of your unions."

"One of my unions?" Stevie asked. He was aware Tommy was looking for Fabian; he was on the same alert that flagged John Lissoni. But Stevie had no idea he even knew anyone in Las Vegas.

"Yes. He is very bad apple."

Stevie bolted up. "Noah, keep a man on this fuck until we work out a plan. Make sure it's one of our guys, not someone from the casino." Stevie rushed out and left the hotel in search of a distant pay phone to give Tommy Herrick the Fabian information.

Dominic had just pulled into the bakery's parking lot when Tommy called him his secret phone. "What's up, Tommy?"

"I got the scoop on Sin City. Where can we meet?"

"Come here, to the bakery. Danny's here, we'll have to meet in the parking lot."

"It's fucking freezing. Why can't he just use the scrambler?" Tommy asked, annoyed.

"Because he's insane, that's why." Dominic hung up and entered the bakery with his cousin Jimmy.

"Why is it every time I see you nowadays, you look like a train ran over you?" Danny asked, drawing chuckles from Angelo.

"He's got a new broad," Angelo said.

"Oh, I haven't seen you with anyone since I been out. I thought maybe things had changed," Danny joked.

"Very funny guys, make fun of the guy with the dead wife for not whoring around like those around him," Dominic responded.

"Always such a dark place with you," Danny said.

"I'm just fucking around. You know, I woke up this morning and she was cooking breakfast," Dominic said.

"You don't sound very happy about it," Danny said.

"It feels like she's trying to hurry a relationship."

"Because she made breakfast? Maybe she was hungry and didn't want to wait for your drunk ass to wake up," Danny told him.

Angelo piped in, "I'd give anything for Angela to cook breakfast just once."

"I've seen your wife cook, Ange. You're better off," Dominic retorted. "And I just don't think we're at a point where she should feel at home going through my cupboards and my fridge. When me and Jimmy left this morning, she never even entertained the thought of getting dressed and leaving. I mean, come on, my wife's clothes are still in her closet."

"What do you hide in your cupboards?" Danny asked.

"Nothing. Why?"

"Then what do you care if she goes through them?"

"You're missing the whole fucking point. It's not the cupboards, it's the going through them, like she lived there."

"I don't think she plans on moving in, Dom," Angelo said.

"Looks that way to me. I'll probably come home and it will be all redecorated, in pink or something. Probably, moved right the fuck in."

"Always such a dark place with you," Danny added, again. "Why the hell did you bring her over then?"

"I didn't. I woke up and there she was," Dominic said.

"He don't remember last night," Jimmy said from the background.

"You don't remember last night? How much are you drinking?" Danny asked.

"You don't remember last night? You were a riot," Angelo said.

Dominic looked back to Jimmy. "Go outside and watch the fucking truck."

"It's like five degrees, Dom," Jimmy said.

"Now!" Dominic yelled. Jimmy scurried off.

"Dominic, you can't be going around being a drunk. You've got too much responsibility," Danny told him.

Dominic dismissed Danny. "Yeah, yeah, I know. I'm not." He turned to Angelo. "Where did you see me at last night?"

"You don't even remember me? We left the Corner together to go to Vince Cusamano's engagement party in Ferndale." Vince worked at the Amicucci book.

"The last thing I remember is drinking with Kenny at the Corner."

"You need to slow down," Danny said.

"You may be right, Danny. I don't remember any of that. I left someone's car on I-696 and had Michelle pick me up. I told her it broke down. Don't remember any of that, either."

"Dumbfuck," Danny said. "How'd your visit with your dad go?"

"Fine, nothing new. Tommy H is on his way here. He says he's got to come by," Dominic reported.

Within the hour, Tommy arrived at the bakery and was let in the back office. "Hey, Tommy, what's up?" Angelo asked at the door.

Tommy walked right past him and stood in front of Dominic, sitting at the table. "My fucking brother just called me. You took his wife's car last night?"

Danny and Angelo couldn't help but burst out laughing. "That's whose car it was?" Dominic asked, not laughing.

Tommy looked at Danny and Angelo in confusion; he didn't know what was so funny. He turned back to Dominic. "What do you mean 'that's whose car it was'? You don't remember?"

The laughter grew, and Dominic replied simply, "No, I really don't."

"What the fuck's wrong with you?" Tommy asked, growing impatient.

Danny and Angelo almost lost it, and so did Tommy. "What the fuck is so funny?" he snapped.

Danny grabbed his chest and was about to double over in laughter. "Stop, stop, I'm going to have a heart attack." He was wiping tears from his eyes.

"Tommy, I swear I don't remember taking Billy's wife's car. I drank way too much," Dominic tried to explain.

"Well, get the car back."

"I don't know where it is."

"This is so much better than cable," Danny chirped in.

Tommy put his hand in the air. "This is so fucked up here with you guys today. Let's take care of business, then you can go bring the car back, Dominic. Or buy her a new one, I don't give a fuck. And the next time you tie one on, stay the fuck on your side of town and leave my family alone."

Danny and Dominic grabbed their jackets and Danny inquired further into Dominic's night. "Where did he get her car from?" he asked Tommy.

"My brother's restaurant. For some fucking reason, he showed up there about two thirty in the morning. Alone, no car, and totally wasted."

"I'm right here," Dominic called from behind as they walked to a point Danny felt comfortable to talk.

Neither responded. "He told Claudia he'd have it back in the morning, that he had a driver outside and wasn't driving," Tommy told Danny.

"The kid's got problems," Danny said.

"That's for sure," Tommy answered. Dominic could only sigh in exasperation.

Finally, Danny stopped and turned to Tommy. "Okay, what's going on?"

Tommy nodded to Dominic. "His buddy, that Fabian, he's the one that got Yamamoto in Vegas involved with the Lissonis."

Dominic thought his knees might buckle and stood in silence, trying the grasp the depth of Tommy's revelation.

"That's right. He conspired to have you killed. It wasn't just some betting scam, he's been fucking with you for years," Tommy said.

Danny put his hand on Dominic's back. "We better hurry up and whack this prick, eh?"

Tommy disagreed, "It doesn't really change a thing. We still need the same information we needed before. We whack him now, we'll be whacking guys for years trying to weed out the bad ones. He shouldn't think anything's changed. Stevie in Vegas says Yamamoto is very much on our side now and will try to set John Lissoni up for us. That includes not tipping off Fabian."

Dominic regained his composure. "The plan stays the same, for now. I'll go with my stepmom to see my father on Saturday and give him the new information. But, like you said, Tommy, he shouldn't think anything's changed. What about that Yamamoto though? We're not still going to let him run the casino, are we?"

"I don't see why not, as long as he helps us get Lissoni. He won't be a majority owner anymore. Stevie already has found someone else he wants to bring in, some Hollywood producer who wants to get into the casino business," Tommy answered.

"You can't ever trust this asshole," Danny said.

"It's not about trust. Right now Yamamoto's scared for his life, he'll help us get Lissoni. He also thinks he'll keep a piece of his casino, which, in my opinion, he will, if he helps us. But if we take his casino and let him live, I think it's a no-brainer that he'll run to the feds."

"It's a dead matter anyway right now," Dominic said. "We need him to help set up John Lissoni and keep his mouth shut that we know about Fabian. John's obviously the threat right now and needs to be dealt with first."

"Fabian might not stay in the shadows too much longer, you know," Danny added.

"That's why we've got to find this Lissoni fuck," Tommy said. "Keeping Fabian alive seems to have some value."

"How so?" Danny asked.

"When was the All-Star game? August? That's five months ago, and look how much you've learned about your family. What was a ploy at grabbing some quick cash before being demoted from a captain to conspiring with Jerry Lissoni and Lenny Silesi to take over your family. And kill me, my brother, and Stevie Turner, if I might add." Tommy's voice has starting to rise. "There's probably still more people in your family he corrupted, and I don't need them chasing me in my car, shooting at me or shooting at my brother and his fucking wife again."

"Okay, Tommy, calm down. We'll get this fucker," Danny said, knowing what was coming next.

"Calm down? If I got to put my life on the line, and lives of my friends and family, then I want to be involved in how this is being run. This is fucking bullshit. What a fucking mess you let happen, Dom."

Danny just dropped his head as Dominic responded, "All my fucking troubles started when one of your guys botched the Vic Mattea hit. That's what started turning people against me. And I'm getting real sick of you talking to me with such fucking disrespect."

"Botched the hit? Your guy's dead and mine's doing life, sounds like it went pretty fucking well for you. And your people turned against you because you ordered the hit, not because the shooter got caught. Your whole fucking family is plotting behind your back and you're going to take a tough-guy stance with me?"

Danny felt this might actually come to blows and that would cause a real problem. "Enough! We're on the same fucking side. You guys just want to throw down right here, right now? How many more problems will that fucking cause? It is what it is, let's stop throwing blame around and get this shit fixed."

As much contempt as Tommy had for Dominic, was matched in his respect for Danny Serafini. Before Tommy was forced to deal with the Club, he only knew them through Doug Sullivan's tales. Doug always spoke with the greatest respect for Dominic's father, Nick, and Nick's top two guys, Danny Serafini and Denny Greco. Tommy had met Dominic a few times on the, when Dominic would drive over to meet Doug and he'd stay for a few drinks. Tommy never considered Dominic to be very sharp, just a fun guy who liked to hang out. He was considered more of a messenger and gopher for his father to them. Doug complained several times that Dominic had trouble keeping up with everything they had going. Doug even had to save his life when he saw an unconscious Dominic being placed in his own trunk.

"Okay, fine, the past is the past. But I must insist on one thing," Tommy said.

"What?" Danny asked him.

Tommy turned back to Dominic. "You cannot be running around like a drunk. For one, it doesn't instill much faith in your men. And two, you've infringed on my family now. You can't be taking my family's cars and showing up somewhere at two in the morning."

"You're right, I'm sorry for that. I'll get the car back, as soon as we're done here. That wasn't right of me," Dominic said.

Tommy stuck out his hand. "Thank you. I apologize for how I spoke to you, that wasn't right of me. Danny's right, we are on the same side."

"Good, now let's go have a drink," Danny said.

"I got to get going," Tommy said.

"Let's go get a drink," Danny repeated himself.

Tommy gave up. "Okay, twist my arm."

"I'm going to sit this one out. Booze doesn't sound too good to me right now. Besides, I've got to get the car back," Dominic said.

"If he gets to leave, then I . . ." Tommy said, cut off by Danny.

"Let's go, Tommy, Dominic's off the hook."

Dominic left and called Michelle, who explained where on I-696 the car was parked. He left with Jimmy to retrieve the car but found out it would not start. Dominic called the mechanic his family had used for years and had it towed to his shop and offered a nice tip if he could have it done ASAP.

To Dominic's surprise, he got a call at four in the afternoon by the mechanic, telling him to come to the shop. He finished his workout at Bally's with Fat Kenny and went to see the mechanic. "What's the problem?" Dominic asked, once finally arriving.

"Whose car did you say this was?" the mechanic asked him.

"My friend's wife's. Why?"

"The battery died. It's a new car and car batteries recharge themselves while they're driving. It's a rarity for a car battery to die while driving."

"But yet, it happens. What's the fucking point?" Dominic asked, not wanting a lecture on car batteries.

"The battery was being drained by an FBI bug and the feds came and took it back when it was stranded on the freeway so that you wouldn't find it. There's a rattle in the dashboard that I'll bet wasn't there before."

Dominic pulled out a wad of cash from his pocket and peeled off ten one hundred-dollar bills. "Here's a grand. Get it fixed and back to the address on the registration. And leave this between us."

Dominic used a pay phone to call Doug's satellite phone and reach him in Paris. He explained what the mechanic had told him to Doug. "Why would the feds be recording Billy Herrick's wife?" Dominic asked him.

"Maybe Billy uses the car, I don't know."

"I would think it would be Tommy they'd be after," Dominic said.

"It could be any stupid theory, who the fuck knows? But you have to tell Tommy, right away."

"This reminds me of my wife," Dominic said.

"I'm not going there with you, Dom."

"Maybe she wasn't having an affair . . ."

"You're on an overseas fucking line, you dumb dick. Don't bother Tommy, I'll call him," barked Doug and hung up.

Later that night, Tommy went to his brother's house and asked him to take a walk. All bundled up and walking down the sidewalk, Tommy started explaining why he had come. "You know if something happens to Doug or me, you're in charge, right?"

"Yeah, I know, Tommy," Billy answered.

"Then, there're some things you should know. You're aware that Dominic's wife was murdered, right?"

"Yeah, victim of a mugging gone wrong. Even you told me that."

"Right. But before that happened, there were issues with her," Tommy said.

"What kind of issues? You telling me Dominic whacked his wife?"

"I'm not telling you that. What I am telling you is that she was fucking an agent."

"So Dominic whacked her," Billy said.

"I'm not talking about her fucking death. I'm talking about the feds."

"How does anyone know she wasn't a rat?" Billy asked.

"It was definitely an affair. At first she was tailed to a hotel where she met a man. The tail followed the man and turned in his information. A background check revealed who he was, and we put a tail on him as well."

"Who's we? You and Doug?"

"Don't worry about that either."

Billy was becoming impatient. "You just fucking said there's things I need to know, but you keep telling me telling me not to worry about it."

"I'm telling you what you need to know. Just fucking listen for a minute, okay? Besides the hotel, there was a photograph taken of Dominic's wife and the FBI agent at a shopping mall, holding hands. The agent was married too and had a daughter. And Dominic swore up and down there was nothing she could even rat about, so it had to be an affair. Time went on, and she had the unfortunate incident with the mugging, and it pretty much went by the wayside."

"I don't know why you're telling me this?"

"It was never thought of that the feds would ever target our wives or families, but something happened that kind of changes that. A bigger problem is that maybe they've been using our wives to get to us for years, ever since Dominic's wife."

"What happened?" Billy asked.

"Claudia."

"My wife? What the fuck are you talking about, Tommy?"

"Billy, her car stalled out on the freeway when Dominic borrowed it last night. He had it towed to his family's mechanic. The battery was drained, most likely by a listening device that was removed when the car was left."

"My wife's car was bugged?"

"Seems to be the case."

"And you think she's having an affair and that's how they get access to place their bugs, don't you?"

"It's crossed my mind. Look, Billy, I'd like to put a tail on her, just to be sure. Plus, we can see if the feds are following her."

"It makes no fucking sense to me that the FBI would waste their time with our wives. Claudia don't know nothing to tell. Put the tail on her, I'd like to clear her name."

"Okay, Billy."

"Whatever happened to the agent fucking Dom's wife?" Billy asked.

"He died, car accident."

"And the feds never came asking about it?"

"That's why I'm pretty sure she wasn't a rat. I don't think the FBI knew he was doinking her, and he didn't work organized crime. There was nothing to link him to Dominic's wife."

"You saying you guys whacked an agent and made it look like a car accident?"

"I said he died in a car accident, and I explained why I believe the feds didn't blame Dominic. That's it, Billy."

"If Claudia's not having an affair, and I'm saying she's not, then why bug her? I don't think I've ever even driven the car," Billy said.

"I don't know why either. I don't get why they want to fuck with our wives, it makes it real personal. And I know Doug firmly believes that if anyone fucks with our families, we're fucking with theirs, tenfold."

"There's a lot going on—John Lissoni, that Fabian guy, and now this."

"Business as usual, Billy," Tommy said.

CHAPTER XIII

Watch Your Back

DOUG SULLIVAN BOLTED upright from his sleep. He had been having a nightmare, and the cell phone on the dresser, that started ringing, brought him out of it. Doug tried to gather his thoughts. He looked to see if he woke his wife, but she wasn't there. It's the hotel suite, he was still in Paris, he remembered. He answered his phone to a French-speaking man, "God dammit, I don't speak French. I don't want to tell you again. Have the English-speaking guy call me."

Doug climbed out of bed and threw some water on his face. He picked up his satellite phone and called Tommy Herrick. "Tommy, wake up."

"It's four in the morning here, Doug. What's the emergency?"

"What if it wasn't the feds that bugged Claudia's car? I mean come on, it drained the fucking battery. The feds ain't better than that?"

Tommy was instantly awake and climbed out of bed to speak privately. "Lissoni?"

"My gut tells me it's something bigger. Someone else is controlling John Lissoni and Fabian and whatever the fuck else is going on."

"Who?" Tommy asked.

"Tommy, honestly, I don't have a fucking inkling. But Billy's wife's car was abandoned on 696, and it's everyone's belief that the feds came and took their bug back, right?" Doug theorized with Tommy.

"Yeah, but Lissoni's crew would have to have been tailing her too. His crew ain't big enough to pull shit like that," Tommy said.

"That's my point, exactly. If it's not the feds, it couldn't be Lissoni."

"Doug, it's got to be the feds," Tommy argued.

"That doesn't sit well with me though. Something's telling me it is much fucking bigger. It looks to me like someone's tailing Billy's family's routines. Could be more than just her, too, have you checked all your cars?"

"Yeah, turned up nothing," Tommy answered.

"Something's just not right. Maybe it doesn't even involve the Club at all, and it's something from our hometowns."

"I don't know, Doug. I'll keep an open mind, but I still got to say it's the feds."

"Just don't let your guard down. Watch your back there and watch every fucking angle, Tommy. That's all I'm saying, don't be blindsided. Anything happens to you and I'm buying a fucking a nuke. Don't let that happen."

"When do you come home?" Tommy asked him.

"I'll be in Sicily in a couple of weeks and in Baghdad after that. I'm planning first week of March to come back."

"Doug Sullivan, gangster and spy for the CIA. Who would've ever thought?"

"Yeah, it's some fucking life. I got to meet the Sicilian Mafia in Sicily and recruit men to send home to the Mafia in Michigan. Then I got to meet with these fucking dirty terrorists in a hundred-degree heat and offer to sell weapons to kill Americans. In the meantime, I figured I'd work on a cocaine pipeline here in Europe and start planning for a Mafia war that we're obviously going to have to fight.

What the fuck ever happened to getting high and playing Madden on the play station?"

"Didn't pay the bills. Don't forget living paycheck to paycheck, shutoff notice to shutoff notice," Tommy reminded Doug.

"Just watch yours and everyone else's fucking backs."

Fabian Bosca pulled into the hotel parking lot and waited for his backup to arrive. Fabian had been driving aimlessly waiting for Dominic's call to tell him where they were meeting. Finally, he had the location: a hotel room in the small city of Saline. Fabian was no dummy and smelled a rat; he called Gary Pizza to bring some guys and wait in the parking lot. They had been driving around close to Fabian while he waited for a destination.

Once he got the text from Gary telling him they were close, Fabian left his car. He had parked in the back row of the parking lot and surveyed the area. Jimmy Amicucci was standing near Dominic's truck; he must have pissed Dominic off again. "Hey, Jimmy," Fabian called out when he was close. "What'd you do wrong to be stuck standing outside in this fucking cold?"

"He can't take a joke, that's all. Go on up, they're all waiting for you," Jimmy told him.

Fabian felt a little better knowing Jimmy wasn't in the room. Fabian had expected that Jimmy would be present when they tried to kill him. Jimmy would have to 'make his bones' soon to be a made man. The good feeling was lost when Fabian entered the hotel lobby and found Scary Scarelli waiting for him. It was Scary that beat Fabian to a pulp in the Bally's parking lot. Fabian nodded and greeted Scary by his real name "Eugene."

"Follow me," was Scary's response. He led Fabian to an elevator and took him to the third floor. From there, he led Fabian down a hallway until they came to the room. Scary opened the door, and Fabian followed him in.

Fabian thought his heart was going to come out of his chest as he tried to peer past Scary Scarelli's huge frame. He was ready for anything. Fabian did follow mob protocol and didn't bring a gun to a sit-down, but he felt he was better than any of Dominic's guys. Even with a bad knee, he was able to throw around Gary Nussman in the bathroom of the bakery. Even Scary, Fabian felt was no match for himself. If Scary hadn't blindsided him in the Bally's parking lot, that fight might've had another outcome.

Scary stopped and turned around. Fabian tightened his muscles, ready to grab the hand that had the gun and point it up, in case he fired. "In there," Scary said, motioning to the bathroom door.

Fabian finally heard another voice; it was Dominic's. Okay, it's starting to seem like a meeting. He understood Scary was taking him into the bathroom to search him for a wire. He braced himself for another challenge in the bathroom, but what Fabian could not let happen was to turn his back on Scary. "Eugene, any chance of you walking in first?"

Scary looked at Fabian with contempt and opened the door. "Please, keep me in your sights at all times." He gestured Fabian to the lighted, and unoccupied, bathroom. Once Scary's huge frame stopped blocking the narrow hallway, Fabian could see into the room. Dominic was with Danny Serafini, and Vinny Jagge was there with his son, Frankie. The world finally came off Fabian's back; it was a real meeting. The odd part, he thought was, that Angelo Rea and Fat Kenny Infelice were there. They had no part in this, and both were already made men, having already done their hits to be initiated.

In the bathroom, Fabian had to remove his clothes before Scary could let him in the room. He also had to leave his cell phone in the bathroom. Once out, he took his seat that was left open for him. "Do you have a number for Vinny for damages on Mexico?" Danny asked him.

What a relief, Fabian thought to himself. "Well, I made fifty million dollars. Twenty percent would be ten million. Do you really expect me to give you ten million dollars?" Fabian asked Vinny Jagge.

"*I'm* talking to you," Danny said.

Vinny held up his hand to Danny, never taking his eyes off Fabian. "Danny, I was addressed and I'd like to answer."

"Go ahead," Danny conceded.

"First off, I will not be spoken to like that from you. And what was that twenty percent bullshit? I expect the usual twenty-five. That's twelve and a half million and I expect interest. Let's just call the interest five million. What I expect is seventeen and a half million dollars."

"You're out of your mind," Angelo told Vinny.

Fabian sat stunned and just stared at Angelo. Vinny also took a moment to digest the interruption. "How the fuck am I out of my mind? And why the fuck do you want to play captain now?"

"Am I not here because I'm Fabian's captain?" Angelo asked Danny.

Danny also looked surprised at Angelo. "Yes. And you're right. Let's come with a real number."

"How is my number not real?" Vinny asked.

"He didn't try to fuck you, Vinny. He didn't know he had to pay for Mexico, just a misunderstanding," Angelo argued.

Dominic finally got his say in. "Vinny, you wanted five million in interest, that'll be your payment."

"Five million?" Angelo protested.

"It's settled. Fabian, you got to pay Vinny five million dollars in an offshore account," Dominic ordered.

Fabian nodded. "Done. I'll have it wired today."

"Once that money is paid and Vinny has control of it, your name in this family is clear. The debts you owed have been paid and your bullshit with the under betting is forgiven. These are the words of my father. Your limitations of not leaving the state are lifted and you are in control of the Mexican rackets again. You are released from Angelo and you are now under Vinny, owing any percentage your new captainso orders. If no one else has any other business, this meeting is over," Dominic announced.

After a few minutes of everyone saying their good-byes, Danny, Dominic, and Angelo had the room to themselves.

"Wow, Ange, I didn't know you had it in you," Dominic told his cousin.

"Think he bought it?" Angelo asked.

"Angelo, he's always looked at you like a little brother. He went way of out his way to send you twenty-five grand for your wedding. He even put his top man in jeopardy to do so. I have no doubt you'll be the one he contacts when he needs some inside information on us," Danny told Angelo.

On his way from the meeting, Fabian called his top man, Gary Piazza. "You should have heard this line of bullshit they fed me. Little Angelo standing up for me, it was a riot. They really think I don't know they're trying to lull me into a false sense of security? It's fucking insulting. Is John ready to go in California?"

"No, Lissoni says he's taking care of Vegas first. He's going to make a move," Gary Pizza told his real boss. Officially, Gary reported to Vinny Jagge's son, Frankie, but he never lost his allegiance to Fabian.

"He can't make a move yet. There's more to do. This'll force their hand in Michigan, and they'll have to come after us. Tell him he's a fucking moron, he's going to ruin everything," Fabian explained.

"He should hear it from you," Gary told him.

"Just take care of it. I'll be in Mexico by the morning, watch your back."

Danny and Dominic went to Nick's restaurant, Cooch's Cucina, for dinner. They never sat at the same table twice in a row, as that way the feds would have to record all the tables. Over pasta, Danny asked Dominic, "When did Fabian find out?"

Dominic looked at Danny with a blank stare. "What are you talking about?"

"About Larry," Danny said.

"Are you talking about Fabian's dad, Larry?"

"Yeah, when did Fabian learn the truth?"

"Danny, I have no idea what you're talking about. What truth?"

Danny wasn't sure if Dominic was pulling his leg. "Who do you think whacked Fabian's father?"

"Moshe Levin. That's what we've always thought." Fabian had always swore up and down that he would avenge Larry Bosca's death, that someday he would kill Moshe Levin. Moshe was a legendary hitman for the mob but in his later years settled into the role of a lieutenant for Benny Mancini.

"I can't believe you don't know. Your father made his bones on that hit. I just assumed you knew and Fabian had finally learned of it."

Dominic was crushed. He knew how much damage his father's death had caused Fabian; they were the closest of friends in their early years. "How the fuck could my father not let me know? How could he keep Fabian around us, planning his attack all his fucking life?"

"It was a secret, Dominic. There was no memo. He probably thought you knew or he never intended for you to know. Maybe as long as you didn't know, Fabian didn't know. Your father really liked Larry Bosca. He really wanted to take care of his family. He had no bad intentions, so don't start with the 'he hates you' bullshit."

"I don't know what to say, Danny. I'm devastated here," Dominic said.

"I don't see the big deal," Danny told him.

"You don't see the big deal? We could pay for this with our lives, Danny. That's the big fucking deal."

Danny's voice raised above the crowd, and everyone stopped to gawk. "That's enough, this discussion's over."

Dominic leaned in over the table. "I say when it's over, I'm still the fucking boss."

Danny leaned in and growled back, "If you're going to pull the fucking boss title on me, you better be prepared to wear it every fucking minute of every fucking day, like your father did." Danny stood up and dropped a hundred-dollar bill on the table. "Here, I got this, boss." He turned and left to a watching audience.

"I hate this fucking shit," Dominic said to himself as he waved to the waitress. "Bring me a drink, will you?"

"Jack and Coke?" she asked, ensuring he wanted his usual.

"Minus the Coke, hon. And bring a couple of them."

Grace Sullivan awoke to a pounding on her front door. Why would the police raid the house while her husband was away in Europe? She thought to herself as she put on her robe. The pounding stopped when her father, who lived on the first floor with her mother, answered the door. Grace looked out the window before going to gather her two boys, who she was sure were also awakened. Instead of police cars, she saw a truck driven right onto her lawn. Her heart stopped. Would one of her husband's enemies try to do him harm here, at their home?

Grace flew open the bedroom door and saw her six-year-old son at the top of the stairs, getting ready to go down. "Graham!" she screamed and whisked up her boy and ran to her one-and-a-half-year-old son's room, slamming the door behind her.

"Mom, what? It's Uncle Dom," Graham told his mother, who was squeezing the air out of him.

"What?"

"It's Uncle Dom. He's at the front door."

This wouldn't be the first time someone had come to Grace's home in the dead of night for an emergency. Now her thoughts were that something had happened to her husband. Again, she flew open the door and ran the down the stairs.

Her father cut her off before she got the door. "He's drunk, Gracie. Stone cold plastered. He thinks Doug is here."

"Well, you can't leave him on the porch," said Grace and walked past her father to the front door and let Dominic in.

"Dominic, what's happened?" she asked him.

"I need to talk to Doug," Dominic slurred.

"Dominic, he's in Paris. Is Doug in danger?"

"We're all in danger," Dominic slurred.

Grace ran into the kitchen and picked up the home phone to call Tommy Herrick.

Tommy groggily looked at the caller ID and saw it was Doug's house calling. Without thinking, he just assumed it was Doug. "You really got to get this fucking time difference down, Doug."

"Tommy, it's Grace. You have to get here right away."

Tommy was now awake. "Grace, what happened?"

"It's Dominic, he's here's and he's wasted. He says we're all in danger," Grace told him.

"Okay, keep him there. I'm on the way."

"What happened with Grace," Tommy's wife asked, also now awake.

"Nothing with Grace, everything's fine. Go back to bed," Tommy said, throwing some clothes on.

"Then why do you have to leave?"

"Because if it ain't one Sullivan, it's the fucking other one. I got to go, bye."

Tommy saw Dominic's truck on the lawn, and his temper was about to burst. Grace had the door open before he even got to the porch. "Tommy, I don't like this. My whole house is in an uproar. I didn't call Doug. I didn't want him to kill him," she whispered to Tommy as he entered the house.

"I'm not so sure you should've called me then. Where is he?" Tommy asked, trying to hold back the rage.

"He's in the kitchen with my parents. He's a lot more subdued than he was when he got here."

Dominic tried getting up when he saw Tommy, but he almost fell doing so; he ended up right back in his chair. "Tommy fucking

Herrick, finally, someone I can talk to. No offense," Dominic said to Grace's parents. His speech was slow and slurred.

"Dominic, let's go outside and leave these nice people alone, okay? They don't need to hear your problems," Tommy said in the calmest voice he could muster. He did not want to have an altercation with the boss of a crime family, even if it was this drunk guy in front of him.

"That's where you're wrong. It is everyone's problem. So tell me, whose side will you be on, mine or Danny's?" Dominic asked Tommy.

Tommy gave Grace an apologetic look. Grace had become friends with Danny's wife, Bianca. And before her death, Grace was friends with Dominic's wife, Angela, as well. Tommy looked back to Dominic. "Shut up, Dominic."

Dominic's voice become a holler. "You shut the fuck up! You work for me, everyone fucking works for me."

Tommy looked again to Grace, who was one step ahead of him and taking her parents out the kitchen, fully aware of what was probably next.

Dominic eyed Tommy the whole time it took for the others to leave the room. Even in his drunken state, he knew what Tommy Herrick was capable of. Once clear, Tommy lunged at him. Dominic meant to sidestep him and counter with a right hand, but his legs didn't do as they were told and buckled instead.

Tommy had aimed at Dominic's midsection; he just wanted to take him down and subdue him without it getting out of hand. Despite the anger flowing, Tommy still knew he couldn't really hurt Dominic. It could put their whole livelihoods in jeopardy, not to mention their lives. But Dominic's knee buckled, and he was already falling when Tommy reached him. Tommy's shoulder collided with Dominic's jaw, knocking three teeth across the room.

Tommy rolled into the stove with a thud, causing a big dent. Despite being hazy from the booze and the shot to his mouth, Dominic was able to grab Tommy's leg, as Tommy got back to his feet, and pull him back down to the tiled kitchen floor. Dominic tried to climb on top of Tommy, but Tommy easily threw Dominic to the side and regained his feet. Dominic tried to get up again, but he got the wind knocked out of him with a kick to his chest.

Tommy pulled Dominic up by his shirt and pulled his face inches from his own. Tommy stared into his bloodshot eyes; he looked at the blood flowing from Dominic's mouth and growled, "Understand this, Dominic, I work for Doug. That's it, nobody else. If you weren't you, I hope you understand, you wouldn't be walking out of here. So when you go back and tell everyone how I disrespected you, remember the respect I did give you. I gave you your fucking life, you piece of shit." Tommy let go of Dominic's shirt, and he collapsed to the floor.

Tommy went to check on Doug's wife and his in-laws. "Everyone okay?" Tommy asked them as they were seated in the living room.

"Tommy, you've got blood on your shirt," Grace said.

"Don't worry, it's not mine."

"I didn't think it was. Is Dominic okay?" she asked him. Grace was fully aware of what her husband and his best friend, Tommy, were capable of. Grace had known Tommy longer than Doug. Tommy was dating her best friend, Valerie, when Grace met Doug through them.

The first night Doug and Grace went out alone, they went to a bar and had some drinks. The date ended with Grace taking Doug to the hospital for stitches after he fought four guys who had insulted her. Many times, Grace and Val had to take Doug and Tommy away from somewhere because they never hesitated to fight. She knew the moment Dominic yelled at Tommy, in the manner he did, what was going to happen. And she knew if it was ever Doug or Tommy fighting someone one on one, it was Doug or Tommy that was going to win. Not that they were the biggest or the baddest, it was just that it wasn't in either of them to lose.

"Yeah, just a little accident. He's got a bloody lip, he'll be fine," Tommy said.

Grace also grew to be good friends with the Amicuccis and knew Dominic had become the boss after his father went to jail. She knew

Dominic had a whole crime family at his disposal and knew Tommy striking Dominic could cause some serious problems. "You know, Tommy, I haven't talked to Doug yet. I'll bet if you just drove his truck home, he wouldn't even remember he was here. I'd hate to see you get in trouble for this."

Tommy smiled his appreciation. "Thanks, but I can't do that. Please tell Doug when you talk to him what happened here. You can talk it down if you want, but I've got to get this problem fixed."

Grace knew he wouldn't do it; she was hoping in her heart that Dominic wasn't about to "disappear." "Be careful, Tommy."

Tommy gave a last smile and returned to the kitchen where he found Dominic washing the blood out of his mouth in the sink. "Dominic, I'm going to approach you. No more trouble between us, okay? I didn't mean to hit you in the mouth, you fell into my shoulder."

Dominic turned the faucet off and turned to Tommy. "You knocked my fucking teeth out."

"You knocked your own teeth out. We have to take this out of here. There are kids trying to sleep upstairs."

"What about my fucking teeth, Tommy?" Dominic asked.

Tommy stopped his movements and raised his hands, as if to be searched. "I don't want no trouble with you, Dominic. But you're way out of line here. This is a man's house. You've disrupted this whole family, just because you can't handle your liquor."

"This is my fucking house, Tommy," Dominic said with his voice rising again.

"This is Doug's house, you drunk motherfucker. I'm not going to tell you again, lower your fucking voice and let's get the hell out of here."

"Fuck you, I'm going to Doug's," Dominic said, walking to door.

Tommy went to follow him, at least he was leaving the house, Tommy figured. But Dominic stopped in front of the stove. "Why are you stopping?" Tommy asked him. It was too late to react once

Tommy realized it was a frying pan that Dominic had spun around and swung at him.

Tommy could feel the blood oozing through his fingers as his hands covered the gash the frying pan made in the right side of his forehead. He fell to the floor and tried crawling on his elbows, away from the danger he could no longer protect himself from, but his legs wouldn't work.

Dominic whizzed the frying pan across the room and into the wall, breaking though the drywall. "Hah, look at you now!" Dominic yelled, towering over Tommy, defenseless on the floor.

Tommy could feel himself losing consciousness, but he had to stay awake his brain kept telling his body. How the fuck did Dominic manage such an agile swing in his drunken condition? Tommy thought. Keep thinking, keep thinking. Tommy cursed himself for underestimating Dominic. He curled into the fetal position as a last hope to protect himself.

His body was lifted from the ground, and he was face-to-face with Dominic. Tommy begged his legs to work, but he still couldn't get on steady ground. He could smell the whiskey on Dominic's breath, but he couldn't open his eyes. It was all black for Tommy as he awaited whatever fate his opponent had chosen for him. His arms! Tommy could move his arms. *Good enough*, he hoped.

He could hear Dominic saying something, but he couldn't make out the words. Tommy reached his right arm back, and with as much strength as he could muster, he swung it at where he heard the voice coming from. His hand collided with what he believed was right above Dominic's eye; at least that was what it felt like to the right handTommy just broke on pure bone. His body fell back to the ground, and he heard the thud of Dominic.

Grace heard the smash from the kitchen; something had just been thrown at the wall. She heard Dominic taunting Tommy. Something had gone wrong, and Tommy was down. The two men Grace always called in an emergency were her husband and his best friend. One was in Paris and the other was in need of help, Grace believed. They didn't call the police—they just didn't believe in it. There was one person Grace had left to count on, and it was herself.

She told her parents to stay put, and that she was calling the police, but that was just to keep them still. Grace ran upstairs and was relieved not to see her son in the hallway. She ran to her room and got the registered firearm her husband kept locked in the nightstand by the bed. She checked the safety and ensured it was loaded, just as Doug had taught her to do.

Grace ran down the stairs and past her parents with the gun in her hand. Her father got up and followed his daughter into the kitchen. He pulled his own gun out of his waistband that he had retrieved when she ran up the stairs. "Finally," he said. Doug had taught them both how shoot and handle a weapon.

When Grace arrived in the kitchen, she saw Tommy on the floor and Dominic was staggering to his feet. With both hands on the gun and shoulders and elbows poised perfectly, Grace aimed the weapon at Dominic. "Get out of my house and get your truck off my lawn." Her father also had his gun targeted at Dominic from across the room. She could see Tommy moving and starting to get to his feet. Tommy had a huge cut on his head and Dominic's mouth was bloody and swollen, and there was cut above his eye. ***These two have been in a huge battle,*** she thought.

"You guys want to play with guns, do you? I'll have a hundred armed men down here with a phone call," Dominic threatened.

"You'll never get to make that phone call," Grace answered. "Don't think for a second that Doug didn't teach me how to use this thing."

Tommy was on his feet now, using the kitchen table to stay up. His vision had returned, and he was trying to make sense of the situation. Tommy's first thought was that he was dreaming. It looked like a movie to him. Was that Doug's wife and her father pointing guns at Dominic, the Mafia boss? ***Can't be real,*** he kept telling himself. How and what would cause a situation like this? ***Doug's going to kill me,*** he thought. He noticed a tooth on the floor under him, and it all came back to him. He now understood: Grace had come to his rescue.

"Put the guns down," Tommy ordered, still holding onto the table for dear life.

"Are you okay?" Grace asked, never taking her eye or her weapon off Dominic.

"I'm fine, put the guns down. I mean it," Tommy snapped. Both put their guns down, and Grace wanted to look at Tommy's head. "Stay there," Tommy told her. Tommy turned to Dominic. "I'm going to give you two fucking options. One, you and me go out back and take care of this like men, just you and me, no fucking weapons. Or, we settle this by going to Danny."

"Danny? I knew it, you're on his fucking side," Dominic said.

With his left hand, Tommy pushed off the table and hit Dominic in his mouth with his right hand. Dominic fell into stove and onto ground, his mouth a bloody mess. Tommy screamed in pain from using his broken hand and still on wobbly legs, hit the ground hard.

Tommy got up first and grabbed Dominic's shirt and dragged him to the kitchen door. Tommy opened the door with one hand and kept hold of Dominic with the other. He threw Dominic out the door and onto the ground outside and followed him out.

CHAPTER XIV

Cracking Up

TOMMY LET DOMINIC get to his feet before he threw another punch at him. Conscious of his broken right hand, Tommy threw a left jab. Although still intoxicated, Dominic blocked it easily. "You ain't so bad, Tommy," Dominic taunted.

"What'd you say? I can't understand what you say, sounds like you're missing some teeth," Tommy answered him. Both men just circled each other with their dukes in the air, waiting for an opening to strike.

Dominic was also aware of Tommy's broken right hand, so Dominic threw his left, knowing if Tommy was going to block it, he'd have to use that broken right hand. He threw his left, and Tommy blocked it with his right, yelling out in agonizing pain. Dominic used the opportunity to land a hard right cross to Tommy's jaw.

Tommy knew his legs wouldn't hold if he stood there going blow for blow with Dominic, so he knew he could no longer protect his hand. Tommy brushed off the shot to the jaw and came back with a serious uppercut with his right hand. Dominic stumbled backward, more blood flowing from his damaged mouth. Tommy could feel the pain shooting through his hand, but he had to end this. He wound his right hand back and was prepared to land it, with everything he had, right into Dominic's nose.

Dominic saw Tommy's hand wind back to hit him. He was stumbling back from the uppercut, so he continued to stumble in order to distance himself from Tommy's punch. It worked, and Tommy almost swung himself to the ground with the miss. Dominic seized the opportunity. Despite his intoxication, although not perfect, his instincts were carrying him in the fight. He landed a right, left, right combination to Tommy's eyes.

Tommy's reaction was to grab onto Dominic, no longer confident he could outbox the drunk. *How is this happening?* Tommy thought to himself. He considered Dominic a pussy when he was sober. Totally wasted; this should've been a breeze. *Way underestimated him,* Tommy kept thinking to himself. He tried to get Dominic in a headlock, but he kept not letting Tommy get his arm around his neck. Even with his own wobbly legs, Tommy could feel Dominic was just as wobbly. No longer fighting from a distance, Tommy found his advantage. He just had to keep hanging onto Dominic and deny him his reach.

With his right hand hanging onto Dominic's shoulder, Tommy started uppercutting with his left. He was behind Dominic and at his waist, but he just kept punching until he saw blood flowing from Dominic's face like a faucet. Tommy stopped punching and pushed Dominic with his other hand. Dominic crumpled to the ground like a sack of potatoes. Tommy stood and waited for Dominic to get up. After about twenty seconds, Tommy collapsed to his knees in pain and exhaustion.

Grace had watched the whole thing from the back porch; she learned long ago not to get in the way of Doug or Tommy when they were fighting. Once Tommy dropped to his knees, she ran to aid her husband's best friend and her best friend's husband.

"Tommy, Tommy, are you okay?" Grace asked him, putting a cloth over the cut on his forehead.

"My god, he is one tough son of a bitch, I had no idea," Tommy said, staring at Dominic, who was starting to stir.

Tommy crawled over to him and rolled him on his back; he reeled back in horror at the damage he caused to his nose. Fifteen punches to Dominic's nose left it in disarray. It was broke, torn open, and didn't even look like a nose anymore. "Grace, call my brother and tell him to get over here and to call the doctor."

Tommy rolled Dominic back over, so he wouldn't choke on his own blood. He covered Dominic's nose with the cloth Grace had given for his own head. It would be at least a half hour before his brother, Billy, would arrive and take them to a doctor; they paid very well for his home services without reporting it to authorities.

Grace told Tommy to go clean up and that she'd stay with Dominic. Tommy took a few minutes in the bathroom pouring peroxide on his cuts and then decided it was time for his buddy, Doug, to be filled in on the situation. *After all, it is his house,* Tommy reasoned.

Tommy forgot his satellite phone when he hurried out the door, so he called from the home phone. Doug assumed it was his wife calling. "Hey, hon," Doug answered.

"Doug, it's Tommy, there's a problem."

Doug was in a car, being driven to the airport. He was going to Switzerland for a few days to do some business and do some skiing in the Alps. His heart dropped when he heard Tommy's voice on his home phone line. "It's got to be four in the morning there, what's wrong?" Doug asked with a panic in his voice.

"Everyone's fine. It's Dominic, he came here about two hours ago, drunk out of his mind," Tommy told him.

"He came to my house, drunk? For what?"

"Looking for you, that's how drunk he was. It's been a trend lately for him. Grace called me to come get him, and we had a problem," Tommy said.

"A problem? Shit, Tommy, he's fucking Nick Amicucci's kid. What have you done?"

"Hey, brother, this ain't my fault at all. He was very loud in your house, had everyone awake. I told him to quiet it down, and he told me I was taking Danny's side."

"Taking Danny's side in what?" Doug asked him.

"Who the fuck knows with this idiot, but he got louder and louder and was swearing up a storm, so I charged him. I just wanted to get him to the floor and subdue him. He stumbled and my shoulder went into his jaw. It knocked some teeth out."

There was only silence from Doug. "Doug, you there?" Tommy asked him.

"Yeah, I'm here. I was trying to figure out how to tell Nick you fucked up his kid. I know it's not your fault, but we got a real situation here."

"There's more," Tommy told him.

"There's more?"

"He pretended he was leaving, and I followed him out. The fucker sucker punched me with a frying pan," Tommy said.

"He hit you with a frying pan? What the fuck?"

"Yeah, dropped me right to the ground," Tommy answered.

"I would think it would. Wow, Tommy, are you okay?" Doug asked, now concerned.

"I got a huge gash in my head, and my hand is fucked up, that's it. His nose is going to need plastic surgery."

"I'll fucking kill him. Is that it?" Doug asked, anger now seeping into his voice.

"Far from, Doug. Your wife broke it up," Tommy told him hesitantly, knowing Doug would blow up.

"Grace? Grace had to break it up?"

Tommy decided to just spit it out, "Grace and her father burst into the kitchen with guns blazing. It looked like a movie, Doug."

"I'm on my way," Doug growled before he ended his call.

Billy Herrick arrived and went to his brother with the man lying on the ground. Billy stopped mid-step once he recognized who it was. “Tommy, that’s Dominic.”

Tommy looked at Billy. “Yeah, I know. Help me get to him to my car. You called the doctor?”

“Yeah, he’s expecting a gunshot, though. What happened to you two?” Billy asked before he took another step.

“We got into a fight. Come on, Billy, let’s go, grab his other arm,” Tommy said trying to lift Dominic. With the adrenaline gone and with his own injuries, Tommy has having great difficulty.

“You did this? Tommy, we’re all fucking dead,” Billy said.

“There’s no time for this, help me or get the fuck out of here.”

Billy still stood frozen. “He’s fucked up, Tommy.”

“Look at me, I’m fucked up too. Just go, I wasted my fucking time waiting on you,” Tommy said, deciding to drag Dominic by his arm.

Grace had had enough. “Goddammit, Billy, help your brother or I will.”

Billy looked at Grace and then walked forward and whispered in Tommy’s ear, “You’re not going to whack him, are you? I don’t want to be a part of that.”

Tommy dropped Dominic’s arm and faced his brother. “What the fuck’s wrong with you? If I was going to whack him, why would I be taking him to the doctor? Now, help me carry him, will you?”

Billy and Tommy finally carried Dominic to Tommy’s car, and Billy started driving to the doctor’s house. Once they were clear of the house, Tommy called Grace from Billy’s cell phone. “Sorry for that stuff. But I wanted to thank you for stepping up for me, like one of the guys.”

“We’re family, Tommy. You’ve proven what you’d do for me and my family, so there’s no need to say anymore. Do you think Doug needs to know any of this?” Grace said.

“That’s another reason I’m calling. I called him when I was in the bathroom,” Tommy told her.

"Why, Tommy?"

"Because I have to, I'm sorry."

"Was he mad?" she asked, already knowing the answer.

"Oh yeah, he's super pissed. Hung up on me, said he's on the way back," Tommy said.

Grace sighed, "Will you at least meet him at the airport so he doesn't kill someone?"

Tommy agreed and drove in silence to the doctor's house. They stopped once, for Tommy to use a pay phone and call Danny. He gave Danny the doctor's address and told Danny he'd wait for him.

At a quarter to six in the morning, Danny arrived at the doctor's house with Angelo Rea at his side. Tommy met him at the back door and led them to the basement to see Dominic. "You sure took your time coming over," Tommy said, hoping to lighten the tense mood.

Without looking at Tommy, Danny said, "We brought some friends." Right on cue, Fat Kenny Infelice and Scary Scarelli trampled down the stairs. Carlo DeMini, another associate of the Amicucci book, stood guard at the front door.

Tommy looked at his brother and grimaced. Tommy wasn't sure if he was going to get a chance to explain. Tommy commended his brother to himself for bringing the guns when he was called; at least they were armed at the moment.

Danny took one look at Dominic, lying on the bed unconscious, and turned away. He looked at the doctor who just returned Danny's stare. "Well, how the fuck is he? Is he going to make it?" Danny asked impatiently.

"Make it? Oh yeah, he's fine. I mean, he's not fine, but he's not in any life-threatening condition. He's out from the surgery I did on his nose. It was pretty mangled, but I did what I could. I set it the best possible way with what was left. Eight to ten weeks, he should be bandage free. I can recommend a good plastic surgeon who'll keep the same arrangement as me, and he'll be good as new in less than a year. His jaw had multiple fractures, and I set it, but he's going need an oral surgeon, like today. He'll have to unset it and reset it, tremendous pain for the kid. Again, good as new in less than year. And I stitched the cut above his eye, twelve stitches, nice one," the doctor reported.

Danny asked the doctor to leave and turned to Tommy. "When does one say one has crossed the line?"

"Can I explain what happened?" Tommy asked.

"How do you explain that?" Danny asked, pointing at Dominic. "That's the boss' kid."

"So I'm supposed to just let him beat on me?" Tommy asked.

"Yes. Those are the rules," Danny explained.

Tommy scoffed, "Not my rules. No one pricked my finger," Tommy said, holding up his trigger finger, which is the pricked one when a made man is being initiated. "No man beats on me."

The two big men, Kenny and Scary, moved closer and stood on both sides of Tommy. Everyone looked to Danny. "Go ahead, what's your side?" he asked Tommy.

"Danny, I'll be up front with you, Billy and me are armed. I just want you to know," Tommy said.

Danny laughed and nodded to the two big men. "Yeah, so are they. Your side?"

"I plead it's not my fault at all. Remember the other day when he was all hung over and couldn't remember taking my brother's wife's car?"

Danny was getting a feeling Dominic had pulled another stunt and with the wrong guy this time. Nonetheless, he couldn't tolerate someone treating a made man in this manner. "Yeah, I remember."

"Same thing, but worse. He wasn't singing and dancing on a bar this time. This time he was the opposite, angry. He kept asking if I was on your side. Did you guys have a problem?" Tommy asked.

Danny remembered his last conversation with Dominic—at Nick's restaurant, when Danny walked out on him for pulling rank on him. *He must've started drinking right then,* Danny thought. "Doesn't matter, what else?"

"I think it does matter if he wants me to pick a side. He showed up tonight at Doug's, looking for him. Woke up his wife, her parents, the kids, and drove his fucking truck on the lawn."

"Doug's in Paris," Danny told him.

"Yes, I'm aware," Tommy said sarcastically. "But that's why he was there. Grace called me when he said everyone was in danger. He fucking said that to someone's wife. I asked him to come outside and he just got louder and louder, saying I was with you," Tommy explained.

"Who threw the first punch?" Danny asked.

"It wasn't a punch. I went to tackle him, to just subdue him. I wanted him to quiet down and stop scaring Doug's family. He lost his footing because he was so drunk and was falling and my shoulder hit his jaw. I knocked out three teeth," Tommy answered.

"Did he fight back?"

Tommy pointed to his head. "Well, yeah. He hit me with a fucking frying pan. Then all hell broke loose. I did that to his nose because I was losing. He can fight."

Danny nodded. "He was quite the barroom brawler in his youth, drove Nick nuts. I don't know what to say. You had to defend yourself and Doug's family."

"Grace even pulled a gun on him," Tommy said.

"Oh no, does Doug know?"

"Yeah, he's flying back. I am off the hook here, right? Clearly, everyone would have done the same when it comes to our families," Tommy said.

"I know my wife would've shot him," Angelo piped in with.

"My wife would've used the chance to shoot me," Danny said. "All right, I've got to get a message to his father. I'll tell him you did everything you could do to prevent this."

Nick Amicucci ate his breakfast in the library office of the prison. Every morning, Nick, his cellmate and fellow Michigan mafioso, Eddie Turco, and three other veteran gangsters from three different crime families ate in the back office. Their breakfasts were prepared with the guards' food and delivered to the office. This morning, Nick had gotten an urgent message from Danny, and Nick was waiting for a clean phone to speak on from the guard. He ordered everyone out of the office so he could speak alone.

Finally, a guard brought him a phone. Nick stopped eating the bacon and took the phone. "Everything all squared away now?" Nick asked, annoyed at the delay.

"Just a little mishap, won't happen again," the guard answered.

"Mishaps lead to you switching that uniform for my outfit, be smarter," Nick ordered.

"I will, I'm sorry," the guard said, scurrying off.

Nick put the phone down and continued to eat as he waited for Danny's call. Twenty minutes later, after not receiving the call, Nick went looking for the guard. "You sure you gave him the right number?" Nick asked him.

"Who, Danny? You're supposed to call him. He's waiting at a pay phone."

"I don't have the number to no pay phone," Nick said.

The guard pulled a piece of paper from his shirt pocket. "I was supposed to give you this."

Nick took the paper and glared at the guard before walking away. Back in the office, Nick dialed the number and Danny answered. "I didn't think you got the message," Danny told him.

"It's like dealing with my fucking kids with theses assholes, total incompetence. What's so urgent?" Nick asked.

"Speaking of your kids, it's Dominic," Danny said.

"What'd he do now?"

"His drinking has taken to new turn," Danny reported.

"What do you mean? The kid's never been a drunk, he'll snap out of it."

"Too late for that, Nick, he messed with the wrong guy."

"Danny, what's happened to my boy?" Nick asked, now starting to think the worst.

"You knew about the incident with Billy Herrick's wife?"

"Goddammit, Danny, is Dominic okay or not?" Nick asked, the suspense killing him.

"He's beat up. Broken nose, jaw, and stitches above his eye," Danny said.

It took Nick a moment to get over the relief he felt that Dominic wasn't whacked. First came concern and then the anger. "Where is he, hospital?"

"He's at your sister's. Marie will take good care of him. They say within a year he will be as good as new."

"So it's all fixable? No permanent damage?" Nick asked.

"Probably, plastic surgery, but that's about it," Danny answered.

Nick let out a deep breath from his relief, now would be the anger. "Okay then, don't tell me my fucking son was fighting in a bar? It's not the example I want set for the men."

"No, definitely not in a bar," Danny hesitated. "Nick, I'm just going to come out and say it. Before you explode, listen to the whole story. Lately, Dominic's been out of control—boozing it up until he can't remember. He went to the west side and took Billy Herrick's wife's car one night, and this morning he went to Doug's house, about 2:00 a.m. Grace called Tommy to come get Dominic because he was keeping her kids awake. Tommy gets there and they get in a brawl. Dominic hit Tommy with a frying pan and they beat each other to a pulp. Dominic gave as good as he got, though. Then Tommy took him to a doctor they keep on the side and he did surgery on Dominic's nose."

"Is that it?" Nick asked when Danny hesitated.

"Dominic had Tommy on the ground, and Grace came running with a gun, ready to shoot Dominic, her father too. Tommy said Doug knows and he's flying in. No one's been able to reach him. This is very bad."

Nick surprised Danny with his calmness. It had been almost a decade since Doug Sullivan brought Dominic home to his wife after saving his life from a hit. There was no stopping Nick on the roads on the way there that night. He didn't stop at one red light, never hit the brakes, and scared the living hell out of Danny on the way to Dominic's house. He didn't expect this reaction from Nick. "I think we both agree Dominic was way out of line going to Doug's house, but rules are rules, Danny. Who threw the first punch?"

"Dominic was cursing at the top of his lungs to Tommy and Doug's wife and her kids upstairs. Tommy asked him to go outside, Dominic wouldn't. Tommy asked him to quiet down, Dominic wouldn't. Tommy had to charge Dominic to quiet him down. He just wanted to subdue him. He's not an idiot, Nick. He's not going to walk up and punch the boss' son. That's where it started, there was no first punch," Danny explained.

"It sounds like you believe Tommy Herrick's justified," Nick said.

"I do. Earlier that day, Dominic found out you're the one who whacked Fabian's dad. Gave me a real attitude, I fucking walked away from him. Tommy said Dominic kept telling him to pick sides between me and him. Nick, there's something wrong with your kid. I've seen him deteriorating from the day I got home. It's more than booze or drugs—he's got something in his head lately. One minute he's a boss and in control, the next he's having a blackout night from drinking."

"He found out about Larry Bosca, huh?" Nick asked.

"I can't believe he didn't know. He started getting loud in your restaurant. And I hear he's been talking about his wife a lot," Danny said. "He needs a vacation, the kid's cracking up. But now, he's all fucked up and can't travel."

"My wife says he's got some brunette he's seeing."

"Let me get him laid, maybe that'll bring him back," Danny joked.

"Maybe there's someplace he can go to heal with the girl, check it out. I'll call Marie when we're done, see how he's doing. What's Doug going to do when he gets back?"

"My understanding is, kill Dominic," Danny answered.

"Well, that can't happen. You need to have a sit-down with Doug and Tommy. Make this right, we can't have a war with them," Nick ordered. "Tell them you're in charge, that'll appease them. Kind of like we planned, eh?"

In February of 2005, when Danny was ready to take his five-year deal, it was Nick's plan that Danny be in charge when he got out. He had only hoped that Dominic could manage controlling the lucrative empire for the duration of Danny's term. It was a job Danny didn't want. The man at top of the family is always the man at the top of the fed list. He was very content to sit in the backseat and let Dominic run around and draw all the attention after he was released, but that was over now for Danny. He now had to take all the reins; at least, until Dominic could heal and clear his head.

"Yup, it's working out like a charm," Danny said dryly.

Early the next morning, Tommy picked up Doug from the airport and met Danny and Angelo at a hotel. Tommy had filled Doug in on what'd transpired since they had talked last, and Doug had calmed down. Danny started the sit-down when they arrived. "Doug, no one condones someone's family being disrupted the way yours was. You have our sincerest apologies for Dominic's actions, and we're here to put this behind us."

"My wife had to pull a gun, and Tommy's got a fucking hole in his head and a broken hand. An apology ain't going to cut it," Doug responded.

"And Dominic looks like the Elephant Man. I'd say he learned his lesson."

"My boys had to witness that bullshit, and I can't get past my wife pulling a gun. Danny, I can never allow a situation like that to transpire again, ever," Doug said.

"I can't allow Dominic to be in danger, so I need assurances from you that you have no problem with Dominic."

"You're not hearing me. I consider Dominic a friend, Nick's been like a father to me, my wife and children consider the Amicuccis family. I'm not going to hurt Dominic, and I'm not going to go to war. But you want assurances from me, and I want assurances from you," Doug said.

"What assurances can I give you?" Danny asked.

"Ten years ago, Dominic came to me and tried shaking me down for fifty percent of my profits. I told him to make it twenty-five percent and we'll call it a partnership. He took it to his old man and he agreed."

"I remember, I was there," Danny told him.

"That was my agreement with Nick, a partnership. I don't work for you guys, never have. You guys needed me to do some things. I did them and was rewarded. When you guys went to jail, it more than served my interests to keep Dominic in power, so we did. You and Nick made your family strong again. Dominic and I took it to the next level. Without me and Tommy, Dominic would've been dead years ago," Doug explained.

"And our family is greatly appreciative of everything you guys have done, but for now, Dominic's going to be out of commission, and I'll be in charge. I want nothing more than to continue working with you. We got to get past this, Doug."

"What I want is for everyone to understand that we don't work for you. We don't play by the same rules as you made men. I don't want any made man thinking he can put his hands on my men, just because he took an oath. Anyone that does is subject to what happens to them, plain and simple. Boss or no boss," Doug said. "And I will personally kill any other fucker that comes to my home and acts like that."

Danny hated being spoken to like this, but for now, he bit his tongue. He had to end this sit-down with the Westide crew on their side, especially with Lissoni and Fabian still alive. "I wouldn't have it any other way." Danny started to stand and shake hands.

Doug didn't move. "And I've got serious objections to some of the management. No offense to you, Danny, I know you've walked into a mess. I want one of my guys at your book, just to make me feel better. And while I'm gone, I want Tommy consulted with weekly."

Danny stared at Doug. "You serious?"

"Yeah, or we walk. No war, no violence, you can have all your rackets that we run for you, but we're out. And you ain't getting my twenty-five percent no more, either," Doug said.

"I can't be strong-armed, Doug. What are you doing here?" Danny asked.

Doug stood up and offered his hand to shake to Danny. "My intent is only to keep my friends and family safe, that's all, Danny. I'm not strong-arming you, good luck to you guys." Doug stood there waiting for Danny to shake his hand and say good-bye.

Danny shook his head in disgust. "I'm not going to forget this. I'll meet your bullshit demands." He shook Doug's hand.

"I'll have my man at your book tomorrow, just in time for the Super Bowl," Doug said. After they left, Tommy dropped Doug off at his home. Four hours later, he was back on an airplane, en route to Switzerland.

CHAPTER XV

One in a Million

NOAH BROOKS ARRIVED home after his eighteen-hour workday. He had left his wife and young son at eleven the previous morning; it was now a 5:00 a.m. His wife had beat him to the garage and parked her car there first. Noah stopped his car by the porch, it was the least amount of distance he'd have to walk, and got out. His day was nonstop, and he wanted nothing more than to just lie down. His first reaction when he heard a noise was to pay it no mind. He heard it again, and he whirled his head around to its location. Lights were on in the front yards of most of the houses on the street; it was lit up very well, and there were no real dark spots. Noah sensed danger when he didn't see anything—something had to cause those two thuds.

He decided to run to his porch; a gunshot rang out with his first step. Noah heard the shot and heard his back window shatter. He had no idea where the shot had come from, so he dropped to the ground and rolled under his car where he pulled out his gun. Noah scanned the area as best he could from underneath his car. Two more gunshots rang out, piercing into his car. He now had to worry about the gasoline being exposed to flying bullets; he had to move.

Noah thought about rolling to his porch; it was a wooden deck with space underneath it. He could break through the lattice and use the cover of the deck to defend himself. But he chose not to take a chance on the shooter aiming any closer to his house than what he was aiming at now. He rolled out from under the car in the opposite direction and ran to cover in his neighbor's front yard. He first looked for a big tree, but there wasn't a tree on this side of the street for four more houses. The shooter started firing again. Noah felt the first bullet whiz in front of him, and it seemed to come from above. Two more shots whizzed in front of Noah, and he realized the shooter was smart enough to shoot in front of a moving object. He was no dummy Noah realized. At least he saw the flashes from the gun and finally knew where the bullets were coming from.

He stopped dead in his tracks and dropped to a knee, aiming his weapon up in the tree across the street. Those thuds from earlier must've been the shooter throwing rocks to draw Noah's attention elsewhere. Noah had his weapon trained on the tree, but he still couldn't see his enemy. Noah knew the shooter was sizing him up, waiting for the perfect shot. Noah was wide open, so he figured the shooter must have a bad angle if he was not shooting then.

Noah fired two bullets into the tree, just to stir it up. A man and a rifle fell to the ground. "No way," Noah said to himself, not believing he had hit him. He kept his weapon trained on the target that just fell from the tree as he ran across the street. He now heard sirens in the background. The man lay motionless face down in the grass, his rifle six feet away.

A cop car sped down his street as Noah stood over the facedown body; he dropped his gun at his side. The officer got out of his car, weapon drawn and ordered Noah to lie on the ground. "Deputy Clark, it's me, Noah Brooks." Noah was well known through the Nevada City by politicians and law enforcement. They knew him as Stevie Turner's man, and they knew Stevie was the mob's guy in Vegas.

The deputy lowered his weapon. "Mr. Brooks, what the hell happened here?" More police cars started rolling in as well as the gawkers now coming out of their houses, now that the shooting had stopped.

"I got home from work and started taking fire from that tree right there," Noah explained, pointing up in the three. "I took a shot in it, and I don't know if I hit this guy or if he was knocked out. If I hit him, I must be the best fucking shot in the world."

The deputy rolled the body over and revealed a bullet hole in the chest. "You know him?" he asked Noah.

Noah nodded his head. "Yeah, his name is John Lissoni."

Doug Sullivan had spent four days in Switzerland after the incident with Dominic. He flew back to Paris for a couple of days and left to fulfill his obligation in Sicily. He landed in Palermo on Sunday and was planning to spend two weeks in the small port town where Nick Amicucci's grandfather was born.

Doug was picked up at the airport and driven the long ride to the town to meet with its Mafia leader, Nino Amicucci. Doug always stayed at Nino's villa, two hours from the downtown. Nino agreed to Nick's request to send him a dozen men for a ten-percent increase of his cut of their multimillion drug business. Doug had spent the following three days interviewing the long list of men who wanted to come to America.

On Wednesday morning, he was having lunch with Nino and his son, Nino III, when his satellite phone rang. It was a Las Vegas area code, and Doug assumed Stevie was calling from a pay phone there. "Excuse me, I've got to take this," Doug said, leaving the table for some privacy. "What's up?" Doug asked Stevie.

"Lissoni's dead. Noah got him in Vegas," Stevie answered.

Doug didn't expect that, and it took a second for it to compute. "No, shit? How?"

"Stupid fucker went after Noah. He climbed a tree across from his house and waited for him. Noah got home, and Lissoni missed him with every shot. Noah took two shots into the tree, and somehow one of them hit Lissoni. One in a million shot."

"I haven't met this guy yet, have I? Where'd you find him?"

"Yeah, you have, he worked for me at that nudie bar. He picked you up once at the airport, he's been top notch. He came recommended from Chicago, their loss in my opinion," Stevie filled him in.

"Where's he now?"

"Police station. He's got his permit to carry a gun, and it was registered. It was clearly self-defense. He'll be home in a couple hours. I've called Tommy, and he's on his way to see Danny."

"The rest of Lissoni's crew should still be in Vegas. You got to lock down the city. These guys have to be running for the hills. And tell Tommy to have Danny check on Fabian's whereabouts," Doug ordered. Then he had an idea. "Hey, I'm going to send you a couple of zips. I'll let you know when they'll be there."

"What the fuck's a zip?" Stevie asked.

"It's what these guys call someone from Sicily. I don't know why."

Stevie was puzzled. "You're sending me a couple of shooters from Sicily? I can handle this."

"That I know. Keep these guys a secret when they get there and let them do the work. You and that Noah should be highly visible, ensure an alibi," Doug explained. "Stevie, this could be the start of a war. The feds are going to be all over us and you got victim number one out there. You're probably going to have a couple more real soon. You might start getting your first taste of some heat from the FBI. Let these guys do the work. Keep them a secret from all your men, need-to-know basis only. There'll be no one to clue the feds in."

"If you say so. Let me know when to pick them up," Stevie said. "What are you going to do, fly home?"

"Tommy don't need me—he knows what to do. He's already done everything I told you to tell him. I'm going to pick the best two zips and put them on a plane tonight. But for right now, I'm going to enjoy my huge lunch and go for a walk and check out this scenery. Even when it rains, it's just fucking gorgeous here," Doug told him.

"Well, enjoy yourself. The rest of us are going to war I guess," Stevie chided.

"Knock 'em dead," Doug said and hung up.

Danny Serafini left his meeting with Tommy Herrick and headed back to Clemency to assemble his crew at their headquarters, Cooch's Corner. He was confident the bar was still under surveillance, but he had to communicate to his men. He entered the bar and all noise ceased, every head turned to Danny, to see what was so urgent. Danny looked the men over and turned to the captain of the crew, Angelo. "Where the fuck is Fat Kenny and Nussman?"

"Gary's running the bakery," Angelo answered.

"Right. And Kenny?"

"He should be here," was the Angelo's answer.

"Call him. I want him here now," Danny ordered.

Angelo pulled out his phone to call Kenny. Danny turned to the crew's bookie, Jackie Beans. "Who's in charge of making sure this place ain't bugged?" Danny asked. The Corner used the same security system as the bakery: top of the line alarm system and twenty-four-hour video surveillance. Every single day someone watched the recordings to ensure no one had entered the building to install wiretaps.

Jackie nodded to Scary Scarelli, and Danny turned to him. "Are you one hundred percent sure the feds never got in here?"

Scary looked to the three youngest members of the crew, Carlo DeMini, Vince Cusamano, and Frank Neri, who all nodded yes. It was their job to watch the recordings every day. "One hundred percent," Eugene Scary Scarelli answered.

"Eugene, we're going to talk openly here and if this meeting ends up being played back to me in a fucking courtroom, it's your life I'm taking in reparations," Danny told him.

Danny turned to face all the men. "That goes for everyone. Anyone ever decides to wear a wire and record me, I will hunt you down like the fucking dog that you are." He turned to Angelo. "Where's Kenny?"

"Ten minutes away," Angelo told him.

"Call him back and tell him if he ain't here in ten minutes, he can put on a fucking tablecloth to wear as an apron and he can be the new busboy. I will have punctuality in this fucking crew," Danny said in a loud voice for everyone to get the picture. "Come get me here when the lieutenant decides to arrive," Danny's use of Kenny's new position was said in sarcasm.

He stormed across the bar and walked into the office in the back, slamming the door behind him. He hadn't been in this office since before he went to jail. After coming home from five years in prison, Danny was fearful of speaking anywhere. Hushed conversations with plenty of background noise were his preference, but he was forced to be the boss now—a job he so dreaded; almost undoubtedly, it meant a long prison term.

To Danny, so many great men had owned this office since its creation in 1934. He thought back to when he was a teenager and his father would bring him in this office and listen to Nicodemo Amicucci give his orders. Before him it was Paul and Pete Lissonis's office. Hell it was even Nick and Danny's office until the feds took them down. His mood lightened with the reminiscing and the bottle of scotch he noticed on the desk. *Fucking Jackie Beans is drinking, lying son of a bitch,* Danny thought to himself. Danny poured himself a glass and took a seat at his new desk.

Six minutes later, Angelo opened the door to announce Kenny's arrival. Danny left the office and stood in the middle of the bar and called out Kenny, "That's one strike, it's two and out with me, capische?"

"I'm sorry, Danny . . ."

Danny held up his hand. "Take the strike and shut the fuck up." He waited to ensure Kenny was clear and started his meeting. "John Lissoni was shot dead this morning in Vegas. We could be at war. He attacked one of the Westside guys and lost. We don't know where the rest of his crew is or if anyone else is involved. Until we know more, everyone's got to be on alert. Watch your tails, it might not just be the feds behind you."

He looked around the room; he definitely had their attention. "Everyone knows what happened to Dominic. Before anyone ever says he got his ass kicked, I know what happened. He fought like a warrior. He lost a fight, a fight that I don't think any of you would've lasted two minutes in." He looked at Scary. "Maybe three for you, Eugene," he said with a laugh. "My point being, anyone says a bad word about Dominic, you'll be in cement shoes. Until it is stated otherwise, I am in charge. I shouldn't be here having to meet with you guys. This really should be done by you, Kenny. But here we are. Despite the feds, my office will be right here. Who better for a bodyguard than the FBI?" Danny turned to Angelo. "The bakery's all yours. Do not fuck it up."

Danny looked at the oldest crew member, huddled up at the bar. Danny had known Paul Amevu all his life, but he had served two long prison terms and just hung around nowadays, retired. "What the fuck do you do anyway?" Danny asked them.

Paul Amevu, driver for Nick's grandfather, Nicodemo, long ago, held up his glass. "I just drink, Danny."

"Well, you're here now, you're fucking involved. Don't just be here, Paul, be *here*. Be a part of the crew, give your advice. For fuck's sake, I'd listen to you, you old bastard. Everyone here, even you, Genie," Danny said pointing to Eugene Evola, who was not a tough guy but an odds expert. "You all have lived this life your whole lives, you know the rules, follow them, the same way I did when I was in your positions. I'll be here most days from noon until midnight. Everyone around me will act as I say, or you just won't be around. It's plain and simple with me: do as you're told."

Danny left the bar and took with him his new driver that had been guarding the front door from the outside, Jimmy Amicucci.

Helena Amicucci still had her oven mitts on when she opened the front door to see who was pounding on it relentlessly. With her mascara running, Sandra Lissoni stood face-to-face with the mother of the man she believed had her son, John, killed.

Sandra lived just a few miles from Nick's house, as did John Lissoni, actually. They all had known each other their entire lives, except for those that had married in, like these two. "Sandra, what's the matter?" Helena asked in all honesty.

"I want blood for my son," Sandra hissed.

"What happened to John? Is he found?" The only knowledge Helena had was that John had taken off a year ago and his wife and two small children moved in with his parents.

"Your son killed him."

"My son? Who Dominic?"

"Yeah, Dominic. May both your souls burn in hell."

"He's not my son," Helena said coldly, before slamming the door. Helena walked back into the kitchen where Sal had started eating out of a pot that Helena had put on simmer to answer the door.

"What was all that? John Lissoni died now? They got some bad luck," he said.

"If anyone ever comes to that door and says that about you, I'll kill you myself. I will not have given birth to a murderer." Helena took off her mitts and went upstairs to cry for the mother's loss. She knew how hard Sandra and John's father, Bobby, tried to keep John, their only child, out of the life. Bobby was the youngest son to Pete Lissoni and was so law bidding, he didn't even speed.

The power, the money, the women, even the blood that flowed in their veins, it all pulled them to the life. Helena prayed every night for Sal to have the strength to resist all those temptations. John Lissoni was always such a good kid; he was a ring bearer at her and Nick's wedding when he was six years old. He was the beloved grandson of Pete Lissoni, the only man she ever saw her husband bow down to. John was pampered since the day she met the cute little boy. How could something like this happen? *Two more Mafia children orphaned,* she thought. It seemed so easy when Nick promised her he could keep Sal out of the life; everything he said just seemed to happen. But now it seemed almost impossible.

The life she was so drawn to in her youth, she now loathed more than anything. She hated Nick's son, Dominic, for what he was, but she knew the good in him. She knew the devotion he had for his father and the commitment he'd take to the grave to keep Sal out of the life, just because he gave his word to Nick. The tragedy with his wife that he adored so much and the pressure of trying to fill his father's shoes at such a young age had taken its toll on Dominic, and she hoped and prayed that his beating might be the incident that changes his path in life. *He could have been such a great person,* she thought, *if Nick would've kept him out of it.* Maybe it wasn't too late.

While the incident with John Lissoni weighed heavily on Helena, it had provoked a rage in Tommy Herrick. After his meeting with Danny, Tommy consulted with his brother in a wooded area they used for hunting. "You see, that's the exact fucking point Doug was trying to make with Danny," Tommy raged.

"What is?" Billy asked. *Tommy can't even say hello anymore?* Billy thought to himself.

"Every fucking thing they do affects us, that's what. Someone wants to make a move at them guys—they always fucking attack us. Shooting at me in my car, you at your house, and now Noah at his house with his family inside."

"You don't even know this Noah Brooks," Billy reminded Tommy.

"I know I don't want someone shooting at me in front of my house. That much I fucking know, Billy. Your own fucking wife had to go through it firsthand, why don't you get it?"

"I get it. So we find the rest of his crew and whack them, what's the big fucking point?"

"The families, the fucking families, Billy, they're why we do it. Maybe it'd be different for you when you have kids, but take Claudia, for instance. You've already risked your life for her, so imagine that times ten. You'd move heaven and earth for your kids, the mere thought of your child in danger, Billy, and you'll understand. And it's a danger we bring on ourselves to give them terrific futures. There's more guilt than can be bore for any tragedy with our families. From now on, it's a zero percent chance of danger rule. If anyone poses any sort of threat to us or our families, they die," Tommy explained. "They're hitting too close to home nowadays."

"What are you going to do, kill everyone?" Billy asked sarcastically.

"Yes, that's the plan. We're not waiting for these assholes to shoot first anymore."

"And Danny's on board? You said he was pretty cold to you today?" Billy asked.

"Danny's fine, time will heal all. I've got all the respect in the world for him, and we're on the same mission: to clean up Dominic's mess. And I ain't bitching about Dominic either. I got a new respect for him. He was just way out of his league as a boss, but I don't want to fight him again, especially, if he's sober. It is what it is, and we got to deal with it," Tommy said.

"How many people do you guys got in mind to whack?"

"Don't know. We'll just kill them as we find them. But you have a job to do," Tommy told him.

"What's that?" his brother asked.

"Doug's sending over two Sicilian shooters, they're going to Vegas. As soon as he lets me know the flight number, you got to pick them up at the airport and drive to Vegas."

"Why do I got to pick them up?" he asked.

"Because this is hush-hush, only you and Stevie will know. They're going to wipe out the rest of Lissoni's crew once Stevie finds them. And you got to drive them, so that there's no paper trail."

"Sure, you know me. Never drove that far, but okay. Do these guys even speak English?" Billy asked, dreading the drive.

"I don't know, but there's a catch," Tommy said.

"You mean a catch other than driving across the country?"

"Yeah, you have to pick them up in New York and drive from there."

"No problem, thanks a lot, big brother," Billy said. "Anything else?" he asked sarcastically.

"That's the attitude. Just be careful."

Danny arrived home late in the evening; he had spent the day meeting with the crime family's captains, throwing his weight around. In his attempt today to ensure all his key players knew who was in charge, he felt confident he had also let the feds know. He felt his fate was sealed; he had to set the crime family up for the future before the feds sent him to jail. He felt more than fortunate when he was offered that five-year deal—it was a steal. The whole time he was away, he hoped Dominic could emerge as a good boss and Danny could avoid the position Nick wanted him to take upon his release. It looked promising at first, but even Danny's own release from prison added fuel to Dominic's self-destruction.

His wife, Bianca, had the dining room table set for dinner, a huge dinner waiting for her husband. "We having company?" Danny asked, hanging up his coat.

"No, I know you've had a long day, and I thought a nice meal would be nice to come home to," Bianca answered.

"You heard about John Lissoni," Danny said, sitting down at the table and pouring a glass of wine.

"I know how much you hoped he would come home safe and sound. I'm sorry." Bianca started rubbing Danny's shoulders.

"You're being extra nice today," Danny said, surprised at the treatment he was receiving.

"Like I said, I know you've had a hard day, and with your new responsibilities, I just wanted to do something nice for you," she told him.

"What new responsibilities? What are you talking about?"

"Danny, everybody's talking."

"Talking about what?"

"Everybody's saying Dominic's out and you're in."

"Who's telling you this?" Danny asked.

"All the wives. Look, Danny, you've been nothing but loyal to Nick and the Amicuccis, you deserve this very much. *We* deserve this very much."

"We? Oh, I get it. Helena's been dethroned and you're the new queen bee," Danny said with a big grin for his wife.

Bianca returned the smile, although sheepishly. "You didn't think I was sticking around because of your loving demeanor, did you?" Danny raised his eyebrows at her. "I'm just kidding, but I am so proud of you."

"You do know my new responsibilities will cost me twenty or more years, right?"

Again Bianca decided to joke with Danny. "Oh, I'll be just fine." Bianca laughed. "I love that we can still joke with each other after all these years. It looks like you'll just have to be smarter than the FBI."

"Easy for you to say," Danny said as started in on his dinner.

Nick waited for his cellmate in their cell. Nick had finished his nightly phone calls to his family, and he was waiting for Eddie Turco to do the same. Eddie's son had taken over his family's rackets until his father forced him to quit. Eddie Turco Jr. was the last Turco on the streets that wasn't incarcerated, and his father wanted to ensure he wouldn't die in jail like the rest of the family. Although retired, Eddie Jr. kept in touch with old friends and kept his ear to the streets. He became an invaluable source of information for Nick in prison, through his father.

When Eddie finally arrived, he told Nick of what news his son gave him. "Well, Danny hit the streets hard today. He met with all the captains, and word has it, lit your crew up pretty good."

"Good. What are they saying about Dominic?" Nick asked Eddie, as the seventy-three-year-old gangster climbed into the top bunk that Nick made him sleep in. Eddie had been here since 1990 when he was sentenced to sixty-five years.

"Nothing good, Nick. One rumor has him doing drugs and trying to bang Doug Sullivan's wife," Eddie told him, finally lying down.

Nick shook his head. "I really fucked him up. Poor kid never stood a chance."

"What are you going to do? Either you got it or you don't."

"Oh, he's got it, and Danny will show him how to use it. I'm up for parole in twelve years, and I figure if Dominic could handle it for five years, twelve should be no problem for Danny. If I get parole, it's three years of parole. That's when Dominic will take over and Danny can retire. Dominic will be well seasoned by then," Nick explained.

"It was that Fabian Bosca thing, it pushed him over the edge."

"All my fault. I handled that all wrong, and Dominic took the hit."

"You ever tell him that?" Eddie asked.

"No. He's been a good son. It ain't his fault he got thrown in that situation. For some reason, it's easier for me tell someone else how good he did than it is for me to tell him directly."

"You asking me to tell him?"

"No, you senile fuck. I was just telling you, forget I said anything," Nick said, climbing into the bottom bunk and calling it a night.

In Las Vegas, Stevie Turner took a seat on his couch and turned on the evening news. There he was, the headline story, Noah Brooks. They showed footage of Noah leaving the police station with his lawyer; no charges were filed in the self-defense shooting of John Lissoni. Noah ignored the press until one reporter asked him about the shot. Noah beamed. "One in a million shot, one in a million." He hopped into a waiting a car and was taken home, where more press were waiting.

"What happens when a gangster from Michigan takes on a gangster from Chicago? The Michigan man loses," the reporter reported. "One Noah Brooks, formerly of Chicago, was attacked this morning by one John Lissoni, who has an address in Michigan. Lissoni was shot dead from a treetop sniper's nest. Brooks's gun was registered, and he has a permit to carry it; he was released with no charges pending. The FBI lists Brooks as an associate of the Chicago mob; he went to work for them at a topless bar here in Las Vegas and has gone on to be their man in recent years. The FBI is not answering questions as to a motive of the attack. One source said off the record that Lissoni was being hunted by the mob in Michigan and may have been spotted here in Vegas by Brooks and that Lissoni tried to kill Brooks before he could alert his superiors."

Stevie couldn't help but smile; he couldn't believe Noah was being linked to the Chicago mob and his name hadn't come up yet. One thing he was certain about, though, the FBI in Las Vegas would be talking to the FBI in Michigan. How much longer could his shroud of invisibility continue?

CHAPTER XVI

Funeral

DANNY SERAFINI ENTERED the funeral home just after one in the afternoon on Monday. He brought his wife, Bianca, his daughter, Sabrina, and her husband, George Lena, to Charley Amicucci's funeral. The funeral would be small, mostly just family, since Charley wasn't mobbed up, but, of course, with Ziggy being a made man and his last name being Amicucci, the crime family's captains would come pay their respects

They gave their condolences to Charley's wife, Lonna, and their five children. Danny gave Jimmy, the oldest child, an envelope with five thousand dollars in it. The Serafinis met briefly with Charley's brother and sister, who had moved away years ago, distancing themselves from this life. Danny received a rather cold greeting from them; they just wanted to say good-bye to their older brother and get back on with their lives, which did not include their gangster father, Ziggy.

Danny handed another envelope to Ziggy. "I'm sorry for your loss, Zig."

Ziggy took the envelope and nonchalantly placed it in his suit jacket pocket. He put his arm around Danny, and they both looked to the casket. "I've never seen him look so peaceful."

"Forty-six, way too young," Danny said.

"In a little bit, I need to talk alone with you," Ziggy told Danny.

"Anytime, just come and get me." Danny met up with his wife, who was with her best friend, Helena Amicucci. Sabrina and her husband had partnered with Valentina and her husband, and Sal stood alone looking through his iPhone.

"Hey, Sal, how's the job at Doug's bar?" Danny asked him.

"It's not open yet," Sal answered, barely looking up.

"I heard you're going to be working security. Tommy Herrick said you were learning some self-defense and working out."

Sal perked up. "Tommy talked to you about me? What'd he say? How am I doing?"

Danny was puzzled by Sal's enthusiasm for Tommy. "You know he's the one that beat your brother up, right?"

"Even Dominic says it's his own fault. He said, well, he wrote because his jaw's still wired shut, that Tommy's the toughest man he ever fought. Over on the west side, Tommy's a legend, him and Doug," Sal told him.

Danny hadn't realized Sal could be used for information on the Westside crew which his crime family had become so dependent on. "How often do you see Tommy?"

"Never, just when he'd come over to our house to see Dominic, before they fought, of course. But, my boss, Matt Young, he's in charge of the security of club, and he's known them since before high school."

"Good, sounds like this job might toughen you up," Danny said, messing up Sal's hair. Angelo and his mother, Marie, entered the group. "Angelo, how long have you been in charge of the bakery now?" Danny asked.

"Five days, why?" Angelo asked.

"Don't you think you could go one week without being late?"

"When was I late?"

"Yesterday, I checked the alarm times. Five ten you took the alarm down. That's ten minutes of our staff was standing around outside waiting for someone to open the door. Ten wasted minutes," Danny said.

"I'm sorry." Angelo had entrusted Kenny to open the bakery on Sunday morning. Kenny had covered for Angelo on the under bet, so Angelo decided not to mention Kenny's tardiness, especially, after arriving late for Danny's meeting.

"I want you there before five," Danny told him, then walked off.

Angelo looked to his mother, who had overheard the whole thing. "I'd be there before five if I was you," she told him.

Later in the evening, Danny reassured Ziggy that his monthly stipend would continue, just as it did when Dominic handled the crime family's finances, when Jack Mattea and his lieutenant, Rocco Gurino arrived. Danny approached them in the parking lot. "Jack, you don't look a day over ninety."

"Thanks, I'll be eighty-five in March, you prick," Jack joked, and the two embraced. "You know, Pete's kid, Carmine, is up for parole next week."

Carmine Mattea was Pete Mattea's middle son; he pled to thirteen years in 1999. He worked hand in hand with his second cousin, Jack, in running the crime family for the short period they did before Jack got ten years and Carmine took his thirteen. "I did not know that," Danny said. It wasn't the best news to Danny. "What do you want to do with him?"

"If he does make parole, he's still off the streets for a few years, but once he's off parole, I thought I could be consigliere and he could replace me as capo regime," Jack told him, campaigning for the job of the crime family's advisor and number three position.

Danny nodded his head. "A decision like that is ultimately up to Nick, so I will make sure it gets to him."

"I've got something too, Danny," Rocco Gurino said.

"What?" Danny asked.

"My son."

"Nicky? How's he doing?" Danny asked. The Gurinos also had lived near Nick and Danny, and their children had gone to school with their kids.

"He's fine. He, Mikey, and little Bruno were all working together with Ziggy's boy, Jimmy." Mikey was his nephew, and little Bruno was Bruno Jr., Rocco's cousin's son. The three cousins were like brothers and had formed a close friendship with Jimmy and Sal. "You guys took Jimmy to your crew, and my son's stuck with that Angie Jars."

"You want permission to move them to your crew? No problem, a son should always be with his father. I don't know why you'd let them go with Angie Jars in the first place."

"Because just like in your family, I forbade my son to be involved in our life, and he was recruited elsewhere. Your cousin Jimmy's a smart one. He's been to dinner at our house a million times. I've grown fond of him. I figured if they were with Jimmy, they'd be okay," Rocco explained.

"I'm not putting Jimmy back with Angie Jars, he's my personal driver now," Danny told him.

"Fuck Angie Jars, I was hoping you'd take them into your crew. You've known all three of them forever."

"Oh, let me think about that one. I'll get back to you." Danny liked the idea of bringing three young recruits to his crew, especially, ones with a bloodline dating back longer than the Amicuccis. But he was concerned because of Jack Mattea. Danny's first thought was that it would give Jack inside information into the Amicucci crew, since Rocco Gurino worked for him. They still had concerns as to Fabian's other connections, and Jack Mattea was a possible suspect. Perhaps, the Matteas would like to have the title of boss back.

"They're good kids, Danny. I personally vouch for all three. I'll put a foot up their asses if they give you any trouble," Rocco said.

"I know they are, but I need to talk to Angie's captain, Vinny Jag. He'll be here today, and I'll try to talk to him about it."

Walking to the back door, Danny saw Fat Kenny and Jackie Beans pull up, so Danny went to talk to them. "Where the fuck you two been?" he asked them.

"Danny, I didn't know there was a certain time to be here, no one told me," Kenny said, scared of strike two.

Danny laughed. "There's not, I'm just fucking with you. But I do need to talk to you, Jackie. It's of a personal nature." Kenny entered the funeral home, and Danny spoke with Jackie, "How long have we known each other now?" Danny asked him.

"Since the sixties when Eddie Kalko brought me around the bar," Jackie Beans answered.

"We used to deliver bread together, remember?" Danny asked.

"Yup, me and Johnny G." John Gioli was Jackie's best friend growing up.

"Where's he at now?"

Jackie looked at Danny as if he was crazy. "You and Nick promoted him, made him a lieutenant. Have you forgotten?"

"I don't forget anything, Jackie, ever. My point is, all of us have been promoted, and all of us have climbed the ladder. You're stuck on the bookie step. Do you know why?"

"I know I fucked up with my drinking. You think my failure in the Club is my most disappointing moment. I failed as a husband and a father, and that keeps me up more at night than being just a bookie, which is what I love," Jackie explained.

"You have given every fucking penny you've ever made to your wife and son. You've more than tried to make that right. You want to drink, that's your call, but if you're going to run this book, you can't be a fucking drunk."

"I'm not a drunk anymore. I go to my meetings, I'm good," Jackie said.

"Scotch? Back room? And where do you get the balls to even sit at that desk? You know as well as I do the people who've sat at that desk."

Jackie hung his head; he was caught. "I don't know what to say. It's not a problem anymore. I just have a drink every now and then."

Danny put his hand on Jackie's shoulder. "Listen, old friend, do as you want, it's your life. But if you're going to handle my money and lead my men, you can't be a drunk. Not a chance in hell with me."

"I won't, Danny," Jackie said.

"Take a moment here, Jackie. If I catch one bad sign that you're not up to your fullest capabilities, I'm tossing you out. I'll put you on a shelf. People on the shelf don't collect a pension. This is a serious decision, Jackie. If you want to stay on, you better be the way I want you to be, which includes not ever fucking lying to me again. Or you can retire, full pension. You'd be at seventy-five hundred a month and keep your full insurance. So don't give me an answer today. Take the night, sleep on it, and tell me tomorrow."

"I don't need to take until tomorrow, I am the Amicucci bookie. The job's an honor and worth more to me than a stupid bottle. If I can't control it, I'll come to you before it's a problem. Thank you, Danny. Or is it Don Daniel now?" Jackie asked jokingly.

Danny stared at Jackie. "Danny's fine. Bust someone else's balls, would you?" Danny said before walking off and entering the funeral home.

Inside, Danny noticed Vinny Jagge arrived with his sons and a special guest. Fabian flew in from Mexico and tagged along with the Jagge trio, most likely an attempt to keep himself in good graces with Danny and Dominic, Danny figured. They must've come in the front door. Danny found Angelo and pulled him away from his wife. "When the fuck is Dominic going to get here?"

"He was here this morning, during the family's hour. He left. He didn't want anyone to see him like he is," Angelo told him.

"I can understand that," Danny said.

"Why would Vinny come in the front door? Everybody knows to come in the back, there could be feds out there," Angelo said.

Danny sighed. "Because if there are feds out there, then they have a nice photograph of Fabian in good graces with us. Gives us a defense for when we whack him, smarten up," Danny said and walked off again.

As the visitation progressed, others came. Valentina's father-in-law, Tom Caruso, showed up. Mario Marconi, Dominic's longtime friend, arrived just before dark. Mario impressed Danny by showing up with two of his crew that he'd been in charge of for a year now. It looked like young Mario was gaining some respect in Jerry Lissoni's old crews.

Danny was watching Ziggy have a few laughs with Vince Apana, the last of his old crew, who showed up with Mario. It was nice to see the old man have a nice moment, Danny thought to himself, when Daniel Amicucci asked him for a minute. Daniel was one of Nick's younger brothers and not involved in the life. "Danny, why is that thug talking to my daughter?"

Danny saw Daniel's daughter, Marie, talking to Rocco DiNapolli, a lieutenant for Mario. "That's just Rocco, he's a good kid."

"He's a thug," Nick's brother said.

"He's not a thug. You see him," Danny said, pointing to the old man Ziggy was laughing with. "That old man works for Rocco, he's what we call an up and comer."

"I'm supposed to say okay to that?" Daniel asked incredulously.

"Your daughter goes to college, she's going to be a lawyer. Your dorky daughter don't want nothing to do with no gangster." Danny stopped. "Oh my god, did I just say that?" he asked himself.

"My dorky daughter?"

"I didn't mean it to come out like that. I just meant, Rocco's not her type. So why worry?"

Daniel shook his head and walked away from Danny. ***I'm going to hear about that one later,*** Danny thought. Angelo tapped him from behind. "Guess who's here?"

"I don't know, your fucking dad, who?"

"Geez, Danny, my dad's doing life," Angelo said.

"Yeah, I know. Who's here, already?"

"That old man, Paul Amevu, that guy that hangs around the bar. He's a whack job, why would he be here?" Angelo asked.

"Why's he a whack job? He used to drive for your great-grandfather. That old man did two twenty-year stints, show him some fucking respect," Danny ordered, then went to say hello.

Paul was talking with Sal when he saw Danny and Angelo approach. "I can't believe this is Nick's kid. He looks just like him."

"Wouldn't that mean you should believe it?" Sal asked the old man.

Danny hit Sal on the back of the head. "Stop it," he told Sal.

"You know, young Salvatore, I missed your great-grandfather's funeral. I missed your grandfather's funeral. It's nice to be able to come show my respects for once," Paul said.

"Why'd you miss all those funerals? Were you in jail for fifty years?" Sal asked.

Paul laughed. "Almost."

"What'd you do? Something like my father did?"

"No. Your father's a great man, I was a nothing. I robbed a bank," Paul explained.

"I remember. I was fifteen. Nick's father was crushed, mine too," Danny said.

"In fact, Salvatore, the last funeral I was at, was your great Uncle Jack's, Giacomo's funeral."

Danny laughed. "Yeah, you were just out on parole, and they busted you for being at a mob funeral and sent you back."

"Funny to you, not to me, I was only out for eight months," Paul said.

"How long were you out after that, two years? I remember you were at your daughter's wedding," Danny said.

"Two years? Eleven months," Paul answered.

"What'd you do to go back?" Sal asked, fascinated.

"Bank robbery," both Danny and Paul answered in unison.

"Again? Why?" Sal asked.

"I needed money," Paul answered, shrugging his shoulders.

"How're you sitting now?" Danny asked. "You got your two hundred grand from Dominic when you got out, right?"

"No, I never got my button. That money's for made men, and I spent too much in jail to be around to get made. Right now, I'm getting by. I'm living with my daughter and her husband. I got my wife's life insurance money," Paul said.

Danny reached into his pocket. "I think that's only a grand. It's all I brought that wasn't stuffed in a fucking envelope. Take it."

"No, I said I'm good."

"You are aware of my position now, aren't you? I'm not asking. Take the money. Like I said, it's just a grand. Buy something nice for your daughter." Paul took the money and put it in his pocket. "I'm willing to bet you wanted to retire, but you can't stay away from the Corner."

"I just got to be a part of it, even if it's just hanging at the bar, listening to the bullshit," Paul said.

"No more just sitting at the bar for you," Danny told him.

"Danny, I was a tough guy, I did the dirty work. Now I'm seventy years old. I'm an old man that never had to use his brains. There's not much I can help with."

"Let's just see about that," Danny told him. He saw his wife walking toward him with a scowl on her face. "Excuse me, I need to see my wife, I think."

"Did you call Daniel's daughter, Marie, a dork?" Bianca asked.

Danny sighed and admitted to it. "I did,"

"Why on earth would you do that?"

"I don't know, I apologized. He's just going to have to get over it. Besides, she is a fucking dork. I think it's time we get going anyway. This whole day's been exhausting." They said their good-byes, and Danny had to listen to Bianca nag him about his name-calling for the rest of the night.

Billy Herrick drove through the desert, carrying his two Sicilian immigrants. He saw headlights turn on in the distance—that would be Stevie Turner. Billy caught up to the headlights and got out of his car, telling the Sicilians to stay put.

Stevie Turner and Noah Brooks stepped out of the other car and approached Billy. "How was the trip?" Stevie asked.

"Miserable. Couldn't count on either of these two to drive, they can't read or write any English. One of the fuckers just kept saying, 'We live here now, we live here now.' I can't fucking take it anymore. Take them and good fucking luck. I'm going to get a room," Billy complained.

"You know you can't stay here, not even one night," Stevie reminded of Tommy's orders. Billy was to turn around and head back home, stopping only at small hotels along the way, paying cash and using a fake ID.

"I'll use my fake ID," Billy pleaded.

"Tommy said you'd say that. You'll still be on camera, no can do, Billy. I've got my orders, that's to deny you any access to Vegas, sorry."

Billy didn't say a word; he just returned to his car and motioned for the men to get out. Alberto and Benedetto climbed out of the car with a bag apiece. "That's all they have?" Stevie asked.

"That's all they got. These guys moved here with just a fucking bag," Billy answered before hopping in his car and turning it around and leaving.

Alberto looked to Stevie. "We live here now?"

Stevie laughed. "No, we'll take you to your home for a little while, come on." Everyone piled into the car and Noah drove them to a desolate rented cabin where the hit men could hide out until needed.

"So what the hell happened with John Lissoni?" Fabian asked Angelo as the two sat at a bar having a beer. Many people left the funeral and met at a bar down the street.

Danny was right. Fabian was using me to get information on the crew, Angelo figured. "He attacked one of the Westide guys in Vegas, got himself killed instead," Angelo answered.

"So what now?" Fabian asked.

"What do you mean?"

"What about Lissoni's crew? They're still on the loose."

"Danny says they fled, there's no way they'd stay in Vegas," Angelo lied.

"Probably right. If you need any help from me, let me know. I still owe you for sticking up for me with Vinny Jag."

"You were getting fucked, and I've known you all my life. Vinny Jag just popped up out of the woodwork like the next messiah," Angelo said. "I'll tell you, ever since Danny got out, it's been fucked up. Everyone blames Dominic for all the bullshit, and you fucked him over pretty good too."

Fabian put his beer down and tried as quick as he could to read Angelo. He thought Angelo's sticking up for him with Vinny Jagge was staged, but now he wasn't so sure. Fabian thought if Angelo was lying, he deserved an award for his acting. "I know. I wish I could take it back. And I'm sorry I fucked you over too. I can't believe nobody's whacked me."

"Your family, Fabian. My Uncle Nick would rather whack Dominic before you I think," Angelo said.

"He's always looked out for me since my father was killed. Look how I repay him? Man, I wanted to get a quick million or two and stash it before Vinny Jag got out. I never thought I'd get caught," Fabian explained.

"That's what I don't get. You've got more money than God, why risk it all for a couple of million dollars. You were making that every two weeks in Mexico," Angelo said. "That's why it looks like you were shoving it in Dominic's face."

"I know. It seemed like the right thing to do at the time. I don't think I was thinking well."

"Well, that's that. Now you just keep your nose clean for a while and it'll be gone from everyone's mind before you know it," Angelo told him.

"I hope so. All I can do now is keep earning," Fabian said before they were joined by others.

CHAPTER XVII

Six to the Chest

"UNCLE ZIGGY, DO you have a minute?" Sal Amicucci asked his uncle at the small gathering at Aunt Marie's house.

"Kid, I'm seventy-two years old, how many minutes you think I got left?" Ziggy asked jokingly.

"Seriously, I've got a lot of questions and no one's allowed to talk to me. You'll talk to me though, won't you?"

"If this is about the birds and the bees, I'm going to be pretty fucking pissed you wasted one of my minutes," Ziggy said.

"I'm good there, thanks. That Paul Amevu guy that came to Charlie's funeral. Why does someone who does twenty years for robbing a bank have to rob another one because he has no money? My father always said they always take care of the guys that go to jail."

"I remember when Paulie got out of jail the first time, in the eighties before you were born. Your grandfather, my oldest brother, just died and your father was in charge. He gave Paulie Bankjob a nice wad of cash, out of his own personal money. Paulie was always a degenerate, he gambled, he could never hang on to money. Paulie had no money because of Paulie. And by the way, the second time he got caught, was without permission to rob that bank," Ziggy explained.

"You guys called him Paulie Bankjob?"

"Yeah, so?"

Sal laughed. "Nothing. I always heard that you and Uncle Ray weren't allowed to be involved, but you did it anyway. What happens if I do it too?"

Ziggy nodded his head in understanding. "You want to be in the life, I get it. Salvatore, it's not something you learn, you either are, or you ain't."

"How come Dominic could and I can't?"

Ziggy laughed. "When Dominic was your age, he was already collecting bets. He was in the life the day he was born. You were raised to not be in the life. Besides, people won't take you seriously."

"What do you mean people won't take me seriously?" Sal asked, offended.

"You act dumb. You say some dumb things. It makes people believe you speak without thinking—a very bad trait in our life."

"How do I act dumb?"

"You just do. Fix the impression you give if you ever want to be taken seriously," Ziggy said. "And a bit of advice from someone who's been around the block. With your job on the west side, Danny's going to try and get little bits of information on them guys, and them guys are going to keep trying to learn things about Danny. Always look for an angle, Salvatore. No one's ever on the up and up in this life, they all want something," Ziggy explained.

Doug Sullivan talked with Tommy Herrick before he left for his meeting in Baghdad. "You're taking them tonight?" Doug asked them.

"We set the meet with the last two of Lissoni's crew for ten tonight. Parking lot of a small restaurant, the zips are going to mow them down and get out of town," Tommy explained.

"You're sure they're all set to drive now?" Stevie had been teaching the two Sicilians how to drive and use the navigation systems.

"Stevie says they're good to go, that's good enough for me," Tommy answered.

"Yeah, me too. I meant to ask you, why'd you send Billy to drive across the country? Anyone really could've done that. He pissed you off or something?" Doug asked.

Tommy chuckled, "First of all, he's miserable, so right there's a good reason. I wanted to see what Claudia did when he wasn't in town, that's the real reason," Tommy said.

"Clever. And?"

"Just fine. She shops a hell of a lot, but nothing out of the ordinary. And we didn't pick up any tails on her or nothing. Maybe her battery just fucking died and Dominic's mechanic is a moron," Tommy said.

"Could be. Anyway, we'll wrap up this Lissoni problem tonight, and we'll deal with Fabian and get back to business."

"That would be nice. You can finish your overseas bullshit and start staying home more, that would be nice too," Tommy said.

"We'll see, but you know I'm always looking for the next big project. I got the bar opening in May, and that shooting at Noah Brooks's house in Vegas got me thinking. Our families are too much in the open. I want to move us to a secluded area," Doug said.

"Even my brother got shot at, at his house. What are you thinking?"

"Buy land, build our own street, we'll all build our own houses, total protection," Doug described.

"Sounds expensive."

"I'll flip the whole bill," Doug told him.

"You're going to buy land, make a road, and have me design my own house?" Tommy asked.

"And your brother and we'll see who else. We'll build another street and put the zips there, we'll make our own little city," Doug said.

"You never cease to amaze."

Danny arrived at Cooch's Corner at five minutes to noon and found his whole crew had already arrived. *They're finally starting to act like a crew,* Danny thought to himself as he said his hellos. Jackie Beans was there, talking with Paulie Bankjob. *Well, that's the old table,* Danny told himself. Fat Kenny headed up the younger table, which included Carlo DeMini, Vince Cusamano, and Frankie Neri. Scary Scarelli kept his usual seat by the entrance and Jimmy Amicucci remained with the car. The book was becoming small and Danny was still considering whether to bring the Gurino cousins on board.

Danny tapped Kenny on the shoulder and told him to come outside for a private discussion. Once outside, Danny asked if Kenny had seen Dominic lately.

"Monday I was by there. Dropped off his money," Kenny told him.

"How was he?" Danny asked.

"He looks fucked up."

"I asked how he was, not how he looked," Danny said.

"I don't know, okay, I guess."

"You need to go see him and give him a message. Tell him, tonight we're ending the Lissoni problem. Tell him Angelo has his hooks into Fabian and let him know his father said it's time to make a list of new inductees this year. We'll have our ceremony in the fall," Danny explained.

"You want me to go now?" Kenny asked.

"Yes, go now. After that, you stay at the bakery with Angelo."

Danny went back inside and headed for his office where the waiter would deliver his lunch; it was to be served exactly seven minutes after Danny closed the office door behind him. Inside, Danny noticed someone else had arrived. Glenn Conway worked for Doug and Tommy; he ran a lucrative book on the west side. Glenn was appointed by Doug to watch his interests at the bar, an idea that

Danny despised, but was stuck with for now. "Jackie, come on in," Danny called for the veteran bookie. Once in the office, Danny shut the door and turned on the airwave scrambler, which he begrudgingly used for discussions of low level, like gambling and loan-sharking.

"How is this Conway fuck?" Danny asked him.

"He ain't so bad, Danny. He's got a good head for numbers, and he ain't cocky or nothing. I don't think he wants to be here at all," Jackie Beans told him.

"Keep him at arm's length. How's Paul Amevu working out?"

Jackie shrugged his shoulders. "I don't know what you want him to do, but he don't cause no problems."

"He's done a lot of time for this family, Jackie," Danny told him.

"Danny, I come from the same school as you. We were all teenagers when he went away. I know what he's done."

"I'm going to put him up for his button this year. He more than deserves it."

"No argument here, Danny. Hey, I got courtside tonight at the Palace, they're playing Indiana, want to go?" Jackie asked.

Danny's eyes lit up, and then disappointment set in. "I can't. I got some business to take care of tonight. Dammit."

There was a knock on the door and a waiter brought in a steak for Danny. Danny gave the waiter a ten-dollar bill and told Jackie to leave; he ate his lunch alone.

Doug arrived for his meeting in Baghdad with his friend from high school. Doug had been friends with Sami Nasser and his brothers for a long time. In the United States, Sami ran an electronics business that used to supply Doug and his friends with beepers, back in the day. The Nassers moved back to Iraq in the late nineties and stayed in contact with Doug.

Doug and Sami took their seats across from one man who was guarded by several armed men. "So you are this Doug Sullivan, an enemy to your country," the man said.

"Hey, you got this all wrong, pal. I'm no enemy to my country," Doug told him.

"Perhaps my words are wrong, my English is not perfect. Enemy to your government," the man corrected himself.

"That I can live with. We don't really see eye to eye on everything," Doug said.

"How would a criminal like you get out of such a long prison term?"

"How did I get out my ten years? Money, bottom line, money. Everybody has a price," Doug answered.

"It must have been a lot of money," the man said.

"I have a lot of money, so it's okay. And speaking of money, can we get down to business or are there more questions?" Doug asked.

"I do have one more question. What was your business in Paris?"

"My business in Paris? I was meeting your guy there, who, by the way, is a rude son of a bitch," Doug said.

The man laughed, and his guards followed suit. "Yes, he can be that sometimes. Very well, let's get down to business. I understand you can be relied upon to supply weapons?"

"I can be. What sort of weapons?" Doug asked.

"Weapons like you have already used. We need rocket-propelled grenades, like your men used on your beloved Christmas Eve. We need surface-to-air missiles, explosives, guns, everything," the man said.

"Guns and rifles are never a problem. Surface-to-air missiles, SAMs? You're going after planes, and I don't think I can be a part of that. I would need assurances that nothing I sell will be used against civilians or U.S. soldiers."

"Your military is no longer our concern. And we want to protect our civilians, not kill them. What we buy from you will be only used on our enemies," the man said.

"Look, I've made bulk sales before and took them home and sold them to friends there and in New York and in Sicily. With them, I knew what they were using them for. With you, it makes me nervous," Doug explained.

"But I have given you my assurances that what you care about will not be targeted by the weapons you supply. Other than that, what do you care what they are used for? You are a businessman after all, are you not?"

"No, you're right. Give me a number, what do you want?"

"Do you have prices for your merchandise?"

"I didn't come here unprepared," Doug answered.

"Two dozen RPGs and SAMs and five thousand pounds of TNT," the man ordered.

"No guns or rifles?"

"My men are equipped fine."

"They're using old and rusted AK-47s. How is that fine? I'll bet they don't even shoot straight anymore. You just want to blow things up and shoot off your rockets and run and hide. You got enemies? Why not arm your men and go get them. I can get you M-16s, silenced machine guns, night vision goggles, bulletproof vests, all of it," Doug said.

"And who will train my men on such advanced devices?"

Sami answered that one, "I will. I am very familiar with them."

"If I buy your M-16s, will you sell me missiles in the future?" the man asked.

Doug stuck out his hand. "You are a wise man, you understand my concerns. Let's do this deal, start small, and we'll agree to do more business in the near future."

The man shook Doug's hand, and they discussed the terms and transfer of money. Doug and Sami left to return home and were stopped by the usual checkpoint when leaving the city. The Nassers lived about thirty miles outside of Baghdad. "What's a civilian from Michigan doing with an Iraqi?" the sergeant in charge of the checkpoint asked Doug as the other soldiers went through the car.

"Sergeant, there's a lot of Iraqis living in Michigan. My friend here went to high school with me and his parents came back here years later. I'm just seeing an old friend," Doug told him.

"Why the hell does anyone come back here?" he asked Sami.

Doug answered for him, "His father died and his mother wanted to go home. Sergeant, I was here about four or five years ago and I had met a lieutenant, Vernon Cooper. Might you know if he's still around?"

"Colonel Cooper? Shit, he's still here."

"Colonel, eh?" Doug asked himself. Vernon Cooper was Doug's connection years ago to exporting weapons home via military channels. Cooper had gotten very rich from Doug, and Doug believed he must still have a few things going on if he had stayed on for more tours. He made a mental note to stop in and see him before he left for home.

The soldiers gave the car the "all clear," and Doug and Sami were on their way. "Doug, I don't get it. If you're supposed to sell these guys weapons, why not sell them what they want so you can bust them?" Sami asked.

"We want to follow the chain, and I need to earn their trust. If I gave them what they want now, they might think I moved too quick to betray my country, and it could draw suspicion. But if I'm battling them at every corner, then it's more realistic," Doug answered. "The goal is to keep building the order and every step we take, I'm supposed to meet the next boss. The bigger the purchase, the bigger the boss. That's the goal. This is going to go on for a few years, Sami."

"I'm really going to teach these guys how to use an M-16?"

"Yes. Think big picture. These fucking jerk-offs we just met with are nothing. We want to get to the top," Doug told him.

10:00 p.m., Las Vegas: Alberto and Benedetto, the Sicilians entrusted with the hit in Vegas, sat in their car waiting for their targets to arrive. In Sicilian, they went over the plan detail by detail. In Sicily, they had killed many, but this was their chance to show their new boss what they could do. Their new boss had promised money, a job, a place to live, and a chance to put their pasts behind them. Their targets were due to arrive within the next ten minutes, and the duo waited anxiously.

1:00 a.m., Michigan: Tommy Herrick worked out with his punching bag in the basement, waiting for his throwaway phone to ring. Once he got word from Stevie Turner that the hit was complete, he was to call Doug on his satellite phone and then call Danny Serafini. Danny would get word to Nick in prison and call Angelo Rea, who was waiting at Dominic's for word from Danny. "The hit call list," Tommy called it.

Danny stayed awake watching TV, waiting for his phone call, as were Angelo and Dominic, at Dominic's house. Even Nick lay awake in his cell, waiting for a guard to come tell him that Danny was selling his stocks first thing in the morning—their code for all went well.

9:00 a.m., Baghdad: Doug stood outside the Nasser household talking with the neighbors, waiting for his satellite phone to ring. Once the neighbors started complaining about inconsistent electricity and water problems, of course, Doug started contemplating how to help these people and make a fortune in doing so.

10:00 p.m., Las Vegas: Stevie Turner sat with his wife at the blackjack table at the Kajino. Stevie, like everyone else, was anxious for the news on the hit. The zips were instructed to call the one number programmed in the phone when they were on their way out of Vegas. The number was to Noah Brooks's throwaway phone, who would call Stevie. They had done the dry run with the zips several times and showed them where in the desert to bury their guns and the phone.

The last two of John Lissoni's three remaining crew members pulled into the parking lot of the small restaurant three minutes early. They thought they were here to meet with the third member, who was supposed to be getting them some fake IDs.

Armed with the pictures for their fake IDs and the knowledge of what kind of car to look for, the zips spotted Paul Vicoppi and Adam Gapland. They waited for their targets to park, and Benedetto put the car in drive and the car crept forward.

Alberto rolled down the passenger window and readied his silenced submachine gun. He squeezed the trigger and put all six silenced bullets into Adam Gapland's chest, killing him instantly.

The car rolled a few more feet, and Alberto took aim of the driver. Paul Vicoppi wasn't sure what had just happened and was looking around frantically when he also caught six perfectly placed bullets to his chest.

Alberto quickly scanned the area before he told Benedetto to step on it. The silenced weapon worked like a charm; it drew no attention. It was a small restaurant away from the strip and was clear of any witnesses. Alberto told him to go and rolled his window back up. He caressed the rifle and looked at the driver. "I love this gun. We can't bury this."

"Put that down," the driver ordered. "Get that map out."

Alberto put the rifle at his feet. "You don't need a map in this country, just listen to the car. You can't read it anyway." He pulled out the cell phone, and the phone calls began.

"You think they'll let us keep this car?" Benedetto asked in their native language.

"I think they'll give us anything we want. We're very important men now," Alberto said.

Stevie got his phone call from Noah and did his job, which was to call Tommy. He told Tommy that the hit appeared to have gone off perfectly. Stevie had someone listening in on a police scanner in case someone caught a description of the car. If that happened, Noah was to call the zips and tell them to burn the car in the desert and wait for another. After calling Tommy, he returned to the blackjack table to keep his alibi going.

Tommy made his calls and went upstairs for a shower. He found his brother, Billy, in the kitchen talking with his wife. "How fucking long you been here?" he asked Billy.

"Yuck. Why the need to swear there?" Tommy's wife, Val, asked.

"It shows an emphasis on my anger," Tommy told her. He turned to Billy. "It's one in the morning. You here to see me or are you here to see her?"

"Okay, I guess I caught you at a bad time. I'll just see you tomorrow," Billy said.

"Good idea," Tommy told him, as he watched his brother walk out the door. Tommy turned his wife with a big grin. "I love doing that."

"What is your problem? Why do you get so angry at him?" Val asked.

"I'm just playing around. It's what big brothers do, they bully their little brothers. I'm not mad at him at all. In fact, I'm pretty freaking happy."

"What if he wanted something important?"

"Then I think he would've come downstairs and told me instead of hobnobbing with you in the kitchen," Tommy said.

"Why Thomas Herrick, I do believe you're jealous," Val teased.

"Why would I ever be jealous? Every man knows I'll tear off their arms and beat them over their heads with them if anyone even talks to you."

Val's shoulders slumped at the vision of Tommy playing the drums on a man's head, using the man's own arms as the drumsticks. She envisioned her husband with the biggest grin while doing so. *Like an ape in a cartoon,* she instantly thought to herself. "Well, there went that mood. Good night, Tommy."

"What'd I say?" he asked his wife as she went upstairs. "I give her a compliment and look how she acts," Tommy mumbled to himself as he went to shower.

For Danny, Angelo, and Dominic, it meant they could finally go to bed. Doug took his phone call with a grain of salt and went on to the next thing. He had Sami Nasser drive him into the city in search of Colonel Cooper.

In Vegas, the police set out to pick up Noah Brooks for questioning. They didn't have to look far. Noah was at home, hosting a small barbecue with some neighbors.

"For the hundredth time, I don't know these guys. I didn't know that John Lissoni guy personally, and I sure as hell don't know why he was shooting at me," Noah pleaded to the feds who had just taken over the interrogation.

"Who said anything about John Lissoni?" the agent asked him.

"They did," Noah said, pointing to the two-way mirror.

"No, they didn't."

"Knock it off. You can play your fucking tape back."

"Okay, relax. If you don't know John Lissoni or these guys from Michigan, who do you know from Michigan?" the agent asked.

"I don't know anyone from there," Noah answered.

"No? What about Steve Turner?"

Oh shit! Noah thought. "Steve Turner? What about him? He's not from Michigan."

"Am I really supposed to believe that one? Noah, you're not fooling anyone," the agent told him.

"Just to get you off my back, I'll give you this. I left Chicago to try and make some money out here. A friend of mine told me bouncing at the hot clubs was very lucrative. This guy talked to that guy, and so forth and I was given a job. My boss was Steve Turner. I assumed he was from Chicago. The guy don't talk much, never about anything personal, that's for sure," Noah explained.

"What kind of orders did he give at the club? It was a topless bar, correct?"

"Top of the line. Turner had me toss people out, make sure the girls weren't in any danger, shit like that."

"Not those kind of orders. Money, anything like that?" the agent asked.

"Yeah, he paid me. You think this guy's connected? I gave him my respect because I was out here on someone's good word. The girls barely listened to him," Noah said, hoping he was throwing the feds off the track.

"Who do you report to in Chicago?"

"If you want to go down that road, I'll ask for my lawyer. Give you guys an inch and you fuck it all up. I'll talk to you about this Lissoni guy and his buddies, and even about this silly Steve Turner theory, but that's it, folks."

"How did you know they were buddies?"

Noah grunted, "On second thought, I think I'd rather shoot myself than do this with you. I'll invoke my right to a lawyer now. You're just too annoying to even play the game with." Hours later, Noah would be released with no charges.

Alberto and Benedetto stopped in the desert to bury their guns and cell phone. They buried them a good three hundred yards from the road. Their next stop would be in Utah, where they would meet with Stevie Turner's cousin, abandon their car, and drive to Michigan with him. Their timing in Michigan was to coincide with the arrival of ten more zips, who obviously, Alberto and Benedetto believed they were going to be the boss of.

Nick Amicucci took his news of the successful hit and stayed up talking with his cellmate, Eddie Turco. "My father was even the godfather to John Lissoni's dad, Bobby. That's how close we were. I feel so bad for the family. Bobby's older sister used to babysit me, it tears me up," Nick confessed.

"I never met Jerry or Tommy Lissoni. They were cousins to John, is that right?" Eddie asked.

"Yeah. The family's a fucking tragedy. All my family's rolling over in their graves. And Bobby Lissoni lives two blocks from my house. His wife came over my house and yelled at my wife for being Dominic's mom. How did it ever come to this?" Nick asked.

"Everything changes. I never thought I'd be doing sixty-five years while my brother's doing thirty. But I was lucky. I got my kid out of it before he took any lumps with the feds, real lucky. And with your kid, Dominic, you can bitch and moan about everything he's done wrong, but he's done what you asked, Nick. He's kept the Amicuccis in power. You got to treat the Lissonis as a result of that. It's something that had to happen for you to stay in power. That's nothing to bust yourself up about. Jerry Lissoni did rebel against the family, nobody gets a pass for that," Eddie counseled.

"The next part is to whack the kid of the man I made my bones with, a kid I've treated like my own, raised him with my son. I love that kid. I'm still in shock that Fabian was able to fool us all for all these years, all these of years plotting," Nick said.

"It's a hard life. It's not for the weak, that's for sure."

CHAPTER XVIII

Electricity

THE PAY PHONE rang, and Danny Serafini stepped out of the car to answer it. Danny and his driver, Jimmy Amicucci, drove a half hour's distance toit. "Morning, Nick," Danny answered.

"Time for the weekly update," Nick said to his underboss.

"Its official, Eddie Batts is retired," Danny said, refering to the retirement of New York's Grazzitti Family's boss, Eddie Battaglia.

"I heard, Bruno Bini is his replacement? Who the fuck is that?" Nick asked . . .

"How've you heard already?"

"There's a guy from their family in here, I found out first thing. I got better access to information in here than I've ever had on the streets," Nick boasted. "Even he don't know who this Bruno Bini is."

"It's Eddie's son-in-law. I guess finding out firsthand doesn't give the best info though, does it?"

"His son-in-law, huh? He wasn't even a captain?" Nick asked.

"Nope, just some poor schmuck that married the boss' daughter," Danny answered.

"And of course, Vito's bent all out of shape that he wasn't picked," Nick said.

"Of course, and he wants us to take out Bruno, so he can be boss. I told you before, he's willing to set us free for it."

"My grandfather married Vito Paganini's aunt, so we're related, but make no mistake about it, Danny, he is a slippery motherfucking worm. You remember, he didn't live this life. He went to college. He was never in the muscle end, started in stocks. He is in it for the money, that's his motivation. And you know how to deal with them people," Nick said.

"Blind them with greed."

"You got to remember, he was the liaison to Eddie Batts when we were making our move. Take Vito out of the equation, we go to Eddie Batts ourselves. Its Eddie Batts we owe, not Vito. Vito made his name off our name. He was fine with his stocks, but we gave him the muscle and the clout to move up and be named a capo."

"No arguments here, but do we take this guy out or don't we?" Danny asked.

"We will, but under our rules. You can't give Vito one ounce of leverage over you. You have to make him think you don't want to do this, that there's too much risk in it for us. And we're definitely not killing Eddie's son-in-law while Eddie's alive," Nick said.

"What if its years?" Danny asked.

"My guy in here says Eddie won't last the year, but if it takes ten years, then sorry, Vito, it'll take ten years. And he concedes any claims to any of our rackets. And he sells his fucking house here and minds his own business in the Big Apple."

"Anything else?"

"Yeah, he needs to get some assurances from his own captains and then the other families. He needs to do this right if he wants us to do it. We're not going to go to war with New York because of Vito fucking Paganini. Does Doug have the zips here yet?" Nick asked, referencing the Sicilian hit men that Doug had recruited.

"Tomorrow night. Four apartments, three men each, all have jobs and temporary citizenships," Danny explained.

"Okay, what about Carmine Mattea's parole?" Nick asked about the old boss' son.

"Parole denied. He'll be out in two years anyway. The feds hang their paroles like some big fucking carrot, but it's like eighty-five percent of your term is gone. You don't get parole, so the fuck what? Two more years, no problem," Danny complained.

"State prison is a lot better for parole. Your parole got denied too when you were in, didn't it? A little bitter?" Nick joked.

"What else is on the agenda?" Danny asked, dead serious.

"What are you fucking kidding me? What's your fucking problem? Danny, I'm the one doing the twenty years, take a minute, have a laugh. You're getting too serious in your old age," Nick said.

"The job sucks. It isn't like before, there's no one left. It used to be you, me, and Denny, every day. Now, they're all fucking kids. And I got to sit there, right in the fucking middle and wait for the feds to make a case that I got to let them make because no one else is even halfway competent. No offense to your son, he was just too young."

"I know it sucks, but it's hopefully for just another twelve years, that's all," Nick said.

Finally, Danny laughed. "That's if you make parole, but at least if you don't, I know it will be only a few more years."

"Okay, so Carmine Mattea didn't make parole. Where does that leave Jack Mattea? I'd like to have the Gurino boys in our crew," Nick said.

"Well, we said, if Carmine makes parole, we wouldn't let the boys transfer, just in case they were using them for information. Without Carmine, I don't think Jack's a problem, but that could change when Carmine does get out," Danny said.

"I agree. Anything else out there?" Nick asked.

"Louis Rubilla," Danny said.

"Who's that?"

"He works for Doug Napier, over in Frankie Jagge's crew, selling guns," Danny told him.

"What about him?"

"He's been selling guns to Fabian on the sly since 2008. Probably even supplied Jerry Lissoni and Lenny Silesi in their revolt against Dominic," Danny explained.

"Who's says that, Vinny Jag?" Nick asked.

"Yeah, Doug Napier came to Vinny's kid, Frankie about it. Says he just found out, someone just mentioned it in conversation like it was common knowledge."

"Guns, eh? He's probably supplied his troops in Mexico. It might be time to start taking action against Fabian's guys. Keep a tail on this Rudilla and set up a plan for the zips to take him out," Nick ordered.

"At the least, it'll eliminate Fabian's access to weapons," Danny said.

"I'd be willing to bet he's got others. I want to see how he reacts. I bet he runs."

"Why would we want him to run? Right now we know exactly where he's at?" Danny asked.

"Obviously, when he runs, he'll run to his assets in Mexico. He'll just lead us to who we've got to kill," Nick explained. "Danny, I've got to go, the guard's waving me down," Nick said before he ended the call.

Doug Sullivan entered the office. "Now that you're a colonel, I can't get an appointment?"

Colonel Vernon Cooper stood and gave Doug a handshake. "Well, you are persistent. What in the name of God would bring you back here?"

Doug shrugged his shoulders. "Money, what else?"

"What's your angle?"

"Electricity," Doug answered.

"What about it?" the colonel asked.

"Where I'm staying, the electricity works only intermittingly," Doug told him.

"What do you mean, intermittingly?"

Doug looked at the colonel like he was an idiot. "Intermittent, it doesn't stay on consistently."

"I understand the word, Doug, I don't understand what you want," Colonel Cooper said.

"I want to know why the electricity doesn't stay on."

"Who are you to question me?" the colonel asked with resentment in his voice.

"Jesus Christ, I'm not questioning you. I want to know so I can fix it," Doug answered.

"Fix it? The United States cannot keep electricity flowing through the country, but you think you can?"

"That's what I'd like to know. All work like that is done from government contracts? Private contractors can't just make a deal with the Iraqis, is that right?" Doug asked.

"What is it that you want to do?"

"I'd like to put a power plant up and start connecting it to local towns or however the hell it works, and be the top electrical producer in the country. Obviously, it'd be like starting from square one," Doug answered.

"It's just not that simple," the colonel told Doug.

"Thus, the reason I come to you. Make it simple for me, who do I got to see?"

"Like I said, it's not that simple."

"Just tell me who I got to talk to about getting a government contract and I'll get you a nice finder's fee," Doug offered.

"Doug, there's a system already in place. The companies already have gotten the contracts, there's nothing else to do."

"Wow, they sure are doing a bang-up job. Let me guess, this is our taxpayer dollars hard at work in Iraq, right? There's no one even working on it, and you're saying it's all done. These companies got their money from our government, paid for by the schmuck citizens, did this not even half-ass job and bolted. Job done, right?"

"You don't see the big picture. These animals don't want us here. There's only so much security we can provide, and companies don't want their workers getting kidnapped or blown up."

"I'll take care of my own security, I wouldn't want the military's help," Doug said.

"You think you can provide better security than the U.S. military?"

"In this case, yes. Instead of you and me debating who can do what, why don't you just give me someone to talk to?"

"Someone you need to talk is me, and like I've been telling you, there's a bigger picture here," the colonel said.

"I heard you. How about this for a big picture: what company do you think of when you think electricity?" Doug asked.

"General Electric," Colonel Cooper answered.

"Exactly. I want to be General Electric," Doug said.

"I don't see it happening, Doug."

Doug sighed, "Look, Vern, I was hoping you could point me in the right direction. I wasn't seeking your approval. You see, I'm doing this, and since we've done business before, I thought I'd give you an opportunity. But fuck it, I'll just go around you. Maybe I'll make a stop at the embassy and see which of those greedy fucks wants to make tens of millions of dollars."

"You're in over your head, Doug. Companies like Sundromeda can't be bullied by the mob, they work with places like the Pentagon. They have civilian and military contracts."

"You're right they probably can't be bullied, but they can be bought. Everyone has a price, Colonel Cooper. You've had one in the past and I'll bet you have one now, just name it. You can be involved or you can be left out in the cold," Doug explained.

Vernon Cooper took a moment to stare down at the man sitting across from him. "Hypothetically speaking, what would my cut be?"

"Welcome back, Vern. But you're still not getting it. I'm not looking for a partnership with you, just like before, I'm offering a life-changing finder's fee."

"You get me ten million dollars and I'll get you a chance to offer a bid. You'll be denied, but whatever company you've submitted your bid with will have their name in the hat for next time," the colonel responded with.

"Ten million dollars to be denied? Who the fuck do you think you're dealing with?" Doug asked with disgust.

"It's the best I can do. Like I said, there's a system already in place."

"Your system sucks. Vern, I'm going to go now. It was nice to see you again," Doug said as he turned around to leave.

"What are you going to do?" Cooper asked, knowing Doug didn't give up this easily.

"Me? I'm going to find a way to fix your fuckups and make some money in the process. Good luck to you and Sundromeda."

"Doug, don't do anything stupid. You don't know what you're dealing with here."

"It's you who doesn't know what you're dealing with here," Doug said as he shut the door behind him.

Paulie Bankjob noticed someone at the grave he was approaching. It looked like an old woman from behind; it looked like she had been here for a while. She was two graves away from where Paulie was going, the grave of Nicodemo Amicucci. Finally, he could see the grave she was at and knew who she was. The grave belonged to Nick's father, Dominic, and the woman must be Nick's mother. "Helen?" he asked.

She turned around and searched her memory for the man that stood in front of her. Finally, she remembered, he was her deceased husband's father's driver long ago. She had heard that Paul Amevu had attended Charley's funeral but that he had come late and Helen had already left. "Paul? Is that you?" The man she remembered that always followed her husband's father around looked like a football player. This man was more than a few inches shorter. He had the remnants of a once-in-shape body, but time had taken its toll on this man.

"Yeah, I'm sorry I missed you at Charley's funeral," he answered.

"Oh my, how you've changed! The last time I saw you was at your daughter's wedding. What are you doing now? Where are you living? How's your daughter?"

"I'm living with her, in her basement. She's doing great, her kids are great, I couldn't be prouder," Paulie beamed.

"That's terrific. Where are you going, Nicodemo's?"

"Yes. I like to come here. It's like the one place that hasn't changed. You must be the one that keeps the fresh flowers at all the graves?"

"There's no one else to. Ziggy's wife, Hillary, used to help until they moved to Florida. My daughter, Marie, comes with me a lot, she's going to have to take over after I'm gone," Helen said.

"I still can't believe George Rea's doing life. Marie's done a fine job, Angelo's turned out good," Paulie said.

"That Georgie was such a good boy. He and Nick and Danny, they were inseparable. I was so delighted when George and Marie started dating. I always said George was the smartest of them," Helen said.

"Yeah, George was a good kid. There's a bright future out there for Angelo, he's got Rea and Amicucci blood."

"Too bad he's an idiot. No one has listened to what Nicodemo wanted. He didn't want Ray and Ziggy in that life—he wanted his American-born boys to go to college. He only wanted the oldest son of his oldest son to enter the life. That meant, my son, Nick, was to be the last one, the last Amicucci to live in that world. But now there's my grandson Dominic, in the life. There's my grandson, Angelo, in the life. Even Ziggy's grandson, Little Jimmy, is in it now. This isn't the way my husband's father wanted it," Helen complained.

"Jack's kids never got involved?" Paulie asked about Nicodemo's second son, Giacomo.

"Involved? Hell no, they moved away, just like Ziggy's other children. All of Nicodemo's children went to jail except for my husband. Jack died there, Ray's going to die there, and Ziggy spent seven years behind bars. Nick has to spend another fifteen years away. What do you think's going to happen to Dominic and Angelo? Prison, that's what. Poor Marie, she and I raised Dominic—he's like a son to her. Both her children will join her husband and brother in jail. It's become such a shame. My husband died young, he died while Marie was still pregnant with Angelo. He never would've let Angelo be in this life. He probably wouldn't have let Dominic either—they could have been so much more."

"So why did Nick let them?"

Helen straightened up with pride as she spoke, "My son reached a height the rest of them never even thought about, to be the boss. My husband, his brothers, his father, all of them, spoke in such awe of men that were above them in rank, never in their wildest thoughts would they have put themselves in such a position. My son came into a power only great men have held, and I believe it caused him to lose sight of some things in order to preserve his power. It's happened to kings."

"No. When I came out of the prison the first time, right before my daughter's wedding, Dominic was already on his path. He was delivering bread, that's how they train them. It's step one, collecting money," Paulie informed her.

Helen seemed to contemplate it before responding. "You're wrong, Dominic wasn't involved until Nick moved up."

"I'm sure you're right then, my time frame is off, I'll bet," Paulie said, letting the woman keep her satisfaction.

"I blame that Raymond. He's the one that started with the defiance. He wanted to be like his older brothers, Dominic and Giacomo. Ziggy would've followed Ray anywhere, so this became his life because that's what Ray wanted. If Ray would've listened to his father, I have no doubt Dominic would not be in this life."

Paulie scratched his head—that made no sense to him. "He always was different," he said, placating her desperate need to justify Dominic's involvement in the life.

"You know who Ray got along with? That creepy Jerry Lissoni that tried to kill my grandson, that's who. The Lissonis were like family, but that boy was just plain bad from the start. He used to leave people's gates open so their dogs would run away. Who does that? But he and Ray could talk for hours with each other. Anyone else, they just sat quiet."

"Well, Nicodemo was like a father to me, and he complained a lot about how Ray dragged Ziggy into the life. He always said Ray was different than his other boys. He thought Ray was completely empty of feelings while Ziggy was too sensitive. Jerry Lissoni was the same as Ray, just a mean person, and I'll bet he dragged his younger brother, Tommy, into it too. I understand what you're saying. How about we change the subject? I don't see a car here, how'd you get here?" Paulie asked.

"I take a cab when I want to be alone. My eyes are no good for driving anymore."

"I don't like to drive either. I hate the cars nowadays. You have to put it in drive from the middle of the seats. What was so wrong with it on the steering wheel? I can't get used to it. And all the gimmicks these things have now. The cars talk, they tell you where to go, the cars decide when the headlights turn on. I just want to drive. Plus, they're all plastic and there's no trunk room anymore. The world has passed me by. People walk around talking to themselves with invisible phones. Do you have one of these cell phones? How do you call a cab from here to pick you up? I could give you a ride," offered Paulie.

"There's a café a few block from here I like to walk to. I call a cab from there."

"Want some company today?"

"Sure," Helen answered.

Billy Herrick pulled into the apartment complex with the two zips, Alberto and Benedetto and parked the car. He turned to his passenger. "Guess what? This is where you fucking live."

Billy got out, and the other two followed, looking around at their surroundings. "You're going to be living with another guy, his name is Franco. You've got your IDs, and Monday you start your jobs, traveling salesmen."

Inside the apartment, both men were in awe at the big screen TV that was supplied for them. "It's a fucking TV, come on, guys," Billy told them.

I expected y," "Does this come from your satellite?" Benedetto, the older of the two asked.

"No, Japan," Billy answered. "Check out the running water too."

Benedetto said something to Alberto in Sicilian, and Alberto laughed. Billy took offense. "What the fuck was that? What'd he say?" he asked Alberto.

"I told him, you think we are cavemen. I understand your running water joke," Benedetto told him.

"We are very important men now," Alberto said. "We want money and our own car."

"You can go fuck yourself, that's how important you are to me. You'll get your car and some money to go shopping tomorrow. I'll send over some fucking gofer in the morning. The other guys will be here tomorrow night, and you get to meet Franco. Until then, enjoy your fucking TV, the fridge is full, cook yourselves some spaghetti and have a blast. Bon fucking voyage," Billy said on the way out the door.

Benedetto looked at Alberto. "I do not understand this man. What are we going to do with a gopher?"

Tommy Herrick looked over the handmade dollhouse with admiration. He had paid a woodworker to build him a huge dollhouse for his daughter's fourth birthday, which was two months away. Five feet tall and five feet wide, all handcrafted wood, it was a beauty. "You outdid yourself," Tommy told the builder.

"Thank you. I'll hook up the electricity and decorate it. I'll be done in a month."

"What about the secret compartment?" Tommy asked.

The dollhouse was built on a six-inch base. The builder removed the staircase from the dollhouse and revealed a tiny hole, highly unlikely to be noticed if you weren't looking for it. He took out a pen and pressed the tip against the tiny hole and an unseen drawer emerged from the bottom.

"Perfect. Eight grand, right?" Tommy asked.

"Yeah, paid at completion."

Tommy's satellite phone rang. "Excuse me, I've got to take this. I'll talk to you soon." Tommy answered the phone while walking out of the shop. "Hey, Doug," he greeted.

"Tommy, I need to find out everything you can about a company called Sundromeda. It's an electrical company the government uses in Iraq," Doug explained.

"Why don't you get your CIA buddies to work on this? I got a lot going on here," Tommy said.

"I don't want the CIA to know what I'm doing. I've got my agreement with them, and I'll abide by it to the letter, but that's it. They want something from me, and I want something from them. There's no partnership here, Tommy. Start looking around for viable electrical companies that can do overseas work. We'll have to start buying some up. I'll talk to you later," Doug said and hung up.

"What the fuck is he up to now?" Tommy asked himself as he got in his car.

Stevie Turner waited for the red light to turn green at the intersection. He was on his way to meet with Yamamoto and deliver the bad news to the majority owner of the Kajino casino, that he was out and would have to sell his shares. The light turned green, and

Stevie waited for two cars to go before he made his left. As always, he watched his rearview mirror to see who else turned left and noticed a dark Chevy Impala two cars back which he had noticed earlier in the day. Stevie spotted a burger joint to the right, so he quickly hit the gas and crossed the two lanes into its parking lot. He spun his head to watch the Impala and see what he does. The Impala hit its brakes, but kept going.

Not one hundred percent sure if it was an FBI tail or not, Stevie called Yamamoto and told him he was going to be late. Stevie took the long way to the diner where he was supposed to meet him and parked across the street when he arrived. He called Yamamoto and changed the meeting place. He told him to meet him at a strip mall, two miles down the road. Stevie watched Yamamoto exit the diner and get in his car. Stevie tailed him to the new meet, and as far as Stevie could tell, Yamamoto had no tail.

Yamamoto, oblivious to being followed by Stevie, was startled when Stevie knocked on his window. "Get out, let's go for a walk," Stevie ordered.

Once they started walking, Stevie delivered the news. "You're out. I've got a buyer for your shares."

"Why? I have followed your rules and not warned your enemies of your knowledge of them," Yamamoto argued.

"And for that, you get to live. And live well, if I might add. You'll walk away with forty million."

"Forty? I invested seventy-five million dollars. You are not a man of your word, Mr. Turner. You told me I could remain in position."

"I told you could remain a minority owner if you helped us catch Lissoni and his crew, you did not help in catching them. You get to live for not tipping them off, I'm keeping my word. I also told you if you run to the feds, you'll die. You can bet, my word stands strong on that too. You'll receive sixty million dollars for your shares, and you'll siphon off a third of that to an overseas account which I will control, leaving you with your forty million," Stevie explained.

"And I lose thirty-five million dollars, not very fair, Mr. Turner."

"You're worth half a billion dollars, you'll be fine. Make the sale and go the fuck back to Japan and enjoy your life. I'm under orders to report if I don't believe you're going to be cooperative, and I must say, I don't believe you are. I'm sure I don't have to explain how my bosses react when they feel threatened, do I?"

"No, I'm quite aware of the savagery of your bosses, Mr. Turner. The sale of my shares will most likely tip off Fabian Bosca that something has changed though," warned Yamamoto.

"We'll take care of Fabian, you take care of Yamamoto. It's what you do best. There'll be a lawyer stopping by your office on Monday, he'll have the paperwork. Good-bye, Mr. Yamamoto," Stevie said before going back to his car.

CHAPTER XIX

THE DAY FROM HELL

DANNY SERAFINI WAS in his kitchen talking with his wife and daughter, who had stopped by to take Danny's wife shopping, when his throwaway phone rang. Right after saying hello, he heard Nick's angry voice. "What the fuck is going on with Paulie Bankjob?"

"What?" Danny asked.

"This motherfucker really thinks he's going to fuck my mom?"

"What are you talking about?"

"I just talked to my mother—she was at my father's grave yesterday, and Paulie was going to my grandfather's. He ends up taking my mom to lunch, in the fucking public. He asked her out at my father's fucking grave, Danny!" Nick hollered into the phone.

Nick's voice was loud enough for Bianca and Sabrina to hear, and they turned their heads to Danny. Danny walked out the sliding door into his backyard to have his conversation. "Nick, I'm sure it's purely innocent. Who else do they have to talk to?"

"My mother can talk to your parents—they live three blocks away. And I don't give a fuck if it's innocent or not, people fucking talk.

I don't want people saying my mother's out dating at her age. You better have a talk with Paulie," Nick ordered.

"Okay, I will. I wanted to put him up for membership this year," Danny said.

"You want to put him up for membership? I'm a hair away from ordering him whacked," Nick said.

"Oh, come on. Your mother used to babysit him, you're not being rational. This guy's done forty years for the family and you talk of whacking him over lunch with your mother."

Nick was silent a moment. "If anything happens between them two, I'm holding you personally responsible. And if you really want to make this fucking failed bank robber, you better make damn sure he understands that the rule of not messing around with another made man's wife applies to my fucking mom. Capische?"

"Yes."

"If he fucks with my mother, I'll hang him by his balls, cut his stomach open, and let him bleed out, you fucking understand?"

"Nick, nothing will happen, you have my word," Danny told him.

"It better fucking not," Nick said and hung up.

Danny went back to join his wife and daughter in the kitchen. "Hey, Danny, Helena just called. Nick's brother's over there, all pissed off because his daughter went on a date with a gangster and that weirdo, Paulie Bankjob, is sleeping with his mom. What the hell is going on?" Bianca asked.

"This can't be happening," Danny mumbled to himself as he walked through his house to the front door, grabbing his keys in the process.

"Where are you going?" his wife asked.

"To go deal with these Amicuccis, they're not normal," Danny answered.

"Hey, Dad, if Valentina's there, tell her to call me," his daughter, Sabrina, added.

"You know, I'm kind of missing my prison cell right now," Danny said to his family before leaving.

Danny drove around the block and pulled into the driveway of the house that was right behind his. As soon as he entered the Amicucci house, Nick's brother started right in on him. "I told you at Charley's funeral that thug was after my daughter," Daniel Amicucci complained.

"And I told you he ain't no thug," Danny said.

"I don't want my daughter involved with . . ." Daniel said before cutting off with a finger being pounded into his chest.

"I don't want to hear about it. Rocco DiNapolli's a good kid. You ever talk to him? He's got manners and morals, he's got integrity. Those are rare traits for any young man of this day and age. Speaking as a father, Daniel, I'd feel safe if my daughter was with him. And I'm sorry I called Marie dorky, it's not what I meant. Your daughter's a smart girl, she does right, she ain't out partying and shit like that. That's what I meant, it just came out that way. Marie's a smart girl. I think you should trust her judgments and let her decide who's good for her," Danny said.

"And if he dies or goes to jail, what then?"

"Like I said, she'll know if it's the life for her. She's been around it all her life, she's fully aware of the damages prison can do to a family. Trust her, Daniel."

"And this Paulie Bankjob, what the—"

Danny held up his and cut off Nick's brother. "I will not hear you speak a bad word about that man. He's seventy years old and your mother's eighty, what the hell is wrong with you guys?" Danny asked. The question drew a laugh from Nick's wife, Helena, who was watching the whole thing.

"My mother's seventy-seven."

"Whatever the fuck," Danny said.

"I don't like the way you're talking to me, Danny," Daniel said.

"When you were fourteen years old and got arrested for stealing that car, who'd you call?" Danny asked his best friend's brother, who was ten years their junior.

"You," he answered.

"And who swore to never tell your parents or Nick, and kept that promise?"

"You did."

"And who got you that Corvette for your prom?" Danny asked.

"You did."

"And saved you from getting your ass beaten by those four guys when you were twenty, and kept it a secret?"

"Okay, you did."

"So don't tell me how to and how not to talk to you. How many Sundays I eat dinner at your mother's kitchen table? More than I can count. I'm not going to let some scumbag play games with her. When your mom was a teenager, she used to babysit Paulie. They're from the same day and age. There's nothing going on there but reminiscing with someone who can reminisce with you. The way you Amicucci's think is crazy. I mean Paulie used to drive for your grandfather, you should think of him as family. Don't forget, the man's done forty years in jail without telling on your grandfather, or your father, or your brother. That should be worth something in your book."

Daniel nodded his head. "Okay, but I don't know how Nick's going to take it."

Danny laughed. "I've already found out how. Now, if you guys will excuse me, I'm going to have a quick word with Paulie Bankjob."

Danny gave Helena a hug good-bye, and she whispered, "You handled that very well. I didn't know you were this good at solving everyone's problems."

He laughed. "It's getting to be second nature. You just tell Dominic to get himself well and get back to work."

"Danny, I'm not sure he's coming back," Helena told him.

"Haven't you talked to him?" Daniel asked.

"Talked to him, what? I'm here every Sunday, he don't come by. He don't call, he's supposed to be taking care of his face," Danny pleaded.

Daniel answered, "He's got that Michelle girl living with him, he's in love. They've been to my house."

"What?" Danny asked, totally puzzled.

"I don't know if it's love, I think she's just taking care of him," Helena said.

"What?" he asked again.

"I must say, Danny, if this incident has shown him the way out of the life, I hope you'd respect that," Helena said. "It doesn't have to be too late for him. Although, he'll never love a girl like he did Angela."

"That's for sure," Daniel said.

"I always ask about him. I don't understand," Danny said. He pointed to the backyard. "My backyard's right there. How do I not know any of this?"

"Maybe the same reasons you don't know that Paulie Bankjob is dating my mom," Daniel joked.

"I'm done here," Danny proclaimed, throwing his arms in the air and walking out the door.

Danny called Angelo from his phone once he was on the road. "If I ask you how is Dominic, what would you tell me?"

"I'd say he's getting better every day, why?" Angelo asked.

"How would you say his progress is?" Danny asked.

"Night and day from before, I mean, he can talk, somewhat," Angelo answered.

"You don't think that's something relevant to say when I ask how he's doing? I was under the impression he was practically bedridden. Why doesn't he go to Sunday dinners?"

"He has to wear sunglasses to cover his black eyes, still. His nose is crooked, he don't want to be in family photos like that," Angelo said.

"Any reason he hasn't contacted me? It sounds like he's avoiding me."

"No, he's just getting better," Angelo answered.

"Anything else I should know?" Danny asked.

"Not that I can think of, Danny," Angelo said.

"Nothing about the girl?"

"Oh, the girl."

"Angelo, either you're lying to me or that Fat fucking Kenny really is the smartest out of you guys."

"I haven't lied to you," he said.

"There's something you need to tell me. Stay at the bakery until I get there," Danny said.

"I'm here every day until four o'clock. You don't think you'll be here in the next six hours?" Angelo asked.

"Just don't leave early."

"I wasn't planning on it," Angelo said.

"You know what, Angelo? Wait for me in the parking lot," Danny ordered, annoyed with his captain.

"Fine, how far away are you?" he asked.

"I'm one fucking minute away," Danny said, although his drive is usually thirty minutes.

"Come on, Danny, it's twelve degrees out there," Angelo complained.

"If you're not in that parking lot when I arrive, I'll have to drive to Pennsylvania and see your daddy in prison, so that I can personally apologize for the beating I put on his only fucking child," Danny hissed.

"I'll be out there," Angelo conceded.

It took Danny forty-five minutes to get there; he was sure to take as long as possible and make young Angelo suffer. When Danny pulled into the parking lot, he was pleased to see that Angelo listened and waited outside. Danny exited his car and walked up to Angelo. "This is your one fucking chance to tell me what's going on with Dominic. Lie to me now and we're done."

"What do you want to know?" Angelo asked.

"Is he talking about not coming back? Because I don't want this fucking job, Angelo. So if he's planning on changing his life, someone better fucking tell me."

"Honestly, Danny, he doesn't say that. He doesn't even ask anymore about what's going on. He asks if we've clipped Fabian yet, but that's all," Angelo answered.

"I know he's been to his Uncle Daniel's house with that girl. I know he's not laid up. I feel like he's jerking me the fuck around here," Danny said.

"Danny, you're like an uncle to him, to me too. He's not doing anything to try to hurt you. He's in a bad place right now," Angelo told him.

"A bad place? It sounds like he's living it up."

"He's not living it up. I don't know what's wrong with him. He'll snap out of it. He went into a funk after Angela got killed, but he snapped out of that," Angelo said.

"Or did he? Angelo, if you really care about your cousin, you won't keep secrets from me. I can't let him have a total meltdown, this has to stop now. If he wants out, fine, but his head needs to be clear to make a decision like that. Come on, we're going over there," Danny ordered.

"I can't leave, Gary's at a store, meeting an owner," Angelo said.

"Is there a problem?" Danny asked.

"Cicirelli's Market decreased our footage on our shelves. Gary went to see why," Angelo answered.

"Why would we lose any space? We've been there forty years."

"These things happen. Maybe another bakery came in with a lower price. Who knows?"

"No, these things don't happen. It's never happened, not to us. I fucking told you not to fuck this up. Goddammit, I've been here since I was a teenager, and we've never once lost one fucking foot. I could strangle you," Danny said.

"What am I supposed to do? You want me to strong-arm this guy? Make him run to the feds?" Angelo asked.

"I really thought you were coming into your own, man I was wrong. We've never lost any footage because we offer the best bread at the best price with the best service, we don't need to strong-arm anyone. Above all the betting and everything else, this can never ever change. It's business 101, Angelo. You call Gary and tell him whatever the competitor's price is, we won't even match it, we'll beat it, no questions asked. And if Gary thinks he's going to get tough with old man Cicirelli, they'll find his body floating in the Detroit River."

"Old man Cicirelli died when you were away. His son's running it now. Maybe he just doesn't know what he's doing," Angelo said.

"Then you have to find out," Danny told him.

"That's why Gary's going over there, everything's under control, Danny."

"Next time go yourself, every customer is that important, Angelo. And don't act like it's no big deal, this bakery is your heritage, treat it like it," Danny said.

"Hey, speaking of heritage, Paulie Bankjob's not dating my grandma, is he? I just saw her on Sunday," Angelo said.

Danny sighed, "They just had lunch, it wasn't a date. I can't believe how fast that rumor fucking spread. Who told you?"

"I ain't no rat, Danny. I think it's good Grandma has someone to talk to," Angelo said.

"Fucking finally someone can see how harmless it was," Danny said. "Let me know about Cicirelli's," Danny ordered and left to see Paulie at Cooch's Corner, just a few blocks away.

Danny walked into the bar and surveyed the room. Paulie was sitting at a table with Jackie Beans. Danny walked over and picked up Jackie's glass and took a whiff. After smelling no alcohol, he put it back down and took a seat.

"It's Pepsi, Danny," Jackie told him.

Danny ignored the answer. "Where's Kenny?"

"It's the last Friday of the month, I'd imagine he's out collecting," Jackie said.

Danny put his hand to his head, he had forgotten. "Its five minutes to noon and this has already been one hell of a day. These Amicuccis got me running around so much, I forgot we're counting money today. Paulie, let me have a word in my office."

"What's up, Danny?" Paulie asked once they were alone.

"Two things, first one, I'm putting you up for membership in the fall," Danny informed him.

"Oh my god, really?" Paulie asked, completely surprised.

"You've earned it," Danny answered.

"I swear my eternal loyalty," Paulie said as he grabbed Danny's hand and tried to kiss his ring.

Danny pulled his hand back. "This ain't no movie, Paulie. We don't kiss rings around here. I will take you up on the loyalty, though. Paulie, I need you to look me in the eye and tell me what your intentions with Helen Amicucci are?"

Paulie was taken totally off guard. "What?"

"Don't fucking what me, Paulie. What are your intentions?"

"I don't have any," he answered. "We went to lunch yesterday, I saw her at Big Dom's grave."

"There are some very unbalanced people who might think lunch is more than just lunch, her sons being one example," Danny said.

Paulie's jaw dropped. "Nick? Nick thinks I'm with his mother? Danny, I'd never, I swear on my own wife's soul, may she rest in peace."

"Say no more, I get it. Just keep one thing in mind, you fuck up with that woman and my life's on the line," Danny told him.

"Look, I was just being nice—she was going to take a cab. I'm only seventy—she's got seven or eight years on me. I'm going to take my button and get me some young tail," Paulie joked.

There was a knock at the door. "That's my lunch, you got to go now. You just keep your nose clean and you'll get your finger pricked this year."

"I can't thank you enough, Danny. How ever many years I got left, I devote them to you."

"Okay, okay, let my food in. Stop thanking me, it's your due from forty years of jail," Danny told him.

After lunch, Danny left to visit Dominic. Within ten minutes, Danny pulled into Dominic's driveway and noticed Kenny's truck there. "Motherfucker," he said to himself as he got off his car. He opened the old gate and entered the backyard, and he instantly smelled barbecue.

Fat Kenny was at the grill, barbecuing some steaks and baked potatoes. His heart dropped when he saw Danny walking toward him wearing a scowl from hell. "Hey, Danny, I'm just in between collections right now. You want a steak?"

Danny patted Kenny on the back. "No. It's good to see you're out enjoying the beautiful day. They say it might even be down to fifty degrees by next week." He opened the door wall and walked into the kitchen.

"Four o'clock at the Malibu Inn, right, Danny?" Kenny asked.

Danny stopped and turned around. "Yes, Kenny, four o'clock at the Malibu Inn. I'll see you there to count." Danny's deadpan response terrified Kenny worse than if Danny had started screaming at him.

Michelle entered the kitchen right after Danny shut the door wall behind him. "Oh hi, Danny. I was just making a salad for lunch, you hungry?"

"No, I already had lunch. Where's Dominic?" he asked, trying to contain the anger that was building.

"He's in the basement," she answered.

"Thanks," he said and walked down the stairs to the basement.

Dominic sat in a recliner watching his big screen TV; he started to get up when he saw Danny.

"No, don't get up," he said, waving for Dominic to stay in the chair. "What are you watching?"

Dominic looked at Danny, waiting for him to yell. "*SportsCenter*," he finally said through his clenched teeth that were wired shut.

"Of course you are. I don't think you've ever missed an episode. Listen, Dominic, I'm not here to yell at you or tell you everything you've done wrong. I'm going to speak to you for a minute, and you're not going to say a word," Danny told him. Dominic just nodded and returned to watching the TV.

Danny leaned in and spoke right into Dominic's ear. "Whatever the fuck is going on with you has to end. You blame yourself for Fabian? Fuck him, he's going to get his and he can burn in fucking hell. There's no blame there, Dominic, not one fucking person can blame you for that. And if they do, fuck them too. Ain't no one walked in your shoes," Danny slapped Dominic's shoulder for emphasis, thinking he was pumping him up. The vibrations from the slap caused vibrations throughout Dominic's body and terrible pain to his head and jaw.

"Ow, Danny, my fucking mouth," Dominic said through the clenched teeth and pain.

Danny laughed. "I'm sorry. I wasn't thinking. I just want you to understand that you don't have to carry that weight. If you're embarrassed that you lost that fight to Tommy, well, I saw him after that fight. I'm telling you, Dominic, anyone else and I think you'd have killed him. You opened his skull with a frying pan, the guy just ain't right."

"I'm embarrassed about how I acted. Look what I did at Doug's house," Dominic said as best he could.

"Dominic, you can simply say you're sorry. You can say you're sorry to Tommy, forgive yourself, because everyone has forgiven you. You got a problem, you need to get something off your chest or need to talk, I'm here, Dominic. I was at the hospital the day you were born. I was one of the first people in your life to hold you. I care about you, Dominic, like I do for my own boy. You want out of this life, I'll support you. But you shouldn't want out just because of your mistakes. Those were rookie mistakes. Guess what, rookies make them—that's where they got their name. You had to learn on your own, and if you take away Fabian and all his undermining bullshit, you did a better job than me and your father did. The fucking money you bring in? For everything you blame yourself for, you're the one that kept everything going and made them bigger and better. I got to be honest though and tell you, you had no forethought to recruiting, but that's okay."

Dominic had to laugh. "Thank you, Danny."

"And if it's Angela, I can only imagine. It wasn't fair you had to go through that alone, well, without me or Nick. I want you to do something for me, go to her grave today. Think some things through, but I need you to remember your other obligations. If you want out, like I said, I'll support you. You did everything asked of you and you did it well and you went through more than anyone should ever have to, there's no shame in it. Just be sure it's because you want the other life, not because of anything else. No bullshit when I say, you were born for this life, you're a natural, you are truly your father's son. If you want to be in this life, then snap out of your funk today and be at the bakery at six in the morning. I'm also pretty concerned about Angelo's lack of sense of urgency, and I kind of need you back there. It'll be you and me, all is forgiven, no baggage and all wrongs are righted. I'm here to stand beside you in both of our worlds, Dominic, no matter what your decision is. Capische?"

Dominic nodded and stood to give Danny a hug. Danny told him one more thing, "And you tell fat fucker upstairs that I don't ever want to see him eating lunch before he's got all our money. And how the hell are you eating steak?"

"I eat the potatoes, mashed," Dominic told him.

Danny left and headed back to the bakery; he wanted an update with Cicirelli's Market. First, he had to stop for gas, as his low-fuel came on. While pumping his gas and cursing himself for giving Jimmy the day off, he saw a van pull up and the passenger got out and ran inside. Thinking nothing more of it, Danny filled his tank and turned to the left, leaving the gas station. Caught at the light, henoticed in his rearview mirror that the van pulled out and turned his way—it was pulling up in the left-turn lane, right next to Danny.

He cursed himself again for not having Jimmy or any other driver with him today when the van's passenger side window started to roll down. Danny's heart dropped as he saw the passenger lean out the window with something in his hand. Danny floored the gas pedal, and his tires spun before his car screeched across the intersection. Looking back, Danny realized what had happened—the man had a map and Danny thought he had heard the man say the word *directions*.

There wasn't time for Danny to regret his rash decision to run the red light. Once he looked back at the road in front of him, he realized he had veered into oncoming traffic. He no longer knew what was in his blind spot and feared that pulling the steering wheel to the right would cause him to lose control and he had to react now, because he saw the two cars coming his way. His only choice was to try to navigate his Lincoln onto the side street he saw on the left.

Danny hit the brake and tried controlling his car onto the street. He succeeded in keeping his car on the cement but failed in controlling it. He made the turn, but his back end crashed into a parked car, causing Danny's airbag to deploy and cracking a rib.

He exited his car and pulled out a handkerchief and spit into it, it was blood. He pulled out his phone to call Jimmy and walked up to the house he believed the car belonged to, so that he could notify the owner that he had just crashed into his car. Before dialing, Danny uttered one sentence to himself, "The day from hell."

CHAPTER XX

The Mother Lode

TOMMY HERRICK KNOCKED on the hotel room door, and for the first time since his fight with him, Tommy came face-to-face with Dominic Amicucci. Dominic wore sunglasses to cover his eyes, and his nose was bandaged. Tommy had a scar on the right side of his forehead, and his right hand was still in a cast from his broken hand which required surgery to repair. Danny was inside the room; he looked hobbled and had a fat lip and some swelling around his eye from the airbag.

"Well, well, well, look at this gruesome twosome," Tommy commented before he hugged Dominic, and they both apologized to each other.

"You guys seem to apologize a lot to each other," Danny noted.

"Nonetheless, it's good to see you back, Dominic," Tommy said. "So we're all ready to start moving on Fabian?"

"Yeah, first target is Louis Rubilla. He works for one of Frank Jagge's guys. He sells guns," Danny explained.

"Do any of your people know of our zips, yet?" Tommy asked.

"Not unless your man at our bar told them," Danny said.

"Then no, perfect. Let's set up a phony gun sale with the zips. Tell him the immigrants are from New York and he's supposed to hook them up with something they can't get there. At the meet, the zips can kill him, throw him in a trunk, and make him disappear," Tommy suggested.

"Beautiful," Danny said.

"He lives in Southfield," Dominic added through his clenched teeth. "We can use Moshe Levin's chop shop there for a car, and we can crush it and dissolve it there with his body inside."

"It's nice when a plan comes together. I'll get Vinny to set it up," Danny said.

"Here's his address and a picture," Dominic said, handing a manila envelope to Tommy. "He's never been married and has no family that anyone knows of."

"Consider it a done deal," Tommy told them.

The next day in Iraq, Doug received his call from Tommy, outlining the assassination plan. Once complete, Doug asked him about his research into the giant energy company, Sundromeda.

"Doug, these guys are huge. I don't think you want to get involved in this," Tommy told him.

"Yes, I do want to get involved. Give me what you got," Doug told him.

"They've got exclusive rights to the energy in Iraq, signed off by the White House. They have publicly listed transactions with the Iraq government, with our government, our military, and even fucking NASA, Doug. What are we doing here?" Tommy asked.

"Do they subcontract their work? Can you find out who exactly did the work here in Iraq? And what about the ownership of this company, are they traded on Wall Street?" Doug asked.

"They do have shares," Tommy informed him. "They have a CEO and different heads for all their foreign operations. As far as subcontracts, common sense would say yes. And there won't be any specific records on who did what in Iraq, at least not available to the public."

"Find a company they've subcontracted work to and buy it. If you can find a few, buy them all," Doug ordered Tommy. "Oh, and Tommy, put one of the zips on that Gary Pizza guy that works for Fabian. If Fabian takes off like expected, Gary can lead us right to him later on."

"Will do," Tommy said.

"What did Stevie ever do with that last guy in Lissoni's crew, the one that set up the other two?" Doug asked.

"He let him leave the country, he went to Canada," Tommy answered.

"How'd Dominic look?" Doug asked.

"To be honest, kind of freakish. I'll tell you what, Doug, I hit this guy with some real hard fucking shots and he kept coming—he's no pussy like I always thought. I realized today, I kind of miss the prick," Tommy confessed.

Doug took the phone away from his ear and looked at it, as though it were broken. Replacing the phone at his ear, he said, "Look, for almost ten years now, Tommy, you've bitched and moaned to me about him. You end up beating his head inside out, and that makes you like the guy? What the fuck's going on with you nowadays? Cracking under pressure?"

"That's my point, everyone bitches and moans about him. He fucked this up, he fucked that up, but I saw a different side to that. He has that instinct, Doug, that desire to fight through and never quit. I only won because I finally got him in a defensive position, and I uppercutted his nose about a dozen times. He probably actually should be dead," Tommy told him.

"What the fuck is this mancrush about?"

"I'm trying to say he has more to offer than any of us thought. I think he can be a good leader over there," Tommy explained.

"Just make sure the hit goes down without any attention, okay? I say six months and the honeymoon's over. You'll be right back to calling him a dumbfuck."

"Only if he is a dumbfuck," Tommy told him.

"Bye," Doug said, and he ended the call.

Danny met two of his captains, at Nick's restaurant, Benny Mancini and Vinny Jagge, for lunch. As always, they sat at a random table, still with the belief the feds couldn't bug every table. "Vinny, it's time to honor your request to whack Louis Rubilla. I'll take care of the shooters. You tell Louis's boss, Doug Napier, that there're these men of respect from Sicily and are living in New York. Tell him these Sicilians want to buy six Mac-10s, but can't find them in New York."

"You know Fabian's going to take off to Mexico, right?" Vinny asked him.

"That's where we want him to go. We need to find out who'll give him aid down there. Benny, we need to use Moshe's chop shop. We'll need a work car and then to crush it and dissolve it with his body inside," Danny explained in a hushed voice, even though there wasn't anyone around their table.

"Which chop shop, he has two?" Benny asked.

"Southfield."

"When?" Benny asked.

"I'll let you know, just make sure it's ready. You might get an hour's notice, just be ready," Danny emphasized.

"No problem," Benny told him. The men had their lunch, and Danny went to the Corner.

Tommy Herrick went about fulfilling his end of the hit. He stopped at his brother's restaurant to give the information to Billy to give to the zips. Billy would get the information to the zip leader, Benedetto, and the stalking of Louis Rubilla would start first thing in the morning.

It would take just two days for Benedetto to say he was ready and the call was made to Rubilla to sell six Mac-10 submachine guns to two Sicilian immigrants. Ten o'clock Thursday night, Benedetto and Giovanni were looking at a Mac-10 in the basement of Louis's house. Benedetto brought Giovanni along instead of his usual partner, Alberto.

"You have all six?" Benedetto asked Rubilla.

"Of course. Do you have the money?" he asked him back.

Benedetto nodded to Giovanni, who threw a duffel bag to Rubilla. Louis opened it and saw it was stuffed with cash. Now realizing he was dealing with some real players, he opened his stash for the zips to see.

"Are you guys interested in anything else? Anything bigger?"

Giovanni was supposed to shoot the target after he threw him the bag, but he paused when Benedetto gave him a quick glance, a signal not to fire.

"What else do you have?" Benedetto asked, hoping Giovanni doesn't shoot until Louis shows more weaponry. Billy told him they could have the cash in the bag and the six Mac-10s, as well as anything else found at the house.

Louis shrugged his shoulders. "Everything, just name it." He walked behind his bar and started placing the purchased weapons on top of it. "Here's the other five and come on down. I've got a basement in my basement. Tell me if there's anything you fellas might want to buy." He opened a trapdoor in the floor that led to a small room full of boxes.

Just as Louis Rubilla opened the trapdoor, Giovanni pulled out his silenced revolver and shot him through the top of his head. Only Louis's feet were visible from their vantage point, and Giovanni closed in for a better look; he gasped in amazement once he was behind the bar.

"What? Is he still alive?" Benedetto asked.

Giovanni came back to his senses. "Him? Alive? No, you got to see all this," he said, pushing Rubilla's body aside so he could open a metal box. "A box of grenades," he told Benedetto.

Benedetto climbed down in the hole and found dozens of metal cases that must have held machine guns. There were metal crates, most likely ammo or explosives. “Start looking for more trapdoors,” he ordered. “We’re going to have to search this whole house, who knows how much we’ll find.”

“How are we supposed to get all this out of here?” Giovanni asked.

Benedetto opened a case, expecting to find a weapon of some sorts, but instead found it stacked tightly with one hundred dollar bills, same with case underneath it. “We need a truck. I’ve got to call this in. This is not what they expected.”

“Call it in? You said we could have what we find,” Giovanni argued.

“They didn’t know all this was here. There’s no honor in stealing, Giovanni,” Benedetto lectured.

“You’re stealing from him,” Giovanni said, pointing to Louis Rubilla’s corpse.

“He’s dead,” Benedetto said, dismissing the body. “You need to get his body to the garage, I’ll call Billy.”

“Done so soon?” Billy asked after answering his cell phone that he just activated and will destroy tonight.

“You need to come here,” Benedetto told Billy, in his broken English.

“I’m not coming there, Benny. What’s the problem? It’s safe to talk on your phone,” Billy told him.

Benedetto hated being called Benny. “The problem is, your information is incomplete and there are stashes of money and weapons. I call you out of honesty and loyalty and you insult me with your disrespect.”

“I call you Benny because I’ve grown to like you. I meant no disrespect. I apologize, Benedetto. Now, how much money are we talking about?” Billy asked, placating the zip.

"I believe it to be millions of dollars. I just opened another case with what looks like a very large machine gun. We are going to need a moving van," he told Billy.

"What about the target?" Billy asked.

"That is done," Benedetto answered.

"His body is gone?"

"No, it is still here."

"Get it the fuck out of there. Get the body in the trunk of his car and get his car and your work car to the junkyard, now. Come back in your car, I'm going to send some people there," Billy ordered.

"With a moving truck?" Benedetto asked.

"Sure, Benedetto, with a moving truck," Billy said and hung up to call his brother.

Tommy Herrick carried his four-year-old daughter, Peggy, piggyback style through the parking lot to his car. Tommy, his wife, Val, and Peggy had just seen a movie and were going home.

"Daddy, can we go for pizza?" Peggy asked her father.

Val answered, "It's already too late. You should've been in bed an hour ago."

"Daddy, please, I'm so hungry," Peggy pleaded.

"Your mother already said no and you had enough junk in the movie," Tommy told her as his cell phone rang.

"Call me back from a pay phone," Billy said over the phone.

Tommy put his daughter on the ground and started digging for change. "Val, I need change for a pay phone."

"Use your cell phone, Daddy," Peggy instructed.

"Yes, use your cell phone, Tommy," Val said with a smirk.

"I don't get a signal here, honey," Tommy explained to his daughter.

"Use mommy's cell phone," Peggy offered, not wanting her father to have to go back in the theatre to use a pay phone.

Val pulled her phone out. "Yes, Tommy, use mine."

Tommy looked at his wife. “A little help here, please,” he begged.

“Fine. Oh look, I don’t have a signal either. I guess you’ll have to use the pay phone that was by the concession stand,” Val said.

“Thank you,” Tommy said and kissed both the women in his life and ran back to the theatre.

“What’s up, Billy?” Tommy asked after buying a soda and getting change.

“Rubilla’s dead, they should be getting rid of the body right now. But the zip says there’s millions of dollars in cash and there’s machine guns and all sorts of weaponry. Tommy, this sounds like we hit the mother lode,” Billy said.

“No shit, eh? This is a Fabian stash, I’ll bet,” Tommy said.

“The zip says we need a moving truck to take it all.”

“Mother lode sounds right. Listen, grab some guys and rent a U-Haul, under someone else’s name, please, and empty the house. Any neighbors get nosy, just tell them he moved and he sent for his things. Maybe no one will even know this fucker’s dead,” Tommy said. “Take everything valuable to a warehouse and destroy the rest.”

Billy arrived at the house shortly after midnight with Dave Worowski. Dave ran a huge bookmaking operation for the Westside crew and was the de-facto boss of their hometown of Henderson. The house was abuzz with men carrying furniture to the truck. Billy and Dave searched out Dave’s right-hand man, Matt Young. Matt ran the book for Dave and was in charge of security at Doug’s new bar, The Four Seasons. Matt Young also was training the staff for the opening of the bar, and one of his staff members was Sal Amicucci, Dominic’s younger brother.

“You guys got to see the basement. There’s over two hundred metal cases filled with money and guns and explosives,” Matt told them.

“Hi, Billy,” a voice from behind him called.

Billy turned around to see a young man carrying a couch with another person. “Sal? Dominic’s brother?”

Sal and the man stopped to put the couch down, and Sal offered his hand to Billy.

Billy shook his hand in pure puzzlement. “Why are you here?”

Sal nodded to Matt Young. “Matt needed some muscle.”

Billy snapped his head toward Matt. “You’re not this fucking ignorant, are you?”

“What? You said to call some scrubs and gut this house,” Matt said.

“You think I’m a scrub?” Sal asked Matt in a hurt voice.

“You’re going to get me fucking killed!” Billy yelled at Matt, and everyone stopped moving.

“Billy, he’s just moving furniture. What the fuck?” Matt asked.

“Billy, what are we doing wrong?” Sal asked him.

“You go the fuck home,” Billy ordered. He reached into his pocket and pulled out a wad of cash. “Here, take this. You were never here,” he said, putting the wad in Sal’s hand.

“I don’t want this. I can’t even move furniture without this shit,” Sal complained.

“That’s right, not around me. I’m not going to be the one that gets blamed for anything that happens to you. You take that money and forget you ever here,” Billy told him.

“What’s going to happen to me here, a hernia?” Sal asked.

“Fall down the stairs, anything. I’m not putting my life on the line. You go. Someone take him home,” Billy called out. He turned to Matt. “What are you thinking?”

“He’s moving furniture, Billy? I don’t get it,” Matt defended himself with.

“Guns, money, and explosives, all words you just used to describe the basement. You don’t think this might be somewhat illegal?” he asked.

“Only I’ve been in the basement. There’s about four or five Italian guys down there lifting the boxes up from the hole,” Matt said.

“To be clear about this, that kid works at the bar. That’s all he does, Matt, he works at the bar. He don’t move nothing, he don’t go wash a car, he does security. Are we clear?”

"We're clear. I apologize, I meant no harm," Matt told him.

"Well, then, let's see this basement," Billy said, clapping his hands in anticipation.

The men piled down the stairs, and Billy stopped in awe at the sight of the metal crates, stacked nearly to the ceiling. Benedetto appeared from behind one of the stacks.

"Those over there," he said, pointing to three stacks of six metal crates, "those are all money, all one hundred-dollar bills."

Billy shook the man's hand. "There's a lot of men who would've kept this for themselves. You're truly a man of respect," Billy told him.

Benedetto beamed with pride and looked back at his men who stopped working to watch. "I try to be an example for them," he told Billy.

Billy leaned in close and whispered, "Louis Rubilla is no more? Not in body or soul?"

"His existence is gone, as is his car," Benedetto reported proudly. "And if I may add, a beautiful plan you came up with."

"Thanks, but it was my brother's plan," Billy confessed, rather enjoying the ass-kissing.

Benedetto pulled out a cell phone. "I almost forgot, his phone. It rang a few times."

Billy looked at four missed calls, all from the same number with a Florida area code. "Okay, let's get this show moving. Who's taking these upstairs?" he asked.

Matt answered, "My guys are taking the first truckload to a chop shop that he says we can use to burn it all," he said, nodding toward Benedetto. "Then his guys are going to load the next truckload with these and some remaining furniture, for disguise. Then we'll store it in a few warehouses covered by the other bullshit."

Billy nodded. "Okay, sounds good. Whose warehouses?"

"Mike Clement's," Matt answered. Mike was a Westside drug dealer, who was away serving a five-year sentence.

"Well, let's start taking an inventory," Billy said, opening up a crate.

Tommy stopped by Billy's house early in the next morning; he was so eager to find out what the entire take was. Billy hadn't slept yet, as he was up counting cash at the warehouse. The brothers stepped in the backyard to have a hushed conversation.

"Well, how much money, Billy?" Tommy asked impatiently.

"I didn't count all the boxes, but the first three I counted had two and half million each. If all eighteen crates have the same, it's forty-five fucking million dollars," Billy said.

"Oh my God," Tommy let out.

"M-16s, sniper rifles, high-powered shotguns, uzis, grenades, C-4, detonators, land mines, bulletproof vests, ammunition, and even a bazooka with four shells. The complete mother lode," Billy said.

"Where is everything?" Tommy asked.

"Mike Clement's warehouses, he had some empty ones," Billy answered.

"Those may have been the empty ones, you stupid fuck, but the ones that aren't empty have tons of fucking pot in them. What if the DEA has it under watch? All that fucking money lost because my retarded brother was put in charge of something," Tommy said. "Move everything the fuck out of there."

"Move it where?" Billy asked.

"Up north, take it to Doug's property in Traverse City," Tommy said.

"Tommy, I got to get some sleep," Billy complained.

"Sleep on the truck. Call the zips, get it all moved as fast as possible," Tommy ordered.

"Why do I got to do this petty bullshit?" Billy asked, irritated with his brother.

"Forty-five million dollars is petty to you? Move the shit and shut the fuck up," Tommy said and opened the gate to go to his car and left.

Tommy left his brother's house and left to meet Dominic and Danny in a faraway city. They didn't want to be recorded meeting the day after a hit went down—it would look like a status report, they feared.

At the small dive of a bar, Tommy told of the hit. "Rubilla's gone, and it might've turned out better than planned. I really think no one's even going to know this guy got whacked, and Fabian could be led to believe that this guy took off with his money."

"What money?" Danny asked.

"Brace yourselves. The zips found three hidden rooms dug under the basement. Firepower like you wouldn't believe and forty-five million dollars in cash," Tommy said.

Neither man said a word for at least thirty seconds. Dominic broke the silence. "What?"

"Forty-five million, cash. My brother's transporting everything up north to Doug's land in Traverse City right now. I talked to Doug. He told me to make sure I told you that it's your money and whack it up anyway you see fit. But we do ask that the zips get five million for not stealing everything," Tommy told them.

Danny finally came over his sudden shell shock at the amount of money that was at hand. "Okay, five to the zips. Vinny Jag has claim to twenty-five percent of the rest, that's ten mil. That leaves thirty—fifteen for us and fifteen for you. Do you agree, Dominic?" Danny asked, ensuring to keep Dominic involved in the decision-making.

Dominic nodded his head as did Tommy, and the deal was done. "What about the weapons?" Tommy asked.

"What kinds exactly?" Danny asked.

" M-16s, uzis, shotguns, sniper rifles, enough for a whole army," Tommy said.

"I want an M-16," Dominic said through his clenched teeth.

Danny and Tommy looked at Dominic, and both said at the same time, "Me too."

"Fifty-fifty on the weapons?" Tommy asked.

"Deal. Turn your truck around and let's split this up," Danny ordered.

"Why not wait, let everything sit for a month or so?" Tommy asked. "We have no idea what the feds might know about this guy."

"Good idea," Dominic said, unintelligibly.

"What?" both men asked him.

"Good idea," he repeated himself, slower and louder.

"Then we shall wait," Danny proclaimed. "You guys can get that kind of cash laundered?" he asked Tommy.

"In an overseas account. The amount of cash don't matter, our guys can move it all," Tommy told him.

"I'll never have to see it?" Danny asked, not familiar with the Westside's money-laundering empire that spanned Europe.

"Nope, I'll just give you an account number and password, do with it from there what you want. Or you can put it with your account for the drug money we manage for your family," Tommy explained.

"What account?" Danny asked.

Tommy looked at Dominic. "You haven't told him?"

Dominic just shook his head.

"When you got out, Doug told me to open an account for you and put a third of Nick's cut from now on into your account. Doug said Nick told him to do it. You got four million dollars in it just from last year's fourth quarter. At the same rate, you'll make sixteen million this year," Tommy told him.

"No fucking shit?" Danny asked, happy with his new windfall.

"I'll tell you, you guys are fucking lucky you're dealing with some honest people. How easy would this be to rip you guys off?" Tommy joked.

Danny looked at Dominic. "You don't know about this?"

"It didn't come out of my cut," he told Danny, with a laugh, as best he could.

Danny held out his hand to shake Tommy's. "I'm real impressed with you guys. I always was, but you know how to live this life. If we could make an exception and make a non-Italian, I swear, I'd be honored to prick yours and Doug's fingers," Danny said.

"Wow, Danny, I don't know what to say. Thank you, that really means something. Oh, Dominic, I don't want you to hear from someone else. One of my guys, Matt Young, he's your brother's boss at the bar. He used Sal to move furniture from the house. Matt didn't know we whacked anyone there and just thought it was harmless. My brother flipped out, made Sal leave, gave him a pocketful of cash, and made sure Matt understood to leave Sal the fuck out of everything. Sal left—he didn't cause no problems. He even tried to decline the money. I'd appreciate it if you didn't say nothing if he don't. He promised Billy he wouldn't say anything. It's a good test of his word."

"Okay, thank your brother for looking after him, I appreciate it," Dominic answered.

Tommy left the bar and checked his watch. He hopped in his truck and started driving north to Traverse City. He couldn't wait to lay his eyes on forty-five million dollars.

CHAPTER XXI

Look at You

"JUST PUSH THIS button here," Benedetto said to Stefano, the fifty-one-year-old former Italian army colonel. Benedetto pushed a button hidden in the trunk door to the Nissan that he was giving to Stefano. Pushing the button opened a trapdoor and revealed a hollowed-out space in the bottom of the trunk. Stefano's eyes lit up at what was inside.

"That is for me?" he asked Benedetto. In the hole was an unassembled sniper rifle with ammo. There was a revolver and five stacks of cash as well as three cell phones.

"Yes, it is all for you. Now, remember listen to the car, it will tell you where to go. You are going to rent an apartment in New York, and you will learn every move of one Bruno Bini. His address and believed hangouts are in that notebook I gave you. When the time is right, I will tell you to kill him. As you will learn, he is a boss in New York, and this is very important," Benedetto explained.

Benedetto outlined the plan as given to him last night by Billy Herrick, who had stopped by while the zips were having dinner. Their relationship had greatly improved since the zips' arrival, to the point that Billy even brought the wine to dinner. Billy wasn't sure if the hit would ever go down, but if the order came, he wanted everything ready. These were serious men, Benedetto thought. Billy already had Benedetto following the routines of a guy named Gary Pizza getting ready to take him out. He was impressed—they were methodical and systematic about their businesses and especially about their murders.

"I will not fail," Stefano answered and left for his trip to New York.

Benedetto returned to his empty apartment; his two roommates were out. Alberto and Franco were out stalking Gary Pizza. Gary had been on the go a lot lately after Louis Rubilla's disappearance.

Benedetto poured a glass of wine, turned on a CD with Italian music, and thought back to home. His Mafia career had started as the bodyguard of the consigliere's son in his Sicilian hometown. Benedetto committed numerous murders after developing into an assassin and provided security for drug shipments from distribution centers to the shipyards for overseas shipment.

He was not happy when he was picked to go to America. He wanted to go, but he wanted to bring his family, his wife, daughter, son and his wife. His orders were to depart immediately, and he could come home in five years. In essence, Benedetto felt he was sold for a bigger cut in the drug profits, which was true.

He didn't care for Billy Herrick when he first picked them up and drove them to Las Vegas. Benedetto liked the men in Vegas more than Billy and was disappointed to learn he was to be under his orders. But finding that weapons' cache and turning it in with over forty million dollars put him in great standing with his new bosses.

It was noon the next day in Iraq when Doug Sullivan was meeting with his CIA handler, an Arab-looking field agent, in a small café.

"What are you doing with Sundromeda?" the agent asked.

"What?" Doug asked innocently.

"Come on, who do you think you're dealing with? We know everything you're doing. We know of your secret visits to Switzerland and Germany when you were in Paris. We know you went to see Colonel Cooper, that crooked son of a bitch. And we know your guys back home are making inquisitions into Sundromeda. I'm here to tell you to knock it off. Your dealings in Europe, we were willing to turn a blind eye. But you're going to fuck everything up messing with these big companies. They'll get you tossed out of Iraq, and where does that leave our mission?"

"What do you want, a cut?" Doug asked, believing the bribe was the answer to everything.

"What we want is for you to be trusted by the fucking terrorists, that's all. You can't be bringing all sorts of eyes on you over here," the agent explained.

"My agreement is for you guys to not worry about anything else I got going other than with these terrorists," Doug told him.

"Unless it affects the mission. We don't give a fuck what you do, unless it affects the mission."

Doug knew he was out of options. He knew he could be tossed out of the country in a moment's notice, and if he failed to help the CIA, he would be returned to prison for the remaining eight plus years he owed.

"After my job's done with you guys, I'm free to do as I please over here?" Doug asked.

"Once the mission is complete, yes," the agent answered.

"That'll give me time to make some moves on Sundromeda," Doug said.

"Why do you even care? Believe me, Doug, these people don't care about us."

"You see people that don't care. I see people that want things fixed, that want better lives, people that are infiltrated by these terrorists. But then, I also see a bigger picture. I see opportunity after opportunity here to make billions, legally. I just a need a foothold, a big one. Sundromeda has a monopoly on the energy in this country. I want a monopoly on everything: energy, construction, water, and communications. I want to own the first Baghdad casino," Doug explained.

"Either way, the first step is the terrorists. We'll meet again after your meeting next week, and stay out of trouble, okay?"

Dominic had his mouth unwired and had surgery on his jaw, thus having it rewired. This Thursday would be his first visit with his father after having his mouth unwired for the last time. "How does it feel to be able to communicate with the world like a normal person again?" Nick asked his son.

"Feels good, I'm getting plastic surgery on my nose over the summer," Dominic told him.

"Listen, Son, I talked to Doug the other day and we're going to be making some moves," Nick said.

"What kind of moves?" Dominic asked.

"You know how Doug has the cement rackets with the state government? He's going to do that in Iraq. It's a completely open territory. Someday, somehow, he says these people are going to become westernized, and he plans on cashing in on it. We're starting with energy companies. Buy two or three small electric anything companies, doesn't matter what they do, as long as it's something to do with electricity. Tell Vito in New York to tell the other families there to do the same—that will help him with them if he does ever want to make a move for boss. When we own enough companies, we'll merge them altogether and start pushing for government contracts. The money the government pays is astronomical. This will take years, but you watch, we'll be the biggest thing in Iraq if this works out," Nick explained.

"And by being the first one to actually finish a job over there, he wins over the people and shows competence with the government, right?" Dominic asked.

"Wow, I think Tommy beat some sense back into your head. It could be the opportunity of a lifetime. It's the ground floor of a total reconstruction, like the first big companies when this country started building. It can be like Cuba in the old days for us, our own country," Nick said.

"Seems far-fetched to me, but what do I know, I'm a bookie at heart," Dominic said.

"I'm glad to see you're thinking right again. Laying off the booze?" Nick asked.

"Well, yeah, whiskey through a straw didn't sound right, plus the painkillers, haven't had a drink," Dominic responded.

"Them pills aren't the answer either, you know. Pain and hurt, Dominic, will only heal when you deal with them straight on. Take it from someone who knows. I was a complete drunk when I lost your mother. I know it's a rare occasion when I say something positive to you, but, Dominic, I am proud of you. Not just for the other bullshit, I'm proud of the person you've become, you're your own man, with no help from me," Nick told his son.

Fabian Bosca sat on a bench, waiting for the pay phone to ring. *Finally,* he thought to himself once it rang. "What the fuck took you?" Fabian asked when he answered.

"I got tails, had them for them about two weeks," Gary Piazza told Fabian. The tails were actually the two Sicilians, Alberto and Franco.

"Still no word from Louis?"

"No, and his house is empty. I talked to his neighbors. They said he cleaned it out in the middle of the night," Gary said.

"If they whacked him, why would they clean out the house? Even the furniture is gone?" Fabian asked.

"Even the living room rug," Gary told him.

"The motherfucker ran off with everything. Probably, bought a fucking island with all my fucking money," Fabian complained.

"What do you want to do?"

"Find him, what the fuck else? Find him and find my money and those weapons. He was supposed to have them shipped here in Mexico. He fucking stonewalled me until he could steal them, and I thought he was just lazy." Fabian hung up the phone with Gary and called another number. He called his captain back in Michigan, Vinny Jagge. "Just checking in, boss," Fabian told him.

"Fly in, we should talk," Vinny said.

"About what? We're both on secure lines," Fabian reminded Vinny.

"Because I want to see you, fly in whenever you can. My boy, Michael, can pick you up at the airport," Vinny suggested.

"Sure, I'll call you and let you know when I can," Fabian said as he got off the phone. ***Well, that sounds like a hit,*** Fabian thought. Fabian was also aware that Vinny wanted to get his youngest son, Michael, made and would have to perform a hit to do so. Jimmy Amicucci and Mike Jagge were now the biggest red flags for Fabian. He didn't want to be anywhere that those two might be. They were wanted by the family to become made men, and Fabian would be the perfect hit for either of them to make their bones.

He left the pay phone and returned to the two waiting cars. He climbed into the back of one, and they both took off. Fabian rode with an entourage in Mexico, not like before, like a celebrity, now it was for protection. He knew it was only a matter of time before the Amicuccis made their move. He was ready to make his own move until his money and his arsenal went missing.

Fabian was under the protection of a Mexican sheriff of a small town that Fabian and his family were residing in. He no longer had his Italians friends around that were sworn to uphold an oath. Now he was surrounded by Mexican mercenaries—men he had planned to start an army with, with his money and weapons that he no longer had. He had planned on taking over the Amicucci drug routes in Mexico, a crippling blow to the family's income.

If the Amicuccis came calling, he had his own personnel to deal with them. Then he would unleash his army in Michigan and wipe out Dominic and Danny and those Westsiders. But his dream would be for his men to break into Nick Amicucci's prison and shoot him dead.

He would rather that the Amicuccis left him alone in Mexico; he didn't really want to kill Dominic—he felt he had to. If Dominic would leave him alone, then fine, Fabian would wait until Nick did his twenty years, and then, he, Fabian Bosca, would have his father's revenge and shoot his father's murderer dead as he walked through the prison doors like the dog that Fabian considered him to be.

But now it appeared all his plans were going to go awry. Every plan was just a minor irritation in the side of the huge crime family. Even diminishing Dominic's reputation as a leader had seemed pointless with Danny's return to the streets. Dumb John Lissoni had to go after Noah Brooks in Las Vegas instead of listening to Fabian and inflicting the terror that he suggested was working. Now his entire crew was wiped out, and Fabian's man in Vegas, Yamamoto, had left the scene. All he had left was Gary Pizza, and Fabian wasn't so sure those were FBI agents following Gary like he thought they were.

Danny walked into the Corner and saw the newest additions to the crew, the three Gurino cousins, huddled around Paulie Bankjob, listening to him to tell a story of the old days. Jackie Beans was in a card game with Vince Cusamano and Carlo DeMini. "Does anyone know why the Lakers game's been pulled off the board?" Danny asked.

Everyone looked around curiously, and no one answered. "That's because everyone's fucking around." Danny grabbed the money on the table from the card game. "My time, my money," he said and put it in his pocket. "Why isn't ESPN on the TV? Who's checking the lines every half hour to see if there's movement?" A gift basket on the bar caught Danny's attention. "What the fuck is that?"

"It's from Cicirelli's Market," Jackie answered. "Old man Cicirelli's kid brought it himself. He said to tell you thanks for the free three days of bread. He said to tell you he gave you more footage than you had."

Danny smiled to himself and silently congratulated Dominic for handling the situation. "Jimmy, take it to my wife," Danny ordered.

"All the way back inEmery Beach?" he asked.

No one dared move, and all eyes were locked on Danny. Danny tossed his keys to Rocco Gurino. "Rocco, take that gift basket to my house."

Rocco caught the keys and jumped up and took the basket. Danny pointed his finger at Jimmy. "You go the fuck home and stay there. I don't want to see your face." Jimmy slumped his shoulders and walked out.

Tommy and Billy Herrick entered the gym for a workout and to do a few rounds of sparring with each other. They had been coming here for almost twenty years, as did Doug Sullivan and Stevie Turner. Today, they found Matt Young there. Matt was Dave Worowski's top man in Henderson and was in charge of running the security at Doug's new bar, opening in May. Matt had brought his staff here to get in the ring and make sure they could fight.

"Holy shit, is that Dominic's brother, Sal?" Tommy asked as he got close to the ring.

"Yeah, he's doing well," Matt answered. "Tommy, you don't have a problem with this, do you? He's just learning to box."

"You kidding me, it's great," Tommy beamed, watching the youngster in the ring. Tommy became engaged in the sparring match. "Move your head, Sal," he yelled.

Matt looked at Billy, who shrugged his shoulder. "He loves boxing."

Tommy actually climbed up to be in Sal's corner. "Don't just stand there, jab and move, jab and move," Tommy yelled. He looked down to Matt Young. "You taught him anything? What the fuck?" he barked and turned back to the action.

The bell rang, and Sal returned to his corner, puzzled to find Tommy there. "Jesus Christ, Sal, are you an idiot? Why take a punch if you don't have to?" Tommy asked him.

"I don't know," Sal answered. The trainer offered him water, and Tommy slapped it away. "You got to earn your water. Don't just stand there, Sal, you look stupid. Move your feet, move your head, move everything. Jab with your left, set up that right. Every punch he throws, come back with two, every time."

"I thought I was doing good," Sal complained.

"Sure, if you want to go through the motions. But you want to win, don't you?" Tommy asked.

"It's sparring," Sal said.

Tommy slapped the headgear the boxers were required to wear. "Don't you have any pride, Sal? You go tell that to your father or your brother and they'd disown you. Now, be an Amicucci and get the fuck out there and knock that asshole out," Tommy ordered.

The instructor walked to the center of the ring to give some instructions to the fighters on the next round; this was supposed to be remedial. "Get the fuck out of the way," Tommy yelled to him.

The instructor looked at Matt, who had hired him and rented this time from the gym, and Matt nodded for him to get out of there. "Someone ring the bell," Tommy yelled.

Matt turned to Billy. "Your brother has completely taken over the gym."

Billy nodded. "That he has."

Sal danced around a bit before he threw his first jab, which his opponent slapped away. His second jab ended in the same result. His third was sidestepped, and his opponent retaliated with an uppercut to Sal's chin, causing his knees to buckle, and he dropped to the canvas.

"You pussy!" was all Sal heard as he got up. He shook the cobwebs and put his dukes back up. The referee, who was the gym manager, asked Sal if he was okay, and Sal nodded yes.

Now Sal felt something he hadn't felt before—adrenaline and anger. Now he was ready. Sal stepped to his opponent; he no longer could hear Tommy in the corner. He couldn't see the crowd that had assembled to watch the lively match. He only saw the man in front of him.

His opponent went for the kill and threw a big right. As if Sal had known it was coming, he ducked and countered the punch with a clumsy right and good left, both of which stunned his opponent. The sounds of the world returned, and he could hear Tommy yelling to hit him. Sal followed Tommy's advice and landed two solid rights to his opponent's headgear.

Tommy was jumping up and down with Sal's burst. "Go for the kill, Sal, get him," he hollered.

With a rage he had no idea he had, Sal reached back his right, and with everything he had, he let it go right into his opponent's jaw. The man's mouthpiece went flying, and he stumbled toward his corner. Sal went after him and hit him with a right, left combo to the back of opponent's head, knocking him down, face first. The ref pulled Sal away and threw him to a corner where he was met by an overjoyed Tommy Herrick.

Tommy was jumping around, raising Sal's arms in the air. "Look at you, Sal. Look at you," he yelled with joy.

Finally leaving the ring and letting the class progress, Tommy asked Sal if he was even twenty-one. "Not 'til May," Sal answered him.

"Well, I know a place where I can get you a beer, come on," Tommy said.

Billy interrupted, "We still haven't worked out for even a minute yet."

"Fuck off, Billy," Tommy said as he walked off with Sal.

"I only do that because he's my younger brother, that's the only reason. Just like Dominic does with you sometimes, so you can't it personally," Tommy explained to Sal as they walked to the parking lot.

Sal returned home in time for dinner with a box of pastries. "Where's everyone at?" Sal asked Helena.

"We're going to your aunt Marie's. I'm waiting on you. What's that?" she asked, pointing to the pastries.

"Pastries for dessert," Sal answered.

"That I gathered, but why do you have pastries?" she asked suspiciously.

"Mom, today I just feel like being an Amicucci. And you guys eat a lot of pastries. Here," Sal said, handing his mother the box. "I don't know what they are, but the lady at counter said they were good."

Helena beamed. "I'm sure they're just terrific, Sal. That was very thoughtful of you."

"You have to drive, my car's at the gym. I had some beers with Tommy, and he drove me home," Sal said.

"You had some beers with Tommy Herrick? He was at the gym or something?" she asked.

"Yeah, he coached me through a sparring match. I knocked a guy out, real bad," Sal said with pride.

"You were boxing?"

"For my job, they've been teaching us self-defense stuff, and today we boxed. Tommy showed up there. I guess he spars there and jumped in my corner. Then he took me for some beers and drove me home. Someone from the staff will pick me up tomorrow."

"And this is all legit?" Helena asked.

"It's more than legit, Mom. It's my job to make sure it all stays legit. If I do well, I might even be able to promote and be a manager," Sal said.

"And you're taking this all very seriously?"

"Mom, it's my job to take it seriously."

"Okay, I don't know where my son is, but you can stay," Helena joked. She leaned in and whispered, "I like you better." Then she gave her son a kiss on the cheek.

Later in the evening, Danny and Dominic had dinner with Vinny and Frank Jagge at Nick's restaurant. "Fabian should be flying in any day," Vinny told them.

"He called Angelo today to pick him up tomorrow at the airport," Dominic told them.

"Crafty fucker! I told him my boy, Michael, would pick him up. He's a smart one all right," Vinny said.

"Be sure to keep him at ease, he's got to know Louis Rubilla's missing by now. Remember our goal is to get Gary Pizza to fly to Mexico to see where Fabian is staying," Danny instructed.

"I've got a pay phone number he called me from, I'll get a trace and find the city," Vinny offered.

"That doesn't mean that's where he's staying," Dominic said. "We drive for an hour just to use a pay phone and then drive back. With his life on the life, I imagine he'd drive for three or four hours. That number could be very misleading."

"Very true, Dominic," Danny said. "Has he used the same number twice?" Danny asked Vinny.

"Not once," Vinny answered. "But all his other calls have been from throwaway cell phones."

Vinny's oldest son, Frank, snapped his fingers. "What number did he use to call Angelo? Obviously, you guys were right, and Angelo's the one person he'll contact believing Angelo will keep it secret. Maybe Angelo can get somewhat of a location—maybe even make a trip to Mexico."

"That's not a bad idea, Frankie," Vinny said.

Dominic disagreed, "I'm going to go ahead and speak for my father and say there's no way in hell I'm letting Angelo go to Mexico by himself to meet Fabian, no chance in hell. We could all be the fuck wrong and Fabian might start killing us all now. Since he can't kill my dad, who's to say he wouldn't take Angelo's life as compensation for Fabian's father."

Vinny and Frankie looked at Dominic and then turned to Danny to get his opinion. Dominic was going to respond but decided to see what Danny's response would be. "What are you looking at me for? If Dominic says no, then it's no, but he does have a valid point, Vinny. You wouldn't send your sons down there either. No one knows for sure what Fabian's going to do next. I'd agree with Dominic that he probably won't keep sitting still, and let's not forget about all those weapons. Obviously, there's something in the works. But we still have to find out who his connections are in Mexico, so all we can do is wait, and not do anything stupid like sending someone to Mexico to be whacked."

"And Angelo will pick him up and keep befriending him, trying to learn as much as possible," Dominic added.

"Look at you with the big words like befriending," Danny joked.

Doug and Sami Nasser sat in a small café with what they believed to be their link to the terrorists. "All together then, what is your price?" the man asked Sami who translated for Doug.

"Seventy-five million dollars," Doug replied, knowing full well he had inflated his price by twenty-five million expecting to be haggled down.

"Okay," the man answered and put out his hand to shake.

Sami smiled and clapped his hands in celebration of completing the deal.

Doug was more hesitant. *Something's wrong here,* he thought to himself before he shook the man's hand.

"Six months would be the worst-case scenario—I figure three or four months and I can have it all here," Doug said.

"You will not need to transport them overseas, we have connections in your country that can take them from you," the man told him.

Doug's heart dropped. "What did that mean?" he asked himself. "No deal," he said and stood up. "Come on, Sami, they're not keeping their word," he said and walked out with his friend.

The man caught up to them and talked in Sami's ear. "What is so wrong?" Sami translated.

"I said I will not sell these for any attacks against my country. You can go fuck yourself, asshole. I ought to kill you myself," Doug scowled at him as he continued walking.

"It is not to be used there, it is coming here. No offense, we have shipping means that I trust more than I trust yours," the man told him.

Doug finally stopped walking. "I'll let Sami know when it's time. You give him an address, you transfer the money, and I'll drop off the weapons. If I find out you're lying to me, I will blow up your fucking whole town and drop you off in the middle of New York City with a sign that says 'I love Osama' and let you see what happens." Doug pointed his finger at the man. "Don't think for a fucking second that I'm in my position because I let anyone ever double-cross me, ever," he said and stormed off, with Sami in tow.

Doug was still irritated when they got back to Sami's house. It irritated him even more to learn there was no air-conditioning—the electricity was out again. Doug walked out of the house and called his wife, "Grace, I'll be home Monday, I hate this place."

CHAPTER XXII

Eggs and Baskets

DOMINIC AMICUCCI AND his girlfriend, Michelle, had dinner with Danny Serafini, Doug Sullivan, Tommy Herrick, and their wives. After dinner, the group headed to a local nightclub to have some more drinks. Doug had been home for three days now, and they were having their own private celebration. The girls were on the dance floor, and the guys were at the bar.

"To us," Danny toasted as everyone clanked shot glasses and drank them down. Doug was the first to notice three guys try to dance with their women. The women paid no mind to the men and tried ignoring them. Doug slammed his beer down on the bar and charged out to the dance floor when he saw one of them grope his wife.

It took a moment for the others to notice what caught Doug's attention, and Tommy, Dominic, and Danny followed suit. Trying not to cause a barroom brawl, Doug grabbed his wife's hand and led her off the floor. The women followed, as did the men that tried to dance with them.

"Hey, what the fuck's your problem?" one of them yelled to Doug as he got closer.

Doug's fuse was lit, and he let his wife go and got in the man's face. "You see that ring on her fucking finger? I put that there, cocksucker. Back the fuck off before you get carried out of here."

There were two men with him, but more of their friends had noticed what was going on, and another six men started circling the situation.

"Let her tell me, asshole," the man told Doug.

"You say one fucking word to her and your parents got to bury a kid. You catching my drift yet, you dumb motherfucker?"

Dominic caught the man's attention. Dominic was right next to Doug; he still wore the sunglasses due to his black eyes that the doctors told Dominic would not heal until he got surgery on his nose and the cavities surrounding his eyes.

"Lose your Guido friends and you and me can go toe-to-toe," the man said to Doug.

Dominic was drinking for the first time since his fight with Tommy, and combined with his painkillers, he was feeling no pain. "Who the fuck are you calling Guido?" Dominic asked him.

Tommy stood behind Doug, trying to gauge who in the drawing crowd was with these guys—a fight seemed inevitable.

Grace grabbed Doug's arm. "Just take me out of here, Doug," she told him.

"Yeah, Doug, listen to your bitch. Get the fuck out of here," the stranger said.

There was no more talking. Doug clocked the man in the nose, sending blood flying and the man to the ground. All hell broke loose. Doug took a punch to his jaw that he had no idea of where it came from because he was going to hit the guy that had just hit Dominic from behind. Doug was satisfied when he saw Tommy come out of nowhere and drop the guy that hit Dominic with one punch from Tommy's left hand.

Doug turned to follow where the punch came from that hit him and saw the man that delivered it. He saw another that was ready to hit him again. Before he could hit Doug, Doug pushed him backward and landed a punch in the other man's eye. He knew he had to get rid of one of the two opponents quickly, so he hit the man again square in the nose, causing the man's eyes to water and rendering him ineffective, at least for a few moments.

Doug quickly turned his head to check on his friends; he only had time to see Tommy throwing uppercuts at two guys while Dominic had two of his own. Doug turned his head back to the man he pushed and saw he was coming back at him. Doug turned his back to his friends and squared up against the man he pushed. Before he could do a thing, he was put in a headlock for a few seconds and was released. Danny had busted a beer bottle over the man's head and had moved in between Doug and his opponent. Danny at fifty-nine years old was poised and ready to fight someone thirty years his junior.

Instead, Doug passed Danny and grabbed the man by his throat and threw him backward. As the man stumbled, Doug went after him, hitting him with three solid right hands that split his left eye open.

What seemed like an eternity was a mere few moments and a gang of bouncers grabbed all the men involved in bear hugs and ushered them to the door. When the bouncer let Doug go, Doug saw the man that had groped his wife and started the whole altercation. His nose was still gushing blood, and the white towel used to stop the bleeding was predominantly red with blood.

Doug went right after him. He tore the towel from the man's hands and wrapped it around his neck, tying it from behind and squeezing in an attempt to choke the life out of him. Doug wasn't through; he drove the man's head into the wall, causing his forehead to split open. Again the bouncers grabbed Doug as the man fell to the floor in a broken heap.

Luckily, everyone got out of there before the police showed up. Danny threw the bouncers a few one hundred-dollar bills to tell the cops they had no idea who was involved in the fight. In the car, Doug and Tommy jumped in the back while Grace drove and Tommy's wife, Valerie, rode up front. The same scenario played out in the car with Danny and Dominic.

Once the adrenaline wore off, Doug and Tommy were enjoying a few laughs. "Wow, you got pretty good with your left," Doug said as he nudged Tommy in the backseat.

"No choice, my right will never be the same, thanks to Dominic's hard fucking head," Tommy said.

"I can't believe you guys find this is so much fun," Tommy's wife said to the backseat.

"I find the whole thing embarrassing," Grace said.

"You know what I find embarrassing?" Doug asked. "Watching my wife get hit on and fondled."

"It was under control," Grace replied.

"No, you're dead wrong. Now, it's under control," Doug told her.

The next day, Doug met with his CIA handler. They chose to meet in a small town outside of Toledo, Ohio. They both knew the FBI was tailing Doug, and neither wanted them to know of Doug's deal with the CIA.

"I'm telling you, these guys are going to double-cross us," Doug told the field agent.

"Everything will have a beacon that we can trace. We'll always know where the weapons go," the agent said.

"Just so that we're clear, anything goes wrong with those weapons, I'm holding you guys personally responsible," Doug said.

"What are you fucking kidding me? Who are you to threaten me? Do you have any idea what can happen to you?" the agent asked.

"Nothing in comparison as to what can happen to you. Do you have any idea why you guys would let someone like me out of a ten-year sentence to do this shit? Because I'm the only one, I'm the only one that has anything going over there. You and your organization can't say that, only I can." Doug pointed his finger at the man. "So it seems whatever you guys can do, I can do better. Trust me when I say, you don't want to fuck with me. You guys need me more than I need you. I'll go and do my eight years, that's fine. But you and your bosses got to watch over shoulders the rest of your fucking lives. Kill me, I guarantee you a bloodbath that my crew is more than willing to carry out. Don't lose track of these weapons, and if they don't leave this country, you got to let me know. I'll go retrieve them, because I can and you can't. I hope we're clear now," Doug said, getting up and leaving.

The same day, Dominic had a visit with his father. Dominic gave the guards their usual five thousand dollars, and they were happy to see Dominic back in action. Nick took his seat and looked his son up and down. "When the fuck are you going to get rid of those sunglasses and get back in the gym. You're getting a fucking gut."

"What's up your ass?" Dominic asked.

"Nothing, take the fucking sunglasses off, you look like a moron," Nick ordered.

Dominic did as he was told, and Nick revolted, "Put them back on. Why won't that heal?"

"It's pressure and blood vessels, it's a whole fucking thing," Dominic answered, putting his glasses back on. "I can't work out probably for another year. I'll tell you, I am out of shape, though. We got into a little brawl last night at a club, and I was winded."

"Who got into a brawl?" Nick asked.

"Me, Danny, Doug, and Tommy. Some guys were fucking with the girls, we had to take care of it," Dominic explained.

"Danny too?"

"Oh yeah, he busted a bottle over one guy's head," Dominic said with a laugh.

Nick shrugged his shoulders. "Well, it's good to see everyone getting along, at least. And Helena says Sal's taking Doug's job seriously. She says he's really into it."

"Yeah, he's learning to box, some karate and shit like that. He's loving it, he's working out. Even Tommy Herrick saw him sparring and said he knocked someone out," Dominic said.

"What about Fabian and the weapons cache?"

"It's all up north, the money too. Doug and Tommy will get it laundered. Forty-five million dollars, fucking amazing," Dominic said.

"Fabian did pretty good in five years, that cocksucker. He's always been a smart kid—you can bet that wasn't his only stash. He wouldn't put all his eggs in one basket," Nick explained.

"He would if he didn't have many baskets left," Dominic said,

"Keep making sure his baskets are diminishing. Everything seems to be running smoothly."

"It does," Dominic answered.

"That's when something gets you in the ass," Nick reminded Dominic.

Early the next week, Doug came barreling into the Corner with a box of Cuban cigars for a meeting with Danny and Dominic. When he entered, there wasn't a sound. Danny and Dominic were sitting with Angelo and Benny Mancini, an Amicucci captain.

"Who the fuck died?" Doug asked jokingly.

"Benny's dad," Danny answered.

"Oh shit, I'm sorry, Benny. He was in California, right?"

"Yeah, doing thirty-nine years, he did thirteen," Benny answered.

"Want a cigar?" Doug asked, earning a hard glare from Danny.

"Actually, yeah, I wouldn't mind," Benny said.

Doug handed him one. "No disrespect, but I really need a word with Danny and Dom," Doug said.

Danny and Dominic took Doug outside to the back parking lot, and Angelo and Benny had a cigar. "What's so urgent?" Danny asked.

"Now you know I was trying to get some things going in Europe while I was there, right?" Doug asked.

Danny eyed him suspiciously, wondering what Doug had gotten into now. "Yeah."

"Well, I just got word something panned out. It's the fucking score of a lifetime, more than we ever hit for yet. It's not the drug pipeline like I was hoping for, it's a onetime deal," Doug said.

"We just found forty-five million dollars and you're talking about the score of a lifetime," Dominic said.

"Half a billion," Doug told them. Neither man said a word; they just stared at Doug. "That's two hundred and fifty million for you and two hundred and fifty million for us."

Danny turned to Dominic. "What's my end of this?"

Dominic had no answer, and he turned to Doug. "Dominic, you personally get a hundred and twenty-five, that's your half with your father. Danny, you get a third of Nick's, forty one and two thirds millions."

"I've got a hundred and twenty-five million dollars?" Dominic asked in disbelief.

"What, are you kidding me? You've already got more than that," Doug told Dominic.

"I do?"

"Don't you check your shit out? Jesus Christ, you really are a fucking idiot," Doug said.

"I knew I had millions, but I had no idea," Dominic said.

"How do I get my money?" Danny asked.

"You can transfer it to any overseas account you want. Or you can leave it where it is, earning two percent a year. It's a low rate, but it's safe," Doug told him. "And if you ever want the cash, just say the word."

"So if I say I want five million dollars cash?" Danny asked.

"I'll have it to you in less than thirty days," Doug answered.

"I had over thirty million from that federal construction deal you were doing, is that part of the one forty?" Dominic asked.

"That's a separate account. The cash that gets washed goes to another account. The drug money gets handled by one group, the construction money is another group, and sending cash overseas is a third. That way all the eggs aren't in one basket. One group goes down, we're not cleaned out," Doug explained.

"My dad and me were just talking about eggs and baskets," Dominic commented.

"So I've got forty one million dollars?" Danny asked, still in disbelief.

"You've got forty-five, you already had four million," Doug said.

"How do we make it legal?" Danny asked.

"That's the near impossible part. We can spend it in the European market, but spend a dollar of it here and I guarantee the feds are all over it. I've got my lawyer working on lobbyists to lessen banking regulations for U.S. citizens, but that's a crapshoot for a decade away," Doug explained.

"What the fuck has happened in five years? Who are you?" Danny asked.

"I'm the guy that uses your clout as the mob to make you richer than beyond your imaginations. And I've got a new plan."

"You're taking over the Colombian Cartels?" Danny joked.

"No, but you should know, we do have a relationship with one of them," Doug said.

"Nope, didn't know that either," Danny said, looking at Dominic.

"My plan is to invest in European companies. If we can find the right people, pool our money together, we can do some real damage. I want to westernize Iraq with these companies. We're going to take over the energy business of the whole country, and we're going to monopolize the rest with our European companies—it's a two-prong attack, and we'll be bidding against ourselves. And then we're going to build an Arab Las Vegas. We'll be mega billionaires, legally," Doug told them.

"If you're not in jail first," Danny reminded Doug.

"Even from jail," Doug said.

The next day, Doug was furious to see the progress on the construction of his new bar, The Four Seasons. "How the fuck is this going to be ready to open at the end of May?" Doug asked the foreman.

"Well, it's not," he answered.

"You're going to get fucking smart with me now?"

"No, I didn't mean nothing smart. It just ain't going to be ready, I'm just being truthful," the foreman said.

"Let's be fucking truthful then. Are you not being more than well compensated for your work?" Doug asked.

"Well, yeah, but we can't work in freezing rain and all this bullshit weather."

Doug clapped hands his together. "What will it take to get it done?"

"There's just no way, we're that far behind."

Doug's phone rang, and it was his wife. "I'd like you to come home," Grace told him.

"Is someone hurt?" Doug asked.

"No, I'd just like you to come home," she repeated.

"Honey, I'm working here," Doug told her.

"That's always a given, believe me, I'm aware, but I'd like you to come home."

"Baby, please, I've got a crisis going on."

"You've got a crisis, I'm pregnant, you asshole," Grace said.

"You're pregnant?" Doug asked. "You're pregnant!" Doug yelled and hung up. He looked to the foreman. "My wife's pregnant, I'm having a girl."

"Congratulations," he said.

Doug smiled. "You're a lucky motherfucker, huh? Look, call your boss, Jason Vance, tell him I want this done, whatever it takes. Work twenty-fours, triple the manpower, fucking rape the hell out of me, just get it the fuck done," Doug said as he took off for his car.

Instead of going right home, Doug stopped by Billy Herrick's restaurant and had a drink with the Herrick brothers before returning home with flowers he purchased at his last stop. He hugged his wife. "I'm just so happy. I can't believe we're going to have a girl," Doug said as he embraced Grace.

"You think it's a girl, eh?" she asked him.

"You said it was," Doug said, releasing his wife and staring at her.

"No, I did not."

"I heard you," Doug told her.

"As always, you heard what you wanted to hear. All I said was that I was pregnant, and you hung up on me. Anything after that, Doug, is all in your head," Grace said.

"Huh," was all Doug had to say as he sat down. "Where are the boys?"

"Well, father of the year, it's Wednesday, so your oldest child is in school. But Little Bobby should be waking from his nap soon. He was wearing his football helmet you got him, earlier," Grace said with a smile. "I got to tell you, Doug, you outworked me on Bobby. You haven't even been out of jail for six months and you taught your son his first word *touchdown*. A mother could never be prouder."

"I'm telling you, this one's going to be a quarterback in the NFL. Just the way he throws his ball, I'll bet he throws farther than any of the other babies," Doug gloated.

"And Graham will be a Hall of Fame pitcher," Grace bellowed, mocking her husband.

"At last, she gets it," Doug joked.

"And if you get your daughter, what about her? Top cheerleader?"

"Whatever she wants. For her, the world," Doug said.

"And if it's Doug Junior?" Grace asked.

"Well, he better be tall, because he's playing basketball," Doug said. Then he snapped his fingers with an idea.

"We're not naming him Joe Dumars Sullivan," Grace said, cutting off Doug.

Later that day, Doug awoke from his nap and found his boys in the living room while Grace and her mother were preparing dinner. "I'd have taken you to dinner, you're pregnant. You don't need to be cooking away," Doug told his wife.

"Touchdown!" Little Bobby yelled when he saw his father.

"God bless that kid," Doug said with pride. He picked up his youngest son and sat on the couch next to his oldest. "You know what tomorrow is, don't you?" he asked Graham.

"Of course, I do, Dad. It's the Tiger's opening day, they're in New York," Graham answered.

"That a boy," Doug said as he messed up Graham's hair. "You ready to throw the ball?"

"After dinner," Grace hollered from the kitchen. "Doug, do you want your messages? I am your secretary after all."

"Sure."

"Tommy called, Billy called, Stevie called, your lawyer called, Jason Vance called, said it's very important. And someone named the Eagle called. I got to ask, who's the Eagle?"

"Ooh, I can't tell you about Eagle," Doug told her.

"Fine, whatever," Grace said.

Doug laughed. "The Eagle is the leader of the local eagle scouts, Graham wanted to join," Doug explained.

"That's actually sounds like a good idea," Grace said.

"Dad, why don't we go to New York to watch the Tigers' first game?" Graham asked.

"Because we don't like Yankee fans, Son, they're bad people," Doug told his son.

Grace stopped what she was doing to intervene, "Doug, stop it."

"Listen to me, Graham, there's no good that can come from a Yankee fan," Doug continued.

"Doug!" Grace said louder this time.

"I'll tell him why, Grace. We don't like Yankee fans because a true baseball fan wants to build his championship, not buy it. And here, Son, we build things. We don't need to go buy the best left-hander and future hall of famers, we build them. That's what makes it special, they're not true baseball fans," Doug explained.

"And I'm going to tell you, Graham, you can like any team you want," Grace told her son.

"Not in this house," Doug said. "If you want to continue to call me dad, there's a list of teams you may not like. You may not like the Yankees, Red Sox, Twins, Indians, White Sox, Blue Jays, Royals, Brewers, Orioles, Cardinals, Mets, Cubs, Packers, Bears, Vikings, Cowboys, Giants, Jets, Bulls, Celtics, Knicks, Lakers, or any hockey team that's not the Red Wings. And as God is my witness, if you ever utter one kind word about Ohio State, you're on the streets. I think that about sums it up."

"You're unbelievable," Grace said as she returned to her cooking.

On Saturday, Doug met Danny and Dominic at Cooch's Corner. "What are you guys all dressed up for?" Doug asked them when he walked in.

"Benny's dad's funeral was today, big turnout," Danny answered. "Let's go out back."

"Here's this," Doug said, handing a piece of paper each to Danny and Dominic. "Those are your account numbers and passwords to your overseas accounts. Next month will have that big score included—these numbers are as of yesterday. You should check your balances, and if you want to move any to different accounts, go ahead, it's your money. As I promised your father, Dom, I've got his accounts. Don't ever log in from anything that can be linked to you. I'd much rather just give you bi-yearly reports if you're not going to move your money. I think it's just safer."

"Thanks, but we called you here to do some work for us," Danny told Doug.

"What'd you need?" he asked.

"It's in North Carolina, one of our bookies," Dominic said. "You know him, Nathan Vind."

"What he do?"

"We found a Fabian connection. It seems Nathan ran the same under scheme in North Carolina, stole almost a million dollars," Danny answered.

"Shit, fucking Angelo pulled the same stunt on your crew in cahoots with Fabian.It's a pass for Angelo and a grave for Nate the Hate?" Doug asked, referencing his nickname.

"He's still kicking a percent to Fabian," Dominic said.

"I started North Carolina. I got a lot to lose there. You really telling me he's giving Fabian money? I don't want Fabian anywhere near there," Doug said, starting to get mad.

"That's why we got to whack him," Danny said.

"Oh, I'll fucking whack him all right. But what the fuck? Dom, I only let you guys have those two books there out of respect and cooperation. That's our drug distribution point there, you know that. Millions of dollars for all of us there, and one of your two fucking books, that I allowed, is trying to fuck that all up. I mean, come on," Doug said in disgust.

"Yeah, but your guy fucked up the gambling in Miami, call it even," Dominic joked.

Doug did laugh. "I started Miami too. I'm allowed to fuck that up. Okay, so we whack this fuck and it's all fixed? Maybe his whole crew is tainted. Let your other book there take it over."

"The other book belongs to another captain, we can't just combine them," Danny said.

"Sure you can. Nathan Vind reports to that old man, Modica, right? He's lost my trust to operate there, so he's out. Combine the crews, pull the old guy out, or take them both right out of there," Doug told them.

"You can't—" Danny started before Doug cut him off.

"Yes, I can. I'm not letting a bookmaking operation jeopardize a multimillion dollar drug operation. Control your crews or get them out. I don't mean any disrespect," Doug said.

"It sure sounds like it," Danny told him.

"Okay, control your crews or get them out, please, with all due respect. You know I'm right, Danny."

"All right, we'll tell Modica he's out of North Carolina. He is the one who came to us and asked for the hit, though," Danny said.

"He figured it out too late. The under scam should've been his heads-up," Doug said.

"You going to use the zips?" Dominic asked.

"No reason not to. I'm going to have them send a message to everyone else in North Carolina and to Fabian. He has to know his time's running out. He's got to act or run soon," Doug said.

CHAPTER XXIII

Lessons

BENEDETTO WALKED UP to the front door and rang the bell. It was ten minutes after two in the morning, and he could hear someone in the house rumbling about. Finally, a man came to the door. "Who is it?"

"It is the FBI, we are here for Nathan Vind," Benedetto said in his thick Sicilian accent.

The door opened. "What the fuck?" the man asked.

"You are Nathan Vind?" Benedetto asked.

The man nodded. "You got a badge or a warrant or anything?"

Benedetto pulled out the shotgun he had underneath his overcoat and fired it into Nathan Vind. He flew backward and into the wall behind the front door, splattering blood everywhere. Benedetto calmly stood over Nathan and fired another shot. Benedetto dropped the weapon; he wore gloves, and the gun had been wiped clean. The gun had never been used before, and the serial numbers had been scraped clear. He got into his car that he parked in the driveway and drove away.

Benedetto was to now drive to another location and swap cars. He was to drive to Miami, and from there, the Westside was to smuggle him into Mexico and await orders. He had his men trailing Fabian's friend Gary Pizza for some time now, and Gary was finally going to meet Fabian. He had purchased a ticket to Mexico City for tomorrow, Saturday, with a return date of Monday.

Benedetto would have to follow Gary Pizza and find out where Fabian was hiding out. Once Gary returned to the United States on Monday, his assassination was to take place. Things were heating up.

The next day, Danny and Dominic met at Mario Zangarra's restaurant inEmery Beach. They were there to meet with captain, Eugene Modica and Mario, his top lieutenant. "You heard about Nathan?" Danny asked Eugene after they were all seated.

"Yeah, I heard it's all over the news down there. I thought it would've been better to make him disappear. I wanted Mario here to handle it. Shotgunning the guy at home with his family upstairs? Draws a lot of attention," Eugene advised.

"It's not your concern anymore, you're out of North Carolina," Danny told him.

"What?" the seventy-seven-year-old captain asked in surprise.

"You've got to hand off all your customers and your monies to Mikey Adini and bring your people home," Danny instructed.

"I've got fourteen people down there. I've got nothing for them here. You're really telling me that you're taking a whole book away from me?"

"Yeah, we can't have bullshit like that going on down there, we've got some other things going on there," Danny explained.

"Hah, you mean the Westside has other things going on down there, this is their call, ain't it?" Eugene's top guy, Mario Zangarra, interrupted.

"You're out of line, Mario," Dominic told him.

Eugene held up his hand for his lieutenant to shut up. "If that is your order, then it is done," Eugene told his bosses. "Is there any other business, or can we eat?"

"You're candidates to be made. Jackie Matts raised a beef about Vito Billini," Dominic said.

"What's his beef with Vito? How does he even know him?" Eugene asked.

"Something about the old days, I didn't get the whole story. Got anyone else other than Vito you want to make?" Dominic asked him.

"Jackie Matts has a problem with Vito, eh? Since Jackie Matts now gets my book in North Carolina, how about you guys ask him to shut the fuck up about Vito and enjoy his new extra income," Eugene said. "That would sound fair to me."

"Plus, he's seventy-seven years old, Eugene. It's like wasting a button," Dominic said.

"I'm seventy-seven years old," Eugene told Dominic.

"Yeah, but you've had your button since the eighties," Dominic said.

"Vito is my choice. Unless, you're giving me another order that's going to cut my legs off, I'm not changing my mind," Eugene said, standing by his man.

Dominic nodded to Danny. "Okay, he can get his button," Danny said.

"Is there any problem with Pete Graziano?" Mario asked them.

"No, Pete's a stand-up guy, runs a classy card game," Dominic answered.

"When are you planning the ceremony?" Eugene asked.

"October, we'll decide the location then," Danny answered.

"Just so that you know, Danny, Dominic has kept the ceremony the same as his father and you did it, it's been perfect," Eugene said.

"Good to know," Danny answered.

"I do have one more thing," Eugene said. "Your sister's father-in-law, Tom Caruso."

"What about him?" Dominic asked.

"He owes me money, but he's asked me to wait for payment until he pays you off for another debt. How much longer do I got to wait?" Eugene asked.

Danny had no idea what this was about and just watched Dominic answer. "What's he owe you?" Dominic asked him.

"A hundred and twenty large, I've been more than patient," Eugene said.

"I'll sit back now and let him pay you, thanks for your patience, Eugene. I didn't know you were waiting to get paid," Dominic answered.

After dinner, Danny asked Dominic about the Tom Caruso debt situation on their way to their car. "Tom was another one who kept the action in Fabian's fucking scheme. I loaned him four hundred grand and ain't seen a penny. And he's got the balls to tell his captain to wait for payment while he pays me off, and he ain't fucking paying me off," Dominic complained.

"Nice job of playing it off in there," Danny told him.

"Isn't that how I'm supposed to play it? Never show what's going on in our house, that's what I was taught. I was also taught not to be fucked with. What am I going to do with Tom?" Dominic asked.

"Well, your father just adores him, so we're stuck with him. How much interest are you charging him?" Danny asked.

"I didn't even charge the fucker any points," Dominic said sadly.

Danny patted him on the back. "Nice one," he said and got in the car, ending the conversation.

A couple hours later, driven by Scary Scarelli and Fat Kenny Infelice in the passenger seat, Danny and Dominic pulled down the dimly lit side street to meet Doug Sullivan. He'd asked them to meet him on the west side, three streets off an exit on I-96. Doug flashed his headlights, and Scary parked the car. Doug, Danny, and Dominic got out and talked in a circle.

"This looks like a fucking hit," Danny complained to Doug.

"I'm kind of thinking we not meet in the open right now. The feds in North Carolina already came by to see one of my guys. I didn't think they had any idea anything was even going on there. I may have made a mistake by making the hit so prime time, but we'll muddle through. The zip is in Mexico, he's on Gary Pizza's track. We should actually have Fabian's hiding spot tonight," Doug explained. "Everything's about to blow up, and like I said, we should meet on the down low for a while."

"Gary Pizza dies when he gets home, right?" Dominic asked.

"He gets home Monday, he won't see Friday," Doug said.

"Then what about Mexico?" Danny asked.

"We'll find who his allies are down there, and they'll either work for us or die. We'll take over everything else Fabian kept hidden, just more money rolling in," Doug told them.

"And what about North Carolina? We just told Modica he was out and we'll just enlarge the other crew there," Danny said.

"I don't care as long it doesn't interfere with my business there. Remember, my business there makes you richer than your business there. We'll just have to ride it out," Doug said.

The next day, Danny, Dominic, Doug, and Tommy gathered at a warehouse in Ann Arbor to divvy up some of the weapons from the cache they had discovered a month ago. "Here you go, an M-16 for each of you," Doug said, hoisting two metal cases and bags that contained ammunition on a table.

Dominic opened his case and gasped in joy, "Wow, ain't this something?"

"I'm sure I don't need to remind everyone that this not something to leave out for the feds if you get raided," Doug said, pulling out his own.

"Everyone's not loaded, right?" Tommy asked.

Everyone checked their weapons and concurred. "Good, you're all dead. Pop, pop, pop," Tommy yelled as he pretended to shoot the trio and run off hiding behind boxes.

Doug ran off chasing his friend in a game of make-believe with their new M-16s. Dominic looked at Danny. "Go ahead, be a fucking kid," Danny told him. Dominic ran off to join Doug and Tommy.

After about ten minutes of playing around, they returned, but Danny was now gone. "Danny! Danny, come on, we were just playing. We're sorry," Doug called out.

"Yeah, you're sorry all right. Sorry, now that you're all dead," Danny called out from the top of a stack of wooden pallets that he had climbed up on and waited like a sniper. "Pop, pop, pop."

"Good one, Danny. Come on down, you want any grenades?" Doug called out, opening another box. "He's like sixty years old, should he be climbing up on a pallet stack?" Doug whispered to Dominic.

Two days later, Tuesday morning, Billy Herrick let himself into the zips apartment. "What's this shit? You're too sick to meet me for breakfast?" Billy called out. He found Benedetto on the couch. "What happened to you? You look like ass," Billy said.

"What happened to me? I'll tell you what happened to me. I drive eleven hours to shoot a man, then I drive down into Florida. Do you think I could sleep? No, I'm whisked off into a boat and taken to Mexico. Not just any boat, I say, a small speedboat, and we're taking that to Mexico in the middle of the night. I'm met by men with machine guns, who give me a car and tell me where this Gary Pizza guy is staying. Still no sleep for poor Benedetto, I've got to stay awake and wait for him to lead me to this Fabian Bosca. No pasta, no tomato sauce, just burritos and tequila," Benedetto complained from the couch.

"Well, what'd you do, drink the water?" Billy asked, keeping his distance to avoid catching the aliment. "Don't drink the water in Mexico."

"What does that mean 'don't drink the water'?" he asked Billy in irritation.

"Because it's bad water, everyone always says don't drink the water while you're in Mexico. You never heard that?" Billy asked.

"How stupid. You don't swallow water when you are in the shower? What a stupid fucking saying," Benedetto said.

"You sure are picking up the language well, listen to you swear. Why don't you just sleep now?" Billy asked.

"I'd like to, but you kept insisting on talking to me," he complained.

"Well, are we all set with Gary Pizza?"

"Yes, yes, I will kill him tomorrow. I've got two men on him now, he's at home. I just need to sleep this off," Benedetto said.

"You're a grumpy fuck when you don't feel well. Just so you know, I was going to treat for breakfast," Billy said as he left.

Benedetto slept through the day and awoke early to join his roommates, Alberto and Franco, who had Gary Pizza staked out. Gary was having a 6:00 a.m. breakfast with one of his guys, and Benedetto had Franco drop him off at Gary's house, while Alberto stayed on Gary.

Gary left the restaurant and headed home, as was his normal routine. Gary normally backed his car into his garage, and Benedetto hid in the bushes next to the driveway, hoping he'd stick to his pattern.

Gary stayed true to form and backed his car into the driveway. Once he passed Benedetto in the shrubbery, he jumped out and fired his silenced revolver twice through the driver window and watched the driver's head slump against the steering wheel, causing the horn to blow endlessly; the car continued to roll in reverse.

This was more noise than Benedetto had planned for. He acted quickly; he reached in through the shattered window and opened the driver's door. He threw Gary Pizza's body to the passenger seat and jumped in, instantly getting his foot on the brake and stopping the car.

He dropped it into drive and sped off; lights were turning on all over the place on this quiet residential street. Gary had a wife and daughter in the house, and Benedetto expected them to see Gary's car speeding out of their driveway. He turned to the right, hoping if

Gary's family didn't see the busted-out window, they still might not think something terrible had happened and wait to call the police.

Turning right got Benedetto confused from his planned escape route, and he quickly became lost in the maze of side streets. He pushed Gary's body to the floorboards as best he could and fired another shot into his temple, just to be safe. He broke away any remaining glass, so that it appeared that the window was just rolled down. Despite the blood on the dashboard and steering wheel, Benedetto was feeling confident he could make it to the chop shop to incinerate the car and the body without any problems, once he found his way.

He tried to take another side street back in the direction he wanted to go, but it twisted him around back the way he was going before. Still remaining calm, he turned the car around and retraced his steps. Once he got near the street of his victim, he turned, hoping to find a busy road. A couple of blocks later, he passed a car and made eye contact with the driver, who gave Benedetto a friendly nod. If he was in his remote lands of Sicily, he'd have turned around and killed the witness, but he was under strict orders in America to only kill people he was assigned to kill. If he was caught with the body in the car or arrested later because of the witness, he'd just have to go to jail. He knew his family would be cared for if he went to prison.

He finally came to a streetlight and turned onto the main road. Benedetto pulled out the address of the chop shop and inputted it into the navigation system. He was there within ten minutes.

Benedetto pulled into the chop shop and gave the car to its boss. Benedetto went inside to get Alberto and Franco, who were waiting for him to arrive. He found them playing cards with some of the employees. He walked over and stood behind them. "What if I needed you?"

Both men jumped in surprise. Alberto answered him, "We'd have come."

Benedetto started yelling in Sicilian at them, and one of the players interrupted, "Yo dawg, calm down. We got a fucking game going here."

Benedetto snapped; he pulled his gun out and put it to the man's forehead. "Call me dog now!" he yelled with his thick accent.

Everyone stood silent, except for Alberto and Franco, who tried to calm Benedetto down. "It's how they talk, he no mean harm," Alberto said.

"Yeah, man, it's how I talk. I no mean harm," the man repeated, terrified.

"Motherfuckers," Benedetto said as he put his gun away. "Let's go," he called to Alberto and Franco.

The next morning, Doug met Dominic at a bar on the west side. "Those fucking sunglasses are starting to get annoying," Doug joked when Dominic sat down.

"You're worried about my sunglasses? You got bigger problems, my friend," Dominic said.

"What problems are those, my friend?" Doug asked him back.

"Your fucking zip pulled a gun on someone at Moshe Levin's chop shop when he dropped off the body," Dominic told him.

"What?"

"Yeah, he started screaming in Sicilian at his guys because they were playing cards and someone told him to calm down and called him a dog," Dominic said.

"Called him a dog? Like a dog dog, or a 'what up, dog?'" Doug asked. "These are men of respect, and they don't take kindly to being called dogs."

Dominic held his arms open. "Come on, Doug, you serious?"

Doug sighed, "No, you're right. I have no idea about this, let me find out."

"Well, you got to find out about it, there's a sit-down tomorrow night about it," Dominic said.

"Okay, I'll get you the info," Doug said.

"Bring it to the sit-down," Dominic told him.

"What are you shitting me? I can't go to no sit-down, I'm not Italian," Doug complained.

"Neither is Moshe Levin. Face it, Doug, if you look at an FBI crime family chart, you're on it, just like Moshe is. You're part of this family," Dominic said.

"And you want me to go to a sit-down against Moshe Levin, that Frankenstein motherfucker?" Doug asked.

"He's a sweetheart if you get to know him," Dominic said.

"Am I going to get to know him?"

"No, he's pretty pissed. And I'll tell you, I wouldn't want him pissed at me. He's a hit man from the Black and White day," Dominic said.

"And you guys are scared and want me to keep you out of it," Doug said.

"It's actually my father's idea. He said you can stand up for yourself. There's no reason for me or Danny to argue with my father's decisions," Dominic said with a smile.

"Terrific, and when is this sit-down?" Doug asked.

"Ten o'clock tomorrow night, at the Cucina," Dominic told him.

"At your father's restaurant, how stupid is that?" Doug asked.

"What?"

"Why don't you just write a letter to the feds and give them permission to wiretap the restaurant. They take pictures of the meeting there, they take it to a judge and ask for a wiretap, and because you gave them the probable cause, they start listening to the next sit-down there. Real fucking smart, Dom," Doug complained.

"You want to fucking plan it then?" Dominic asked.

"Yes, I do. Let's all just head out on the highway, find an exit an hour away and get a hotel room. It's totally random, and we'll have plenty of time and room to shed any tails," Doug explained.

The following night, the meeting took place in a hotel suite two hours from their homes. Danny and Dominic were there. Moshe Levin was with his captain, Benny Mancini, and Doug was there by himself.

Doug shook hands with everyone, and Moshe spoke to him first, "I met you at a wedding, years ago. Whose wedding was that?" he asked Doug, in his deep and loud voice with words always spoken slowly.

Doug nodded to Dominic. "Dominic's sister, Valentina's."

"Oh yeah, Nick's daughter. You were away, Danny, it was a beautiful wedding," Moshe told him.

"I've seen pictures," Danny said, bored with the small talk.

Dominic started the meeting. "Let's get down to business. Moshe, you've got a gripe against Doug. We're all in agreement that Doug's man put a gun to Moshe's guy's head?"

Moshe and Doug nodded their agreements. "Then how say you, Doug?" Dominic asked.

"What do you mean?" Doug asked him.

"What's your story? What's your defense of your man?" Dominic answered.

"I'm new to all this here with you guys. Where I come from, I ask the questions, so I want to be clear. There's no question my guy did what he did, what else am I defending him from?" Doug asked.

Danny answered, "Doug, once the facts are on the table, Dominic will decide a punishment for your man or reparations for Moshe."

"My guy was offended when your guy called him a dog. He was already hot from his lazy men playing cards, and he snapped. There's no excuse here, he was fucking wrong. I'm responsible for him, and I'm apologizing for him. If this asshole is a loose cannon, then I'll send him back where the fuck he came from, but I'll deal with that. To you, Moshe, I'm sorry he did that. I do appreciate your shop there, and I'd never do anything to jeopardize it," Doug said, extending his hand for a handshake.

Moshe shook Doug's hand. "I accept your apology."

Doug sat back down. "Good, then we're done here?"

"I still have a decision to render," Dominic said.

"I want death," Moshe said.

"What the fuck? You just said you accepted my apology," Doug told him.

"I do accept your apology. But I can't forgive the actions of your man. And if he's from Sicily, why does he work for you?" Moshe asked.

"Because he just fucking does. You're nuts if you think I'm whacking him for this. I agree a hundred fucking percent he was wrong, but your man ain't dead, and mine ain't going to be either."

"Hang on, Doug," Dominic said.

"You guys want an eye for an eye? Fine, give your guy a gun, have him put it to my guy's head for a minute or so, and call him a few names," Doug said, shrugging his shoulders.

"No one needs to die here," Danny interrupted.

"Let's talk reparations," Dominic said.

"If he's gets a pass, I want 250 grand," Moshe said.

"For what?" Doug called out.

"For the lack of respect," Moshe answered.

"If it was about respect, an apology and a handshake would do," Doug said.

"What would you do if it was one of your guys?" Moshe asked Doug.

"None of my guys would ever let someone walk away if they put a gun to their head and didn't pull the trigger. I got nothing else to say other than my guy was wrong and I'm sorry. You want gas money for driving all the way here, fine. I'll even pay for a new pair of drawers if your man shit himself or the tissue box he bought to cry himself to sleep that night. Other than that, ain't no one getting a fucking penny from me or my guy," Doug claimed.

Silence overtook the room. Moshe stared at Doug. "You know, it took me a long time to agree to play by their rules," he said, nodding to Danny and Dominic. "But it came down to it one day. Either I play by their rules or I don't play their game. You might think you can start your own game and make your rules and keep them around for their names. You're not the first to think that, but their thing will always take center stage, it will always prevail. I see you got balls, have enough brains to learn these lessons when you're young."

"What are you telling me?" Doug asked him.

"I'm telling you Dominic still has a decision to make, and he knows that at a minimum, I'm entitled to some cash," Moshe said.

"Twenty grand," Dominic decided.

Doug wanted to grab him by his throat. "Twenty grand? Okay, fine, twenty grand. I'll have it to you tomorrow. And you're right, Moshe, I did learn a valuable lesson here today," he said and walked out.

CHAPTER XXIV

PRIORITIES

TOMMY HERRICK MET Dominic Amicucci on a side street off the freeway, halfway between both their houses at four o'clock Saturday morning. "What's up, Tommy?" Dominic asked.

Tommy handed him a knapsack. "Here, Doug said this is for Moshe Levin," Tommy told him. "It's twenty grand."

"It's twenty grand, why's it so heavy? Oh no, Tommy, is there twenty thousand singles in here?" Dominic asked, hoping Doug didn't go through all this trouble just to anger the infamous hit man.

Tommy nodded his head. "Yeah, Doug sure is hot at you guys."

"I already paid him the twenty grand, and that was my plan all along. I just needed Doug to make me look good. Give this back to him," Dominic said.

Tommy put his hands in the air. "That's all between you guys, my job here is done. I'll see you next Friday with our monthly cut."

"Fine, I'll deal with Doug. Let me ask you something about those Swiss accounts before you go," Dominic said.

"What do you want to know?"

"How the hell does it work?"

"I don't know the actual drug routes, but the money system is a thing of beauty. Doug set that up. We pay the Sicilian Mafia and the Colombian Cartel through those accounts. We get our money from our man in Miami, Virgil Boyle, who transfers the money back into the accounts. He gets his money from the streets. He's the one that washes all those millions in cash. We never see it, we never touch it. We just give the okay and collect the money in overseas accounts," Tommy explained.

"I hide my money until I get over seven hundred grand in cash, then I give it to you or Doug and you guys give me an account number. Where does that money go?" Dominic asked.

"That's my creation, my guys handle that. There's no need to know there," Tommy said.

"I'm not a fucking rat. What's wrong with you?" Dominic asked.

"It ain't about that. No offense, you just don't need to know," Tommy told him.

"Whatever. You wait until next year when I'm back in shape. You and me are going to do a little sparring. I hear you spar a lot," Dominic said.

"You really want to get a match going when we're both a hundred percent? Because I got to tell you, that was the best fight of my life. I'd love to do it again, in a ring, though. I wouldn't want you to get your hands on another frying pan," Tommy joked.

"We'll set some odds and get some action going on it," Dominic said.

"I love that thinking," Tommy told him.

"Done, I'm going to set up my fucking surgeries so I can get back in the gym," Dominic said.

"Hey, just don't kill yourself doing this. I want you at your best when I knock you out," Tommy joked as he got in his car.

It was close to five in the morning when Tommy arrived at Doug's house. As usual, he walked to the backyard, but this time he heard something going on back there. At first, he was alarmed and wished he had a gun on him. But he heard Doug's voice and it wasn't distressed, so Tommy entered the yard.

There was Doug on the patio, and he had his oldest son, Graham, running the four corners of the yard. Doug heard Tommy open the gate, and Tommy looked on disbelief. "It's five in the morning, Doug, what's going on?"

"Just getting him ready for his first game on Tuesday," Doug told him.

"He's in tee ball," Tommy said, still puzzled.

"Nonetheless," Doug said.

"You got to relax on this kid, Doug. He is my godson, after all."

"Relax? He needs to pick up the pace. Besides, he was in bed early," Doug said.

"Not to give credence to the 'pick up the pace' comment, but I was here at nine o'clock last night and you were throwing the ball with him. You got your kid sleeping five hours or something?" Tommy asked. "Grace can't be okay with this."

"I'll have him back in bed before she wakes up in another hour," Doug said.

"She don't know," Tommy said laughing. "That's great, she will kill you, Doug."

"Why is everyone bitching at me? You got another kid coming, could be a boy, you should be writing down what I'm doing. What I'm doing here, Tommy, is giving you and everyone else a recipe for success," Doug boasted. "This kid's going to be in the major leagues. And I'll have Bobby in the NFL, it's perfect parenting.

"You know these kids are going be emotional cripples, right?"

Doug gave Tommy a curious look. "Tommy, I said the major leagues. That boy right there will be a major league baseball pitcher."

Tommy just nodded his head. "Okay."

"You're his godfather, and you should be on him too," Doug told him.

"Nope, I'm his only hope of having a normal male figure in his life," Tommy said.

"Nah, his grandfather babies him too. And I know you're the one that gives him those twenty-dollar bills I keep finding in his room," Doug said. "I take them all."

"Poor, poor kid," Tommy joked, sort of. He had no idea about the twenties; he gave his godson fifties and hundreds that the boy kept well hidden. "Well, don't worry, I'll take care of your kids when Grace goes to jail for killing you."

"What do you want anyway?" Doug asked, irritated now. "Graham, three more times around and get upstairs," Doug called lightly to his son.

"Dominic paid Moshe the money, you weren't supposed to pay," Tommy told him, watching his godson finish another time around the yard, wishing the lights would come on in the house.

"What kind of bullshit is that? He just doesn't want to give him the singles, fucking pussy," Doug scoffed.

"I don't think it's bullshit at all. He seemed surprised you thought you had to pay," Tommy said, another lap complete.

"Could he be that dumb and not tell me he had a plan?"

"Yeah, obviously," Tommy said.

Graham finished his laps and walked up the stairs to the deck. "Hi, Uncle Tommy," he said as he saw his uncle.

"Nice job, there," Tommy said as he high-fived the out-of-breath six almost seven-year-old.

"Come here," Doug said, giving his son a hug. "Great job, I'm proud of you, Son," he said as he ran a towel over Graham's head, drying off the sweat. "Take this." He handed him bottled water.

"What're you learning in school, Graham?" Tommy asked.

"I spelled necklace, and that's a third grade word. And I'm only in kindergarten," Graham boasted.

"Well that's pretty smart," Tommy said.

"Hey, Graham, I'll bet you your Uncle Tommy can't even spell it," Doug joked.

Graham laughed and got a kiss from his father and uncle as he went to his room before his mother got up.

Doug and Tommy continued their talk. "Want to have some fun?" Doug asked him.

"What?" he answered, cautiously.

"Go back and tell Dominic I'm furious. I insist he gives Moshe the singles or I'll do it myself," Doug said. "Tell him it's not the money, it's the message I want delivered."

"Oh no," Tommy said, shaking his head.

"Oh yeah," Doug said, nodding his head. "Tommy, it'll be hilarious."

"Don't we have enough going on?"

"When is it ever going to be enough?" Doug joked. "Come on, do it. I'll let Danny in on it, that way he can make the peace."

"Make the peace, well, at least, you seem to know it'll come to that," Tommy said.

"This Moshe guy is going to be so pissed at the mere thought that someone would disrespect him like that, to give him ones. Dominic's going to be terrified, it'll be great. Well worth the ramifications, believe me," Doug said. "Come on, do it."

"Okay, I'll do it," Tommy said, giving in to the pure pressure.

"Yes," Doug said, slicing his fist through the air in celebration.

"I'm not so sure your priorities are really in order anymore," Tommy joked.

"Oh, sure they are."

Lights started coming on in the house, and the men departed. Grace came into the kitchen as Doug came in through the door wall. Grace looked at Doug. "Tommy?" she asked, knowing who her husband's early morning meeting must've been with.

"Tommy," Doug answered.

Grace went to the coffeepot. "Don't you think you could've at least started a pot?"

Doug looked blankly at her. "I'll be honest, yes, I could've, and yes, I should've, especially because I'd really like a cup."

"You were a considerate man when I married you," Grace said with her back to Doug.

"Just a ruse to lure you in, and now you're stuck," Doug joked.

"Not if I kill you," Grace said, still with her back turned.

"That's odd," Doug said.

"What's odd, your lack of consideration?"

"No, not that. Tommy was just saying that you were going to kill me," Doug said.

"You can tell Tommy that I've never forgotten it was him that introduced me to you. Tell him he's on my list too," she said, turning around and pointing a kitchen knife at Doug.

"Why do you have a knife if you're making coffee?" Doug asked.

Grace looked at the knife and back to Doug and smiled. "No reason, honey."

Doug smiled back. "I knew you'd be my downfall from the moment I laid eyes on you."

Tommy met Dominic on another side street and relayed Doug's message. Dominic went to the Corner to consult with Danny, who had already been let in on it by Doug. Danny told him to take Moshe the singles.

They met Moshe at night and used the side street meeting. Moshe looked in the bag and back at Dominic. "Is this all singles?"

"Twenty thousand of them," Dominic said.

"But he already paid me. I do not understand," Moshe said.

Dominic was getting nervous. "It's another twenty grand to show how sorry his man was."

"In singles? Who does this?"

"The singles are like a joke," Dominic said, as he realized he might not be helping matters.

"Joke? Where's the joke?" Moshe asked as Dominic started to sweat.

"Look, I fronted the money that day so that you'd get it right away. He paid me the next day, he gave me the singles to give to you," Dominic said.

"He was paying me singles? Why?"

"I'm not sure, he thinks it's funny. And not in a funny, ha-ha, Moshe or nothing way. You know, just a joke, like between friends," Dominic stammered, trying to not anger Moshe.

Moshe was getting angry though, and Dominic nudged Danny. "Anything?" Danny didn't answer.

"Why does a man pay another in one-dollar bills when he doesn't have to? He's this angry about the money that he'd actually do all this work?" Moshe asked.

"I don't think he's mad. Like I said, a friendly joke," Dominic stammered.

"This is no joke, Dominic. This is a fuck you to me," Moshe said, voice rising.

"No, not a fuck you. Danny, you got anything to say here?" Dominic asked, hoping.

Keeping a straight face, Danny said, "No, I really don't know why someone would count out all those singles. That is a lot of effort, I just have no opinion."

"Thanks," Dominic said to him.

"I'm calling my captain, and we need to have a sit-down. I'm not backing down this time, someone's dying for this," Moshe warned.

"Moshe, come one, it's not like that," Dominic said.

"Is this the sit-down? Because, I've requested my captain, remember?"

"No, this isn't the sit-down, we're just talking here," Dominic said.

"Well, I want a sit-down," Moshe screamed.

Danny couldn't hold it any longer and burst out laughing. He dropped to his knees on the grass in his suit—he was laughing so hard. Tears were rolling down his eyes as he tried to explain. "It's all a joke, it's all a joke. You guys reacted perfectly, oh man. Perfect."

After a few minutes of this, everyone grew silent. Moshe held up the bag. "So what about this?"

Dominic smiled. "I guess Doug and Tommy's little joke just cost them twenty grand."

Danny grabbed the bag. "OK, let's split it up in the truck."

The next morning, Danny met with Doug and Tommy for breakfast to give them the details of their joke. After everyone enjoyed the story, Doug asked who took the money, fully expecting to not get it back. "We split it up," Danny told him.

Doug was surprised. "Who's we?"

"Me, Dominic, and Moshe. Why?"

"I'll be honest with you, Danny, I don't really see why you got a cut of my money," Doug said.

"You being serious?" Danny asked him back.

"Well, yeah, what'd you take, sixty six hundred?"

"Flat six grand," Danny answered.

"I think I want that back," Doug said.

"You think you want that back?" Danny repeated.

"Yeah, it's like I just gave you six g's," Doug explained. "That means you went into this whole thing expecting a third of that money. That's not right. Don't get one over on me. You know the number I could do over on you?"

"Let me ask you something then. What are you giving Dominic and Moshe ten grand apiece for? For the laugh? For their expenses of setting up a meet? Just for the enjoyment, right?" Danny asked.

"Pretty much, yeah," Doug agreed.

"Then here's the best joke of them all: The reason Dominic didn't tell you that you didn't have to pay Moshe, was our joke on you. And, oh my God, Doug, look how you reacted. Twenty thousand singles? I got to tell you, sitting back and watching both these jokes play out was priceless." Danny laid his six thousand dollars on the table. "Worth every penny, Doug. Priceless."

After Danny left, Doug looked at Tommy. "Did that really happen or is he just saving face?"

Tommy was amused. "And you lose fourteen grand."

"I only had to even tell Danny because you were so scared," Doug said.

"Well, then you'd have lost the whole twenty grand, then wouldn't you've?" Tommy joked.

The next night, Doug received a phone call from Dominic needing to meet with him. At 1:00 a.m., Doug saw his truck on the side of the freeway. Doug pulled over and reversed his car and got out to talk to Dominic who was with Danny.

"We got another hit for the zips," Danny told him as cars zipped by on the freeway.

"Cleaning house, eh? What do you got?" Doug asked.

"A guy in Miami, he's actually not one of ours. He's an enemy importing drugs for Fabian. Benny Mancini's crew down there found out about it," Dominic explained.

"Benny Mancini?" Doug asked suspiciously.

"You know Benny," Danny told him.

"Yeah, I've met Benny a few times. But I do know Moshe Levin works for Benny," Doug said.

"So?" Danny asked.

"It sounds like the set up to a joke," Doug said.

"Oh come on," Dominic let out with a laugh.

"This is a hit, Doug," Danny said. "No one plays games with this shit."

"Okay then, are you sure that this guy isn't part of Benny's crew and no one wants to tell me that another of your crews that I let operate in my area is fucked up?" Doug asked.

"He's Cuban, Doug," Danny told him.

"Is he part of a Cuban operation? I'd like to know more about what kinds of aftermaths are coming after this guy goes down. I say it again, I got a lot to lose there," Doug reminded them again, just like with North Carolina.

"Small-time crew, just a few guys," Dominic said, shrugging his shoulders.

"This is what Benny says from his crew there?" Doug asked.

"Yeah," Danny answered.

"Okay, you got his name and address?"

"Here," Dominic said, handing Doug a folded piece of paper.

"Okay, I'll talk with you guys later," Doug said, walking back to his car.

"That's it?" Danny yelled to him.

"Yeah, I'll talk to you later," Doug said, getting in his car and pulling back onto the road.

"What's with him?" Dominic asked.

"He doesn't believe us. He still really thinks it's a joke. He's going to have his people in Miami look into it, guaranteed," Danny said.

"Suspicious fucker," Dominic joked.

Doug left there and met up with Tommy's brother, Billy. Billy took him to the zips' apartment, and they were buzzed up at three in the morning. Benedetto opened the door and let him in. "Benedetto, this is Doug Sullivan," Billy introduced.

Benedetto looked embarrassed to be in just his pajama pants for the first time he met Billy's boss. "I am honored," Benedetto said, shaking Doug's hand.

"I'm honored, anyone that turns in forty million dollars deserves respect," Doug said. "Go ahead, throw a shirt on." Doug took a seat at the kitchen table with Billy. Benedetto's two roommates, Alberto and Franco, were pleased to meet Doug, as well.

After everyone gathered at the table, Doug spoke to the group. "You guys done a great job since you been here. But I got to ask," Doug said to Benedetto, "why'd you pull your gun on that guy?"

"He called me an animal," Benedetto answered. "Apparently to be a dog here is to be cool. I will not ever understand that one."

"Next time, if you're going to cause me all this grief, pull the fucking trigger and make it worth my while," Doug told him.

The men all laughed, and Doug began again, "I do have to know though, that that'll be the last incident. Understand that your fuckups can cause me and Billy our lives," Doug explained.

"I would die for you," Benedetto said.

"That's not what I'm asking here. I want to know if I have to worry about you. Do I?" Doug asked.

"No, no worry," he answered.

"Good. Then after all this bullshit calms down, you're going on a vacation. You've got five million dollars of the money you turned in to get home and get to your families," Doug told them.

"What?" Benedetto asked, shocked.

Doug looked at Billy. "You didn't tell him?"

"I told him we'd take care of him. Five million's a lot to promise. I just wanted to make sure before," Billy said.

"So anyway, you'll get a million dollars and all your men will get three hundred and fifty thousand. It's all been laundered in overseas bank accounts, which you'll be emptying out when you go to Europe and then back home as a rich man. If you want to bring your family back with you, that'll be fine," Doug explained.

"I don't know what to say," Benedetto said.

"Don't say nothing, yet there's still plenty of more to work to do," Doug told them. "Billy and I need you to go to Miami and see a friend of ours. His name is Virgil Boyle, and he's one of my top men. I need you guys to track someone down and find some things out for me. Take one of your guys with you and head down tomorrow. Virgil will tell what to do while you're there. He speaks for me," Doug said.

"I am at your service," Benedetto said humbly.

"Oh, there was a little cash left over from your stash, it didn't get laundered. Give it to him, Bill." Billy tossed an envelope to Benedetto. "A hundred and fifteen thousand dollars cash for you. Have some fun. But, remember, you guys can't cause no trouble."

"Never," Benedetto told him.

"One more thing, you've got a tail on Fabian Bosca since he flew in last night?" Doug asked.

"Of course," he answered.

"Take the tail off," Doug told him.

A few hours later, Fabian Bosca entered the dimly lit bar. It was just after six in the morning and only the two people he was meeting with were there, Vinny Jagge and his son, Frankie.

Vinny greeted him and kissed him on both cheeks. "How was your flight? You're just getting in?"

"No, flew in last night, I stayed at a hotel near the airport. Flight was fine," Fabian answered. Vinny already knew Fabian had stayed the night at his mother's house. He knew because Angelo Rea had picked up Fabian at the airport and dropped him off.

Fabian handed Vinny a thick envelope. "How much is this?" Vinny asked.

"212 grand, normal month," Fabian reported.

The door opened, and Vinny's youngest son, Michael, entered with a pot of coffee and four mugs. Michael Jagge was the one Fabian feared the most. He feared he was the guy pegged to kill him so that Michael could make his bones and get his button later this year. Fabian's senses were already heightened, but now he was scared to even blink. He took a step backward to get closer to the wall and kept his eyes on the three Jagges. "None for me, thanks," Fabian said as Michael poured him a cup.

"We're all drinking from the same pot, it ain't poisoned," Vinny joked.

"Free breakfast at the hotel this morning, I had plenty of coffee," Fabian said.

"Suit yourself," Vinny said. "Frankie, you had a question for Fabian, didn't you?"

"Yeah, when Gary Pizza worked for you, did he have any secret spots that you knew of?" Frankie asked.

"Secret spots?" Fabian asked.

"He's missing. He hasn't checked in with me in almost two weeks. His wife reported him missing to the cops, and I was wondering if there was somewhere you knew that we could check," Frankie explained.

Yeah, he's missing because you fuckers killed him, Fabian thought to himself. "No idea, we weren't that close," Fabian lied.

"Well, if you can keep an ear out, we'd appreciate it. You want to get some breakfast with us?" Fabian asked.

"No, in fact, if there's nothing else, I got to see my mother," Fabian lied again.

"Sure, see you later," Vinny said. None of the Jagges moved, they just kept their eyes locked on Fabian.

This is it, Fabian thought to himself. His only choice of walking to the door on the other side was by walking by Michael Jagge. Fabian locked his eyes on Michael and started walking. Michael never moved an inch, and Fabian now had his back turned to the trio, and terrified.

"Fabian," Vinny called out.

Fabian almost started running but turned instead, expecting a gunshot. "Yeah?"

"Here, your smokes," Vinny said and tossed Fabian's pack to him that he left on the table.

Fabian's knees almost buckled to the floor; he was so relieved. "Thanks," he said as he caught the cigarettes and turned back around for the door. This was the last time he was going to come here, he thought to himself as he finally heard the gunshot that he feared was coming.

CHAPTER XXV

The Card Game

"GIVE ME YOUR gun," Frankie Jagge said urgently to his brother Michael. Michael still hadn't moved a muscle, he was frozen.

"Give me your fucking gun, Mike," Frankie yelled to him.

Michael gave his brother his silenced revolver. Frankie took the gun and ran over to the wounded Fabian. After Fabian had turned his back on the Jagges, the plan was for Michael to shoot Fabian. When he couldn't, Frankie pulled out his gun and fired. He wasn't expecting to use the gun, so he hadn't put the silencer on it; the bang was loud, and he was worried.

Frankie's shot hit Fabian in the back. Fabian seemed to have only the use of his left arm, and he was trying to pull himself across the floor and to the door with it. He had a gun strapped to his right ankle, but Fabian could only think to pull himself across the wooden floor. He pulled himself another couple of inches toward the door when he saw the shadow cast over him.

Fabian gave up the fight. He flopped onto his back to look his killer in the eyes. Frank Jagge placed the gun to Fabian's forehead and "Fuck you, Fabian," were the last words Fabian heard.

"Goddammit, Michael, it wasn't supposed to go down like this. Get the blankets," he ordered his brother.

Vinny pushed his comatose son into life. "Move, you fucking nitwit."

"Let's go, Mike, that fucking gunshot was loud, anyone could've heard it. We got to move," Frankie said, as he already grabbed the blankets from under bar.

Frankie covered the head while Vinny covered the bleeding from the back shot. There was a blood trail from where Fabian had crawled; there was a lot more blood than they had expected. Vinny grabbed some bleach and started pouring it on the bloodstains. Frankie grabbed a mop and kept bitching at his brother.

"Leave him alone, he's in fucking shock," Vinny told him. "You're no better with your fucking bad shot. He didn't have to die like that."

"Fuck him," Frankie said as he started mopping.

Vinny knocked the mop out of his son's hands and grabbed Frankie by the face, squeezing his cheeks. He got right in his son's face and hissed, "He didn't have to die like that." He pushed Frankie away. "You're a fucking monster if you enjoyed watching him crawl across the floor like that. Fucking Michael's now fucked up. You got to get out and practice your shooting."

"All right, all right, we got to get this body out of here," Frankie said. He went into Fabian's pocket and pulled his car keys out. He tossed them to his father, who stopped to talk to Michael before he left to pull Fabian's car into the ally.

"Michael, it's okay, it's okay," Vinny told him.

"I'm sorry, Dad, I just couldn't move," Michael told him.

"It's okay," Vinny repeated. "It'll be our secret, okay? Don't tell anyone what happened here. We'll just say you did it, and we'll still get you your button. Can you help Frankie carry the body to the trunk? I'm almost seventy, Son, I don't think I can."

Michael slowly nodded his head. "That a boy, everything's okay," Vinny told him and hurried out the back door.

"I'm sorry, Frankie," Michael told his brother from across the room.

"Don't worry about it. Just help me with the body. I'm going to take the car and get rid of it and the body. Dad's going to follow me. You've got to stay here and keep cleaning," Frankie told him.

Within an hour, Fabian Bosca's body was crushed inside of his car and the remnants melted down and incinerated at Moshe Levin's chop shop. Vinny stopped at a pay phone to phone Danny and tell him that the hit was a success and his son, Michael, was the shooter. The Jagges returned to the bar and took Michael out of there. Vinny and Frankie spent the rest of the day looking at new floors to replace the bloodstained ones. Even though it was cleaned up, the feds had the ability to still find where blood was spilled.

Dominic was at the bakery when he got word that the deed was done. He grabbed his cigarettes and went for a walk in the beautiful May day. Four blocks later, he took a seat on the old bench across the street from the apartment complex Fabian used to live in. As far back as Dominic could remember, he was a regular guest at the Bosca apartment. It was just Fabian and his mother, the best of friends.

His poor mother, Dominic thought, *she's not going to get over this*. She's buried a husband, a granddaughter, and now she'll bury her son—except, she'll never have a body to bury, and that bothered Dominic. She now lived in a nice house not far from here.

His throwaway phone rang; it was his father from prison. "You okay, Dominic?" Nick asked him.

"Yeah, yeah, it's not like some surprise. I should be happy, the way he fucked me over," Dominic said.

"He fucked you over because of me. There's never any happiness in days like these. Go be with that girl of yours," Nick told him.

"I broke up with her."

"You what?" Nick asked.

"I told her there ain't no future, she started with the marriage talk," Dominic said.

"Already? She really moved fast. Damn Dominic, you're getting it from all sides," Nick joked.

"You know what, Dad? It doesn't even matter. I'm ready for it all. I'm a new man," Dominic boasted. "And soon, I'll look like one."

"Tommy's beating made you see how you were acting?" Nick asked.

"Actually, it was when Danny put it on the line for me in my basement. He told me to go to Angela's grave and clear my head. I did, and she talked to me," Dominic said.

"Oh she did, did she? What'd she say?" Nick asked skeptically.

"She forgave me," Dominic answered.

Later in the evening, Dominic was at the Corner, hanging out with Danny and the crew when Fabian's mother stopped by. They sat with her at a table as she asked if they knew Fabian's whereabouts. "He said he had some business, but that he'd be here at the Corner with you guys," she explained.

"You know Fabian, Kristina, he's always working. I didn't even know he was in town," Danny told her.

"He said Angelo picked him up at the airport and dropped him off at my house last night," she said.

"No, I was with Angelo last night," Dominic said, giving his cousin an alibi.

"Why would he lie to me unless something bad was happening?" Kristina Bosca asked, starting to panic.

"Relax, he's a big boy. We'll ask around, see what we can come up with. He could be on a plane to Mexico right now for all we know," Danny said.

After a little while, they finally convinced her that Fabian was all right and she left. "Seems like just yesterday when she was running in here for help with her bills after Fabian's father was whacked," Danny told Dominic.

"She's had it rough," Dominic said. "She's a good woman."

"It's a sad day. Even when you know it's coming and it's something that has to happen, it doesn't make it any easier," Danny said, getting up to get a drink. "Your dad said you broke up with that brunette. How'd you do it?"

"I just told her she had to go," Dominic said.

"And she just left?"

"Well, she did the whole crying thing, and I just told her I was never marrying again and that she's an idiot if she wants to be with someone like me. I told her if some hot blonde threw herself at me, I probably wouldn't hesitate. That got her to go," Dominic said.

"So, you're all set then, no woman, no kids? Just going to ride this thing out, huh?" Danny asked.

"Until jail," Dominic answered.

"Then you better make sure Angelo's ready by that day," Danny told him.

Dominic stopped by his father's house after he left Danny. He had just missed dinner, but he grabbed a piece of tiramisu. His sister was there with her husband and his parents. Dominic took her father-in-law outside for a discussion.

"Tom, why can't you make any money?" Dominic asked him.

"What do you mean?" Tom Caruso asked.

"You can't pay your captain, and you tell him you can't pay him because you got to pay me? And you ain't paid me nothing. What the fuck, Tom?"

"That's not what I told him. I didn't tell him I was paying you. I told him I owe you a lot of money," Tom told him. "I swear, I think Eugene's getting senile."

"Shut the fuck up about Eugene. He shouldn't have to not get paid from his own lieutenant. I asked you a question, why can't you make any money?" Dominic asked again.

Tom didn't answer, so Dominic continued drilling him. "You only got three fucking rackets, you got no headaches. All three have always been healthy and profitable. Your Southfield book was a cash machine. You got the education union, nothing major, but you should be eating well on that alone. And your insurance rackets with those chiropractors, again, nothing major, but enough that you shouldn't lose money. I don't get it, Tom, where's the money?"

Tom's silence was enough for Dominic. "Okay, you mute fucker, you don't want to answer? That four hundred thousand family loan that I loaned you, you know, that no interest loan, you now get the asshole rate of three percent." Dominic computed his interest in his head. "Twelve grand a week, Tom."

"I'm gambling, Dom," Tom confessed.

"You're kidding me?" Dominic laughed. "I didn't expect that. I was thinking something horrible, and it turns out you're just a stupid degenerate. I can't even tell my father that one. He'd lose every ounce for respect for you. Drug addicts and gambling degenerates, the two most important people to keep out of our life, is a favorite line of his."

"I'm sorry, I've gotten in so deep, I can't seem to find a way out," Tom said.

"You want a way out, then don't bet. How much do you need to get out of the hole?" Dominic asked.

"Two hundred large should get me out," Tom said.

"Big hole. I'm going to loan you the money, still with no interest. That's six hundred grand. If I hear that you placed another bet before I get every penny back, well, I really hope you're not stupid enough to think that my sister's marriage to your son is going to save you," Dominic told him.

"Thank you, I—" Tom was cut off.

"You want to thank me? Just be a good fucking lieutenant and show some fucking respect, okay?" Dominic said and walked back in the house.

Sal was watching the Tiger game with Valentina's husband, Nathan. Dominic walked over to Sal and pointed at him. "What is that, Sal?"

"What?" Sal asked, looking himself up and down.

"That . . . that . . . bump on your arm? I think it's a fucking bicep," Dominic joked.

"Hey," Aunt Marie yelled from the kitchen.

"Watch that word in this house, Dominic," Helena scolded. "I've got fifteen more years of a cuss-free home before your father comes back. And I will have it that way until that day. Are we clear?"

"Yeah, sorry. Geez," Dominic complained and turned back to Sal. "What's wrong, tired of being picked on by the bigger kids?" Dominic joked.

"Hey, if you ever want to get in the ring?" Sal taunted.

"Sal, please tell me that when I can fight, you and me can get in the ring. It would be like a lifetime of revenge for you being such a pain in the ass," Dominic said.

"Name the place and time," Sal said.

"This whole house is full of surprises today," Dominic said to himself. "Sal, I am so looking forward to pounding on you, and no one can say shit."

"Don't forget, I've got a lifetime of revenge too, for you being such an asshole," Sal said back.

"You're like a whole new person, I love it. I couldn't imagine actually having a brother that's not such a sissy," Dominic joked.

Sal got up and went to kitchen. "Hey, Mom, me and Dominic are going to have a boxing match when he can fight."

Helena put her coffee down and called out to Dominic, "Dominic, just go somewhere else if you're going to stir up this crap."

"What? Why are you all over me today?" Dominic asked, also going to the kitchen.

"Because Kristina Bosca called here and asked if I'd heard anything about Fabian, that's why," Helena answered.

"She stopped by the Corner, asking about him too. Why didn't you tell me she called?"

"What's the point? It's obvious what happened," Helena said.

"What happened to Fabian?" Sal asked.

"Nothing's happened to Fabian. He hasn't talked to his mom since last night and the world's in an uproar. He's a grown man, he's got a wife, he's got a daughter. He has to call his mom every day?" Dominic asked.

"She says he flew in last night and stayed the night at her house. So yeah, you'd think he'd have talked to her if he's staying at her house," Helena said.

"I'm lost here. It's eight o'clock at night, why does anyone even think he's missing? The guy comes and goes like you wouldn't believe. Miami, Mexico, wherever the hell else he goes these days," Dominic explained.

"Dominic, I'm sick and tired of these phone calls, or they just come by and yell at me and curse me to hell. I'm tired of the only mothers who call me or come over outside of my friends and family, are mothers who've just lost a son."

"What are you saying?" Dominic asked.

"I'm saying that boy ate dinner right at this table, he was like a brother to you. You had your chance to change your life, but obviously, you made your choice. Like I said, I'm just sick of it. You can get out of here now," Helena said, dismissing Dominic, who did as she said and left.

"Dominic!" Marie called out.

"Oh, let him go, he is his father," Helena said. "You can't save him now."

"Save him? I can still love him. What's the matter with you?" Marie asked as she ran out after Dominic.

She caught him getting into his truck. "Dominic, give me a ride home," she said, opening the passenger door.

"What about your car?" Dominic asked as she struggled to get into Dominic's big truck.

"Valentina picked me up. Come on, help me up here," Marie ordered. "Why do you need something this big?"

Dominic sighed, got back out, ran around the truck to help his aunt, got back in the truck, and started his F-350.

"It's too loud. Why do you want something so loud?" Marie asked.

"Aunt Marie, what are you going to do, torture me for the few miles to your house?" Dominic asked.

"I'll slap the Amicucci off you if you want to talk to me that way. I just wanted to see if you were okay. You know Helena didn't mean that," Marie said.

Dominic shrugged his shoulders. "No one ever does. I've heard that since as far back as I can remember hearing anything at all. I'm sorry I didn't mean that."

"We all were just so hopeful that you might've left that life," Marie explained.

Dominic put his finger to his lips to silence his aunt. "Can't talk about that here."

"Whatever the case, I'd like you to do something for me," she said.

"What?"

"Come to church with me this Sunday."

"Oh no," Dominic replied quickly.

"Dominic, please, one time. How long has it been?" she asked him.

"Since the last time I was there, that's how long," Dominic said.

"I need you to come with me, Dominic. You have to do this for me," Marie pled.

"I just can't do it, I'm sorry," Dominic told her.

"Even your friend, Doug, goes to church. He doesn't go for communion or confession, but at least he goes. He drops five hundred dollars in the basket every week," she said.

"How do you know?"

"His wife, of course," Marie answered.

"Twenty-six grand a year? He's trying to buy his way into heaven," Dominic said.

"Whatever the reason, just go with me," Marie said.

"Hey, look, you're home," Dominic said as he pulled onto Marie's street. "Let me think about it, okay?"

"I'll be expecting you," she told him as she kissed him good-bye and got out.

Tommy Herrick arrived at Doug's house the next day at midnight. They talked in the backyard. "I'm glad to see Graham's not doing any laps," Tommy said.

"Grace is still up. How many zips we got in Mexico watching that village that Fabian stayed at?" Doug asked.

"Three. And I talked with Virgil in Miami, and he knew of these Cubans that Danny and Dom want to whack. He said it makes sense that Fabian was their supplier, as he couldn't figure out who it was," Tommy told him.

"Okay, I guess it's not a joke, whack the fucker. Have Benedetto do it, he's already down there with another zip. Make sure there's no body," Doug said.

"Plus we got one zip in New York watching that Bruno Bini," Tommy added. "These guys are working out like a charm."

"We'll wait to see how long until the feds get a whiff. They always fuck everything up," Doug said.

"What the hell's going on at your bar? I was driving by it at three in the morning, and it was going full tilt. You got them working around the clock?" Tommy asked.

"Fucking right they're working around the clock. I'm going to be paying through my ass on this one. We're opening up May thirtieth and that's that," Doug said.

"You know that's Memorial Day, right? Not a big bar day," Tommy told him.

"It's a Memorial Day bash—it's got to be on Memorial Day. We're grilling in the parking lot, free burgers and hot dogs. It'll be madness. That's actually just the kickoff. Friday will be the huge grand opening. This way the staff will have some training," Doug said.

"Okay, not bad. I guess we covered everything, you going to offer me a drink?" Tommy asked.

"Let's hit the basement," Doug said as they went into the house and to Doug's bar downstairs.

The week went by, and on Friday night, Doug and Tommy met Danny and Dominic at Nick's house. The men were waiting for Dominic's uncle, Daniel, to head out for a card game. Marie and Helena had made up from their minor tiff and had made a huge buffet for the men. They met out back first to discuss some business after they ate.

"The Cuban's dead and gone," Doug told him.

"Everything went okay?" Danny asked.

"Doesn't it always?" Doug asked him back.

"Well, no actually," Dominic answered. "Your guy that shot Little Vic Mattea's doing life for it. In fact, you got another guy in jail for another hit."

"He got five years for involuntary manslaughter. Both hits though went down, the targets are dead, and my men went to jail and kept their fucking mouths shut, even after a life sentence. I'd say they went okay," Doug told him.

"Nonetheless, it's something you'd want to mention," Danny said.

Doug looked at Tommy. "Okay, Tommy, give them a report."

"The hit went fine," Tommy said dryly.

"Very well, thank you, guys. Let's go have a drink for another successful hit," Dominic said with pride. "We're on a roll."

"You better knock on a lot of wood, you stupid fuck," Danny joked.

"We just have to deal with Fabian's friend in Mexico, and the whole fucking caper can be done," Doug said as they walked back across the spacious backyard to the house.

"Sometimes loose ends you don't even know exist seem to pop up time and time again through the years. We should really consider the fact that we might never know how deep Fabian's corruption ran," Danny said.

In the house, they found that Daniel had arrived and was having a plate. "You've been nagging us for years to play some real cards, I hope you're ready," Danny said to Daniel Amicucci.

"I got my big boy pants on, thank you," he joked. "Where's Sal? Out on a hot date on a Friday night?"

"He's working," Helena chipped in with pride.

"My brother is actually is in charge of security for the overnight construction crews at his new bar that he's building," Dominic said, pointing to Doug. "I'm rendered speechless."

"He's doing very well. My man, Matt Young, says he's his second best guy," Doug told him.

"Like I said, speechless," Dominic said again.

"And it's a high-end nightclub, not a bar, Dominic," Doug reminded.

"And you want my brother to be in charge of anything there?" Dominic asked.

"Oh, knock it off, Dominic. Don't make me throw you out again," Helena joked. She had called Dominic the next day and apologized for what she said to him.

"Get a few glasses of wine in her and look at her go," Dominic joked back.

"Well, anyway, Doug, I thank you for giving my son a job and looking out for him," Helena said.

The men left for the card game, which to Daniel's surprise was a mere ten minutes away. They pulled down an alley behind a strip mall and stopped behind a laundromat and got out. "How long has this card game been here?" Daniel asked.

"Well before either of us was born," Danny told him.

Doug and Tommy pulled up behind and got out of their car. Waiting outside the laundromat were Scary Scarelli and crew member,

Carlo DeMini. Carlo, it was recently announced, would be getting his button this fall with Paulie Bankjob.

Both men took a car and moved it to another location. The door to the Laundromat opened and a man held it open for the card players. Danny led the way in and walked down the stairs that were immediately to his left. He knew the situation was safe because not only had Scary and Carlo checked it out, Angelo and Fat Kenny were already there waiting for them to play cards.

"Oh, look what the cat dragged in. What're you guys, slumming it?" Carmine Luna asked as the men came down the stairs. Carmine sat by the stairs and checked the players as they came down. Heavyset and with a course voice, Carmine ran the card game at eighty-one years old.

Danny and Dominic hugged and kissed Carmine, and they introduced him to Doug and Tommy and then to Daniel.

"Oh, the good brother, huh?" Carmine joked with his loud voice and laughter.

"Actually, there's four of us, what you call, good brothers," Daniel answered.

Carmine laughed. "Go ahead, you guys, your table's back there," he said, pointing to the back.

"I've never seen anything like this in my life," Daniel said in awe as he walked through the beautifully finished basement of the strip mall. The basement was carpeted and housed four plush card tables, a huge bar, a buffet, and a stage for a band. Waitresses in short skirts and fish nets catered the three active tables as one sat empty.

Danny took a seat at it, and Doug complained, "Hey, I thought we were drawing numbers for seats."

"We are, I'm just sitting the fucking down for a minute, you mind?" Danny asked, irritated.

"Just so that you know, I'm watching you. All night, Serafini," Doug taunted.

The five men all took their seats and ordered their drinks. "Talk about a lucky sign, I'm the only single guy at the table," Dominic joked after their waitress left.

Angelo and Kenny got out of the cash game they were playing and joined the others. The room came to life when a young man, in his late twenties, came out of the back room. Almost everyone at every table and every employee of the card room wanted to say hello. The man walked over to the bar and was handed a drink that was ready when he got there.

"Daniel, come on," Danny said as he and Dominic got up to go say hello. Daniel got up and followed.

"Rocco, this is my Uncle Daniel," Dominic introduced. "Uncle Daniel, this is Rocco DiNapoli."

Daniel's heart dropped, as this was the man his daughter was so infatuated with. Daniel shook his hand. "I take it there's something you'd like to talk to me about besides a card game."

"Yeah, there is," Rocco answered.

"First of all, how old are you?" Daniel asked him.

"I'm twenty-eight."

"Marie's not even twenty."

"She will be in four days. And before you say it, it's not too big an age difference," Rocco said. "Marie is mature well beyond her years."

"I hope you're not implying something."

"Sir, I've not even kissed your daughter. That's not the maturity I meant," Rocco said.

"Look, I see you're a nice young man, you've shown me a ton of respect by speaking to me like this, but I don't want my daughter near this life," Daniel explained.

"Isn't she already?" Rocco asked him. "Marie has her own mind. I'm just asking that you let her use it. She knows what this life entails, and she knows what she wants."

"She wants to be a lawyer," Daniel said.

"And I'm not asking her not to be. I know your daughter is the one for me. I knew the moment I saw her at Charley Amicucci's funeral. She knows it too. I'd like to take her out when she's back for the summer from school. I'd like her to take the time to know for sure I'm the one for her. I only want to encourage her schooling, not detract from it," Rocco told him.

"And if you go to jail, like my whole family has?" Daniel asked.

"Then we'll deal with it. I've got enough money to take care of her and any kids right now, and like I keep saying, she's a smart girl and will more than likely have her income," Rocco said. "I just want to care for your daughter, Mr. Amicucci."

Daniel looked over to Danny and Dominic who waited at the bar, and they both nodded to him. "We both vouch for him," Danny said to him.

"I'll let her decide. But you know my family, and I will give my brother and nephew carte blanche with you if you fuck up," Daniel threatened.

"Fair enough, sir. I think you'll find me to be a more honorable person than most people who are considered solid citizens," Rocco said.

"Time will tell. Are you playing cards with us?" Daniel asked the man whose charm had perhaps won him over.

"Playing? It's my game," Rocco said.

"I thought it was the old man at the door."

"No, Carmine runs this one for me. I've got a bigger one across town, twelve card tables. Packed to gill twenty-fours a day on the weekends," Rocco boasted.

"This is yours?" Daniel asked in awe again.

"Not bad for twenty-eight, eh? I figured you'd be pushing Marie off on me to pay for her law school," Rocco joked.

"You probably could afford law school, couldn't you, if this is small to you?" Daniel asked panning the room.

A few minutes later, everyone was seated with one empty chair. "We missing someone?" Doug asked.

Carmine Luna walked to the table and took the empty seat next to Doug. "Okay, who's giving me their chips first?" he asked, very loudly.

"This is going to be a long fucking night," Doug let out.

Carmine rubbed Doug's back. "Let me get some of that luck of the Irish."

"Is there any chance of that voice of yours coming down some?" Doug joked. "And there's got to be a 'no touching the other players' rule."

Carmine laughed and turned to Dominic. "When is your Uncle Ziggy coming back up?"

"He's coming for my brother's twenty-first birthday. Since Charley died, he doesn't come up much anymore," Dominic answered.

"And how is your Uncle Ray? He never could stand my voice either," Carmine said.

"He never could stand anyone's voice. To be honest, I haven't spoken to him in years. I haven't gone down and seen him since I bought his house in 2002," Dominic said.

"And you haven't gone to see your Uncle George since before I did my time. You should take a trip and visit your godfather," Danny told him.

Carmine was still stuck on Dominic's living conditions. "You're still living in Ray's house? Dominic, it was a dump, I can only imagine it now. You need to buy a real house."

"Can we just play some cards? I don't want to hear this guy call my house a dump all night," Dominic chided.

"I agree, and Danny's right, Dom," Angelo said. "It's been too long since we took a trip to see my father. I'd like to set something up."

"We'll go this summer, before I get my surgery," Dominic told him.

"What kind of surgery, penile enhancement?" Carmine asked.

"You're like an eighty-year-old kid," Doug told Carmine. The two would banter the rest of the night, even after Carmine was the first to be eliminated.

CHAPTER XXVI

Luck of the Irish

DOMINIC AMICUCCI WATCHED the last card, the river card, get flipped and realized he had lost. "Tough luck there, kid," Carmine Luna laughed in his raspy, loud voice.

Tommy Herrick stood up and shook Dominic's hand. "I got lucky there."

"It happens," Dominic said.

"Hey," Carmine yelled to one his men. "Pay the guy, would you? What do you get for third place, Dominic? Oh yeah, nothing," he laughed.

"Everybody, I've got to go, have a nice night," Dominic said to the group watching the game. "Carmine, go fuck yourself," he joked.

Two players were left in the game, the two Westsiders, Doug and Tommy. Tommy had a huge lead over Doug, who offered to play the next hand for "winner takes all." "How much does first place get?" Tommy asked Doug, already knowing the answer.

"Thirty grand," Doug answered.

"And fifteen for second? Let me think about it, and no," Tommy said. He had taken out Dominic in the elimination tournament and

Rocco DiNapoli before him. Danny had left with Daniel Amicucci after they were eliminated, as were Angelo and Kenny before them. Loudmouth Carmine was the first one out and hadn't moved a muscle since he sat down by Doug, over five hours ago.

"A table full of diegos and the two Irishmen take home the money," Carmine joked in Doug's ear. "Guess I was right earlier about the luck of the Irish, too bad I couldn't get some of it," Carmine said, still in Doug's ear.

"You know why you're at the smaller card game, don't you, Carmine? It's that voice and your whole demeanor," Doug joked as the dealer shuffled for the next hand. "I can't believe I haven't shot you yet."

"I can't believe you think you guys are getting out of here with forty-five grand. Luck or no luck of the Irish," Carmine played back.

The game lasted a little over ten minutes more before Tommy claimed first prize. With everyone from the Amicucci crew gone, Doug and Tommy prepared to leave, but Rocco stopped them at the door. "I'm heading to my other game if you guys are up for playing some more," Rocco told them.

"You playing?" Tommy asked him.

"No, I rarely play. I just wanted to meet Dominic's uncle, so I asked a favor, and Danny and Dominic set this game up. I'm guessing you guys play a lot of cards, and I think you'll find the competition at my other game a little better," Rocco said.

Doug and Tommy looked at each other, and each knew the other was thinking how mad their wives would be. "Let's go," they both said almost in unison.

Dominic was having lunch with Angelo and Fat Kenny when Gary Nussman, who ran the bakery's operations, entered the back office. "Hey, Dom, there's an FBI agent here asking for you," he told him.

"What'd he say?" Dominic asked.

"He said he needs a word with you," Gary answered.

"We can go out the back," Kenny offered.

Dominic put his sandwich down and wiped his mouth before he went to speak with the agent. "Agent Centers, long time no see. I thought you retired," Dominic said.

"Retired? I've never been busier listening to wiretaps," the agent joked, hoping to make Dominic think there was a bug recording him.

"Oh yeah? I'll give you a hundred thousand dollars for the transcripts," Dominic joked back.

"A hundred grand? Your old man used to offer me half a million," Agent Centers said.

"Hey, it's a bad economy these days. So what do you want? You didn't come to tell me Louis Cardoni's location, did you?" Dominic asked about the rat that put his father away.

"That's not funny, and I hope you were kidding," the agent threatened.

"Whatever, are you going to tell me what the fuck you want or not?" Dominic asked.

"All right, all right, relax. I came to ask you when the last time you talked to Fabian Bosca was."

"Why?" Dominic asked.

"His mother has reported him missing. She says he's been missing for a week now."

"You've been demoted to missing persons? Ain't that a job for the local cops?"

"I'm just asking a question here," the agent said.

"So this is an unofficial visit?" Dominic asked suspiciously.

"It's a question. Why are you so defensive?"

"I'm not defensive, I'm just curious as to why the feds would be investigating a missing person, that's all. You want to know the last I talked to him, fine. It's been awhile. Like I told his mother when she asked me, I thought he bought a villa and moved to Mexico. That's the extent of my knowledge. Dominic said.

"Like I said, it's just a question."

"Then, you've got your answer. Now, buy some bread or get the fuck out of here," Dominic told the agent and went back to the office.

An hour later, Gary came in the office with a delivery, a dozen dead roses with a card. "What the fuck is that?" Dominic asked as Gary laid them on the table. "Someone actually delivered this?"

"Yeah, a real florist. He said some woman paid full retail for them and to deliver it to you, Dom," Gary said.

"If this is that fucking agent," Dominic said as he opened the card. "I know you did it, love Kristina," Dominic read aloud. "Oh my god, this is from Fabian's mom. That's fucking eerie," he said tossing the card on the table. "Gary, get this shit the fuck out of here," he ordered. "Kenny, let's take a walk and go see Danny."

Dominic and Kenny walked the three blocks to Cooch's Corner, and Dominic talked to Danny out back. "I heard Doug and Tommy cleaned up at Rocco's this morning," Danny said.

"Yeah, about a hundred grand they cashed in between the two of them. But listen, an agent stopped by the bakery today and asked me about Fabian," Dominic told Danny.

"What'd you tell him?" Danny asked.

"I told him Michael Jagge shot him and then disposed of the body," Dominic joked. "What do you think I told him? I told him I haven't talked to Fabian since he moved to Mexico and to get the fuck out. It was Agent Centers."

"Wow, Dave Centers. I haven't seen him since the night I was arrested with your father. He was always a pain in the ass," Danny said.

"And then, a dozen dead roses get delivered to the bakery with a note that says, 'I know you did it.' Care to guess who sent it?" Dominic asked.

"Centers?"

"No, I thought the same thing," Dominic laughed. "Fabian's mom."

"Kristina?"

"Yup, love Kristina," Dominic answered.

"Well, that could be Kristina Kalko as well. You did whack her husband, Nino," Danny reminded Dominic.

"Three years ago. Centers stopped by because Fabian's mother filed a missing persons report," Dominic said.

"Did the prick show his badge?" Danny asked.

"I don't think so actually."

"I'll bet he's retired and working as a private investigator now, hired by her. Have Doug track him down, see what old Agent Centers is doing nowadays," Danny said.

"Sneaky fucker," Dominic commented.

Dominic met Doug in a deserted parking lot at one in the morning to relay the request to find out information on the FBI agent. Doug didn't even need to make a phone call. "Dave Centers? He retired, last year during my trial," Doug told Dominic.

"How the fuck do you know that, you were in Miami, weren't you?" Dominic asked.

"My lawyer told me when we were going over some FBI files for my case. Centers had a lot of notes of meetings with your father and me, my lawyer mentioned he had just retired," Doug explained.

"So, Danny was right. He must be working as a private investigator," Dominic said.

"I'll ask my lawyer," Doug said. He tossed Dominic an envelope. "Thanks for the invite to the card game last night. Rocco took us to the bigger game and we cleaned house."

"How much is here?" Dominic asked.

"Ten grand, six from Tommy and four from me. You guys can't play cards on the east side or what?" Doug joked.

"Maybe Rocco was letting you guys win to draw you back and clean you out for more," Dominic suggested jokingly.

"Either way. The kid's got some nice card games, though. They're nicer than mine, very classy," Doug confessed.

"Rocco's what we call an up and comer. He got his button right at twenty-five," Dominic said before they called it a night and went home.

In the morning, Dominic drove to Aunt Marie's house, where he found her making breakfast for Angelo and his wife, Angela. "Got another plate?" Dominic asked as he entered the kitchen, dressed in one of his best suits.

Marie stopped what she was doing to hug her nephew. "Last week you broke my heart, but I knew you'd come to church." She gave him another sincere squeeze and whispered in his ear, "Thank you, Dominic." She then set another spot at the table and quickly filled him a plate.

"You'll explain to Father Lassia about the sunglasses being a medical condition and not me thinking I'm Joe Cool?" Dominic asked.

"Of course," Marie told him.

"You even remember the prayers?" Angelo asked with his mouthful.

"Manners, Angelo. This is my house, not yours. Please don't speak with food in your mouth. It's like you're regressing in life. And the only thing that matters, Dominic, is that you're there," Marie said.

"Yeah, yell at me and commend him. The only church I've missed is when he wouldn't let me out of work," Angelo complained after swallowing his food.

At the church, they were the last ones to arrive. Waiting in the parking lot were Helena and Sal, Valentina and her husband, Nathan, Danny's wife, Bianca, and their daughter, Sabrina, with her husband, Greg. "What's up, Shades?" Sal asked Dominic.

"What?" Dominic asked.

"Shades, it's my new nickname for you," Sal told him.

Dominic didn't say a word; he just stared at his younger brother. "Don't like Shades? How about Glasses? Or how about Dark Eye?" Sal joked. "I got my new nickname at work. They're calling me Punchy, probably because of my sparring."

Dominic laughed. "I'm sure that's why. You're a good kid." Dominic rubbed Sal's head, messing up his hair.

"My hair, you fucker," Sal said, quickly trying to pat any stray hairs down.

His repair work was interrupted from a slap to the back of his head from Helena. "Language young man, language." She pointed to her son and stepson, "You two behave. I didn't plan on confession today, so do not give me a reason."

Marie gave the men the same reminder she gave every Sunday before they entered the church, "Turn those cell phones off."

"I always just turn mine to vibrate," Sal said to Dominic, who did just that before putting it back in his pants pocket.

A little bit into Father Lassia's sermon, Dominic's phone went off and vibrated against the wooden pew, echoing throughout the church, causing the sermon to pause.

The entire row with him lowered their heads in shame. Marie whispered in his ear, "Okay, go home now."

"Yes, ma'am," Dominic said as he got up, silencing the vibrating. He walked out of the church and looked to see who called him. He stopped dead in his tracks and looked back at the church doors. "Son of a bitch," he said to himself. It was Sal.

It was a full house at the Amicucci household later in the day. It was a gorgeous day, and everyone came to enjoy the first big barbecue of the year. Doug brought his son, Graham, with him to show off his fastball. "Faster than any kid his age, guaranteed," Doug boasted as he played catch with Graham.

"Grace said he was in tee ball, his fastball don't mean shit," Danny joked.

"Tee ball," Doug complained. "They don't even keep score. What the fuck is that?" he asked. "I took him right the fuck off the team."

"You took him off the team? What kind of dick are you?" Danny asked.

"I'm not teaching my kid that kind of shit. Winning does matter. Why the fuck else do you play?"

"Tee ball's just supposed to teach fundamentals, Doug. You hit a ball on a tee, where's the competition?" Dominic asked.

Doug stopped playing catch and sent his son to see his mother. "It's all competition. Shouldn't they be learning fundamentals in practice? What are they doing in practice?"

"Anyway," Danny said, changing the subject. "I heard you got kicked out of church today, Dom."

"Hey, you went to church? Good for you," Doug said.

"Yeah, I went, and my stupid little brother tells me to leave my phone on vibrate, so I do. The little fucker calls me in the middle of the sermon, and it starts vibrating in my pocket against the pew. Even the priest stopped. I cannot believe Sal did that," Dominic said.

"He's growing up, Dominic. And I think he wants to kick your ass," Danny taunted.

"I got to get him back for the church joke first," Dominic said.

"You got to admit, though, that's a good one," Doug offered as they headed to the grills to get some burgers.

Dominic's uncles, William and Daniel, were the grill masters since Nick's departure to prison. Doug walked up to Daniel, who had lost five grand for his entrance to the card game two nights ago. "How'd your wife feel about you dropping that five grand?" Doug asked him as he slapped his back.

"Shh . . .," Daniel said putting his finger to his lips. "I've been to hell and back with that woman in the last two days for that. She still won't talk to me, but please don't get her screaming at me again," Daniel pleaded.

"My bad," Doug said.

"I got my oldest son's wedding in June, and in the fall he starts law school. My daughter, Marie, goes to U of M, and she wants to go to law school. My other boy, James, is graduating high school in two weeks, and he's off to a college in St. Louis for biochemistry. I couldn't afford to lose that five grand," Daniel complained to his new friend.

"I offered to pay it for you," Dominic said.

"Fuck that, I don't need your charity, Dominic. Everything I own, I earned on my own," Daniel said.

"All right, all right," Dominic said, throwing his hands up in surrender. "Can I at least have a burger?"

The men got their food and went back off on their own. "He says he earned everything on his own?" Dominic scoffed to Doug. "That and the half million he inherited when my grandfather died."

"Ain't that the American Dream, though?" Doug asked. "Your grandfather lived his life his way, and he was able to give his kids a better life than he had. Your uncle's going to have what, two lawyers and some kind of biochemist? I think it's great. I mean, isn't that our goal?" Doug asked.

"For most people," Dominic said quietly.

"You'll find the right girl, Dominic. You'll still be able to have kids," Danny told him.

"Danny, it wasn't Angela that couldn't have kids, it was me," Dominic confessed.

"No shit? All those years she told everyone it was her. She did that for you, huh?" Danny asked.

"Yeah, she was the best," Dominic said. "I don't ever want to get married again, fuck it."

"So, Sal's the last chance to carry on your father's seed? Lord help us," Danny joked.

"Gentleman, I think it's time the shots started," Doug said, trying to change the topic.

When they reached the bar in the basement, Sal and Jimmy were already there having a drink.

"Sal, what the fuck are you doing?" Doug asked him.

"Drinking a beer, why?" Sal asked innocently.

"You got to be to work in two hours and you're having a beer?" Doug asked.

"It's cool, I know the owner," Sal joked.

"Motherfucker, is that a joke?" Doug asked, getting angry and drawing laughs from Dominic and Danny.

"Yeah, I'm kidding. I'm off tonight," Sal said. "I go back to days tomorrow."

"You see, just like in church," Dominic said. "He's becoming a little fucking jokester."

"So, Sal, Wednesday you'll be twenty-one, huh?" Doug asked Sal. "What do you got planned?"

"Working, and then my mom's having a party here," Sal answered.

The men toasted a shot, and Jimmy got up enough courage to ask Danny a question. "Will you please let me drive for you again?"

"I was wondering if you'd ever ask, too bad it took a few drinks to get the courage. Ask me in a month, without the booze. Until then, keep delivering bread," Danny told him.

"Sal's going to have to toughen you up, Jimmy," Dominic joked.

"I'll buy the next round," Doug said, picking up the bottle to pour.

"Doug, you don't have to pay for it here, it's all free," Sal said.

Dominic patted his younger brother on the back. "Just when you think they grow up so fast, something happens and you want to say, 'Grow the fuck up,'" he joked.

The next day, Eugene "Scary" Scarelli questioned a stranger when he came into Cooch's Corner. "You need something?" Scary asked him.

"Can a guy get a beer?" the stranger asked.

"You got ID?" Scary asked the obviously over fifty-year-old man.

"You serious?" he asked.

"Everyone gets carded here," Scary said, holding his hand out, waiting for the ID.

"Sure," the stranger said and handed Scary his driver's license. "And you can tell Danny Serafini I'm at the bar," he said and held out his hand for his ID back.

Scary gave it back and went and whispered in Jackie Bean's ear. Jackie got up and knocked on Danny's door and entered when given permission.

"Danny, there's an agent here, Dave Centers. I remember him from when Nick was out," Jackie said.

"He ain't no fucking agent no more, Jackie," Danny told him, getting up from his desk and walking to the bar. "What's up, Dave?" Danny asked him, as Scary stayed close.

"Danny Serafini, long time no see," Dave Centers said, putting his hand out to shake, but Danny never extended his. "You never were one for small talk. I'm looking into Fabian's disappearance."

"Fabian hasn't disappeared," Danny said with a sigh. "Where's your badge, Agent Centers?"

"My badge? I'm not with the bureau on this one," Dave answered.

"You're not with the bureau on anything anymore—you retired, lying asshole," Danny said. "Why are you asking about Fabian? You're a private dick now or something?"

"Actually, yes, I'm a private investigator now. It's going good," he said, stopping to take a drink of his beer while Danny glared at him. "I have a few clients."

"Good for fucking you," Danny told him.

"You should sit down, have a beer, enjoy life a little bit," Dave told Danny.

"You got anything else for me?" Danny asked.

"I was talking about my clients. I know it probably breaks some kind of code or something to talk about my clients, but oh well. The weirdest thing about my clients is that they all have something in common," Dave said.

"What's that, Dave?"

"They're all families of people that were close to Dominic Amicucci and are either dead or missing and presumed to be dead. I'll tell you, it's the weirdest thing." Danny said nothing; he just stared at Dave. "It's amazing the information I can get now without being bound by all those rules and regulations. For instance, some new information I've gathered concerns Dominic's wife. Did you know she was having an affair?"

Danny looked at Scary. "Eugene, after this gentleman finishes his beer, walk him the fuck out of here."

Dave turned around and looked at Scary. "Eugene? Eugene 'Scary' Scarelli? Wow, you haven't aged well."

"Now you can get the fuck out," Danny said.

Dave got up. "Okay, all right, I'll leave."

"You didn't pay for your fucking beer," Danny told him. "And don't forget to tip the bartender."

Dave dropped a ten-dollar bill on the bar. "Keep the change. You know Danny, it's quite a list: Fabian, Gary Piazza, and Louis Rubilla. And what did ever happen to Nino Kalko while you were away? His family sure wants to know."

Dave got to the door and gave his parting shot as he left. "That's okay, Danny, I'll just head down to the bakery and see Dominic. I must say, he's a much better conversationalist than you are."

Danny watched the door close behind him and looked at Scary. "You want me to catch him and break his fucking neck?" Scary asked. "It would be my pleasure, believe me."

"Yes, I do want you to, but you can't," Danny answered. "I guess we better take a walk to the bakery," Danny told Scary.

Danny gave Jackie an instruction before he left. "Jackie, if that cocksucker comes back here, make sure he gets a beat down."

Danny and Dominic talked in the parking lot. "Dave Centers came to see me today," Danny said. "It's official, he's a private investigator, and it sounds like he's working for Fabian's mom," Danny said.

"He made it sound like he was still with the fucking feds," Dominic said. "Rotten bastard."

"I think he's working for Kristina Kalko as well," Danny told him.

"No way, Kristina's as old school as there is. Pete Lissoni was her fucking dad, Danny," Dominic said.

"Yeah, I'm aware, Dom. I've know her longer than you, don't you think? And he mentioned Gary Pizza and Louis Rubilla," Danny said.

"He's working for all their families? Fucking impossible."

"I think he's working for Kristina Kalko and Kristina Bosca. I do believe his other client is your former in-laws, Dom."

"No. They never thought it was me, even when the feds tried telling them it was," Dominic said.

"He said she was having an affair," Danny told him.

"Never, I'll never believe that. Not even if someone has a fucking video, no fucking way," Dominic said.

"He's building a motive, probably handing everything he has to the feds," Danny said.

"So what do we do with this guy?" Dominic asked.

"You need to go see your father today," Danny told him.

"Danny, it costs me almost fifty grand to get in on a non-visiting day. This can wait until Thursday, can't it?"

"How much harm can he do in a few days?" Danny asked, shrugging his shoulders.

CHAPTER XXVII

Twenty-First

GLENN CONWAY TOOK a seat at his usual table at Nottingham's. Decorated in a Robin Hood theme, the bar was the former headquarters for Doug Sullivan and Tommy Herrick. Nowadays, it was headquarters to Glenn Conway, a bookmaker for the Westside. Glenn was in charge of the gambling in the small city of Veeling. He was also assigned to watch the Westside's interests in the Amicucci book at Cooch's Corner after the Fabian debacle. Today, he just returned from there and ordered the Friar Tuck Cluck for lunch.

He waited for his sandwich with one of his men as he watched a man approach his table. The stranger was met by two of the bouncers before they were told to let him through. "I'm looking for Doug Sullivan," the stranger told Glenn.

Glenn laughed and looked around to his men in disbelief. "He ain't here."

"Call him, tell him Dave Centers is here," the former stranger said.

"What? Are you kidding me? You want to talk to Doug Sullivan, you call Doug Sullivan," Glenn told him.

"What was your name?" Dave asked him.

Glenn laughed again and nodded to the bouncers. "Get him the fuck out of here."

"Call him, tell him Dave Centers from the FBI is here."

"Let me see your badge," Glenn ordered.

"Just call him, he knows who I am, believe me."

Glenn looked the man up and down and didn't really know what to do, as this was a first for him. He didn't even have Doug's number. "Have a seat at the bar, I'll make some calls. But if you're not who you say you are, you're not walking out of here," Glenn threatened as he got up to use his phone in private.

Glenn called Dave Worowski at his bar in Henderson and told him of the agent. Dave told him to keep him there. It took forty minutes, but Doug Sullivan came walking in the door. Glenn met him at the door and pointed out Dave Centers, eating a steak and drinking a beer at the bar.

Doug walked over to the retired agent and took a seat next to him. He nodded to the bartender who brought him a beer. "We've never been formally introduced," Dave said to Doug.

"I remember you from sitting outside Cooch's Corner," Doug told him.

"I see you've come a long way," Dave told him.

"And I see you're out of touch since you retired. I don't hang out here anymore," Doug told him.

"I see that, forty fucking minutes it took for you to get here," Dave joked. "I had some questions I wanted to ask you."

Doug held up his hand. "I don't give two shits about your questions. I came here to tell you something."

Dave laughed. "Oh yeah? This is a new one. What'd you want to tell me?"

"I came here to tell you that Dominic Amicucci is a very dear friend of mine, as was his wife. You're going around tainting her name, and I got a serious fucking problem with that," Doug told him.

"Is there a threat coming?" Dave taunted. "Careful, Doug, no one's frisked me for a wire."

"Then be sure to play this back to yourself every night before you go to bed. You didn't do yourself no favor by coming here, you asshole. Stay the fuck away from the Corner and the bakery. Leave Dominic and Danny alone," Doug said.

"Oh yeah, I forgot, you're the Amicucci muscle. You're the guy that protects Dominic and Danny. That's how the Christmas Eve Massacre happened, right?"

"I was in jail," Doug told him.

Dave laughed. "Right, locked up with Nick Amicucci, cells right next to each other, wasn't it? Besides, it's common knowledge that your buddy Tommy Herrick did that with the okay from you and Nick in jail."

Doug leaned in close and whispered, "Don't think that I'm like Danny and Dominic, I will hurt you. You ain't protected by that badge no more. Now you're just a pain in the ass, and if you ever set foot in one of my bars again, you're not coming out."

Dave looked Doug in the eyes and thought that he might really be serious and decided not to get tough back. "What am I supposed to do then? I got to work."

"You need money? Why the fuck didn't you say so? I'll give you a million dollars cash to go the fuck away," Doug told him.

"That is the record for the biggest bribe I've ever been offered," Dave told him.

Doug shrugged his shoulders. "Well, it gives you options. You can be rich and have a nice life or end up in the hospital, or worse, the morgue."

"I'll tell you, if I was wearing a wire, this would be the perfect score."

"Don't you get it, Dave? I don't care if you're wired. Wear a wire against me and you're a dead man. You want to put me in jail and deal with Tommy Herrick? At least, I'll kill you quick, Dave." Doug nodded to the men around them, and Dave became surrounded by six large bouncers. “It’s time to go. Think about my offer,” Doug told him as Dave was led away.

Doug finished his beer, and before he left, he was given Dave’s license plate number that one of the men was instructed to take down. From there, he visited his lawyer, Carl Voight, whom Doug gave the license plate number to. Carl used his resources and gave Doug back the address that the car was registered to.

He gave his lawyer ten grand as a thank you and gave the three secretaries fifty-dollar tips as well, as he usually did. Thanks to Doug, Carl Voight, the independent misdemeanor lawyer, became the founder of Voight & Kribbs Law Firm—the firm recognized as one of the best in the state, with dealings across the nation.

Leaving the law firm in Southfield, Doug found the nearest hotel and called Tommy, Danny, and Dominic to come meet him in a room. It only took a little over twenty minutes for everyone to convene.

“That cocksucker Dave Centers showed up at Nottingham’s today and had them call me,” Doug told them. “He’s the asshole I was telling you about, Tommy. The asshole that retired from the feds but thinks he’s still one.”

“Why Nottingham’s?” Tommy asked.

“I don’t know, because he’s a fucking idiot. He was going to question me about Fabian, but I cut him off and told him to leave you guys alone and stop talking about Angela,” Doug said. “I offered the prick a million dollars to go away.”

“He ain’t going to take it,” Danny said.

“No, I agree. You guys know this guy has to go,” Doug said.

Dominic answered first, “I agree. I don’t want to go through this Angela bullshit again.”

“This kind of hit can only be okayed by Nick, face-to-face,” Danny said.

“I agree. So what’s the problem?” Doug asked.

Tommy had already figured the reasoning on the delay. "He's waiting until Thursday to avoid paying more for a special visit."

Doug laughed and looked at Dominic. "You cheap fuck. We should be digging his grave by nightfall."

"What's two days going to hurt? Even if I was meeting my father today, he still would've stopped by at your bar," Dominic answered.

"Okay, fine, save the money, but if this asshole steps foot in another of my bars, he dies. Right then, right there," Doug told them.

"Time is always of the essence," Tommy informed everyone.

"What the fuck do you two think he can possibly do in two days?" Dominic asked.

"He's obviously relaying information to the feds, that's just got to be common sense," Tommy said.

"And look how fucking irritating he's already been! Who the hell knows what he might stumble on? We should be prepared anyway. You visit your father Thursday morning, and he should be dead Thursday night," Doug added.

"Agreed, go ahead and start the groundwork. Maybe put the zips on it?" Danny said.

Doug handed the address to Tommy. "That was already our plan, Danny."

The next day at Doug's bar, The Four Seasons, Tommy and Billy Herrick stopped by to meet someone there. Walking in the unfinished bar, today the carpet was being laid, and they found Matt Young and Sal Amicucci talking in a corner.

"This place is really coming along," Tommy said as they approached.

"We open in twelve days," Sal said. "What are you guys doing here?"

"Had to meet someone in the parking lot, just thought we'd take a look around," Tommy answered. "Happy Birthday, by the way."

"Today's your birthday?" Matt asked. "Why didn't you say something?"

"It's no big deal," Sal said.

"You're turning twenty-one, you should be out at the bars, causing some ruckus," Tommy told him.

"Nah, it's a big family party at my house," Sal said.

"It's not all family, me and Doug will be there," Tommy informed him.

Sal perked up, "Wow, thanks, Tommy. I didn't know."

Tommy and Billy said good-bye and left out the front door. "You got to let me buy you a beer," Matt told Sal.

"I really got to get home," Sal said.

"Right upstairs, come one, it's one fucking beer. That's an order," Matt said.

"There's no beer up there."

"First delivery came an hour ago, let's go."

"Okay, but just one beer, I'm driving," Sal said.

Matt and Sal went up the stairs to the upper bar and restaurant. "What the hell?" Sal asked himself as he could see the large gathering at the bar. Almost the entire security staff was present, then he saw his brother, Dominic, and his Uncles William and Daniel. His Uncle Ziggy was there, up from Florida, and Doug was there with the Herrick brothers.

"Sal, get your ass over here and do this shot," Dominic ordered.

Sal walked to the center of the group, saying hello and getting his "happy birthdays." "What about my mom's party? Everyone will be expecting me."

"You idiot, there is no other party. You're my responsibility tonight, and believe me, my life is on the line with your mother," Dominic said.

"You, Sal, are the first official guest at the Four Seasons," Doug told him. "You have your party here now, and then, you'll have your party in a few hours at the nudie bar."

About a half hour into the party, a party crasher somehow had gotten in and raised a shot and offered a toast at the bar. "To Salvatore Amicucci, may he not grow up to be like his brother or his old man," Dave Centers bellowed, drawing everyone's attention.

Doug grabbed Dominic by the arm. "Get your brother out of here now. Take him to the strip club."

"What are you going to do?" Dominic asked.

"I'm going to kill this fucker," Doug answered, walking away from Dominic and taking a seat next to Dave. "Dave, what are you drinking?" Doug asked him.

It was obvious that Dave had already had a few, his eyes were bloodshot, his necktie undone, and his speech was slurred. "Are you buying?"

Doug put his arm around his newfound friend. "I don't even want to see you put your hand in your pocket, it's all on the house."

Without uttering a word, Tommy disappeared to find a vehicle to haul the body out of the bar and sent his brother, Billy, to find an ice bin or something they could transport the body in without it being seen. Matt Young went in search of how Dave Centers had gotten up there in the first place.

"I brought a gift," Dave said, putting a gift wrapped box on the bar. "It's a stun gun for the kid's new job."

"That's actually a pretty cool gift, very considerate of you, Dave," Doug told him. "You want to see the rest of the bar?"

Dave agreed, and the two were quickly alone in a room on the first floor. "This is a gorgeous bar," Dave said.

"Thanks, but you found out about it. Do the feds know about it?" Doug asked.

Dave shook his head with little thought. "I don't think so. I left on the outs with bureau. I don't have much in the way of connections left there."

"I thought you were giving the feds any info you were getting," Doug said.

"Not at all, like I told you yesterday, I got to work."

"I got forty grand in my pocket. I'll give it to you for some information," Doug offered.

"Ask away, I'll tell you if I can help or not," Dave told him.

"Dominic's wife, you sure she was having an affair?"

"Her parents told me themselves. They said she was leaving Dominic after his father's trial," Dave answered.

"Do they know who she was having the affair with?"

"No, but I do. It was another agent, a friend of mine. I knew about it the whole time," Dave said.

"But no one else knows?"

"No, I never wanted to taint his name. He died later that year in a car accident, no foul play could be found," Dave told him.

"But you don't think so," Doug said.

"My friend's wife received a hundred thousand dollars in cash that she only told me about. To me, that means the mugging was staged and he was killed, like she was for having an affair."

"Let me ask you this, was she informing on Dominic?" Doug asked.

"I asked him to get information a million times from her, but he wouldn't. He loved her, and he knew from day one that Dominic had staged the mugging."

"What about her parents?" Doug asked. "They never thought Dominic did it."

"They still don't. If it wasn't a mugging, they say, then it was the guy who was having the affair. I went to them when I started my business and offered my services. I tried to sell them on Dominic, but they won't believe it," Dave said.

"And the feds aren't looking to reopen the case?"

"They would if they knew about the affair," Dave said.

"How much info they got on Fabian or anyone else you mentioned to Danny?"

"I have no idea, I was bluffing with Danny. I don't know if they even know as much as I do."

Doug thought for a moment and decided he had no other questions. "Here's your forty grand." Instead of handing Dave a stack of hundreds, Doug punched Dave right in the Adam's apple, causing him to drop to his knees in pain and gasp for breath.

Doug came up behind Dave and put his arms around his head and neck. "Two things I told you are coming true right now. I told you if you ever set foot in one of my bars again, I'd kill you, and that's happening right now, Dave. I did say I'd kill you quick, though," Doug told him as he snapped Dave's neck, causing his instantaneous death.

Doug walked out of the room and grabbed the first employee he saw. "Guard this room. If you or anyone else goes in that room, you're fired, at a minimum."

He found Billy and Matt Young upstairs, waiting for Tommy. "Where's Tommy?" Doug asked them.

"Outside, getting some transportation. Is he dead?" Billy asked.

"Yeah, he's dead. His body's in the farthest bar. Get Benedetto to take care of this. Fuck getting any other transportation, why take a chance on putting his DNA in one of our vehicles. Tell Benedetto to take the body and his car and crush them at Moshe Levin's chop shop. I'm grabbing Tommy and going to the strip club. Meet us there after Benedetto gets the body out of here," Doug ordered.

At the strip club, Danny and Dominic separated from the party when Doug and Tommy arrived and got their own table. "He's dead," Doug told them.

"Where's the body?" Dominic asked.

"On its way to Moshe's chop shop," Doug answered.

"You shouldn't have killed him," Danny said. "Dominic's seeing Nick in the morning."

"This ain't my fault," Doug complained.

"What, he attacked you?" Danny asked.

"No, I told him to never set foot in my places again, penalty of death. This is his fault not mine," Doug said.

"This is going to bring heat from the feds," Danny said.

"We buddied up before I whacked him, he had no friends left at the bureau," Doug told them.

"Or he was just playing you," Dominic added.

"Possible, but I believe him. He said your in-laws never thought you killed Angela, it was him that tried convincing them and they wouldn't waver."

"Nick isn't going to like this, Doug," Danny told him.

"Dominic, you want me to go tomorrow and tell him? Whatever it costs, I got it," Doug said.

"Yeah, I'd love it," Dominic said happily.

"No, that's not how we do it. Dominic, it's your job, you deliver the news," Danny said.

"Danny's right, Doug," Dominic said.

"You know what? I don't need either of you to talk to Nick. I'll just call him myself. I did nothing wrong. I took care of a problem that needed to be taken care of. Fuck him and his pretending to be a fucking agent," Doug said.

"That's right," Tommy added, trying to lighten the situation.

"We just can't react, we're not animals," Danny told him. "There're rules."

"I didn't react like an animal. My reaction was strategic and brilliant if I may add. I received the information I desired before I terminated the threat. There was no blood, and it was a complete surprise to the asshole, another perfect hit," Doug said.

"And if someone knew he was there?" Danny asked.

"Nobody gives a fuck about this degenerate," Doug told him. "All he did was go around and antagonize families that lost someone close to them. He'd tell them Dominic killed their kid or husband and he'd keep working on it for a fee. It gave the prick a reason to do what he loved most, follow you guys around."

The men returned to the party, and Billy and Matt Young arrived to inform Doug that there was no more Dave Centers. The party closed the bar, and Dominic took his younger brother to his house to spend the night. He took him home in the morning before he left to visit his father.

"Sal had a good time last night?" Nick asked Dominic.

"Great time, he's never seen so much tits and ass in his life," Dominic told him. "But there was a problem. Dave Centers, the ex-FBI agent is dead, Doug killed him."

"Doug killed him? What the fuck?" Nick asked, totally bewildered.

"Dave Centers retired from the feds and became a private eye, or tried to be. He went to Angela's parents and convinced them to hire him to find out if she was really mugged or if it was staged. He'd tell them I did it, and when they wouldn't believe him, he'd say okay and tell them he's working on a different angle. He also got hired by Fabian's mother and we think Kristina Kalko," Dominic explained.

"Why didn't you come see me?" Nick asked.

"I was, today. I didn't think two days would matter," Dominic said.

"Two days? Dominic, I'm not understanding," Nick told him.

"Last Friday, Dave came by the bakery asking about Fabian. Monday he goes to the Corner and talks to Danny and starts talking about my wife, Nino Kalko, Fabian, Gary Pizza, and Louis Rubilla. All people he named. So me and Danny agreed to wait until Thursday to talk to you and see what you wanted to do," Dominic said.

"Let me guess, two days ago, he talked to Doug and Doug killed him," Nick said.

"Close, Tuesday he went to the west side and had them call Doug. Doug meets him and before Dave could ask about anyone, Doug told him to stop asking questions and if he went to one of his bars again, he'd kill him. Well, he showed up at Sal's birthday party."

Nick sat there for a moment. "Tell me this did not happen in front of Sal."

"No, Doug buddied up with Dave, and we took Sal downtown. Doug got Dave to talk about what the feds knew, and Dave said he was on the outs with the feds. Doug whacked him with his bare hands, and the zips destroyed Dave's car and his body," Dominic explained.

"And Doug couldn't wait a day?" Nick asked.

"Once Dave walked into Doug's bar, Dad, I'm telling you, he wasn't coming out alive. Doug told him what would happen, and that's what makes Doug Doug. He keeps his word down to the littlest sentence. I can't blame him here. Dave had to die. He's got no badge, and I don't want to relive Angela's murder again."

"Once the feds find out one of theirs is missing, even the retired ones are still theirs, Dominic, they'll be all over you guys," Nick said.

"Then we'll deal with it," Dominic answered.

"Next time, spend the fucking money and come see me asap," Nick told him.

"Doug said he'd call you last night, but I doubt if he's even awake yet. Him and Tommy got pretty fucked up, they're bad together when they go to party," Dominic said.

"Well, that's about it for the spur-of-the-moment hit. What's going on with Fabian's crews in Mexico?" Nick asked.

"We need to knock off his strongholds. We've got a small village with a crooked sheriff that Fabian used for protection at the top of the list. Doug's got the zips on it," Dominic reported.

"New York?" Nick asked.

"Nothing new," Dominic answered.

"What about the making ceremony?"

"We're all set, twelve inductees, every one of them approved by every captain. We're sending Carlo DeMini and Paulie Bankjob."

"Danny's got some mancrush on Paulie. You know he took your grandma on a date, right?" Nick asked.

"It wasn't a date, Dad, it was lunch. And he saved Grandma money on a taxi," Dominic told him.

"He drove my mother home? I didn't know that, I thought it was just lunch. Fucking neighbors got to see my mother getting out of some strange man's car like some kind of fucking hooker?" Nick raged.

"Whoa, I think you just called Grandma a hooker," Dominic told him.

"I didn't, that motherfucker Paulie Bankjob fucking did. I'll kill him. You tell Danny there ain't a one percent chance that Paulie's getting his fucking button."

"Dad . . ." Dominic got out before Nick continued on.

"Who the fuck does he think he is to ask my mother to get in his fucking car?"

"A family friend who was nice to one of the few familiar faces left that he knew after forty years in the fucking can," Dominic told him.

"Oh, I see he's won you over too," Nick said. "This is your grandmother we're talking about here, Dominic. Don't you care?"

"Of course I care, but I'm not a caveman. I understand that an old man and old woman can have lunch together. Could you imagine instead of Grandma having to sit alone, she could invite a friend over and have a conversation? It don't mean they're having some affair. The guy's been in the can forty years, he's going chase Grandma?" Dominic asked, trying to reason with his father.

"That better not mean he's been in her house," Nick said. "And you better not have just called me a caveman, either."

"No, he hasn't been in her house, I was just saying. And yeah, Dad, you are being a caveman if you think Grandma can't have a male elderly friend that she's not sleeping with. And I don't ever want to say that again," Dominic said, thinking of his grandma having sex.

"I agree, this discussion's over, find another inductee," Nick ordered as he got up and ended the visit.

Dominic sat there stunned. "Is this guy for real?" he asked himself.

One of the guards joked with Dominic on the way out. "Dominic, you waited longer to see him than you actually got to see him for."

"Yeah, there went five grand down the tubes," Dominic told him.

"Not for everyone," the guard told him with a smile.

CHAPTER XXVIII

A New Boss

AS DOMINIC DROVE home from his father's prison, his brother, Sal, finally awoke from the celebration from the night before. He went down the stairs and found his mother and sister, Valentina, having coffee at the kitchen table. "What are you doing here?" he asked Valentina as he walked to the fridge.

"Hello to you too," Valentina answered.

"How was your party?" Helena asked with a knowing smile.

Sal found a ginger ale for his hungover stomach. "It was a good time," he answered as he poured himself a glass.

"Oh my god, Sal, is that a hickey?" Valentina asked once she could see his neck.

"By a stripper, Sal, really?" his mother asked him.

Sal rubbed his neck. "I don't know. I don't remember any hickey."

"You don't remember?" Helena asked.

Valentina was up and getting a closer look at Sal's neck. "Look, Mom, there's still lipstick on his neck."

Sal covered his neck, grabbed his glass, and went back to his room. He took a moment to look at his neck in the mirror and gave himself a smile, too bad he couldn't remember who the girl was.

Doug Sullivan had the same rough morning from Sal's birthday party and after breakfast, or an attempt at breakfast, took off to start his day. He had already talked to Nick Amicucci, who read him the riot act about patience and following protocol. Doug explained that he considered the situation with Dave Centers to be an immediate threat, and he felt he made the right decision by executing the former agent.

Doug was meeting his CIA handler today, and he was driving to a small bar in Ohio. He'd be on the road for over ten hours today.

Russell Gorman assembled his men in the meeting room of the FBI building in downtown Detroit. Russell had worked in the Detroit office in the early 2000s and was promoted after Nick Amicucci's conviction. Today was his first day back in Detroit, as he was assigned to take over the whole organized crime division.

"Is it true that you guys don't have a single confidential informant and not a single wire throughout the organization?" Russell opened his first meeting with.

Everyone in the room nodded their heads in embarrassment. "After Louis Cardoni turned, everyone pretty much tells us to go fuck ourselves," one of the agents responded.

"We'll have to change that. Tell me there's at least surveillance," the new boss said.

"After Fabian Bosca was declared missing, we stepped our surveillance again."

"Who are your targets and with what priority is the surveillance?" Russell asked.

"Dominic Amicucci, Danny Serafini, and Jack Mattea are priority number one. Vinny Jagge and Mario Marconi are next. We have a separate group for the Westside, but their top priorities are Doug Sullivan and Tommy and Billy Herrick."

Russell took a seat. "Okay, let me hear Dominic Amicucci's day."

George Nelson was assigned Dominic. "At ten this morning, Vincent Jagge and his son, Frank, showed up at Dominic's house. They stayed about an hour. At twelve noon, Dominic drove to Cooch's Corner and stayed two hours. At two o'clock, he left and returned home."

"Cooch's Corner," Russell scoffed. "The place was Eddie's Bar. The crew hung out there forever. We busted Nino Kalko. He inherited the bar from his dad, and we confiscated the bar. I'm still amazed at how Nick Amicucci was able to purchase it. We couldn't take it when he went away. I'd like to take another shot at confiscating it again. How about Danny Serafini?"

His assigned agent answered, "I lost him on the freeway. So I went back to Cooch's Corner, and he showed up there at noon. He's there until about midnight most nights."

"Why is Jack Mattea such a high priority?" Russell asked.

"He is a Mattea," one agent answered.

Russell knew he had some reorganizing to do here. "The three other captains, Angelo Rea, Eugene Modica, and Benny Mancini, they're a no priority?"

"We have only so many people, sir."

"I understand. Who's got the Westside?" Russell asked.

Agent Jackson knew the Westside crew better than anyone, and he was in charge of their surveillance. Chris Jackson had worked with Russell before on a case involving Doug Sullivan. "I'm still here," Chris answered, raising his hand.

"Excellent, some experience. Tell me about Doug Sullivan's day," Russell said.

"Well, our agent followed him for an hour and a half on I-75 into Ohio before he turned around," Chris answered.

"Not very enlightening. How about his buddy, Tommy Herrick?" Russell asked.

"Not much better. At one o'clock, Tommy Herrick, his brother, Billy, and crew members, Dave Worowski and Matt Young teed off at a golf course in Livonia. It seems everyone took the day off today," Chris Jackson told him.

"Louis Cardoni told us that Doug Sullivan did the dirty work for Nick and ran some union corruption," Russell said.

"Which he was acquitted for," Jackson reminded him.

Russell ignored the comment. "I've poured over his bank accounts, how have these guys come this far?"

Jackson went on now, "I don't think the Westside's actual value to Nick and his family has ever been appreciated. These guys have kept Dominic Amicucci in power."

"And all wiretaps and videotapes prove unfruitful?" Russell asked.

"The warrant expires from lack of results every time, it's like they know," Dominic's agent answered.

"What about prison visits from Dominic and Nick?"

"Same thing, never heard a thing to keep our surveillance going," Agent Nelson answered.

"Okay, this has been very enlightening. We'll meet again Monday, and I'll lay out my changes. And for everyone that doesn't work weeknight or nights, enjoy this upcoming weekend, it'll be your last one off. These guys work long days, they work weekends, they work nights, and some don't even sleep. We will work the same hours as them, and we will work as hard as them if not harder," Russell told his men.

Monday's evening meeting started off the same as his first, with Russell Gorman asking for the surveillance reports. The agents finished their reporting, and Russell informed everyone that Chris Jackson would be his second in charge and combined the Amicucci group with the Westside group. "After all, they act as one, we should treat them as one," he explained. He gave out new job assignments and changed up the scheduling. He ended the meeting by outlining their new attack on the crime family.

The next morning, Doug left his house and drove to a small bar not far from his house. What Doug didn't know was that three undercover agents were going to keep tabs on him today, and Doug had no idea he was tailed to the little bar. What the FBI didn't know was who Doug was meeting there.

Inside the bar and away from the eyes and ears of the FBI outside, Doug took a seat at a small table across from a well-dressed man in an expensive suit.

"How quickly these election years come," Doug said to the man.

"It is that time again," the man responded. The man worked for a state representative in Lansing.

"How much are you looking for?" Doug asked in a bored voice.

"Two hundred thousand," he responded.

"I think I'll pass. Tell Representative Colman that I'll be supporting his opponent this year," Doug told him.

The man was shocked. "Can I give him a reason why?"

"He's not doing what he's supposed to be doing. I give a hundred grand his last election, and I ask for him to work on just two things. Here we are again, he ain't done a thing for me and he asks for double, what the fuck is that? I don't even know who his opponent is, but I'm going to give him a lot of money," Doug told him.

"What two things? Maybe I can help. I do want to run for office myself someday," the man said.

"Well, if you can help me with what I want to do, I'd be happy to help support any campaign you're in," Doug told him. "Two things I asked your fucking boss to work on. I understand he isn't going to get legislation done, but the process can start."

"So tell me the two things," the future political hopeful said again.

"One was to start work on easing the financial regulations for U.S. citizens and the other was to start pushing for mandatory drug tests in high school," Doug told him.

The man was stunned; he had done his homework on Doug Sullivan, and he knew he was a suspected narcotic trafficker. Why he would want to apply some moralistic view to drug test high school kids was beyond him. "First off, banking regulations are never going to ease off, so long as there is terrorism. And you are seriously breaking the Constitution and a lot of civil rights to drug test those kids."

"I disagree on both counts: the process just needs to start and then it can nurture. Everyone has a price, and you should learn that if you want to play in politics," Doug told him.

"So you'll give Representative Colman another chance and donate to his campaign?"

Doug laughed. "No, not a chance. I only give to those that need. The money for your boss was to do something for me. He won't get a dollar from me again. But, like I said, if you run for something and can help me, I'll take care of you," Doug told him as got up to leave.

Outside, while walking back to his car, something caught Doug's attention. He noticed someone sitting in their car while it ran. What struck Doug as odd, though, was how the man looked away. They had made eye contact, and the man went out of his way to seem like he wasn't looking.

Doug patted himself down, pretending to have forgotten something. He went back inside and told the man who paying his bill that he needed to stay for another hour.

"Why should I stay here for another hour?" the man asked.

"Because there's an FBI agent outside and I'm sure he's following me. He might sit around to see who else comes out of this bar after I leave, or if he's here because of you, we're already pretty much fucked," Doug explained. The man nodded and sat back down. Doug left again and went back to his car. The man and the car were gone. Doug drove home and saw no signs of any other tails, which he knew didn't mean that they weren't there.

Dominic Amicucci met Benny Mancini for lunch at a small diner on the east side. Benny explained to Dominic that everything was moving smoothly after the Cuban drug dealer was put out of business.

Dominic saw his tail early on and decided to continue on his day. He told Benny to stay behind at the diner for a little while after Dominic left. From there, Dominic drove to his father's restaurant and met Danny.

Danny also saw his tail early on but took measures to lose the agent. He didn't go to Cooch's Corner today because of the tail; instead, he went to Cooch's Cucina where he thought he was clean from any tails. He was other than the one that Dominic had led to the restaurant, which was not under constant surveillance by the FBI like the bar and the bakery now were. Dominic and Danny both went downtown to the casino after they left the restaurant.

"Dominic, you've got a tail," Danny told him.

"Oh, I know, he's been there all day," Dominic said.

"You led him to your father's restaurant?" Danny asked in disbelief.

"What's the harm? They know we go there, and they know I've known you all my life," Dominic told him.

"You don't know the hell I went through to lose my tail this morning," Danny told him. "Just for you to not even give an effort and take them right to me. Thanks, Dominic."

Dominic looked at Danny. "We're going to the casino, is there something illegal about that? Tell me now, Danny, because I can lose the tail."

"Fuck it, let's just get to a craps table," Danny said.

The delivery truck pulled up outside of Cooch's Corner's back door; the driver got out and rang the bell. Vince Cusamano, one of the Amicucci crew members, opened the door. "Who are you?" he asked the driver.

"I'm the driver. I've got your beer delivery. Got held up, there's an accident on the freeway," the driver said. Vince told him to hold a minute and closed the door and went away.

Jackie Beans and Scary Scarelli came back out the door with Vince. "Now, who are you?" Jackie asked him.

"I'm delivering your beer," he told him. "I'm just covering this route for a day."

"Why didn't they call?" Jackie asked, sizing the man up.

"Do they call you every time there's a different driver?" the man asked.

"Yes, they do," Jackie answered.

"I don't know what else to tell you. Are you taking the delivery or not?" he asked.

Jackie didn't say a word; he just turned around and walked back in the bar. "Get the fuck out of here," Scary told him as he followed Jackie and Vince inside. The driver got back in the truck and exited through the back parking lot.

Later on at the FBI, the driver of the delivery truck sat with Russell Gorman and Chris Jackson. The driver/agent had laid out several pictures detailing the back alley and back parking lot. "There doesn't appear to be any outside surveillance cameras," he informed his new bosses.

"So they really wouldn't take the delivery, eh?" Russell asked.

"Nope, not without the beer company calling them first, which they failed to do for the first time ever by the way it seemed," he told Russell.

"Obviously, their non-phone call was a tip to the bar," Jackson added.

"Good pictures nonetheless," Russell told his agent. "Good work. We can definitely formulate a plan from these."

"They probably already know it was us that tried to get inside today. I'm sure Jackie Beans called the beer company right away, and I doubt they'd cover for us," Jackson said.

"Who do we have a nighttime tail on?" Russell asked Jackson.

"Just Doug and Dominic," he answered. "But it doesn't matter, they're all together. Doug, Tommy, Danny, Angelo Rea, their wives, and Dominic are all at Cooch's Cucina right now. Easy surveillance tonight," he said.

"What's the occasion?" Russell asked.

"No idea," Jackson answered.

"Send the agents inside and have dinner, tell them to have a look around," Russell ordered.

"Sir, they're with their wives," Jackson reminded.

"Our agents can get a look at how they're treated in there and how they act. It's important to know as much about these guys as possible. It won't hurt to see how they act with all their wives present. Plus, their guards will probably be down," Russell explained.

What they were celebrating at the Cucina was the opening of Doug's new bar in four days. Doug was planning on burying himself at the bar, starting tomorrow, and this would be the last of his free time.

Doug finished with another toast and downed his drink when Tommy leaned over and whispered in his ear, "Look at the two dudes that just walked in. Feds?"

Doug looked the two men over and answered Tommy, "I'd have to agree, good eye." He caught Dominic's eye and motioned toward the strangers. Dominic spotted the agents and whispered it to Danny. "Want to have some fun?" Doug asked Tommy.

"You know I do," Tommy said as he followed Doug to a booth next to the agents' table.

"He just texted me, and it's all set for tomorrow," Doug said in a whisper, but loud enough for the agents to hear. They of course were puzzled as to their good luck that Doug and Tommy had something to talk about that they didn't they want to speak of in front of everyone, and they would be here to hear it.

"Fucking finally," Tommy said, playing along. "I thought this was never going to go down."

"Oh, I know. There's going to be some fallout. I hate to say it, but we might have to start carrying guns," Doug said.

"Don't forget, we got that guy who can get those things. I'll give that one guy a call and tell him to start collecting some things," Tommy said.

"Good, we got to consider the feds as well," Doug said.

"Fuck them stupid fuckers," Tommy said.

Doug almost broke out laughing there, but was able to contain himself, at least until the waiter got to their table. "Nonetheless. Hey, I heard the feds found that body."

Both agents almost fell out of their chairs when they heard the word *body*. A waiter stopped at their table and dropped off a bottle of champagne. "This is on the house, compliments of the owner."

Doug and Tommy finally lost it and broke out in laughter and got up to return to the party. "Gentlemen, enjoy the bubbly and your meal's on the house. Thank you so much," Doug said, still not recovered from the laugh. He put his arm around Tommy as they walked away, still laughing. "Oh man, Tommy, ain't they fun," he said for the agents to hear.

Both agents sat there glum and vowed to not tell their boss this and swore to each other that they'd nail these bastards.

CHAPTER XXIX

THE FOUR SEASONS

DOMINIC AMICUCCI AND his cousin, Angelo Rea, came up the stairs from the basement into the kitchen and found their grandma had just arrived. She gave Angelo a hug, and when Dominic reached down to hug his grandma, she grabbed his ear and marched him out of the kitchen into a guest room.

"Grandma, what?" Dominic complained as she held his ear tight still in the bedroom.

"Does your father think I'm having an affair with Paul Amevu?" she asked.

"I don't know, Grandma."

She tugged harder. "Don't you lie to me. Who is he telling this crap to?"

"Just me, just me. Come on, let go of my ear, this is humiliating," Dominic pleaded.

"Why did I hear it in church this morning? Huh, why Dominic?" Instead of letting go of Dominic's ear, she pulled even harder.

"I tried to tell Dad that there's nothing wrong with it," Dominic let out, waiting for his ear to separate from his head in any moment.

"You told your father that there's nothing wrong with me having an affair with Paul Amevu? I'll strangle the both you," she hissed.

"Grandma, please, I'm going to have to get tough with you," Dominic joked, hoping to not need plastic surgery on his ear as well.

She let him go. "In your dreams."

Dominic rubbed his ear. "I told him you two were just friends and that there's nothing wrong with that."

"He's such a Neanderthal," Helen Amicucci complained of her son.

Dominic snapped his fingers. "That's the word I was thinking of. I could only call my dad a caveman."

Helen had no patience for this. "Thursday when you visit your father, you'll take me."

"Oh no, Grandma, he'll kill me. He can't know I said a word to you—he'll never forgive me," Dominic said.

"You two are not at the top of my list right now, same with Nick's brother, Daniel. You'll just have to find a way to not have Nick kill you. And the next time you ever hear of me anywhere or with anyone, you better have enough respect for me not to think I'm sleeping around. The thought makes me sick," Helen said before she left the room.

Dominic found his way outside where everyone was for the big Sunday gathering; this one was on Memorial Day weekend, and the day was beautiful. He found his Uncle Daniel at his usual spot on Sundays, at the grill.

"Hey, did your dumbass say something to Grandma about Paulie Bankjob?" Dominic whispered to him.

"If Paulie Bankjob is Paul Amevu, then no, I didn't. My wife did," Daniel said solemnly.

"Aunt Louisa told Grandma that my father thinks that she's having an affair with Paulie Bankjob?"

"Yes."

"That's it's, eh, yes? You got nothing else?" Dominic asked him.

"What do want me to say? He shouldn't have taken my mother to lunch in the first place," Daniel complained.

Dominic had had enough, and he stormed off to find Danny, who he found talking to Marie and Rocco DiNapoli. Rocco was invited to the gathering by Daniel's daughter, who was home from college for the long weekend.

"Can I have a moment?" Dominic asked Danny, who walked with Dominic to have a private conversation.

"So refreshing to see a nice blossoming relationship before it turns to shit," Danny said.

"Whatever, Danny. Your fucking boy, Paulie Bankjob, is causing such a fucking uproar," Dominic told him.

"Fine, you guys want me to shoo him away, put him a shelf? Okay, just leave me the fuck alone about him," Danny said.

"No, this is all bullshit. I got your back on this one. My dad's flat wrong here, and we're going to make Paulie no matter what he says," Dominic said.

Danny raised his eyebrows. "All right, kid. But it's the other way round, I got *your* back on this one."

"You didn't tell him yet that he was out, did you?" Dominic asked.

"No, I ain't had the heart," Danny answered.

"My family's fucking Neanderthals," Dominic complained as he walked off.

"That a boy," Danny said to himself.

The next day was Memorial Day and Doug's bash at his new bar. He had a dozen grills going in the parking lot, and everything was free outside. Doug even had his boy, Graham, handing out cold colas and water, free of charge. Inside, Doug only opened the lobby bar. Besides the lobby bar, it consisted of four theatre-sized first floor bars and another bar and restaurant upstairs. The plan was to open just one bar a day until the grand opening was announced on Friday, which will have everything open and live bands for each of the four major first floor bars.

Doug manned one of the grills himself and shook the hand of every adult and played a moment with every child. "Thanks for coming, if there's ever anything I can do for you, come and see me," Doug told almost every person. Thirty-two jobs would be given from Doug as thirty-two people told him what they needed was a job. "If you can wash a dish and it'll help, I got a job here for you." Dishwasher, parking lot sweeper, window washer, towel folder, Doug found something for everyone that asked.

"Doug Sullivan, cooking burgers, who'd have thought?" Doug heard someone say from behind him.

"Agent Jackson," Doug sighed after he turned around. "Even on Memorial Day? I commend your dedication." Doug threw a burger on a bun and handed it the FBI agent. "Here, happy Memorial Day."

He took the burger. "Thanks. I got to ask you, how in the hell are you going to make any money giving everything away for free?"

"It's all loss today. Today I give, I can afford it, you know that," Doug said, knowing full well the government had examined every penny in Doug's bank account and scrutinized every line of his tax returns. "Besides, I'll make it all back ten times over on Friday."

"Give me a tour of the inside?" the agent asked.

"I ain't giving that much today," Doug told him. "Don't tell me you came all the way here for the free burger instead of being with your family, what's up?"

"Actually, I thought I'd check the place out. I didn't expect to see you cooking on the grill. But since we're together, do you remember an agent, Dave Centers, used to work Dominic's father's case?"

"Dave Centers, I don't need to remember back that far—the prick's been bothering the fuck out of everyone lately," Doug told him.

"You've seen him? Personally?"

"Yeah, he went to my old hangout and had them call me. I had to stop what I was I doing and drive the fuck out there," Doug answered.

"He had called me and said he had something on Angela Amicucci's murder. He said he went to see Dominic and Danny Serafini, but he never mentioned you."

Doug laughed. "That's probably because I told him he wasn't no agent no more and had six big motherfuckers escort him out. He never mentioned Angela to me. Is there something new on the case?"

"That's what I'd like to know. I can't find Dave," the agent answered.

"You can't find him?" Doug asked convincingly and pretended to think for a moment. "Hey, when I called him a prick, I didn't mean nothing personal by it. I always heard he was a stand-up agent and the men that walked him out weren't really that big," Doug said as he pretended to panic.

"Doug, I don't think anything's happened to him," Agent Jackson laughed. "I think he's full of shit. He still thinks Dominic killed his wife. I personally, with the whole organized crime task force, worked that case to try and find that your friend did it. For once, it's not a murder that we just can't prove—it's that we honestly believe he lost his wife to a murder/mugging. No one deserves that."

"That's good, because, I speak from my heart here. He truly died on that day too. I spent many nights listening to him cry, even sob. It literally broke him," Doug told the agent.

"So if you could tell Dominic and Danny not to talk this guy, I'd appreciate it. Tell them just to send him away. I worry he'll take things too far."

"I'll tell them. You want anything else to eat? You want to invite your family?" Doug asked.

Agent Jackson couldn't help it. "I'll take another burger and maybe a hot dog or two."

Doug smiled and gave the agent his wish. "There's macaroni and potato salad and shit like that on those tables at the end. It's Memorial Day. Don't forget the apple pie, Agent Jackson."

Doug watched the agent fill his plate and thought to himself, *Not one clue*. Doug knew the agent had no idea that Dave Centers was even dead and that his killer had just given him his Memorial Day barbecue.

On Thursday, Nick Amicucci entered the visiting room, expecting to see only his son, Dominic; instead, his mother was there with him. Nick glared at Dominic.

"Oh, don't get mad at him, he wants me here as much as you do. Sit down," Helen Amicucci ordered to her oldest son.

Nick sat down. "I don't like you to be in this place. You shouldn't be subjected to this."

"Then don't make me come here," she told him.

Nick looked at Dominic. "Well, Son, mother's going to speak in riddles. You want to fill me in?"

"Paulie," Dominic answered.

"How dare you tell people I'm having an affair with Paul Amevu," Helen scolded.

Nick spoke to his son, "That's not what I said."

"Why do you keep looking at him, he's only here for the ride," Helen said. "I want to know why you'd do such a thing."

"I only said that I don't want people thinking you're having an affair, that's all. I know you're not," Nick said.

"After church today, Phyllis comes up to me and asks how sex is with an ex-con, and all the other women giggled. It was like we were in school again."

"Mom, I—" Nick started.

"Your father has been gone almost thirty years now. I was married to him for thirty-one years. I met him two years before that, that's sixty-three years since I've ever thought of another man. That doesn't deserve enough respect that if I have lunch or get a ride home from Paul, that it wouldn't be anything more?"

"I never thought you were, and I never said that, Dominic," Nick told his son.

Helen defended her grandson. "He didn't tell anyone, he's like a mini you. You've complained about it to someone other than your son, that's who you need to blame if you must blame someone other than yourself. To even give credence that someone would think that because Paul gave me a ride home is silly and it's disrespectful. Do you know what your father would do to you?"

"I think he'd say I was looking out for you," Nick answered.

Helen held her hand up. "I do not need you to look out for me. And assuming everyone thinks I'm having an affair because I get out of a car, what's the matter with you? You're going to be sixty years old next year. You were smarter when you were sixteen."

"Okay, I'm sorry," Nick said.

"And I don't want you to hold any ill will to Paul. Your grandfather and father thought the world of him, and to me, he's a part of this family," Helen said.

"Grandma, I need a word with Dad alone?" Dominic cut in.

Helen looked around the waiting room at the other full tables. "Where am I going to go, sit with a stranger?"

"Mother, they've got the potato chips you like in the vending machine, that's all the time we need," Nick said, and his mother left for a moment.

Dominic looked his father right in the eye and said, "I'm making Paulie Bankjob."

"I appear to be wrong here. I don't think I am, but you've got my blessing on Paulie, for my mother," Nick said. "I give you a pass on disobeying me this time, but remember this, my young son: you better be able to stand on your own two feet before you cut mine out from under me."

"I'm just trying to do the right thing here, and Paulie's earned it," Dominic said.

"I'm like half mad and half proud right now. I don't like the defiance, but I'm oddly proud of you for it," Nick said.

"I think that's the nicest thing you ever said to me," Dominic told him.

"Don't think that doesn't make you not a fuckup," Nick said. "Now go help your grandma, she can't figure out the machine."

"Yes, Dad," Dominic told him, smiling.

"Will you look at this?" Danny asked as they pulled into the parking lot of the Four Seasons for its grand opening. It was packed. Jimmy Amicucci pulled the car as close to the front as he could get—they didn't use valets for fear of FBI intervention. Danny and Dominic got out of the back, and Angelo got out of the passenger seat. Pulling up behind Jimmy, new crew member Rocco Gurino Jr. dropped off Scary, Fat Kenny, and soon-to-be made man, Carlo DeMini. Jimmy and Rocco would stay with the cars.

There was a long line to get in, but Matt Young was out front and let the mob bigwigs pass the line. At the door, Sal Amicucci was working as a bouncer and checking IDs. He cringed when he saw his brother and everyone approaching; he didn't want to be embarrassed in front of the staff.

The mammoth bouncers watched as an even bigger specimen come in the door. Scary Scarelli led the way. The bouncers watched as the man gave Sal a quick man hug and tipped him twenty dollars. Several other men followed, each giving a bigger hug and a bigger tip than the guy before him with Danny and Dominic pulling up the rear.

Sal watched everyone walk into the bar with a feeling of accomplishment, like he finally had earned some respect.

Inside, the club was happening. They saw a bar where they could get a drink across the room and made their way their through the crowd. They walked around the dance floor and spotted Doug coming out of a room. When Doug saw them, he motioned them back into the room he just left.

Danny, Dominic, Angelo, and Kenny followed Doug into the office. Doug was in pure shock as to how busy the bar was. "I expected busy, but holy shit! I'm going to run out of beer, I got two whole fucking trucks coming. Tommy's already been in an argument with some guy, so he's all pissed off. His brother's upstairs in the kitchen, the restaurant's overbooked, it's out of fucking control."

"And you're in here," Danny noticed.

"Oh yeah, I ran for the fucking hills," Doug joked. "Dom, you promised me you'd make Sal look good when you came in, did you?" Doug asked suspiciously.

"He did very good, Doug," Danny answered.

"Against every fiber of my being, I did it," Dominic said.

"Can we get out there and see this club?" Angelo asked.

"I only came out because you guys were here. I'm staying in here a bit," Doug told them.

Danny laughed. "I've never seen you frazzled before."

Tommy burst into the room. "Hey, guys," Tommy said, acknowledging the crew. "Doug there's some asshole in the 1980s bar doing the moonwalk all over the place and getting in everyone's way. Let me toss the fucker."

Everyone but Doug laughed, much to Tommy's annoyance. "Tommy, I've got a staff to handle this shit, leave it alone, will you?" Doug asked despairingly.

"I heard there's a live band," Angelo added, earning a glare from Tommy.

"There's actually four live bands, Angelo. You guys go ahead, check them out," Doug told them. "I'll be out in a bit." Everyone left Doug to himself.

The men walked to the other side and to the hallway that adjoined the four bars. "Which one?" Danny yelled to Dominic over the music.

"You got a recommendation?" Dominic asked Tommy.

"Don't go to the eighties bar," Tommy told them as he took off.

"Okay, Ange, which one?" Dominic asked him. "Modern, reggae, or the Rock Out Loud Bar?"

"Let's rock out loud," Angelo told him, and the men headed for the bar all the way on the right.

Half an hour later, Doug left his office and caught up with Dominic and them. "Doug, this place is fucking great," Dominic told him.

"I called my wife, she's grabbing Valentina and Sabrina and they're coming here," Angelo told him.

"Terrific, that's terrific. Come on, shots are on me," Doug told him and beelined it to the bar.

Danny stopped Dominic as they followed Doug. "You notice how fast he was just talking? Look at him go," Danny said, pointing to Doug flying down the aisle.

"You won't see Doug do much more than smoke a joint, if that's what you're implying," Dominic told him.

"Dominic, I've done my share of cocaine in my earlier days. I know what the symptoms are, and I'm telling you, Doug just did some lines," Danny said with certainty.

"Danny, since the day you and my father were arrested, my life has been in Doug's hands. If he's doing coke, so be it," Dominic said. "We've all done it."

"We've never relied on it to get through a day like he's doing," Danny said.

"Like you ***think*** he's doing," Dominic reminded him.

"What the hell are you two talking about?" Doug asked when Dominic and Danny arrived for their shot, which they had already missed round one.

Dominic laughed. "You, you're all wound up. You look like you just did a couple of lines," he said, much to Danny's surprise that Dominic came right out and said it.

"I haven't slept in three days, how the fuck else do you think I'm still going?" Doug joked to two surprised faces. Doug realized that they really thought he was in the office doing drugs. "I'm fucking kidding, you retards. I slammed two Red Bulls, but I prefer to call it a second wind, or in my case, a fifteenth wind. You guys really think I'm a cokehead?"

"Not me," Danny said, looking at Dominic.

"No, I really do not, Doug. Next round's on me," Dominic said, glaring at Danny for hanging him out to dry.

Doug shrugged his shoulders. "Whatever," he said, and something caught his attention. "Look at the blonde your cousin's trying to pick up," Doug said pointing.

Dominic looked. "What an idiot! His fucking wife's on her way here."

Danny nudged Dominic. "Go get him. My daughter's coming with Angela and your sister, and I don't want to go through this."

"And he's your captain," Doug joked to Danny after Dominic left to get Angelo.

"I know," Danny said solemnly.

As the night went on, the girls showed up with their husbands and enjoyed VIP treatment at the new hot nightclub. It was a big stress relief for Doug once his upstairs restaurant closed; he was disappointed his staff was not ready. The bars were packed though, and even toward one in the morning, there was still a line to get in.

Doug was having a beer in the closed upstairs bar with fellow Westsider, Dave Worowski, when his phone rang—it was Tommy. "What, some girl at the door not matching the picture on her ID?" Doug asked, totally annoyed with his best friend.

"Doug, you want to come to the lobby, believe me," Tommy said.

Tommy's voice sounded like he had something he really wanted Doug to see, so he went to the lobby and found Tommy talking to someone Doug thought he knew.

"I know you from somewhere," Doug told the man as he put his hand out to shake.

The man didn't return the handshake. "Are you the owner?" he asked.

Doug put his hand down and asked Tommy, "Who's this guy?"

Tommy smiled. "He's here to help. For five grand a week, he can ensure we're safe from any crime and law enforcement, and he can ensure we always get our deliveries."

"You're here to shake me down?" Doug asked in disbelief.

"It's a nice joint. My son's inside. He called me and said there was this new club here. He said it was great, and he was right. You should protect a nice investment like this," the man told Doug.

"What was your name?" Doug asked, still in disbelief.

"Don't worry about my fucking name. If you must, call me Tom."

It came back to Doug who this man was. It was Tom Caruso, Valentina Amicucci's father-in-law. Doug had met him a few times over the years, but they never once said anything more than hello to each other. And here he was to shake Doug down.

"Five grand a week? Not bad. What do you think?" Doug asked Tommy.

"Yeah, not bad. It is a good idea to protect your investment," Tommy agreed, playing along.

"I'll take my first payment today," Tom told Doug.

"Sure, come on in. You want a drink? Where's your kid, I'll make sure he doesn't pay a dime?" Doug asked.

Tom was impressed with himself. "I'll take a drink."

When they got in the door, Tommy quickly whispered a question in Doug's ear, "Are we whacking him here?"

Doug almost broke out laughing and decided not to tell Tommy who the man was; he just shrugged his shoulders to answer Tommy's question.

Doug took him right to Dominic and the party. They were all very surprised to see Tom, who was more surprised to see them. Doug stood between Tom and Dominic and pulled out a wad of cash and handed a stack to Tom.

"What the fuck is that for?" Dominic asked, knowing that Tom personally owed him over a half million dollars.

"This, Dominic, is to ensure my bar will be protected," Doug said.

Tom didn't take the money. "Dominic, I didn't know this was a friend of yours."

"We've met before, I'm Doug Sullivan."

"Oh, yeah, you look a lot different," Tom stammered.

Everyone but Dominic and Tommy laughed. Dominic was without a doubt that the father of his sister's husband, whom his father made him promote, was an incompetent fool. Tommy was starting to understand the joke.

The men gathered in Doug's office for last call, and Dominic was still mad about Tom. "I don't get how the man is so dumb," he complained to Doug, Danny, and Tommy. Everyone else had gone home. "I'd think you'd agree, Danny."

"I think it's funny," Danny said.

"It is funny, but let's not forget the most important fact here," Doug said.

"What's that?" Dominic asked.

Doug motioned to Tommy. "Go ahead, Tommy, tell them."

"That one of your guys just tried to shake us down. That means that someone of the level of a lieutenant isn't aware of where he can operate and where he can't operate," Tommy answered.

"And he can't operate on the west side," Doug reminded them.

Danny looked around the room. "You don't fear wiretaps? I don't see any scrambler."

"Look at your phones," Doug said. Everyone pulled out their cell phones, and all had nothing. "It's built in, the whole office is unbuggable. One million dollars it fucking cost."

Danny didn't answer; he just looked around the room and wondered.

"So, we're all clear about what happens the next time one of your guys comes here to shake us down?" Doug asked.

"Doug'll Dave Center him," Tommy joked, nobody laughed. "It's unbuggable," he reminded them.

"Tommy's kidding, we'll come to you, and I'll let you know if it happens. But I will want you to let me kill him, that I guarantee," Doug warned.

"Or just make sure your people understand your rules—that's probably the best road," Tommy added.

"And here we are again, being lectured by Doug and Tommy," Danny said, getting irritated.

"Name one of your bars that have been shaken down by one of ours," Doug said. "You can't because it hasn't happened. We don't mean to boast, Danny, we just offer advice from a well-oiled machine, that's all," Doug chided.

"You did have the zip that put his gun to one of our guy's heads," Dominic added.

"And I dealt with him. If it happens again, it won't for a third time, he'll be gone. Dominic's right about Tom Caruso—he is a moron and he's in way over his head. Tom's not a very intimidating person, and he don't bring no muscle to shake down a big club like this. Who the fuck is he scaring? But he'll stick around and keep fucking up," Doug said.

Danny had a brainstorm. "Dominic, you stood up to your father with Paulie. Take a stand here. Doug's right, Tom's in over his head, and you know it too."

"What take a stand? I'll call him and tell him," Doug said. "What's everyone so scared of? Run your fucking business the way it should be run. Your father will understand if you tell him Tom just can't do it."

"Incompetence only breeds more incompetence," Tommy added.

"What the fuck is it with you and these one-liners?" Danny asked Tommy.

"Tommy's right though—you want me to send someone over there and maybe teach him some things?" Doug joked.

He could tell he took Danny to his limit. "Okay, I'm just busting balls, Danny. I'm sorry, we're just fucking around. Look at the camera—Sal's having a beer with some of the guys, let's go join them." The men spent about another hour drinking before Doug left to count up the money from his grand opening.

CHAPTER XXX

TROUBLE ON THE HORIZON

"MIKEY, WHAT'S WRONG?" Danny Serafini asked Michael Jagge. Danny, Dominic, and Angelo returned to Doug Sullivan's new bar, The Four Seasons, and invited the Jagges to join them. "You should be dancing around, on top of the world. I'll tell you, when I learned I was getting my button, nothing could bring me down."

Michael was sitting at the lobby bar alone, while everyone was gathered in the 1980s bar. "Just not feeling well, can't shake it," Michael told him.

"You're going to drink it off, huh?" Danny asked when he noticed Doug and Tommy Herrick coming through the door that led to the upstairs. They looked to be in an argument, and they went into Doug's office followed by a door slamming. "I'll be back," Danny told Michael and went to check on Doug and Tommy.

He knocked on the door and was greeted by a "What?"The door was opened, and the two seemed very angry with each other.

"You want to give us a fucking minute, Danny?" Doug asked.

"Everything all right?" Danny asked.

They ignored Danny and continued with their argument. "How the fuck was that my fault?" Tommy now asked.

"The man was leaving, Tommy, and you call him a dumb nigger? What the fuck's the matter with you?" Doug asked.

"That was my bad, I admit it. I was wrong there, but he fucking belittled the whole staff because he had to wait. He brought it up first, saying, 'A nigger can't get a table here?' he asks. The situation was already bad. I only made it worse," Tommy explained.

"Okay, fine, let the staff handle it. Why do you got to be involved in every fucking problem?" Doug demanded. "If you're not there, that fucker keeps walking and doesn't turn around and take a swing."

"I missed some action, eh?" Danny said, again, no one paid any mind to him.

"He was only leaving because of me. If I wasn't there, he probably would've killed someone," Tommy told him.

"That's just more bullshit to feed your fucking ego," Doug said.

"Fuck you, Doug," Tommy said as both men started inching their way toward each other.

"That's enough," Danny said as he got in the middle. "You guys need to go the fuck home and get some sleep. You two don't act this way with each other, knock it off."

Danny's next thought was that he had made a mistake by getting in the middle of these two, but they both let the air out after a few seconds. "You're right. Tommy, please, no more on the racial slurs, okay?" Doug asked.

They shook hands. "I'm sorry for that, it won't happen again."

"And I'm sorry for the ego comment," Doug said.

"You really think I got a big ego?" Tommy asked.

"Little bit," Doug told him with a smile.

Danny interrupted, "Now that everyone's all made up, can we go get a drink? And Doug, I've never seen a bigger ego than yours, by the way," Danny said as they left the office.

Danny led them to Michael at the bar and introduced Vinny Jagge's youngest son to Doug and Tommy. "This is the guy that shot Fabian," Danny whispered to them.

"Oh, I heard it was a solid piece of work," Doug said, shaking his hand.

Michael just nodded and lifted his glass to Doug and turned back to the bar. "Okay then, where's everyone else at?" Doug asked Danny.

"1980s bar," Danny said, and they left to go there.

"He didn't whack him," Tommy whispered to Doug on the way.

"Maybe he just hates himself for doing it, it ain't for everyone," Doug said.

As last call approached. Doug and Tommy held a quick meeting with Virgil Boyle, as he had something to talk them about. "I heard something disturbing the other day, and I wanted to make sure I didn't sit on it. One of the retired DeCarlo's in Miami told me that Sammy Braga will be looking to take Miami back after his old man dies—his old man's eighty-nine," Virgil told them.

"Who the fuck is Sammy Braga?" Tommy asked.

"Vinny Braga's kid. Vinny's the boss of the DeCarlo Family of New York. Sammy runs the family I imagine. He's the one Dominic had to arrange a sit-down with for us to move in to Miami. We had permission, what would be his problem?" Doug asked Virgil.

"Jilly's a retired DeCarlo captain, and he told me Sammy disagreed with his father on letting us take Miami. He says his father just did it because the other bosses pressured him," Virgil said.

"This don't sound too good," Tommy said.

"Let me see if I got this straight, Virgil. The DeCarlo Family had rackets down there that dried in the 1980s and disappeared in the 1990s. We go down, even ask permission first, and whack a bunch of Mexicans or Cubans," Doug was saying.

"Cubans," Virgil answered.

"Okay, and their claim is that it was theirs' first?" Doug asked.

"I think so," Virgil said.

"This Jilly guy, he's on the up and up?" Doug asked.

"He loved the old man, but he ain't no Sammy Braga fan. He said he's really the reason he even retired. I like the guy, he's well respected," Virgil told him.

"Then don't mention his name to anyone else, under any condition. We might need this guy someday in the future," Doug said.

The next day, Doug skipped out of the bar early and took his wife and oldest son, Graham, to the Amicucci household for the Sunday gathering. They left the youngest son, Bobby, at home with Grace's parents. Doug, Danny, and Dominic gathered by the horseshoe pits, away from everyone.

"I think I got some trouble brewing on the horizon. I'm hearing that Sammy Braga's going to make a move on me once his old man dies," Doug told them.

"Any attack on you is an attack on us," Danny said.

"Because of Miami?" Dominic asked. "Vinny Braga said he had no problem. They had nothing going on down there anymore."

"I can only tell you what I hear," Doug said.

"Who's your source?" Danny asked.

"My source is my source, leave it at that," Doug answered.

"What do you want to do?" Dominic asked Doug.

"Well, I don't want to go to war with a fucking New York family, that's for sure. But, I'm not going to kiss their ass either," Doug answered.

"Sounds like we need to hope Vinny Braga lives until he's a hundred," Danny said.

"That's only ten years away from what I hear. I'm not going to act until the old man dies, but I will have a plan in case Sammy decides he really is going to attack me," Doug said.

"I was at the meeting in 2006 with Vinny Braga, and he literally said no problem. I don't get why his kid thinks he's got any rights to Miami," Dominic said.

"Doug, if he does do something, the other bosses in New York won't be happy. We'll have a sit-down," Danny said.

"You guys love your sit-downs. Anything happens to any of my men, I'm not sitting down, I'm shooting back, New York family or not," Doug said. "I already got one zip in New York watching Bruno Bini. I'll flood the fucking streets with Sicilian shooters."

"We'll deal with it if something happens to Vinny Braga," Danny said.

"Rest assured, I'll be ready," Doug told them.

"I'll put a bug in Vito Paganini's ear in New York. It couldn't hurt," Dominic said.

"Okay, I'd love to not have to fight," Doug said as they walked back to the house.

The next day, Doug arrived at the Four Seasons at noon and left by three for a three-hour drive to meet his CIA contact. He immediately noticed he had a tail, and it cost him another hour to lose it. What he didn't know was that the same car had followed him from his house to the bar without Doug seeing him.

He met his contact in a hotel parking lot, and Doug got a room when he arrived; the agent followed after a few minutes. "You're late," the CIA agent said when Doug opened the door to the hotel room.

"I had a tail, fuck off," Doug told him.

"Bad day?" the agent asked. "If so, take it out on your wife, not me."

"I got shit to do, and if I leave now, I'll be home around ten o'clock. I told you I didn't have fucking time for you," Doug said.

The agent ignored Doug's complaints. "The weapons are ready. You need to reach out and set up a meeting with your friends in Baghdad and make the deal."

"And if I'm supposed to deliver them inside the country?" Doug asked, still not wanting to give these terrorists any weapons.

"Deliver the fucking weapons, or go back to jail, okay?" the agent said.

Doug bit his tongue. "Sure."

The agent tossed a manila folder on the bed. "These are the account numbers to deposit the money. Do not deliver the weapons until you have the money in the accounts. We'll meet again, and I'll introduce you to the agent you'll be bringing with you."

"I'm bringing an agent with me?" Doug asked.

"Yeah, you just write him off as one of your top men," the agent said, shrugging his shoulders.

"This deal seems to be getting worse by the minute," Doug said.

"This is a good thing. The weapons all will be tagged with homing beacons and will lead to the people that intend to use them, overseas of course," the agent explained. Doug had voiced his opinion several times that he didn't want to do this deal unless he personally knew the weapons weren't staying in the United States.

"How long do you think this will continue?" Doug asked.

"Three to five years, depending on how well you can infiltrate. It's still better than the eight you were looking at in jail," the agent said.

"Are we done?" Doug asked in disgust.

"The field agent that you'll be working with, he should probably start hanging around at your new bar. In case these guys start checking up on you, his will be a face they've seen before."

"Sure, tell him to grab a tape recorder, and I can start introducing him to all my friends," Doug said sarcastically. "Find a different plan in other words."

The agent shook his head. "Not your show. This is the plan. Have him work the door or stay fifteen feet behind you at all times. He doesn't need to hear your conversations."

It was Doug that shook his head this time. "No, you're going to get me pegged as a rat. Send me back to jail, but at least my best friend won't put a bullet in my head that way. I should have known better," Doug said as he walked to the door.

"Wait," the agent said.

Doug turned around. "If you think you're arresting me now, I'm warning you, you'll be adding resisting arrest and assaulting an asshole to the charges."

"I need your connections, let's find another way," the agent conceded, and Doug walked back.

Doug arrived at his bar a little before midnight and found that even on a Monday night his bar was still packed, no line at the door, but still packed. He found Billy Herrick sitting at the lobby bar having a beer. "No work in the morning, Billy?" Doug asked.

"Just got done upstairs, there's still people sitting," Billy told him, despite the upstairs closing at eleven. "I thought I'd enjoy a beer before I head home and open my restaurant in six hours."

"Billy, whose restaurant?" Doug joked. He was one-third owner with the Herrick brothers.

"Whatever, a thanks would be nice," Billy said.

"Thanks, Billy," Doug said.

"Great, you got anything for the zips? I think they're getting restless."

"Nothing much for now. The zip in New York, the one watching Bruno Bini, I need him to start gathering intel on Sammy Braga out there. Tommy will fill you in," Doug told him.

"Will do. Oh, Benedetto says they'll be ready to make a move in Mexico in about a month," Billy told him. "And another thing, Dominic's little brother, Sal, he really helped out upstairs today."

"Sal? What'd he do upstairs? He's supposed to be working at the door for now," Doug said.

"We had problems again in the kitchen, a line going down the stairs, again. I come out for a smoke, and I see Sal bussing tables, wiping them down, seating people. The kid even knew the specials. Then he added an extra pair of hands in the kitchen when the prep ran out and Sal started slicing and dicing. Like I said, a big help," Billy told him.

"He must've worked in father's restaurant when he was young. I didn't think he worked a day in his life," Doug said.

"If you don't want him here, I'll take him to my restaurant. Our restaurant," Billy said, correcting himself.

After counting the day's money, Doug never noticed the FBI tail that followed him home at three thirty in the morning. They all knew the feds had stepped up the surveillance on them, but had no idea to what extent the feds had stepped it up to.

On Thursday, as usual, Dominic went to visit his father. This Thursday, as Dominic started to reach for the usual five thousand-dollar payment to the guards, he received a different interaction from them. "ID please and name of inmate," the guard said to Dominic

Dominic knew something was up and followed the guard's instruction. After the checking in process and being searched, one of the guards finally whispered a clue to Dominic, "There're agents everywhere here. You'll be directed to a table, it's wired. Your father knows too." Dominic nodded, and the guard continued with his job. "Okay, go ahead. You got table number five," he said to Dominic.

Dominic spent two hours talking with his father about anything but their rackets or people they knew. He also knew his father would not have access to cell phones while this investigation was going on. Dominic had been through this before. The timing was bad with everything going on, but for now, Nick Amicucci was unavailable.

Dominic met Danny for lunch at a distant restaurant. Dominic had finally picked up the tail that followed him to the prison; he hadn't noticed the surveillance prior to that. He was able to lose his tail before meeting Danny, as did Danny on the way to meet Dominic. The FBI was the topic of conversation.

"They're spending a lot of resources on us," Danny said.

"I've been through worse with these guys. They've recorded prison visits before, but thankfully, the guards have always let us know. It's the new guy you said was in charge now, he's just doing what every other one before has. We just wait them out, Danny. Their warrants all have time limits to gather information to keep them going. They get nothing, the warrants expire, and everything starts returning to normal. I went through it after Angela, I went through it after Nino Kalko's fuckup, and I went through it after Tommy blew up Jerry Lissoni," Dominic explained to the veteran gangster.

"We need to tell all the crews to be smart as well. It's evidence even when someone else mentions your name. I need to tell you? Danny and Sally are doing forty years for Jack Russo's murder that you and me did. I don't want to go back to jail because someone can't keep their mouth shut," Danny said.

"I didn't figure you to panic about something like this," Dominic joked.

"I've made no secret that I didn't like my time, and I'm going to give a hundred percent not to go the fuck back in," Danny said.

The next day, Danny and Dominic held a neighborhood barbecue, which they knew would be under the eye of the FBI. On Saturday, it was the graduation party for Dominic and James Amicucci at Marie's house. Dominic, another namesake for Big Dom, was the son of Charley and younger brother to Jimmy. James was Nick's brother, Daniel's, youngest son, going to college for biochemistry

Whereas Danny and Dominic spent their day on Marie Rea's lake, Doug and the Herrick brothers met in Doug's office at the Four Seasons. "We need to be prepared in case we got to fight New York. Billy, just like you've done before, hire a bunch of people to start renting apartments. Get them furnished and livable if we all need to go underground. Get fifteen apartments, some close, some real far away. Here's a 120 grand," Doug said as he tossed him an envelope.

"Where do I get the time? I'm at our restaurant at six in the morning, and I'm at your restaurant by three. I'm handling the zips now, on top of everything else I got going," Billy complained.

"Delegate," Tommy told his younger brother.

"We'll need to establish who's who in their organization and make a hit list," Doug said.

"It wouldn't hurt to find an inside to their family. If we do go to war, there could be people that are against it and would help us end it," Tommy explained.

"Virgil got his information from a retired DeCarlo captain in Florida—that sounds like a good place to start," Doug said.

"Who do you want me to delegate to?" Billy asked, frustrated.

"Dave Worowski," Doug answered. "Matt Young can start taking more of his duties in Henderson, and I'll start lightening Matt's load here at the bar soon."

"You'll need to have someone be able to replace you at both restaurants, Billy," Tommy told him. "If we all take off, everything can't just go out of business."

"Weapons will have to be distributed," Doug said. "Billy, you can have the zips take care of that. Put something in every apartment. Move the cache from my cabin in Traverse City to somewhere down here, maybe down by Toledo."

"It might be smart to get some extra apartments for more zips in New York or maybe New Jersey," Tommy suggested.

"There are some rough-looking years ahead. When Eddie Batts dies, Danny and Dominic are going to want us to kill Bruno Bini. Who knows how that will end up! And when Vinny Braga dies, it sounds like his kid is going to war with us," Doug said. "Plus, it sounds either or both of these two could go any day."

After the war planning session, Tommy and Billy left for home. Walking to their cars in the parking lot, Billy had a question for his elder brother. "Honestly, Tommy, do you really think we can win a war with one of the Five Families?"

Tommy shook his head. "Honestly, no, I don't. I think that while we're hunting Sammy Braga and his captains, their soldiers will roll right through us. I think we're all very dead if we go to war."

The next day was Sunday, and Dominic arrived at his father's at two o'clock. "Where is everyone?" Dominic asked Helena, who was putting together the outside tables.

"Probably still at Aunt Marie's on the lake. Everyone went there after church. You might have gone too if you went this morning," Helena added.

Dominic dipped a spoon in the pot of pasta sauce on the oven. "I had to open the bakery this morning, as Kenny's out of town," Dominic said as he tore a piece of bread to dip in the sauce now. "Valentina's not even here?"

"Valentina and Sal at least are not here because of jet skis. Valentina went to see your father since she couldn't go yesterday morning. And your brother is working," Helena answered. She looked at Dominic and grabbed two glasses and poured each of them some wine. "You know, Dominic, I've said some really mean things to you over the years, and I'm sorry for that," she said, handing him a glass.

Dominic took the glass. "What'd you do, already have a few of these today?"

"Stop it, I'm serious. I must say, I'm very proud of Sal and his job, and how you've kept him out of your life," Helena told him. She lifted her glass to toast. "You have really kept your word with Sal and I thank you, Dominic, from the bottom of my heart."

Dominic gave his stepmother a big hug, and they enjoyed the time they had together before everyone broke away from Marie's and her lake and drove the short distance to Helena's for the usual Sunday gathering.

For the Westside, this Sunday was "Sticking It Day." Once a year, normally in the summer, Westside stolen goods guru Vic Larsen, put on a huge sale for the wives of the crews. Vic kept an organized warehouse for his stolen good business that he turned into a small empire. On Sticking it Day, the wives were given free reign of the warehouse with prices below half the market value and stick their husbands with the bill. He even had a room with jewelry cases that looked like a real jewelry store. Jewelry, furs, electronics, furniture, ovens, washers, dryers, anything that gets shipped on a truck was present in Vic Larsen's warehouse.

Vic personally greeted Grace Sullivan and the Herrick brothers' wives, Valerie and Claudia. Last year, Doug's wife dropped a 150 grand on her shopping spree, with the other just shy of six-digit bills.

"Ladies, where shall we start this year? Jewelry as usual?" he asked them.

"Jewelry," all three agreed in unison and followed Vic to his showroom.

Vic went behind the counter and pulled out his special box that he was saving for the top three wives of the Westside. "This, Grace, I put aside just for you," Vic, the salesman, said. "It's Italian made, and those are real diamonds," he explained about the gorgeous necklace.

The women gasped. "How much?" Grace asked.

"Fifty grand retail, but since I know who your husband is, I'll go sixty grand," Vic teased.

"Stop playing, Vic," Grace said, slapping Vic's hand. This was a day the women were truly giddy.

"Eighteen grand," Vic told her.

"Put it on me," Grace said with anticipation to her best friend, Val Herrick. They put it on, and Grace looked in the mirror. "I'll take it."

The women spent the next twenty minutes in the jewelry showroom, and Vic made a 128 grand on a dozen pieces of jewelry. "I've got a new showroom, purses, perfumes, and crap like that," Vic told the ladies.

"Too bad you don't sell cars," Tommy's wife, Val, said.

Vic stopped in his tracks. "I've got cars. What do you want? Cadillacs, Escalades, Lexxus', you name it."

"Are they legal?" Claudia asked.

"Legal enough to get you a registration and legal plates," Vic said.

"I'd love to see them," Billy's wife told him.

Grace intervened, "Billy can get you a car at a dealership. No offense, Vic."

"None taken, just tell me where to next," he said. "Any furs?"

"I never wear mine," Grace answered.

"I think we're good on the furs," Val said.

"Your husbands lack class, I see," Vic joked.

"I don't have a fur," Claudia said.

"How about sunglasses? I could use a new pair," Grace said.

Not the sale Vic had in mind. "Sunglasses? I'll toss in a pair of sunglasses. What about big screens?"

"I got two last year," she answered.

Vic sighed, "Okay, I was going to save this for last, but I'll show you now. Follow me," Vic said. He led them past aisles and aisles of stolen merchandise.

"This is new, lawn furniture," Val said as they walked.

"I've really expanded in the last year," Vic said as he stopped at a door. "Ladies, behind this door is your dream come true—racks upon racks of the newest lines of clothes, dresses, and shoes. Yes, that's right. There are thousands of totally expensive shoes behind this door. You'll be the only ones that'll be shopping in this room today," Vic told them as he opened the door and watched the women start running through the racks.

Vic looked at his watch. "Well, that should tie them up for an hour or two," he said to himself. He walked back through the warehouse, checking out which wives were there. He spotted two wives that had husbands in Dave Worowski's crew. *They're not even bookies,* Vic thought to himself and kept walking.

A few more wives he saw, but their husbands didn't bring in the kind of money Vic was looking to spend his time on. He invited Stevie Turner's wife in Las Vegas; he even offered to fly her in first class and pay for her hotel. But he knew she wasn't coming. Only once did she fly in for Sticking it Day, she holds the record for money spent. Stevie never let her come back after being stuck with that bill.

Bingo! Vic spotted perhaps the next best prize after the three first ladies. He spotted Virgil Boyle's wife, and everyone knew Virgil was raking in millions down in Miami. "Tina, man, that Florida sun treats you great," Vic said as he greeted Virgil's wife.

FBI agent Tom Stone and his partner, Joe Baker, sat perplexed in their car, watching all the women scurrying to and from this warehouse. They had been sitting down the street from Tommy Herrick's house, waiting for him to leave. They saw the limo pull in his driveway, but, weren't able to see who got in. After the limo rolled past them on the street, they had assumed Tommy Herrick was in it. They had no idea the limo was sent for the three wives by Vic Larsen; they didn't even know who Vic Larsen was. After they watched the limo drop off three women in the warehouse down an industrial road, they stayed to watch the warehouse.

Women were coming and going, and when they left, they all had something. Some had a box of dishes or silverware. Most carried clothes on hangers, a lot of clothes on hangers to their SUV or full-sized vans. Workers loaded TVs, dishwashers, and all sorts of appliances into the vehicles.

"I think we stumbled onto something here," Stone said.

"We better call the boss tonight," Baker answered.

CHAPTER XXXI

Sticking It Day

GRACE SULLIVAN CAME home from "Sticking it Day" and found her husband on his laptop at the kitchen table. "What are you doing?" she asked, waiting to tell of her day at the warehouse.

Doug kept looking at the screen. "My stocks are down."

"Well, you wouldn't be the first," Grace told him.

"It's a first for me. I've never lost money on a stock. I got to make a phone call tomorrow," Doug said, more to himself. He logged off and shut the laptop. "So what am I on the hook for with Vic?" Doug asked her, wondering how much she spent and hoping she didn't beat last year's number.

"Don't say it like that, Doug. We're not newlyweds, I know Vic works for you and he only does it because you let him," Grace said.

Doug disregarded her comment. "What'd you spend?"

"Less than last year," Grace answered happily.

"Nice. Under six figures?"

Grace didn't answer; she just shook her head sheepishly.

"Okay," Doug said with his own smile.

"You got to see what he's done with the warehouse, Doug. It's like a department store," Grace said.

"I've been to Vic's warehouse," Doug told her.

"He's done a lot in a year to it. It seems so much bigger, but it's the same warehouse."

"He bought the building adjacent to it and knocked the walls down, it is bigger, goofball," Doug joked.

Their soon-to-be seven-year-old son came into the kitchen. "Hi, Mom."

She hugged her son and looked at Doug. "Why is he still up?"

"To unload your truck," Doug told her.

Grace stood back up. "It's midnight. You kept him up to carry things from my truck? It's parked right there in the garage."

"I didn't notice it," Doug said. "Who drove there and where's the stuff?"

"Graham, go to bed," Grace told her son and turned to deal with her husband. "My father drove me to Val's, and we took the limo that Vic sent. Vic's having everything delivered tomorrow."

"You mean your father drove you to Tommy's," Doug corrected her.

She raised her eyebrows, and Doug knew what just he did. "Are you telling me, I can't call this my house?"

"Val's house," Doug corrected himself.

"And I don't want Graham up this late."

"I didn't have a choice, your father already went to bed," Doug joked.

The next night, Danny Serafini left Cooch's Corner early for an hour-long drive for a meeting with captain, Benny Mancini, and his lieutenant, Tony Iannetti.

Jimmy was driving Danny, and they knew they had a tail and thought they had lost it, but an hour later, the tail popped up again.

Danny called Benny and told him he had to cancel, as he couldn't shake his tail. To anyone's knowledge, Benny wasn't feeling any of the new heat from the feds, and Danny thought it was better to not get Benny's name in a write-up of a meeting with the crime family's underboss.

"That's a whole fucking hour wasted. Now we got to drive another fucking hour home, dammit!" Danny complained to Jimmy as they made their way back home. "These assholes are getting under my skin."

They did everything they felt they could to lose the tail; they pulled over on the freeway, and the tail sped right by, just to reappear again. They went up an exit ramp on the freeway, same result, the tail reappeared.

It would be two more days before Danny tried to set up the meeting again. Thursday morning at four o'clock, Danny crept through the gate in his backyard that separated his yard from his imprisoned best friend's yard and ran all the way to the awaiting car in Nick's driveway. Danny jumped in. "Go, go, go," he said to Jimmy Amicucci, who threw the car in reverse.

They spent half an hour looking in the mirrors for tails, and once Danny decided they were clean, they left for the meeting, an hour's drive. There was no sign of a tail for the whole ride, and Danny finally felt some relief. They met at a bar near an automotive plant that was open early, at six thirty in the morning; the place was packed.

There were no tables available, and the men had to stand. Jimmy came in with Danny, and Benny's driver watched the cars to avoid any feds tampering with them.

"Okay, so what's up?" Danny asked Benny and Tony Iannetti.

"Anthony wants to move to California," Benny answered.

"That's what's you wanted to meet about? I thought you wanted to whack someone," Danny told him.

"You guys have ordered everyone away from your headquarters except your own crew, and I can't just send him out west without permission. What am I supposed to do?" Benny inquired.

"All right, all right." Danny waved him off. "This is life nowadays, just got to get used to it. The fucking feds are all over me and Dominic—it's getting to be nerve racking," Danny said.

"They got their jobs to do, and we got ours," Benny said.

Danny agreed, "Why California, Tony?"

"My wife's out there. She's been there for two years, since Leo got sick, and now she wants to stay there," Tony told him.

"Leo who?" Danny asked.

"My dad, you were at the funeral," Benny told Danny.

"I know I was at the fucking funeral, Benny," Danny snapped. "I'm confused. I thought my wife said that your sister was out west with Leo," Danny said to Benny.

"Yeah, Stephanie, that's his fucking wife, Danny," Benny said.

"You two are brother-in-laws?" Danny asked.

"By God, I think he's got it," Benny said.

"Knock it off, you little smart ass, or you can go to California with him," Danny told his captain.

"I'm just kidding around, Danny, I apologize," Benny said.

"You'll have to work for Dontae Marino out there. Let's be clear, Tony, you'll be taking a demotion, you understand that?" Danny asked.

"What can I do? My wife's been through enough," Anthony said.

"And is there a replacement in mind, Benny?" Danny asked.

"I'd like it to be Georgie Polizzi if my opinion counts," Tony said.

"Sally Gravila's old driver, he's running the Mancini book now, ain't he?" Danny asked.

"Yeah, and he can be a lieutenant, no problem," Tony recommended.

"His opinion counts with me," Benny said. "That was my uncle's book, not my dad's."

"Okay, all sounds good. I'll run it by Dominic, but you've got my blessing," Danny said, and he and Jimmy left for home.

"Still no tail?" Danny asked Jimmy.

"Feds must have a day off," Jimmy answered.

"Them cocksuckers don't take days off. It's more important for them to play James Bond than to spend any time with their families.

Danny called Jackie Beans into his office. "Jackie, any more attempts by the feds to infiltrate the building?" Danny asked, referring to the agent that posed as a beer deliveryman to gain entrance to the bar.

"Nothing, and we're being super vigilant when we watch the surveillance videos of when no one's in the building," Jackie answered.

"And we got those cameras up in the alley and the back parking lot?"

"Done, we're watching those too. The only talk in the bar is of gambling, we'll take that hit when we have to," Jackie said.

"They've got to get zero information or they can keep the wiretaps and video surveillance going," Danny told him.

"This place ain't wired unless the invisible man came in and set up wiretaps," Jackie said.

"Good, keep doing like you said, being super vigilant. This new fed boss is going to want to make his name here, on us," Danny told Jackie and Jackie left the office.

"Okay, so it's next Friday, Saturday, and Sunday that you got to open the bakery," Dominic told Kenny. Dominic and Angelo were taking a trip next weekend to Pennsylvania to see Angelo's imprisoned father, George, and then they were headed to Memphis, to visit their Great Uncle Ray in his prison.

"I got it," Kenny said.

"This is very important, Kenny, nothing stupid can happen," Dominic warned.

"What could go wrong?" Kenny asked innocently.

Dominic looked at Angelo, who was sitting at the table with them. "Did he just ask that?"

"Seriously, Dom, don't worry about nothing," Kenny told him.

"I'm having my surgery at the end of June, and I could be out of action up to six weeks. Next weekend is your chance to show Danny that you're not just a collector," Dominic said. "If you fuck up next weekend, there ain't a chance in hell you'll get another shot while I'm gone."

"Danny thinks I'm just a collector?" Kenny asked.

Angelo answered, "Kenny, he tells you that all the time."

"I didn't think he told that to other people," Kenny complained.

Dominic rubbed his eyes. "Just make it a nonissue, okay?"

Kenny said okay and left. Dominic looked at Angelo. "Danny's going to kill him while I'm gone."

"Danny's going to kill us all while you're gone, maybe even himself with the way he's handling this surveillance," Angelo said.

"Yeah, he doesn't handle this shit well, does he?" Dominic asked.

"Frankie Jag told me that Danny told Vinny Jag that the feds would have to kill him to take him to jail," Angelo said.

Dominic scoffed, "Danny fire on a cop? That'll be the day when he breaks a rule. Did you know that Danny never even wanted to take his five-year deal, his lawyer wanted to fight it, said there was no case? My father made him take the deal so that at least one of those three miserable pricks would be back on the streets within a decade. That's a tough order to swallow," Dominic said.

"I think I could do five years better than he did his," Angelo said.

"That's because you and me, that's all we've known, death and jail. Danny's going to be sixty next year, and both his fucking parents are still alive. His biggest losses in his life were when your father and my father went to jail," Dominic complained.

"Well, that's not right, Dom. He's lost both his oldest brother and youngest sister. Are you mad at Danny for something or what?" Angelo asked.

"No, not mad, I love him, he's like an uncle," Dominic said. "None of us would be anywhere without Danny Serafini, but it's like he doesn't get it. He's going to go back to jail, I'm going to go to jail, and you're going to go to jail, it's what happens."

The next morning, a guard at Nick's prison gave him a tip he had heard. "Rumor has it you're getting shipped out next week, I heard—to Virginia," the guard told him.

"I appreciate the tip, but you might want to consider the fact that agents let that leak to a few of you, seeing who might leak it to me. Keep everything on the up and up right now, I don't want to give them a reason to ship me to Virginia," Nick told the guard.

After the guard left, Nick questioned his cellmate, Eddie Turco. "And you're keeping your mouth shut, right? I'm sure they're listening to all your calls and visits, seeing if you're passing messages for me."

"Just like the last time you asked me, keeping it shut," replied the seventy-three-year-old. Twenty-one years now Eddie has been locked up. "Just forty-four more years," he joked almost daily. Eddie was sentenced to sixty-five years for his RICO crimes that involved a murder and the trafficking of massive amounts of drugs from Canada into Michigan. Three years later, Eddie's elder brother received thirty years, he's eligible for parole at least when he's eighty-nine.

"I thank God that Danny's on the streets now. I can have peace of mind while I can't communicate to no one about nothing," Nick said.

The women assembled at the reception as the men gathered at the bars. They were waiting for the bridal party to enter after the ceremony for Daniel Amicucci's oldest son, Raymond.

"Grace, that necklace, it's to die for," Danny's wife, Bianca, said to Doug's wife.

"I've never seen anything like it. Where'd you get it?" Helena asked.

"Sticking it Day," Grace answered.

"What?" the women asked.

"Sticking it Day?" Grace asked, sensing she had just made an error.

"What is 'Sticking it Day'?" Helena asked.

Grace realized she had let a cat out of a bag. "It's just something one of Doug's friends does for some of the wives."

"We're wives," Valentina told her.

Helena realized they weren't going to get too much more from Grace, and she looked around for her stepson. The women followed Helena as she marched across the huge reception room and tapped Dominic on the shoulder. "What is Sticking it Day and why are we excluded?" she demanded.

Dominic knew all about Doug's Sticking it Day. He knew it was actually Doug's idea and that Doug split twenty-five percent of whatever Vic Larsen made with his buddy, Tommy. He also knew how much the husbands of the wives that go to the warehouse complain about the special day for the women. He had no intention of listening to the gripes of his own men.

"That's Doug's gig, ask him," Dominic told her.

Doug was not far away, and he received the same question from Helena. Doug glared across the room to his wife who mouthed the words "I'm sorry" to him.

"It's not my thing, Helena, it's a friend of mine that runs it," Doug told her.

"Doesn't Vic work for you?" Dominic asked, trying to antagonize the situation.

"You're right, Dominic, he does," Doug said. Doug had no problem making another profit from these ladies; he was just trying to avoid a headache for Dominic, so much for that. "Helena, I'm going to talk to Vic and see if we can't set something up. Tell everyone you know, the more the merrier," Doug said. "And make sure all the women tell their husbands, they have Dominic's blessing."

Doug patted Dominic on the back and whispered in his ear, "And if any of your idiot associates think they're going to rob the warehouse once they hear of it, you're going to owe me a ton of cash and be short a lot of men." And he walked away.

Dominic realized he had just cost himself some future headaches and gave one last try to avoid it. "You know that stuff's hot, right?" Dominic whispered to his stepmother.

She nodded her head. “I’m pretty sure my engagement ring from your father was stolen, much like anything else that I didn’t pick out myself.” Helena turned and walked back across the reception hall, mission accomplished.

After dinner, the men huddled again at the bars or sat together at tables. Danny, Dominic, Doug, and Rocco DiNapoli sat together when they heard a roar from the reception. The men rushed to the scene only to find that Fat Kenny had caught the garter and was making quite the scene putting it on the leg of the single woman that caught the bouquet.

“Always a good time,” Dominic said with a smile as he watched the show. Danny didn’t find the humor in what he considered embarrassing behavior.

After Kenny entertained the crowd, he spent the rest of his time with the woman whose leg Kenny placed the garter in, and the two actually seemed to have hit it off. Jimmy had brought a date and spent his time avoiding the fellows, but that eventually had to end.

“Jimmy, who’s your date?” Dominic asked once they finally had the couple cornered.

Jimmy looked at Dominic, Danny, Doug, and Angelo and prepared to be embarrassed. “Everybody, this is Katie. Katie, this is my cousin Dominic. That’s Danny, he’s like an uncle, this is Doug, he’s just some wedding crasher,” Jimmy joked. “And this is my other cousin, Angelo.”

“It’s nice to meet everyone. Jimmy’s told me so much about you all,” Katie told them.

“Good, now let us tell you all about Jimmy,” Danny said as he put his arm around the girl and started to walk her away.

“Danny,” Jimmy called.

“I’m just kidding around, kid,” Danny said.

“Katie, you just let us know if Jimmy gets out of line with you,” Dominic joked, and the men left Jimmy to his date.

The men hit the bar and got a drink. “Hey, Dominic, look who just strolled in and is heading this way,” Danny said as he nudged Dominic.

Tom Caruso joined the men at the bar. "Dominic, can I have a minute?"

"Really, Tom, at a fucking wedding now?" Dominic asked, disgusted.

"Scary's not here, is he, Danny?" Dominic asked jokingly.

"No, he's not," Danny said laughing, knowing Dominic was joking about getting Tom beaten up.

"That's too bad," Dominic joked.

"It's nothing bad, Dom," Tom told him.

"Oh sorry, I don't know why I would think that," he said as he walked away with his sister's father-in-law.

Tom covertly handed Dominic an envelope. "Here's a hundred grand toward my debt."

"You serious?" Dominic asked in disbelief.

"I am. And I'm all squared up with everyone and my captain, Eugene. I got a little something for myself, so here you go," Tom told him.

"I'm impressed. And I'm not going to hear any shit from anyone about you owing them money?" Dominic asked.

"I'm turning it around, Dominic. And I imagine Eugene Modica might be retiring within a few years, and I'm sure you wouldn't consider his psychopath, Mario Zangarra, to be a captain. I thought if I did like you said and be a good lieutenant, I might get a consideration when he hangs it up," Tom said.

Dominic was stunned. Tom Caruso a captain? Dominic didn't even want him to be a lieutenant. Dominic didn't want to make him in 2007, but his father ordered him to. "Let's be clear here, you *do* still owe me a half million dollars, correct?" he asked Tom.

"It's all coming, and sooner than later, I promise. You'll see. I'll be the best man for the job when the time comes. I'll prove it to you, Dom," Tom declared gleaming.

"Let's just worry about that money right now," Dominic told him. "And if I was you, I wouldn't say a word to anyone else about wanting to be a captain. What do you think Mario Zangarra would do if he heard you were campaigning for his boss' job? It would upset my sister greatly if something happened to you, and I can't have that."

"No problem, Dom, you'll see," Tom told him, and they rejoined the men at the bar.

That night, two men crept down the alley behind Amicucci Breads. They followed the alley until it emptied into a smaller parking lot, that the feds believed was used by the Amicucci crew to talk privately. The feds had done a few surveillance ops prior to this and found no video cameras on the roof or anywhere else. They had not been back since the crew installed the cameras to inspect the parking lots of both the bakery and Cooch's Corner.

Each man carried a backpack and two duffel bags full of equipment for their missions; they were installing their own cameras to watch the crew meet in the parking lot. They were installing listening devices on a telephone pole and on a wall that encompassed the lot. The listening devices were more of shot in the dark; they could only hope to pick up a conversation out there.

After about forty minutes of surveying the area and beginning to install the first camera, one agent happened to notice something on the wall above the back door to the bar. "Oh shit, is that a camera?" he asked the other agent who flipped on his night vision goggles.

"Yup, I wonder if that was missed or if it's new," he answered. He radioed his boss to get direction and was told to abort the mission. The feds were made aware by Louis Cardoni when he turned rat that the crew diligently watched footage of the bar and the bakery from the night before to ensure no one had entered the premises. The special agent in charge knew the operation would be a bust as soon as the crew reviewed the footage tomorrow; they'll probably even have a good laugh at the feds' expense.

CHAPTER XXXII

Loose Ends

AGENT GEORGE NELSON entered the interrogation room and sat across from Gino LaPurti. "You've been pinched with six ounces of coke, I work organized crime, how can you help me?" Nelson asked. DEA contacted the organized crime division and told them someone they had just arrested said he worked for a mobbed-up card game and was willing to wear a wire to escape his charges. Agent Nelson was sent to check it out.

"I work at a big card game. I work for a mob guy. The game gets into the hundreds of thousands," Gino told the agent.

"Who do you work for?"

"Pete Saratelli, we call him Petey Grass, he's going to get made this year," Gino answered.

Nelson didn't recognize the name, but he was working Dominic Amicucci's case. He was sure that Pete Saratelli wasn't in the Amicucci crews. "Who does Petey Grass work for?"

"I know Eugene Modica's the captain, but I think Petey works directly for Anthony Inserro," Gino told him.

That got George Nelson's attention. He was aware of whom Anthony Inserro was, but he knew that Eugene was a big fish. "Where do you fit in?"

"The bottom unfortunately, I work security. Sometimes, I'm just patting people down when they come in," Gino answered.

"Not much of a reason to let you off the hook for the six ounces," Nelson told him. "Sounds like you're of more use to the DEA than us."

"I talk with Petey Grass every night. I'll wear the wire. He's got to be worth something," Gino pleaded. "I'll try to hang around other bars, meet more people. I've got respect. I just don't have a job."

The agent was becoming bored of Gino. "I have no idea what that means."

"In North Carolina, I was second in charge of a book. The book closed, and I was sent back here to Michigan, where I'm not needed. I'm surely not earning, and that's why I've been peddling a little dope to help ends meet. I got a daughter that just graduated high school and a younger one who acts like she did. I got to earn," Gino said.

George Nelson remembered a hit that occurred earlier this year. "Do you know who Nathan Vind is?" he asked Gino.

Gino scoffed, "Nate the Hate? I was his second in command. He's why the book closed, when he got whacked. Dominic Amicucci had the Westside whack him because we were dealing with Fabian Bosca, and then they whacked him too."

This is what they needed, some inside information on the crime family. "I'll be right back," Nelson said.

Behind the two-way mirror, Nelson was ecstatic. "I want him. Let me debrief him for today and then you guys take him. Do what you need to track his source for the coke, and I'll take him when you're done. I appreciate you guys calling."

"We need to get him back on the streets as quick as possible," the DEA agent said. "Let me debrief him now, quickly, for what I need, and we'll set him free. You can take it from there. I'll let you know if I need anything else. If I use him to set up a meet with his supplier, it could blow the cover for any case you can build."

"This really is the day and age of agencies working together, huh?" Nelson joked.

Danny Serafini's arrival at Cooch's Corner on a Sunday was a rarity, but this one he showed up and was ushered to the back room by Fat Kenny Infelice and Jackie Beans Pinto. They directed him to the video system. "The feds were here last night," Kenny said as he played the video.

Danny watched the two men creeping onto the camera shot from the alley. "Watch this, this is the best part," Kenny told him after a bit of watching the feds start their operation. All three men broke out in laughter as the agent on the screen noticed the new camera the crew installed.

"Oh shit." They could see the words on his mouth as his shoulders sagged and the air was taken right out of the agent.

Danny was wiping tears from his eyes; he was laughing so hard. "That's great, I actually feel like we won one." He patted his lieutenant and bookie on their backs and told them, "Real good job, guys, real impressive. They're not done yet, not by a long shot, so don't let up," Danny told them as he left for his fifteen-minute drive home to spend the rest of the day at Nick's house.

On Wednesday morning, FBI agents tailed Doug Sullivan to a Coney Island restaurant and into another car, leaving his car there. Doug and the unidentified male traveled onto the freeway and doubled back a few times, to cleanse their tail. The feds were using five cars to follow Doug this morning and were able to continue surveillance every step of the way.

"You're not wired, are you?" Doug asked his CIA driver. "They'll probably frisk us."

"I'm not," he answered. He was posing as Doug's bodyguard and driver for Doug's big meeting with supposed terrorist associates. The two had met two times prior to get know each other a bit so they wouldn't be complete strangers. "Once I make sure the money's in the account, you give them the key to the storage unit and we wait there for them to check it out."

"Where's the money go?" Doug asked suspiciously.

"Into an escrow account and it'll be confiscated by the government and used at trial if necessary," the agent answered. The agent's cell phone rang, and he delivered the news to Doug. "We got a tail," he said after ending the call.

"How do your people know? They're tailing us, and they're right next to a fed?" Doug asked.

"Actually, yes," he admitted. "They'll run interference and get us clean."

The CIA tail car did just as Doug's driver said, and they were back on track to a meeting at a house in unknown territory without the FBI watching.

"Does anyone have them?" the FBI agent in charge yelled into his walkie-talkie to the other cars that were following Doug.

"No. Who the hell was that car that cut us off? I think he had another tail, sir," the agent told his boss.

"Circle the area for ten minutes and then head back home if no one sees them," was the order.

Doug and the CIA agent were let into the house by a younger male of Middle Eastern descent. Doug and his bodyguard took off their shoes and waited for a much older man to enter the room.

"Sit, sit," the man said when he entered. "Do you want something to drink?"

Doug sat on the couch as the agent remained standing at the door, holding his laptop. "No, thanks, I'd just like to get this done," Doug told him.

"Good, my wife is at work, and I need you guys out of here before she comes home, or I'm dead," the man said.

Doug laughed. "I expected a lot more people here," he said.

"Who do you want? It's just me and my grandson until his mother comes home."

Doug pointed at his bodyguard. "I'm sorry, I wouldn't have brought him then."

"It is fine, he looks like the computer guy of the two of you," the man joked. "My grandson handles that stuff for me. You can check the account, the money is there now."

Doug nodded to the agent, who did as told. After a few minutes, he confirmed the money was in the account. He quickly transferred it to a different one.

"Here's the key and the address," Doug said, giving the items to the old man.

He gave them to his grandson and sent him to check the contents of the storage unit.

It took an hour of small talk in the home before the grandson called and confirmed the arsenal. "Gentlemen, I believe our business here is done," the old man said. Doug and the agent said good-bye and left the house.

"I don't believe for a second that old man was alone," Doug said as they walked to their car.

"Across the street, second story, window on the right," the agent said.

Doug looked where the agent described and noticed the curtains pulled back some, and the light in the room revealed a shadow—they were being watched. Doug looked at the house next door. "Same thing with the house on the right," Doug said.

They reached the car, and both men were noticing all sorts of indications that they were being watched from several locations. "We are getting the hell out of here," the agent said as they drove off.

"When will we know when they moved the weapons?" Doug asked inside the car.

"You won't, so don't worry about it."

"Are we done for the day then?" Doug asked him.

"I just need to drop you off," the agent answered.

"Pull the car over and drop me off here," Doug told him.

"I'll take you home, it's not a problem," the agent said.

"Pull the fucking car over, asshole. If I don't got to be with you, then I'm not going to be with you," Doug said.

The agent started pulling the car to the side of the car. "You're real lucky there, pal, that I can't get out and teach you a fucking lesson or two."

The car stopped, and Doug didn't get out. "Well, you sure can, I won't tell a soul."

"Yeah right, a shithead like you would sue in a minute," the agent scoffed.

Doug's look turned serious, and the agent mocked on, "Oh, is this where you threaten my family? Don't worry, Doug, we know all about Grace, Graham, Bobby, and the baby on the way."

"Let me ask you this before I get the fuck out of here: why is it that I put my life on the line, my family's life on the line, to deal with these sick fuckers just to be treated like this from you? Because of me, you now know where a cell member lives and what looks like a whole street full of them. I ask a simple question and you tell me don't worry about it. I ask to be dropped off to avoid your poor treatment and you just want to antagonize me more. I still don't utter back and you threaten my family. You tell your bosses that if they want to do business with me, I never want to see your fucking face again."

"I hope they put you back in jail where you belong," the agent said in disgust.

"They can't now, stupid. Take me off the streets now and your targets will think you only let me out of jail to do this deal with them and that would be as far you get with that case," Doug said. "Ha-ha, shit for brains."

"Get out of the car."

Doug got out of the car and called Tommy to see if he could pick him up.

Tommy picked up Doug, and they went to the Four Seasons. They went to Doug's office and called in Dominic's brother, Sal.

"Sal, I'm moving you out of security," Doug told him.

"I done something wrong?" Sal asked.

"No, you done something right. You got a good understanding of the security works?" Doug asked him.

"Inside and out," Sal answered.

"Good, then it's time to move one. Tommy's brother, Billy, says you help out upstairs in the restaurant a lot, so you're moving up there. You're going to work for Billy and learn how to run a restaurant," Doug said.

"I can cook a little," Sal said.

"If you'd spend some time in the kitchen with your mother, you could cook a lot. I'll tell you, Helena would be great in here. Plus, your dad cooked all the time, Sal," Doug said.

"Maybe I could run my dad's restaurant someday," Sal said.

"Maybe you could open your own restaurant someday, Sal," Tommy told him.

"Something that you built with your own hard work, something you can be proud of," Doug told him. "Billy also runs another restaurant that me and Tommy own with him. You can spend some time there learning too. We'll teach you everything you need to know on running a business, Sal."

"The honest way," Tommy added.

After Sal left, Billy joined them for a meeting. "We're all set to go in Mexico," Billy told them. "The whole distribution key for Fabian's network lies in a small town. It's run by a crooked sheriff who dresses like a general. The town's set on low ground surrounded by hilly terrain. There're five zips there, and they're going to pick off the sheriff's men sniper style before rushing the town," Billy explained. "And it is believed to be another Fabian stash of money, drugs, and guns."

"And taking this town will put Mexico totally under our control?" Tommy asked his brother.

"Looks that way," Billy said.

"Okay, get it done," Doug told them.

"It'll be done in a week," Billy said.

"We're moving Sal Amicucci up to the kitchen with you, teach him the best you can," Doug told Billy.

"And Doug's taking Matt Young out of here. Matt's going to run Dave Worowski's rackets in Henderson," Tommy explained. "You can start letting Dave take some of your responsibilities. I'm going to start working with Virgil Boyle. If you, me, and Doug get plucked off the streets, Virgil and Dave will be in charge."

"Expecting some indictments?" Billy asked.

"Always," Doug answered. "Plus, with this bullshit with New York, you never know if just might have to take off one day."

Later in the day, Doug met with Danny and Dominic on a random side street off a freeway exit. "We're moving on Mexico next week, what do you guys want to do with it?" Doug asked them.

"Mexico belongs to Vinny Jag," Danny said.

"Then he needs to get someone down there, so the zips can show him what's going on down there," Doug said.

"You can't keep a zip down there?" Danny asked.

"That's not what the zips are for, and I can tell you this, I'm not working for Vinny Jag. So, no, I can't keep a zip down there to run it for him if that's what you mean," Doug answered.

"Let's let Vinny decide," Dominic told them.

"If whoever he picks needs any help, he can contact my crews in Miami, and they'll help him," Doug offered.

The next day, Dominic visited his father for the last time before his surgery, and after that, he tied some loose ends before hitting the road with Angelo and leaving Kenny in charge for the weekend.

First, they visited Angelo's father, George Rea. George grew up with Nick and Danny and married Nick's sister, Marie, and helped raise Dominic after his mother died when he was three.

Before Angelo was born, George committed his first gangland hit:

1977: Twenty-five-year-old George Rea sat across the table from Mafia royalty. Philip Lodulli was the grandson of the crime family's underboss. Philly, as everyone called him, was two years younger than George, and the two had met each other just today.

They were brought together today to kill a man in the bar and open the doors for both men to be inducted into the crime family. In a booth to their right sat the mastermind of the hit, Joe Fiber, crime family hit man; he was there to supervise the hit and grade the youngsters' performance. George and Philly watched the door to the bar; they waited for Giacomo Amicucci. Giacomo was to enter the bar and find the man he was meeting; this would point to the shooters who the target was. They were to open fire on the man once Giacomo was done talking to him. They were then to run out of the bar and into a car they parked around the corner.

Finally, Giacomo entered and took a seat at the bar next to a heavyset man. George knew Giacomo; he had known him and the Amicuccis his whole life. Giacomo was Nick's father's younger brother, and Giacomo and Big Dom Amicucci were legends in the neighborhood that George grew up in.

Giacomo had previously explained the hit to George. The man was a rival bookmaker, who wouldn't come under the Amicucci thumb. Bygones were bygones until he started taking customers away from Big Dom and Giacomo, and the time had come to end the problem.

It seemed like an eternity watching Giacomo have a discussion with the man, but it was actually not even ten minutes. Once he got up and headed for the door, George jumped up, gun in hand. Without thinking, he undid the safety and fired into the man's back, which was turned to George and Philly, who fired next.

The man fell into the bar and rolled off his barstool. George fired three more shots into his back and turned to run out the door. Giacomo grabbed George by the arm. "You got to finish the job, kid, like this." Giacomo fired a bullet into the back of the man's head, and they both ran out of the bar.

Philly was far ahead of George and reached the car first, so he was driving. George watched Giacomo get into a car that was waiting at the front of the door. He saw that Denny Greco, the crew's bookie guru and tough guy, was driving the getaway car that peeled away.

Three months later, Giacomo and Denny were picked out of a lineup and put on trial while the other two shooters were still sought. Giacomo got a life sentence for the bullet that he delivered to the back of the man's head. Denny got ten years for driving the getaway car. Philly, with his blood lineage, received his button two years later, while George wouldn't get hisfor another ten.

Joe Fiber became a government witness after his 1993 arrest and put George Rea away for life, and Philly Lodulli received twenty years. Joe Fiber put the feds onto a whole slew of murders, and another one was by Ray Amicucci, also in the 1970s. In 1999, after a year in jail waiting for trial, Ray was sentenced to life in prison for the murder.

Dominic loved visiting Uncle George, even if it was through a plexiglass barrier and on a telephone. George was his godfather, and

Dominic's happiest memories from his youth contained more of his uncle than his father.

When he visited Uncle Ray, it was a different story. Ray was the difficult one in the family. It was a joke in the family that Ziggy had stolen all of Ray's personality when they were little. Ray and Ziggy were the best of friends, and there was never a more opposite couple.

Angelo was fifteen when Ray went to jail and never really knew him. He said his hellos to his great uncle and let him and Dominic talk alone.

"How's my house?" Ray asked him. Dominic bought Ray's house in 2002 when Ray's wife died.

"Pretty much the same, I'm thinking about moving, though," Dominic told him.

"If you do, sell it to my brother, Ziggy, will you? Let him give it to one of his grandkids, keep it in the family, at least until I die," Ray said; he was seventy-four now.

"Okay, sounds good. Can I ask you something personal?" Dominic asked.

Ray shrugged his shoulders. "Ask away, let's see what happens."

"I can't have kids. I was wondering if that's why you didn't have any kids or was everyone right when they said you hated children. Uncle Giacomo's son, Dominic, no kids either. My dad's brother, William, also has no kids. Is it a gene or something?" Dominic asked.

Ray's face softened. "I never looked at it that way. Yeah, Dominic, I cannot have children. It must be some fucked-up gene thing."

The rest of the visit, Ray was the nicest Dominic had ever seen him. "Maybe I'll call you once in a while, if that's okay?" Ray asked before the visit ended.

"I'd like that, but you run the risk of being on an FBI wiretap," Dominic joked.

"That's okay, I've been on them before," Ray said before the guard took him away.

Dominic returned home late Sunday, and on Wednesday, he went in for his first surgery for his face. In Mexico, the zips prepared to infiltrate the small town that they had been watching. Benedetto was in charge, and it was his plan. His team consisted of his roommate, Alberto, Stefano, and Antonio and Giovanni.

Every Wednesday, the town's sheriff, who was target number one, held a meeting with his six deputies at three o'clock. This is when they prepared to strike. From their vantage in the high ground, they could watch the movements on the streets below and planned on pegging them off one by one.

Antonio and Giovanni took the north and south sides, respectively, and Stefano handled the east, he was the former Italian army colonel and sniper. Benedetto planned on driving a jeep that they equipped a machine gun to the back that pivoted 360 degrees into the town from the west. Alberto was to handle the machine gun.

It was ten minutes to three when Stefano confirmed their first six targets were on the streets. Simultaneously, the three snipers fired their silenced high-powered sniper rifles, killing all three targets. Stefano was able to drop two more, and Giovanni got the last deputy. Within a minute, all the deputies were dead, and no one had any idea that an attack was under way.

"Targets down," Stefano confirmed as Benedetto started the jeep and entered the town, ready to engage Fabian's small mercenary army. Antonio and Giovanni dropped their sniper rifles and picked up their assault rifles and charged the town while Stefano stayed above to watch the rooftops of the town for enemy snipers.

A man with a rifle opened a front door to a building when he heard the jeep roaring toward the town. Benedetto shot him with the pistol in his right hand before Alberto could fire a round from the machine gun.

Benedetto stopped the jeep in front of the building that the man came from, and Alberto opened fire on it. The few stragglers that walked the streets in this small town now ran for cover.

Once Alberto stopped firing, gunfire could be heard in the distance. Benedetto punched it and continued straight ahead on the town's main road heading for the jail. At the next intersection, they saw Antonio pinned down from gunfire coming from the windows above. Benedetto turned left, and Alberto confirmed he could reach the windows, which he did so once in range.

As Alberto sprayed bullets into the windows, he saw something coming out of the corner of his right eye. "RPG!" he screamed as he jumped out of the jeep, grabbing Benedetto's leg on the way.

A rocket-propelled grenade missile exploded the jeep into pieces. Benedetto had rolled far enough away from the jeep to avoid any injuries, but Alberto was not as lucky. Benedetto crawled to Alberto while Antonio was trying to make his way to them.

"I'm hurt," Alberto told Benedetto. "Go, you got to get to the jail."

It occurred to Benedetto that the enemy had not seen them exit the jeep and thought they were dead, because no one was shooting at them. He picked up Alberto and threw his arm over his shoulder, dragging him to a door. He shot off the handle with their only weapon, Benedetto's pistol, and entered the room ready to shoot anyone there. The shot did draw attention to them, and bullets quickly followed their way.

He dropped Alberto to the floor and out of harm's way as Benedetto took a quick look around the three-room building.

"Leave me here, Benedetto, you have to get to the jail. It's a war zone now, and we're pinned down. You can't stay here and I only will slow you down. Go," Alberto pleaded.

Benedetto grabbed some blankets he found and tried to stop the bleeding from the gash in Alberto's stomach caused by flying debris from the jeep. "Shut up, you fool."

The gunfire got closer as Antonio made it to the building. "I'm getting low on ammo, how much do you have?" he asked them.

Benedetto showed him his gun. "This is all I have."

Antonio's face said it all. "Well, we can't stay here."

Stefano called out over the walkie, "Where are you guys?"

Benedetto answered him, "We are pinned down and cannot get to the jail, I repeat, we cannot get to the jail."

"I am at the jail, the sheriff is dead. Me and Giovanni are here, and there's something you need to see," Stefano told him.

"We're a little busy. Perhaps you can make your way here," he told Stefano sarcastically.

"I'm sending Giovanni. I will remain here," Stefano answered.

Benedetto put his walkie away. "Hold your ammo until Giovanni arrives from the opposite direction. This appears to be the last of any resistance, Stefano and Giovanni have killed sheriff and taken the jail," he told them.

Giovanni arrived, and he and Antonio took out anyone that still fired at them. The men helped Alberto down the street to the jail where they found a women and her daughter in a cell. "Who are they?" Benedetto asked Stefano as he laid Alberto down on a cot in the cell next to the women.

"She says her husband is Fabian Bosca and the sheriff had taken her and her daughter prisoner. They were locked in separate cells when I got here," Stefano told him.

"If you can't get a hold of Fabian, please, call Dominic Amicucci, he'll come and get me," the woman cried from her unlocked cell where she held her ten-year-old daughter.

Benedetto walked to the cell and gestured for them to leave it. "Ma'am, you're safe now. We'll take you home."

"Can I have a word outside?" Stefano asked Benedetto. "Are you sure it is wise to treat them this way?" he asked him once they were outside. "Fabian was the enemy," Stefano reminded him.

"His wife and daughter are not," Benedetto replied.

"I think it is a mistake, just like the mistake you made when you turned off the road for Antonio. You lost the jeep and put the mission in jeopardy. Antonio and Giovanni were to just draw forces away from the jail, they were distractions. Antonio was doing his job, so you didn't need to take the jeep off the main road. What if I would've stayed put and not entered the town?" Stefano asked.

"Antonio was in need, and I tried to help him. I'd do it every time. That is the last time you will get an explanation from me because that is the last time you will question me. The next time you do, I will slit your throat," Benedetto threatened. "And did you get to question the sheriff before you killed him?"

"No," Stefano spit out.

"Then we will have to turn this town upside down looking for stashes," Benedetto said he turned around and returned to the jail. "Giovanni, find us a car to take us to the ocean. I will have Virgil Boyle get us to Miami. Antonio, find a house where they can shower under your guard," Benedetto ordered. "Stefano, you will return to New York from Miami, and I will escort these women to Michigan. Giovanni, you are in charge, you and Antonio are to start searching every building in this town. I believe some men from Miami will be on the boat from Miami to help control the town." With that, everyone moved into motion, and Benedetto sought privacy to make his phone call to Billy Herrick.

CHAPTER XXXIII

Meet the Geek

DANNY SERAFINI BURST into the back office at the bakery, causing Angelo and Kenny to almost jump out of their shoes. "Outside," Danny ordered as Angelo and Kenny followed in tow. "No one knows anything about Fabian's wife's location?" Danny asked.

Angelo shrugged his shoulders. "Got no idea."

"She was being held in a prison cell in Mexico with her daughter. Fabian's own mom files a missing person report on him and no one fucking knows she's a hostage? What the fuck?" Danny asked.

"Danny, I'd kind of say it's Fabian's own fault," Angelo said.

"Weren't you a participant in his under scheme? Didn't everyone cover for you? Even Fat Kenny covered for you," Danny scolded. "Perhaps if the bosses weren't your family, that's an offense you can get clipped for. Would you want everyone in the world to not give a fuck about your wife, Angela, because of your fuckup?"

"No, no, I wouldn't," Angelo answered solemnly.

"Women and children are always innocent, and it's our duty to always protect them, even if it means our lives. You're the next generation. Don't ever let that code die, ever," Danny preached.

"Okay," Angelo answered. "What do you want to do with his wife and daughter then?"

"Doug's zips are bringing them back here. They should have what they want. Probably best if they go to Fabian's mother's house. The bright side is we got someone to blame for Fabian's death," Danny said.

Benedetto waited outside while Alberto slept off the anesthetic from the doctor. "I appreciate the doctor," Benedetto told Virgil Boyle. Virgil had met them at the docks when the boat rolled in, and he supplied the services of a doctor who works under the table.

"That's not a problem. What are you going to do with the girls?" Virgil asked, pointing to Fabian Bosca's wife and daughter, who were just sitting on a parking block, staring out to space.

"I'm taking them back to Michigan as soon as I can speak with Alberto. It will be fine if he stays with you until I can bring him home?" Benedetto asked.

"If you want, I can put you and the girls up for the night, and I'm sure he can travel tomorrow. I'll get you a nice custom van with lots of room. He can even lay down," Virgil said.

"Thank you. You Americans sure do give away a lot of cars," Benedetto joked.

"You do understand that probably 90 percent of them are stolen, right?" Virgil asked. "The custom van sure as hell will be."

Benedetto nodded. "I was told that someone would be sent to take over the town," he said, changing the subject.

"I've got a dozen men there now with your two, for now it's my town. Dominic Amicucci is supposed to be sending someone down there to take over," Virgil explained. "Come on, I know a house you can stay at. I'll drive. I'll keep a man here. Your friend will be safe."

The decision of who Vinny Jag wanted to put in charge of Mexico was wearing on Danny's patience. He called for Angelo to come meet him at the Corner, and they stepped out back. "Is Dominic coherent?" Danny asked him.

"Yeah, he's fine. He's going to stay at my mom's for a while," Angelo answered.

"Go see him. Give him a message. Tell him I think we should give Mexico to the Westside and fuck Vinny. He really already should have someone down there if he wants it. Tell him instead of Vinny giving us 25 percent of his share from the Westside's trafficking, let's take the 25 percent right from Doug and cut out the middle man," Danny said.

"I'll go see him right now," Angelo told him.

Gino LaPurti was quickly turning into a real asset for the FBI. In his short two-week stint of wearing a wire, he had already given the feds a case against his boss, Petey Grass Saratelli, and the whole card game. But he also gave them the source for his cocaine that he was selling; he was driving down to North Carolina and buying it directly from some Westside members there. He supplied all he knew about their trafficking operation there, and while the crime family decided on what to do with Mexico and Benedetto drove the woman north on I-75, the feds raided Gino's source in North Carolina.

Alex Groyer sat handcuffed and surrounded by FBI and DEA agents in his kitchen. The raid had yielded seven kilos of cocaine, five thousand pills of ecstasy, eighty pounds of marijuana, seven weapons, and four hundred thousand dollars in cash.

"Life in prison, Alex," the lead agent told him as he sat across him at the kitchen table. "This is your one chance, your one moment to save your life. Work with us, wear a wire, and testify in court and you'll do less than ten years."

Alex sat in silence, looking down at the table, and the agent continued. "Look, pal, you're not the only one on our list. We'll take you in and hit another house until someone rolls, and someone will roll. This whole thing is coming down, and there won't be anyone left to take care of your family like you're thinking. You're protecting no one. We don't care about you. We know you work for the Monroe brothers. We want them and their bosses."

John, Kevin, and Greg Monroe worked for Virgil Boyle in Michigan. They were part of the bloody takeover in Miami and were picked to run the Westside's drug distribution in North Carolina after that. John was serving for four years, and Kevin and Greg were the ones who found out about Nathan Vind's secret dealings with Fabian, leading to his public murder.

Alex sighed in defeat. "Yeah, I work for the Monroe brothers. Everyone does here, but I barely know them. There's still a layer between me and them. I can give you them."

"For now," the agent answered. "But you do know who the Monroes report to in Michigan, don't you?"

Alex nodded. "Yes, they report to Billy Herrick."

The following Sunday, the Amicucci gathering was without Dominic, and Doug conferenced with Danny since he was totally in charge while Dominic was out.

"So if I give you Mexico, how long until I start seeing any money?" Danny asked Doug out by the horseshoe pits.

"Next month. We've already got product rolling through, and they've almost finished searching the town. We've found all sorts of weapons, kilos of cocaine, and about two million dollars so far. Fabian's wife and daughter are going to stay at his mother's?" Doug asked.

"Yeah, poor thing still thought he was alive. I told her we believed the sheriff had killed him and we were there to avenge Fabian's death. She thought we had come to rescue her," Danny explained.

"Do you want me to handle Mexico?" Doug asked.

"Yeah, take it. Are you doing anything at your bar for the Fourth tomorrow?" Danny asked him.

"I got a permit from the city to put on a fireworks show. The city had theirs last night," Doug answered. "Oh, and I have to go back to Baghdad at the beginning of September for a couple weeks," Doug remembered.

"Great, you complained for weeks about it the last time you went," Danny joked.

Their discussion was cut short when they noticed everyone gathering around the back deck. Danny and Doug made their way there and joined the crowd as Helena was offering a toast.

"Everybody, this is one of the happiest days of my life, and I want to share it in a toast," Helena told the crowd as she wiped tears from her eyes. "My baby's having a baby," Helena said as she lifted her glass. "To Valentina and Nathan, you've made me the happiest woman in the world."

"Nick's going to be a grandfather," Danny said aloud.

"And you're probably not far behind," Doug reminded him.

"I haven't even been home for a year yet. I'm still having a hard time thinking of Sabrina as being married, let alone being a mother," Danny answered.

Over the next two weeks, things started settling down; the biggest headache was the FBI. One of the Amicucci lieutenants died, and Danny was forced to attend the funeral, which he despised due to the FBI surveillance. Frank Luisi was only fifty-nine years old and had just dropped dead one day. The coroner couldn't even determine the cause of death, which of course became of interest to the feds.

Danny brought the deceased's captain, Angelo, with him and Kenny came along as did the other Amicucci lieutenants. Other than them and Luisi's crew members, the funeral was kept minimal. Kenny dropped Danny and Angelo off at the front and went to park the car. Even for the shortest walk possible, Danny could still see the agents camped out across the street.

All the other lieutenants gathered to say hello to their bosses when Danny and Angelo entered. ***Man, we are old,*** Danny thought to himself, meaning the crew. Frank Noutten and Mike Urnstein were independent bookies in their day, but when the mob needed more income they were consumed and assigned to Nick Amicucci way back in 1998. Both men were about eighty years old. Bobby Rubelli followed them at seventy-two years old; Bobby was a well-respected member throughout the entire family. Greg Rizzo came last and was the youngest at fifty-six. Greg spent seven years in jail and had an elder brother serving twenty-five. With Frank Luisi dying, a new lieutenant had to be picked, and the choices were there as well.

Vinny Casselli, John Giolli, and Andy Gerardi led Luisi's three crews. Johnny G came from the Amicucci crew, but Vinny was more respected. Andy ran the family's influence in the transit union and was in his seventies; he was not in consideration for the job.

After greeting his men, Danny and Angelo met with the family members and then conducted their business. They met with Vinny Casselli and Johnny G in a back room; Andy Gerardi did not attend the funeral as union guys were not allowed to attend mob events.

"We've talked with Dominic and we have a decision," Danny told them. "Even Nick has given his blessing from his cell. Does anyone have anything they want to say first?" Danny asked.

Both men shook their heads and Danny nodded to Angelo. "Vinny, congratulations," Angelo announced. "You'll be my new lieutenant. We offer a gift to go along with your promotion."

Vinny was ecstatic; he had assumed that with Johnny G's background with the Amicuccis he was a shoo-in. Johnny gave Vinny a big hug; he had never even wanted the job. Johnny, like his best friend, Jackie Beans, just wanted to take bets on football games and call it a day.

"We're going to release your future son-in-law, Vince, to you," Angelo said.

"He's good in our book. Maybe he can get his button in a year or two," Danny suggested.

Vinny gave both men hugs and many thanks and smiled to ear to ear. "Vinny, don't fucking forget we are at a funeral," Danny joked.

Another lieutenant, Frank Noutten, asked for a minute with Danny and Angelo after Vinny came out of the back room. Kenny joined the meeting since he was Frank's lieutenant. "I'd like to put in my retirement papers, fellows," Frank announced.

"Ready to hang it up, eh, Frank?" Danny asked with a smile.

"I think I've earned it," Frank answered; he had been one of the biggest bookies in the state in the 1980s.

"I think so too," Danny said. "Got a replacement in mind?" he asked.

"Billy Dadano, real sharp kid," Frank said.

Danny was taken aback. "I didn't expect an Italiano," he said. "You know him?" he asked Angelo and Kenny.

Kenny nodded. "He's supposed to be some kind of whiz kid with the odds, not a tough guy at all."

"Thirtysomething, married, got a young girl, I think," Angelo added.

"Look, even Mike Urnstein loves the kid. He wants to train the kid to run his book too so he can retire. Then you can combine the two books under one of yours, and your takeover can be complete," Frank said.

"You can retire, Frank. Like you said, you've earned it. You've also well earned the right to name your replacement, but I'll speak with Mike Urnstein about what's going on in his book and not you, no disrespect intended," Danny said.

"None taken," Frank said.

"And Kenny's going to come by your book tomorrow. Have this super whiz kid there," Danny ordered.

"Okay, will do. I'll see you tomorrow," Frank said before he left.

"Hold on, you guys," Danny said as Angelo and Kenny started to leave. "Since I got out, I busted both your balls and, well, really, thought pretty poorly of you," Danny continued. "I know I don't say a lot of good things, but I'll say something now. In the past year, you guys have grown, and Kenny, you did great while Dom and Ange were gone. You're really on a lieutenant level with me. That's amazing after what a fuckup you were."

Kenny beamed. "Thanks, Danny. That means more than you can ever know."

"And Angelo, your father is my best friend and I miss him dearly. But he can be proud of what you've become. You're almost to a captain level with me," Danny told him.

"Thanks, I guess," Angelo joked.

"Now let's say our good-byes and get the hell out of here," Danny ordered.

Two days later, Kenny and Angelo were waiting for Danny at the Corner; when he arrived, they took him outside. "What's so fucking urgent?" Danny demanded.

"I went and saw that Billy Dadano yesterday morning," Kenny said.

"And?" Danny asked impatiently.

"I say he's a geek, real thin, and nerdy like, but when I asked him what the fuck was so special about him, he gives me a list of the day's baseball games and starts circling teams. Every team hit," Kenny answered.

"Every team hit?" Danny repeated.

"Fucking amazing, ain't it?" Angelo added.

"So he should be in Vegas handicapping games. Can he run a crew is what I care about," Danny said.

Kenny shrugged his shoulders. "I think so."

Danny sighed. "Set up a meeting. I'll meet the geek."

At eight o'clock the next night, Danny, Angelo, Kenny, and Scary Scarelli entered Frank Noutten's bar in Roseville. Danny was immediately greeted by Frank Noutten's right-hand man, seventy-two-year old Joe Vucker. "Joe, I didn't know you were still around," Danny said.

"Thanks a lot, Danny," he joked. "I heard you were coming here tonight and wanted to say hello."

"Well, it's good to see you," Danny told him and turned around to address his men. "This is who Denny Greco taught us to lay off bets to that no one else would take."

"That was until you guys made us come work for you," Joe Vucker reminded Danny. When Nick was a newly appointed captain, he was the one who had to tell two of the state's biggest bookmakers—Frank Noutten and Mike Urnstein—that they no longer worked for themselves, that they now worked for him. Danny and Joe Vucker were both present at the meeting when the takeover was announced and when some tempers had flared.

"Law of the land, Joe," Danny told him.

"This doesn't have to get ugly again, does it?" Frank Noutten joked as he walked up on the men.

They said their hellos, and Danny demanded two things, "I need a drink and I need to meet this whiz kid."

"I am this whiz kid," Billy Dadano said from behind Danny. "And I can get you that drink."

When Danny turned around, he didn't see a tall, thin geek as Kenny had described him. Standing before Danny was a well-dressed, well-groomed young man. "You're not what I expected," Danny told him.

"Kind of nerdy, is that what you were expecting?" Billy asked, and Danny nodded. "I like it that way, keeps me underestimated. But when I hear I'm going to meet the likes of Danny Serafini, nerdy ain't the look I'm going for."

Billy led them to a table that housed the other former independent bookmaker turned Mafia lieutenant, Mike Urnstein. "Why are you here, Mike?" Danny asked.

"I'm here to vouch for young Billy. You know me and Frank always been close forever, and we sort of adopted Billy when he was a teenager. Both our rackets our similar. Frank runs three books and that education union. I've got two books and the nurses union. Billy can run them all. You can combine the crews, and me and Frank couldn't be happier," Mike Urnstein explained.

"And I believe I've got the respect of both crews," Billy added.

"No one was speaking to you," Kenny reminded the unmade man.

"He's right, Billy. Don't interrupt when your bosses are speaking," Frank Noutten told him.

"Billy, leave the table," Danny ordered.

"Okay, so he's got some learning to do," Frank conceded.

"I don't consider step one something to learn. Either you have it or you don't," Danny said. "Now, Frank, you've got two other books besides this one. One is Jimmy Rezza, who grew up not far from our bakery and someone we know well, and Vinny Ansara in Warren. Why wouldn't we just pick one of them to replace you and have Billy just run your book officially?" Danny asked.

"Neither Jimmy Rezza or Vinny Ansara are made men either, and Billy's pretty much been running my book for years," Frank said.

"And mine," Mike said.

"Are you retiring, Mike?" Danny asked.

"No, not yet," he answered.

"Good-bye, leave the fucking table," Danny ordered. As much as Mike wanted to protest, he knew he couldn't, and the eighty-one-year-old legend walked away from the table silently.

"I knew you would pick Jimmy Rezza," Frank said to Danny.

"I haven't picked anyone. I asked you why you didn't pick any of them," Danny asked.

"Because Billy's like a son to me and I know what he can do. Jimmy and Vinny are as far as they should go, bookies," Frank told him. "If I can't have Billy, I'll name Joe Vucker my replacement. He's probably got about another five or six years left."

"Here's the resolution. You're not retired until there's a resolution. I'll speak with Dominic and we'll have an answer real soon," Danny told him and walked out.

The rest of July was event-free, and Frank Noutten was given his way and Billy Dadano was promoted to lieutenant upon Frank's retirement. In mid-August, Dominic returned to the crew, much to Danny's relief. Danny showed up at the bakery in the morning to check in on him. "Where is he? I heard he's back in action," Danny yelled as he came through the door into the back office of the bakery. "What the fuck?" Danny asked once he saw Dominic.

His eyes were no longer black, but the sockets around them were swollen; his sunglasses didn't even cover his eye sockets. Dominic's nose which was broken before and blocked was now clear, and fluids were running through his nose at a fast pace, causing him to be constantly wipe his nose. "I know I'm hideous. You should've seen me six weeks ago," Dominic joked through his nasal voice.

Danny was stunned. "You got to go home."

"I'd like to hang out for a while," Dominic answered.

"You look like a sick version of the Elephant Man. You're going to scare the women and children," Danny joked.

"And the men for that matter, I'm terrified," Angelo added.

"Your forehead, and your nose, they're huge," Danny continued.

"I get it. I won't stay long," Dominic told them.

"When is this going to heal?" Danny asked.

"Next week I'm having another surgery. I should look human and be okay by October," Dominic said.

"So get the fuck out of here today, and we'll see you again, ready for work, by the making ceremony then," Danny said.

"I'm going to stay for a bit," Dominic told him.

"I got to eat lunch soon. What are you doing?" Danny kept joking.

"Fine, I'm going back home," Dominic said.

"Now you're calling my mother's house home?" Angelo asked.

"Don't be mad that Aunt Marie loves me more than you," Dominic added as the door shut behind him.

"If we can get back to being adults now, what's on the plate?" Danny asked.

"Tony Iannetti moved to California, and Georgie Polizzi is officially a lieutenant. Other than that, it's the same old," Angelo answered.

"Nothing going on feels like impending doom," Danny said.

"Or maybe things are just running right," Angelo suggested.

Danny patted Angelo on his shoulder. "I'm going with impending doom, but I like your optimism."

CHAPTER XXXIV

COLONEL COOPER

"WHAT THE FUCK are you doing here?" Angelo Rea asked his cousin, Sal.

Sal had shown up at the bakery, somewhere he was not supposed to be due to the rule of Sal not being allowed to be in the family business. "I can't come to my father's bakery?" Sal asked.

"There's fucking FBI surveillance 24-7, and you walk right into it. They're going to call you an associate and you're going to get me whacked. So, no, I'd rather you didn't come to your father's bakery since I'm in charge here, and that makes me fucking liable for you," Angelo told him.

"I've got a business proposition," Sal said.

"Every Sunday I'm with you at your father's house. Why not bring it up then?" Angelo asked.

"Because I was ready to come to you with it now," Sal reasoned.

"If it ain't a legal business, turn around and walk the fuck out of here right now, Cousin," Angelo scolded.

"It's delivering bread, Angelo," Sal told him. "I know what Doug's paying on his bread for his restaurant at the Four Seasons. You can come in cheaper and I'll take a cut. I can start hitting all the grocery stores over there. The west side can be a whole new market."

Angelo held up his hand to stop Sal. "Do not go to any grocery stores on the west side without me asking Doug and Tommy. They are beyond protective of their areas. But the idea sounds pretty smart."

"The idea is great," Sal boasted.

"I'll talk to Danny, but we do it all on the up and up with Doug. You'll tell him of any percentage you're taking. Honesty is the best policy, Sal," Angelo told his younger cousin.

"Not always," Sal said.

"It is when dealing with friends and family, Sal. Doug's put a lot of trust in you, and you should hear him blab how good you're doing there. He's teaching you how to run a business, his business. Don't abuse someone's trust, Sal, especially not someone like Doug," Angelo said.

"I didn't think taking a cut was some underhanded thing," Sal said.

"He doesn't let you see his invoices so that you can bring a lower bidder and get a cut. If you can find a better deal, you should do it because it's your job and not to get a cut under the table. That's abusing his trust, Sal," Angelo told him. "There's no problem with the cut, but he should know."

"That's not very gangster like," Sal said.

"That's not your life. You've got a great opportunity to learn how to run a restaurant and a bar. You've got a chance to make some money by expanding the bakery to the west side. Why fuck that up by wanting to be 'gangster like'?" Angelo asked.

"You're right, I know, and I wouldn't abuse Doug's or Tommy's trust," Sal said.

"I'll talk with Danny and your brother, and we'll talk about this on Sunday," Angelo told him. Sal got up and opened the door to leave when Angelo stopped him. "Oh, Sal, well, since you know, how much is Doug paying for his bread?"

In a small town outside of Baghdad, Doug and Sami Nasser were picked up in a car and driven three hours to a small, remote house. The house was busy with men rushing back and forth, most of them carrying rifles. Doug and Sami were led to a table which sat three elderly men.

One man spoke, and he was translated by one of the other elderly men. "Thank you for the previous deal you have conducted with us," the translator said as they awaited a response from Doug.

Doug looked around for a moment and gave the simplest answer he could think of. "You're welcome," Doug said as more of a question.

"We would like more. We would like missiles," the man said.

"I've never talked with you gentlemen. I only work with the strictest assurance that the weapons I sell you are not to be used against my country in any way," Doug said.

"Your country is not our target. We need to protect ourselves. We need to destroy our enemies here before they destroy us. It's become every man for themselves since you Americans have come and messed up our country again," the man said.

"Let me guess. You want surface-to-air missiles," Doug said.

"Yes," the man said.

"But, yet, your enemies have no air force for your missiles to shoot down. It's not enemy planes you want to shoot out of the sky," Doug said. "And all we did here was try to help you. We gave the lives of our own soldiers to try give you guys some sort of freedom."

"Sure, you did what you do best. Your armies came, and they killed and they destroyed, then the promises to rebuild, but no one rebuilds. Big machines come, electricity works, and the water runs. Big machines leave, the electricity goes out, and the water doesn't run."

"I'll agree there's some bad stuff there, but that can be fixed. What I don't understand is why you don't build your own electricity then or make your own water run," Doug told him.

"It's all been destroyed," the man simply answered.

"Instead of crying about it, why not show some real leadership? Don't buy weapons. Invest this money in your infrastructure. Don't wait for the greedy American companies who take the taxpayer dollars to put on a show over here. Take your pride and do it yourself. Talk with your enemies and combine your men and money. It's really that simple," Doug said.

"You do not want to do business with us?" the man asked.

Doug gave up. "I do. I thought I'd just try and help. Let me see what I can get and what they cost." With that, Doug and Sami were driven back to the small town, and Sami drove Doug into the city, where Doug had a hotel room this time instead of staying at Sami's with the on-again off-again air-conditioning.

Doug turned on his laptop; he didn't keep anything important on it or anything of importance in his room. He was sure his room would be gone through a few times before he went back to the States.

After logging in, his son, Graham, was available on the screen. "Graham, why are you on the computer? It's dinnertime there?" Doug asked his boy, who was so happy to see his father on the computer screen via the webcam.

"Mom said I could wait to eat until after you called," Graham said.

"That was very nice of her. Be sure you thank her," Doug said.

Graham leaned in and whispered, "She's in the doorway."

Doug laughed. "How was your first day of school?" he asked.

"I don't like it," Graham answered with a frown.

"Boring?"

"No, the kids that were on my tee-ball team made fun of me," Graham said.

"For what?"

"They said you took me off the team because you couldn't pay off the umpires. I don't understand," Graham whined.

"I took you off the team because they don't keep score. There's no point in playing the game. You tell those kids tomorrow that you're going to strike each and every one of them out next year when you *are* keeping score," Doug told his son. "And then you tell them that your daddy can beat up all of their daddies."

"Doug!" Grace hollered from the doorway.

That cheered Graham up, and he laughed and whispered into the computer, "You're going to get in trouble."

"That's okay," Doug joked. "You'll be fine, and take advantage at recess time to meet some of the other kids."

"I will, Dad."

"Be sure to throw the ball with your brother after dinner," Doug reminded Graham.

"I will, Dad."

"Than play catch with your grandpa," Doug said.

"I will, Dad."

"Tell your mother you love her, and I'll talk to you tomorrow after school."

"Not at bedtime?" Graham asked.

"Not tonight. I got to work."

As Graham prepared for bed, it was 4:00 a.m. in Baghdad, and Doug left his hotel room to meet secretly with his CIA handler. He cursed himself for walking out the door onto the street too quickly; he hadn't surveyed it first. "That's him," Doug heard immediately as he exited the hotel. He saw a U.S. army jeep with three soldiers waiting for him to leave. Two soldiers got out of the jeep and approached Doug.

"We've been ordered to bring you to our base," one soldier told him.

"Whose orders? Colonel Cooper's?" Doug asked.

"Yeah, get in the jeep," the soldier said.

Doug got in and left with the soldiers; he was curious what the crooked army colonel wanted. The ride was short, and Doug was dropped off in a courtyard with only the colonel present.

"Four in the morning and still in uniform, I'm impressed," Doug said, greeting the colonel.

"Save the small talk. Why are you back here?" Col. Vernon Cooper demanded.

"I'm here for business, Colonel," Doug replied dryly.

"Where are you going at four in the morning?" the colonel asked.

"For a walk," Doug answered, becoming irritated with it.

"Don't think you're at home in the States, Doug. Nobody but me and those soldiers that picked you up even know you're here," Cooper warned. "You may be some big shot with your gangster friends back home, but here you don't come close to a soldier. Here you're just the fucking criminal that you are. So lose the smart-ass bullshit and answer my questions."

Doug laughed. "You had me going there. For a second, I really did think you were just doing your job. But let's face it, I admit what I am, and you soil the honorable uniform you wear. What's your angle here? You want a piece of what I got going?" Doug asked.

"I know what you got going. You're selling arms to terrorists," Cooper said.

Doug was floored, and he knew he showed it; he couldn't keep a poker face on that one. He did the first thing that came to mind; he got angry. Doug got in the colonel's face. "I'll ask you one last time, what the fuck do you want?"

"Or what?" the colonel asked. He pointed to a guard tower. "There're all sorts of rifles pointed at you right now." Doug didn't respond, nor did he back away; he just glared at the colonel. Cooper laughed and stepped back. "Never saw that side of you. That's the side the mob likes, eh?"

Still without moving, Doug growled, "Is there something you want from me?"

"I want your business. If you're selling arms, you should buy from me," the colonel said.

Now Doug laughed. "I didn't see that coming. What are you doing? Supplying the terrorists on the other side of the town too?" Doug joked.

"Yes, I am," Colonel Cooper admitted. "I've never had a contact with your side. You're dealing with some real mean motherfuckers over there."

"You want to supply both terrorist sides with arms?" Doug asked.

"They're fighting each other right now for control. Once we're gone, let them blow each other the fuck up instead of us," the colonel answered. "I don't know where you get your weapons from, but with me, you eliminate the middle man, I'm sure. Unless you're getting it from a general," Cooper joked.

"Fine, let's talk about prices," Doug said.

Doug couldn't talk with his CIA handler until dark, and when he did, the agent was upset about waiting all day for him. The agent was the only one of the agents that Doug had worked with that he liked. "Don't give me no shit. I was tied up all day bagging you a dirty colonel, a colonel selling arms to another group of terrorists," Doug told him.

"No shit? Who's the colonel?" the agent asked.

"Cooper," Doug answered.

"No way, he's one of the most powerful men in Iraq," the agent responded. "You've done business with him before?"

"I've used military vehicles and ships to move some stuff in here," Doug said.

"What kind of stuff?" the agent asked suspiciously.

"I set up a casino in the back of Lucy's, back in 2007," Doug answered. Lucy's was a small store Doug had bought next to an army base, turned it into a small tavern, and provided some entertainment for the soldiers.

"That was your casino? I've been there," the agent told him.

"It was my bar for a while. My buddy here, Sami Nasser, ran it for me, and I sold it when I went to jail in 2009," Doug explained. Doug didn't tell the agent that the colonel had sold Doug hundreds of Soviet AK-47s that the army had stockpiled during the invasion.

"I'm amazed."

"So, anyway, I'm ready to make a deal with him, and I'm waiting on a time frame from you for the other terrorists. I'd like to get this done and get home. My best friend's wife is due very soon, and I've got my own baby on its way," Doug explained.

"Roger that. Next time we meet, I'll have a date you can give them and the account numbers to wire the money for both groups. This is going to be huge, nice job. You got some nicely placed connections. And congrats on the baby," the agent told him. "Boy or girl, do you know?"

"It's a boy," Doug said, disappointingly.

"Wanted a girl, huh?"

"Yeah, I already have two boys. We'll have to try again. Now if that one's a boy, I'm going to have a pro baseball, football, basketball, and hockey player. That's pretty cool," Doug explained.

The agent just nodded his head and said, "Sounds great."

It took Doug three days to hear back from the CIA, and it took another three to arrange a meeting with the terrorists. The price the CIA told Doug to collect was $200 million. On the last deal, Doug had exaggerated the price, and the buyer never blinked; the CIA had kept the extra money Doug came up with. This time he tried an ever bigger exaggeration and asked for $250 million with the same result from those buyers, and this time Doug handed them a second bank account number and told them to deposit $50 million of the quarter billion dollars into it for himself.

The next day Tommy's wife, Valerie Herrick, gave birth to their second daughter, Caitlyn. As much as Doug wanted to come home, he had one more job to do overseas.

On Wednesday, Doug met with Colonel Cooper and gave his order. On Saturday, Doug drove off in a covered truck carrying a full arsenal of U.S. military weapons after the colonel confirmed his payment, which was made by the CIA. Doug delivered the truck to his handler and arrived home Monday at noon.

He rented a car at the airport instead of having someone pick him up; he'd just have one of his men take the rental back. The first place Doug went to was Graham's school and took his son out of his first grade class for the rest of the day. Before returning home and going to sleep, exhausted from the flight, Doug spent the day with his son, whom he had missed for the past two weeks.

The next day, Doug went to see Tommy's new daughter and catch up on current events. At eleven o'clock at night, Doug drove himself to the Corner and met with Danny in the back parking lot.

"Doug, you remember how we had two books in North Carolina and you made us condense it down to one?" Danny asked.

"Yeah, why?"

"Because the one we now have left wants to whack someone in the crew. He's been branching out on his own and starting his own book," Danny told him.

"Now, that book belongs to the father of one of those new kids in your crew, right?" Doug asked.

"Right—Rocco Gurino, he works for Jackie Matts. Jackie's the one that came to me asking for the hit. But he doesn't want to get thrown out of North Carolina," Danny explained.

Doug shrugged his shoulders. "Okay, I'll take care of it. What else you got?"

Danny didn't expect that; he expected Doug to start his lecture about how Danny and Dominic crews ruined everything Doug tried to do. "You interested in selling Amicucci breads on the west side?" Danny asked him.

Doug mulled it over for a moment before answering, "Yes, yes, I am interested in selling Amicucci breads on the west side. Talk to me."

"It's actually Sal's idea. I'd like for us to sit down and include him," Danny told him.

"Sal?" Doug asked.

"He thought it was a good idea if you bought from us for your restaurant at the bar. And you do have that other restaurant that Tommy's brother runs," Danny said.

Doug laughed. "What happened? That little shit see one of my bread invoices or something?" Doug joked.

"Angelo has already given him the lecture on trust. He didn't mean no harm, Doug," Danny said.

"Danny, I'm not mad. I'm kind of proud of the prick," Doug said. "You guys are family. He didn't betray me. Hey, give me a better deal on bread. I'd love to spend less. This shows me Sal does have some business sense."

"When do you want to meet?"

"Sal's working tomorrow morning. Let's meet for lunch in my office there," Doug answered. "And bring the info on the guy you want whacked. I'll talk to my guys down there and see what they know about him."

The next day, Doug met with Tommy and Billy in his office at the Four Seasons before Danny came. "Billy, we need you to go to North Carolina for a few days, maybe a week," Doug told him.

"I have no time," Billy told him. "What about the restaurants?"

"It's time to put your people to the test," Tommy told him.

"This is crazy, you guys," Billy said.

Doug waved him off. "Just make it happen. I need to know what the hell's going on down there. Danny wants to whack another mob guy down there."

"Are you kicking that book out too?" Billy asked.

"No, this time they caught someone collecting customers for himself. Main point is they caught it this time. That's a good thing. That means at least that book has some leadership," Doug explained.

"What we're concerned about is Kevin and Greg Monroe," Tommy said. "Ever since John Monroe went to jail, it's become a pain in the ass down there. You got to see why and talk with Virgil Boyle. He needs to keep an eye on them."

"They are from his crew," Doug reminded Billy.

"Fine, what about this hit? Are we doing it and who's the target?" Billy asked.

"We'll know after Danny gets here, but let's get Benedetto on the road down there," Doug ordered.

Billy pulled out his cell phone, and it was blank. "This office's so fucking irritating," Billy complained of Doug's million-dollar built-in scrambler.

"Would you rather do life?" Doug asked.

There came a knock on the door; it was Danny, Angelo, and Sal. After the men agreed to a price for the Amicucci bread, the question came of how to get it into the west side grocery stores. "I'll have my guys talk with the owners. I think we can guarantee almost a 100 percent of the stores in Henderson and Veeling," Doug said.

"For sure," Tommy added.

"And our guys will deliver it, or do you want to be involved after the stores agree to carry it?" Danny asked.

"We'll just take our cut after that," Tommy answered.

"And I don't want your thug, Gary Nussman, anywhere near there, only legit guys on our side of town," Doug said.

Danny nodded in agreement. "Sal, congratulations, you just completed your first business deal," Danny told him.

"Hey, Sal, Billy's going away for a few days, and you'll be second in charge of my restaurant," Doug said.

"And if you want, you can help at Karma," Billy offered for his restaurant.

Sal said he would and left the office. "Billy's off to North Carolina. Do you have that info on that thing?" Doug asked.

Danny handed him a piece of paper. "He works for Mike Ardini down there."

"And he reports to your Texas book, right?" Billy asked; he was the most knowledgeable of the Westside's out-of-state rackets.

"You have a Texas book?" Doug asked Danny.

"Yeah, Frank Losia," Billy answered for Danny.

"It's just about five grand a month," Danny told them. "Just something that never went away, I guess."

"When Dominic set the books up for North Carolina, he sent Mike Ardini, who was from Texas and worked for Frank Losia," Angelo said.

"But Mike Ardini still reports to Frank Losia in Texas," Billy told them.

"This is very confusing," Doug said. "I've got the paper. Can we move on to something else?"

"Hang on," Tommy said. "Who does Frank Losia report to?" Tommy asked, finding humor in it.

"Rocco Gurino," Danny said.

"Who does Mike Ardini report to?" Tommy asked.

"Rocco Gurino," Danny answered.

"Frank Losia," Billy said at the same time as Danny.

Doug and Tommy laughed. "This is insane," Doug said.

Danny looked at Angelo. "I don't really know," he said. Danny turned back to Doug. "This all happened when I was away. I'm not too sure how Dominic set this up."

"Does Ardini give his money to Losia, who sends it to Rocco Gurino?" Tommy continued.

"I don't fucking know," Danny said, irritation setting in.

"From North Carolina to Texas and back up to Michigan to Rocco Gurino to Jackie Matts to you, it sounds like Texas is taking a cut it shouldn't be taking," Tommy told him.

"All right, I think we're done here," Doug said before Tommy made Danny blow a gasket. "Billy, you got to fucking go. Go," Doug told him.

"Now? You want me to go now?" Billy asked incredulously.

"Yes, now, and get Benedetto on the road too. Do not be seen with him down there, understand?" Doug asked in all seriousness.

"He's got no family. Just make him disappear," Danny suggested, and everyone agreed.

By midnight, Billy was at a steakhouse with Kevin and Greg Monroe. "You guys don't know nothing about this?" Billy asked after he had questioned them about the mob's book wanting to kill someone.

"We don't talk to those guys," Kevin told him.

"You're in charge here. You're supposed to talk to them," Billy told him. "Didn't you learn anything from your brother?" Kevin was Billy's age and had graduated together. John Monroe, the imprisoned brother of the threesome, was Doug and Tommy's age. The most likeable Monroe was the youngest, Greg.

"It's always been that they got their thing and we got ours," Kevin said.

"No, not that way at all," Billy corrected him, shaking his head.

"What should I do about it now?" Kevin asked.

"Your job would be nice," Billy said. "Like I don't have enough fucking things going on, I got to come down here and make this right. And how often is Virgil Boyle here?"

"Virgil doesn't come here," Kevin said.

Billy took a drink from his beer and said, "I guess I'm going to be here longer than I thought."

The next night, Benedetto followed his target home and shot the man that wanted to open his own book with his silenced pistol in the driveway. Benedetto boldly carried the body to his car and drove away, burying the body and burning the car given to him to burn.

Three days later, the North Carolina rat, Alex Groyer, met with his FBI handler. "Billy Herrick's in town," he told the agent.

"He is? Why?"

"I heard that one of the mob guys went missing. I imagine he's here because of that," Alex answered.

"Slow down," the agent ordered. "What missing mob guy?"

"One of Mike Ardini's crew. I heard he went off on his own, you know, started his own thing, and they made him disappear. It'd be a hell of coincidence if Billy Herrick wasn't involved."

"What's his name?" the agent asked.

"I don't know. I just heard it was some guy from Ardini's crew," Alex told him.

"Where's he staying?"

"How would I know?" Alex asked him. "I'd think he'd be hanging around the Monroe brothers, though."

"Find out what you can about who would've done the hit," the agent told him. "Billy wouldn't have done it himself, would he have?"

"I wouldn't think so either, but like I said, he's here for a reason," Alex answered.

CHAPTER XXXV

A Man of Honor

FAT KENNY INFELICE waited at a bar a few miles from Cooch's Corner. He was waiting on Paulie Bankjob, who was due to arrive in ten minutes. Paulie arrived five minutes early, and Kenny was disappointed in Paulie's appearance.

"I told you to wear your best suit," Kenny told him.

"This is. It's my only suit. Why do I need an expensive suit when I only wear it to funerals?" Paul Amevu asked.

Kenny sighed. "Don't tell a soul I told you what I'm going to tell you. You're getting made tonight."

Recruits were not allowed to know when their ceremonies were. Jackie was overcome for a moment before reality hit him. "Kenny, please, I don't want to go like this," he said, referring to his suit.

"I agree, but where the fuck are we going to get you a suit at one in the morning?" Kenny thought aloud.

"Jackie Beans is my size. Maybe I can borrow from him?" Paulie suggested.

"Jackie's there. He can't leave. Besides, I wouldn't think Jackie would have anything nicer than what you got on," Kenny told him. Kenny pulled out his cell phone and called his captain, Angelo, for advice.

Angelo called Kenny back a few minutes later after speaking with Dominic and told him to call Doug and see if Doug's stolen goods guy had any suits available right away. After a half an hour of phone tag on pay phones, Kenny and Doug finally talked, and Doug gave Kenny directions to Vic Larsen's warehouse. Kenny hung up the pay phone and got back in his car. "We got to haul ass to get to this warehouse. Fucking Carlo is running late. He's going to have to meet us at there," Kenny complained.

At the warehouse, a good forty-five-minute drive from the induction ceremony, Vic Larsen was not very happy on being sent for at that late hour. It took Vic about two minutes to size up Jackie, and he pulled a suit from a rack. "This will fit. Grab a tie over there, and there's shoes on the wall over there," Vic told them, pointing around the room.

"How much is it?" Jackie asked.

"Twenty-five hundred for everything," Vic answered.

"How do you know how much the tie and shoes are? He hasn't picked them yet?" Kenny asked him.

"It doesn't matter. I'm not doing this for any less than twenty-five hundred," Vic demanded.

"I don't have it" was Jackie's answer.

Kenny pulled out his wad of cash and started counting out hundred-dollar bills. "You owe me, Jackie."

Kenny and Jackie found Carlo DeMini waiting in his car in the parking lot. He got out of the car when he saw Kenny. "Why the hell are we all the way out here?"

"Carlo, you're getting made. Shut the fuck up and get in my car. We're running way late as it is," Kenny ordered.

Both Jackie in his new suit and Carlo in the backseat grew nervous with anticipation during the long drive and half expected to be told to go home for being late. Kenny finally arrived at the bakery and told the two to get out. "I'm going to park the car. Go inside and do what they say," Kenny ordered.

It was almost three thirty in the morning when Carlo DeMini walked into the bakery first, not knowing what to expect. There were men standing in front of the bakery in the dark, light being provided only by the outside street lights and the moon.

Paulie had no idea who the four men were, but Carlo kept in touch with the gossip of who was who in the crime family, and he identified all four men. "You, come this way," Mario Zangarra, top lieutenant to mob captain, Eugene Modica, said as he pointed to Carlo. Mario led Carlo to a storage room, and Rocco DiNapoli, who was the top lieutenant to Mario Marconi, joined them.

"You're with us," Matt Mancini, lieutenant and cousin to Benny Mancini, said to Paulie Bankjob as he motioned him to the bathroom. Frankie Zocola, lieutenant to Jackie Matts, was the fourth man, and he waited for Kenny to enter the bakery before he joined Matt in strip-searching Paulie.

When both men passed their strip search, Kenny led them into the back offices of the bakery, which they knew so well. There were six tables set up, and Kenny and his recruits sat at the remaining empty one. Each table represented a captain, and they had to wait to be called to be inducted. One at a time, all six tables would be called to go the three blocks to Cooch's Corner and become a made man.

"Where the fuck you guys been?" Frank Jagge called out from his father's table. Frankie sat with his younger, Michael, and Jimmy Rolanacia, the other recruit.

"We got lost," Kenny joked, and a chuckle went around the room.

"Real nice. It's your fucking hangout all your lives," Frankie joked.

"So this is why Danny told everyone to take the day off from the bar," Carlo noted. "I thought we assume the bar and bakery are under surveillance?"

"That's why we're doing it this way. They'll just think it's unusually high traffic if they're watching. They'd never expect us to hold a making ceremony right under their noses," Kenny explained.

"What about the bakery? It opens in two hours?" Paulie asked.

"That's the problem. We were supposed to start long ago. The ceremony can't start until everyone is present," Kenny told them. "Here's a good one for you guys. Only made men are allowed anywhere near the ceremony, other than you guys of course, so Scary's working the parking lot of the bar and Jackie Beans is inside. Jackie's got to serve the drinks to all the captains like some gopher."

"This I can't wait to see." Carlo laughed.

"Laugh now, but that's you and me next time," Paulie said.

"That's right, Paulie. Actually, you'll be inside with Jackie, and Carlo will be outside with Scary. That's how few made guys we got left in our crew. There's Danny, Dominic, Angelo, and me other than them two. Johnny G and Mario aren't in our crew anymore, so hopefully, Paulie, you can live long and keep our numbers up," Kenny joked.

"If he can stop robbing banks and stay out of jail," Carlo added.

"Hey, I can't say if the right score came around I'd say no," Paulie answered seriously.

The door opened, and it was Mario Zangarra. He walked to the table of the men from his crew. "You're first," he told them.

Lieutenants Anthony Inserro and George Zito both stood from the table, as did their two recruits Vito Billini and Petey Grass Saratelli, who had a rat in his crew. All four men followed Mario out of the room.

The tension continuously grew in the room. It was twenty minutes later when the door opened, but to all the recruits, it seemed like two hours. Matt Mancini came through the door next and was followed out by lieutenants Georgie Pirelli and Henry Agosto with their two recruits in tow.

"We'll be last," Carlo complained.

"We'll be last because we're not going to get this done before the bakers start showing up and they know us, so we'll be the last ones to leave," Kenny explained.

Rocco DiNapoli came next and took the two men from the only table that had no lieutenant present at it. Rocco had to represent those two men because they had non-Italian lieutenants and couldn't be present at the ceremony. Made men working for non-Italians was a sure road to ensure the racket would pass to the Italians in the event of jail or deaths.

The first baker arrived for work and was greeted by Mario Zangarra at the door. "Get to work," he ordered. The baker did as ordered and did as the employees had done for the almost century that the building had been a bakery—gone to work and not asked any questions.

Frankie Zocola entered the room next. Rocco Gurino, whose son was a new Amicucci crew member, and Donnie Vallero led their recruits out with him.

Two tables were left—Frank Jagge and his recruits and Kenny Infelice and his. "Flip you for it," Frankie suggested to see who'd go next; it wasn't Kenny.

It was twenty minutes to six in the morning when Mario Zangarra entered the room and called the last table. Kenny got up, and Paulie and Carlo followed. Once in the front, Mario said good-bye to Kenny, and the bakery was left in the hands of the bakers. Kenny led his recruits to the back alley where a car was waiting, but Gary Nussman was showing up for work. "Kenny, who the hell was that coming out the front door?" Gary asked.

"Doesn't matter. Don't look at the surveillance videos from last night. Erase them all. That comes from Dom and Danny," Kenny ordered, and Gary left.

Kenny got into the front seat of the car driven by Jackie Beans, and Paulie and Carlo rode in the back for the three-block drive. Jackie dropped them off in the back parking lot of Cooch's Corner, and

Scary Scarelli walked them to the back door. The door seemed to open on its own, and its opening only revealed darkness. Kenny led the way; Carlo went next, and Paulie came last.

For Paulie, it was a dream come true. As a teenager, Paul Amevu worked at the bakery; back then it was owned by Paul Lissoni, and he worked his way to collecting bets for Nicodemo Amicucci. When Paulie was given the task of committing his first hit, he came through with no problems. From there, he started driving for Nicodemo during the day and was appointed his representative on a burglary crew that started knocking off banks in distant cities. Three hits and eight banks later, Paulie was as respected in the crew as Nicodemo's two sons, Big Dom and Giacomo. Becoming a made man had become an expectation for Paulie in his twenties.

His last bank job got him arrested four months after it went down, and after going to trial, he received twenty years for it. Getting out in the 1980s, Nick Amicucci, after taking over for his father, Big Dom, after his death, told Paulie he'd get his button the next year with Denny Greco, when Denny's parole ended for driving the getaway car in the murder that landed Giacmomo Amicucci in prison for life. Paulie didn't make it that long, and it was another twenty-year sentence for trying to rob another bank; all hope of becoming made vanished.

The scene was magical for Paulie as Kenny opened the next door. The room's, the bar in reality, only illumination was from what seemed to be hundreds of candles. A big round table engulfed the center; Dominic Amicucci and Danny Serafini sat next to each other in the middle on one side of the table, a candle on either side of them. Next to Dominic sat the three youngest captains—Angelo Rea, Mario Marconi, and Benny Mancini, all under forty. Next to Danny sat the eldest three captains—Vinny Jagge, Eugene Modica, and Jack Mattea, all seventy years old or older. The other half of the table was empty. In the center of the table were a gun, a knife, and two cards of a saint.

Angelo rose and walked around the table to join his lieutenant and his new inductees. Angelo and Kenny stood before the table while

Paulie and Carlo stood behind them. "Come forward," Danny ordered, and the inductees stepped past their lieutenant and captain.

"Do you know why you're here?" Dominic asked. They both shook their heads no as they were instructed.

"You're here to join a brotherhood, an honored society built on honor, loyalty, and secrecy. Whatever beefs you had or hold are squashed. Today is your rebirth. Our brotherhood has rules and obligations, obligations that may have you put the brotherhood before your wives, or your kids, or anything else. If you're called, there's no second-guessing. There's no asking why. Even if your child lays on its deathbed and you're called, you got to come without a second thought. Our society can cause you long jail terms, life sentences. Our life can bring you great pain and sorrow, but you know the rewards. That's why you're here. Knowing what you know, knowing the penalty for not meeting your obligations, and knowing the penalty for violating our rules that will be set forth is death, are you prepared to enter our brotherhood, our society and pledge your life?" Dominic asked Paulie and Carlo.

"I am," they both answered.

Dominic stood and walked around the oversized table. He slid the lace placemat that held the sacred items toward him. "The gun and the knife you see before you are weapons to kill and to defend. Sometimes we have to kill to defend our brotherhood. Sometimes we have to kill to punish those that break the rules of our society. You two have already killed for our family. Will you kill for me?"

"I will," they both answered.

"Paulie, which hand would you hold the knife to stab someone in?" Dominic asked. Paulie held out his right hand. "Which finger would you use to pull the trigger of a gun to kill someone?" Paulie clenched a fist, leaving only his index finger exposed.

Dominic grabbed one of the two cards and nodded to Angelo. Angelo handed Dominic a needle and squeezed Paulie's finger. Dominic jabbed it with the needle, drawing blood. He held the card under the finger, and drops of blood splattered the card.

Dominic did the same with Carlo. He pulled out a matchbook and lit a match; he lit the two cards on fire while Paulie and Carlo held them. As the cards caught fire, they juggled them in their hands to avoid getting burned.

Dominic spoke fast and loud, echoing though the room. "There is one rule that is above all others. There is one rule that breaking it will be worse than getting killed. You may not reveal the secrets of our brotherhood. Repeat after me. If I betray my family and I inform on our brotherhood . . .," Dominic stopped and waited for the men to repeat the oath as the fires increased in their palms.

"May my soul burn as does this blessed saint with the blood that I have shed," Paulie repeated Dominic's next line. The fire seemed so big and yet he felt nothing. The whole thing was so surreal; he wasn't even sure if he was actually saying any words.

"If you're feeling pain, you're not worthy," he thought he heard Dominic say. "You're going to burn in hell."

Paulie for the first time looked away from the flame that seemed to generate no heat to his hands, but he suddenly felt very hot everywhere else. He looked up to see Dominic saying something, but Paulie couldn't hear any words. Juggling the flame was becoming a problem and he couldn't keep his eyes on Dominic. It was dying down, but his arms were getting heavy. But he couldn't drop the flame and burn in hell.

"Paulie!" Angelo's yell brought him back.

Paulie didn't even realize he was leaning against Carlo for support. Carlo was tossing his flame in the air with one hand and holding Paulie up with the other.

"You're sweating bullets," Dominic told him.

"He's having a heart attack," Danny called out from the other side of the table.

Finally the flames died out. "I'll call an ambulance," Kenny said, reaching for his phone.

"No ambulance. Finish the ceremony," Paulie said.

"Take him to the hospital," Dominic ordered Kenny.

"We're not finished," Paulie cried out.

Dominic turned to Danny. "What? Five, ten more minutes?" Danny said, shrugging his shoulders.

"Give me my introductions, please," Paulie pleaded.

Dominic relented and returned to the other side of the table. He whispered in Danny's ear, "Fucking quickly, please."

Danny stood, as did everyone at the table except Dominic, who remained seated. "Everyone here is considered administration. You know you're captain, Angelo. You know you're lieutenant, Kenny. To my right are Vinny Jagge, Eugene Modica, and Jack Mattea. They're capo regimes or captains. To Dominic's left are Mario Marconi and Benny Mancini, capo regimes. Dominic is your boss. I am his underboss. You will always obey your chain of command. You report to Jackie Beans. Jackie reports to Kenny. Kenny reports to Angelo, and Angelo reports to me. We all report to Dominic, and you know Nick Amicucci is our godfather that the government has imprisoned."

Danny looked around and then back to Paulie. "You know all the rules. Is it okay to skip them?"

Paulie nodded his okay, and Danny asked Carlo the same question. Carlo was fine with it.

Dominic sprang out of his chair, and all the captains followed him. They formed a circle amongst themselves and held hands. "Our brotherhood welcomes two new members, and the chains shall be broken to accept them," Dominic said, and the men stopped holding hands. Carlo carried Paulie to the circle, and they then held hands with the others. "Now our society is complete again and the chains are restored." Dominic kissed Paulie and Carlo on both cheeks, and the ceremony was complete.

"Now, I don't want no fucking ambulance. This is supposed to be a secret," Paulie told everyone. "I just want to be driven and dropped off at the hospital by another made man."

"I'll take my new brother," Carlo said. "But I'm not dropping you off. I'll wait."

"A made man is never alone," Danny told his friend.

Paulie was taken to the hospital, and the night, or morning, came to an end. "Well, that's one for the books," Dominic said after he was alone with Danny and Angelo.

"We did the right thing by continuing," Danny said.

"Sure, unless he dies," Dominic said.

"Even then, to him today justified his whole life, all of his forty years being locked up. Today made it all worth it to him," Danny explained.

Dominic shrugged his shoulders. "I guess. I'll give Carlo a call and check on Paulie."

"I'm going to take a nap and I'll head to the hospital," Danny said.

At the hospital, Danny found that almost the whole crew had showed up to check on the newly made man. Jack Mattea and Benny Mancini, two of the captains at the ceremony, gave up going home after being up all night to check on the new inductee. Even several of the new inductees that were made before Jackie and Carloleft their own parties to come to the hospital once they heard. Danny was momentarily overcome by the response. *This is what it's all about,* he thought to himself.

Danny gave Angelo a hug and asked on Paulie's condition.

"Still no idea," Angelo told him.

"I got to say, Ange, I'm proud of you for getting the crew here," Danny said.

"To be honest, Danny, I got here about a half hour ago. They all came on their own. I should've been here first. He's one of my men," Angelo said.

Danny patted him the shoulder. "You're fine, kid."

Danny quickly worked the room, giving his men hugs and thanking the two captains for coming. "A real man's man," Benny Mancini said to Danny.

"I'm very proud to be a part of this thing today," Jackie Matts told him.

"I've got an order to give you guys," Danny told them. "Tell this story. Tell everyone what happened today. Paulie Bankjob chose possible death over not getting his button. He wouldn't even call a fucking ambulance because he didn't want to give away the ceremony's location. Tell them how his new brother held him up during the induction. Tell them how everyone showed up at the hospital. That's what getting made is all about, to become part of a family. This is a direct order. Tell everyone and tell them to tell someone else. There is no greater story to tell. This shall be a part of our history," Danny ordered.

Paulie's daughter and her husband arrived about an hour later, and a doctor came out and told them that Paulie was fine and that they could see him. "How long have you known this?" Danny asked him.

The doctor mumbled something and ran off. Paulie had been cleared over an hour ago, but the men in the visiting room terrified the doctor, and he wasn't going to talk to anyone but family.

Eventually, Danny was let in to see him, and Paulie, somehow, looked great. "I feel like a new man." Paulie beamed.

"You look like a new man," Danny agreed. "What'd you do? Fake a heart attack?"

"Oh, no, I had one, a mild one. But there's this nurse," Paulie told him.

Danny looked at him like he was crazy. "You serious?"

"That blonde one out there," Paulie told him.

"You just had a heart attack and you want to talk about this?"

"Wait until she comes back in here. You'll see how nice she is to me," Paulie said.

"She's nice to you," Danny said in amusement. "Which blonde?" Danny said as he looked in the hallway and came back in. "You mean that twentysomething blonde out there?"

"Yeah." Paulie beamed. "You think she knows I got my button?" he asked seriously.

Danny looked at him curiously. "You medicated?"

"Danny, I'm a made man now. I feel young. I feel good," Paulie boasted.

"You just had a heart attack."

"That was nothing. That happened before I was made. Dominic said that everything before was squashed, so this never really happened," Paulie said, waving around the room. "I'll be back to work on Sunday. There's some big games. Did you see the Cowboys were favored? There's something wrong with that one," Paulie said.

Danny took a seat on the bed. "Look, Paulie, what you did today brings tears to my eyes because I'm so proud and so in awe of you. Nick's grandfather, Nicodemo, was one of the greatest men I ever knew, and he had you at his side for a reason. You truly are a man of honor."

CHAPTER XXXVI

BUSTED

PAULIE BANKJOB WAS released after his heart attack two days later and returned to the Corner that day, a hero. That morning, Doug was awoken to a phone call. His throwaway rang; it was Dominic. "Get packed. We got to go to New York."

"Wrong number," Doug replied groggily.

"Wake up. Eddie Batts died, and we got to go the funeral tomorrow. We're leaving in a few hours," Dominic told him.

Doug was halfway awake then. "I understand about him dying, but why do you think I got to go?"

"Vito says so," Dominic said. Then he remembered Danny's advice on getting Doug to do something he didn't want to do. "I mean Vito would like you to attend with Danny and myself," Dominic told Doug. "He considers you a part of our family, a top part, and you should be there to bury a top boss," Dominic said, playing to Doug's ego.

"Fine," Doug growled. "How are we getting there?"

"Driving," Dominic answered.

"Who's driving?" Doug asked.

"You are and me. It's just you, me, and Danny," Dominic told him.

"You're not taking any muscle?"

"Nah, not for this," Dominic said. What Doug failed to realize was that *he* was the muscle. The other families knew of the Amicucci's Westside army. They knew of Doug Sullivan's connections in Sicily and in Europe. They knew of his crews in Miami and his drug pipeline that ran through North Carolina; New York was one of its destinations. And they knew of his secret crew of Sicilian assassins.

What Vito Paganini wanted of Doug Sullivan was to show off to the other bosses of the four families what Vito had in his pocket. He wanted to show them that he had more power and respect than Eddie Batts's son-in-law, Bruno Bini, the boss named by Eddie Batts, and that he, Vito Paganini, should be the boss of the Grazzitti Family and be the most powerful boss in the country.

Doug attended the funeral with Danny and Dominic. In the night, they stayed at a small hotel and shared a room. "I see I have a new best friend," Doug said as they entered the room.

"Vito?" Danny asked.

"Sure did parade me around those other bosses like I was a new toy or something," Doug complained.

Danny and Dominic remained silent; they thought it was a little overkill by Vito as well. And neither knew what Doug was going to do once he figured it out.

"I mean, why would any boss in New York care if I was with Vito? Because of the Zips?" Doug asked.

They still didn't respond; they just let Doug go.

"I figured I was going to have to whack Eddie Batts's son-in-law, Bruno Bini, for Vito, but I figured I'd let him take it from there. But, now, every single fucking person is going to know I did it. I just got played," Doug said in disbelief. There was still no response from Danny or Dominic. "I take your silence to mean you knew Vito was going to put me front and center with the other bosses."

"I don't what to say, Doug," Dominic said sheepishly.

"I do," Doug told him. "I got duped, and you guys helped to dupe me. That's fine. You want to do business that way. Okay, we'll do business that way," Doug said. "I don't like being treated like some schmuck." Doug grabbed his bags and slammed the door as he stormed out. He took a cab to the airport and took the next flight he could for home.

A month later, Doug still hadn't talked to Danny or Dominic; he even stopped attending the Amicucci Sunday gatherings. Tommy now handled the mob for the Westside.

Tommy Herrick stood outside of the bakery with Danny and Dominic.

"Wow, your face looks much better," Tommy told Dominic.

"Thanks, still a little bit more to do, but it'll work out," Dominic said.

"You should've done something with those ears, though," Tommy joked.

"Okay, already," interrupted Danny. "Still no Doug?"

"What do you want me to do?" Tommy asked. "He'll settle down. Give it time."

"Tell him until Vito is boss and he sets us free after Doug kills Bruno until then Vito really is our boss. When it comes down to it, if Vito tells us to do something, then we got to do it," Danny explained. "And Vito hopes using Doug now will prevent him from having to kill Bruno. He thinks he can take control without violence just by the threat of it. He'll understand that," Danny told him.

Tommy shook his head. "Doug understands the reasoning behind Vito unveiling his so-called secret weapon. It's to avoid having to use it. What he doesn't understand is why you two didn't talk to him about it."

Danny stepped forward. "I take full responsibility. I didn't think he'd go to the funeral. I told Dominic to make sure he gets there. I knew if we told Doug that Vito wanted to show off the arsenal and the earning power that he could muster, Doug would've gone berserk. But it's got to happen, Tommy," Danny continued. "Bruno's not going to step down, and you guys are going to have to whack him. And nobody's going to do nothing. Vito's going to become the boss of the biggest crime family in New York. Do you know what that means for us? And nobody's going to fuck with Vito because everyone knows who killed Bruno Bini. No one's going to fuck with you guys," Danny said with emphasis.

"Nice speech, but I'm not Doug. Things aren't all personal to me. What's done is done. Our concern is what happens now. We'll do the work. We'll whack Bruno if need be. We said we would. Hell, we've had a zip on him for months. We could do it tomorrow. We were even aware of the risks if we were retaliated against for it, but we didn't know we would be put out there like that," Tommy explained. "All is well. Me and Doug understand. We wouldn't have done that to you, but we understand. No ill will. But if you're wrong and somebody does fuck with us and we do go to war, we want out of our 25 percent commitment with you, just as our favor for you will get you out of your 25 percent commitment with Vito and New York. That's a huge loss for you guys. It's in your best interest to keep us out of war."

"It is in all of our best interests," Danny agreed. "And like I said, it was the only way."

"No, not the only way, just the chosen way," Tommy said as he turned to leave. He stopped and added one more thing, "And for the record, neither Doug nor myself think any of those families in New York would be scared of us for a second."

"Tommy, we do need something from you guys," Danny said. "Business is still business, right?"

The balls, Tommy thought to himself. "What do you need, Danny?"

"Another hit," Danny answered.

"Who the hell do you want to hit now?" Tommy asked.

Dominic answered, "Sam Brister, he's a pimp. He runs a prostitution racket for Benny Mancini. He's been selling some heavy coke on the side."

"You guys setting an example to stop breaking rules after the Fabian ordeal?" Tommy asked.

"Pretty much, Tommy," Danny answered. "We'd like him to disappear and avoid any kind of exposure other than in-house."

"That's smart," Tommy said. "I'll talk to Doug."

Three days later, Sam Brister disappeared, and he was replaced by another pimp. Benedetto let another zip do the job on his own, and he felt Giovanni's performance was perfect.

The next day, Billy Herrick garnished a plate for the pass in his restaurant during the noontime lunch. "Table seven's coming now."

"Billy!" he heard his hostess yell from the dining room.

Billy dropped what he was doing and ran to look into the dining room. "Oh shit," he said as he saw FBI agents running through his restaurant. They ran right into the kitchen and threw Billy on the ground.

"William Herrick, you are under arrest on a warrant from the State of North Carolina. You've been indicted on drug trafficking and other charges. We're taking you in and shipping you out," the agent said with his foot on Billy's back and his gun pointed at the back of Billy' s head. "Go peacefully and we won't close your restaurant and raid it."

"Okay, okay," Billy pleaded. They picked Billy up off the ground and handcuffed him. "Can you take me out the back way, please?"

"Just be thankful we're not raiding it and kicking your customers out," the agent told him and marched him right out the front door and past his full dining room of customers while reading Billy his Miranda Rights.

It didn't take long for Billy's wife, Claudia, to get a call from the restaurant. She called the lawyer and her sister-in-law, Val, who in turn called Tommy.

Tommy was having lunch at the Cucina with Dominic, informing him of the hit's success from the night before, when Val called.

“My brother just got arrested on drug charges in North Carolina,” Tommy said after he got off the phone. “I got to go.” Tommy got up and went.

Tommy met Doug at the Four Seasons and joined him in his office. “Kevin and Greg Monroe got plucked today too,” Doug told Tommy. “I talked with Carl,” Doug said, meaning Doug’s lawyer who represented Doug and the Herricks, Carl Voight. “He’s talking to some lawyers in North Carolina, and one said the feds picked up four others down there. If that includes the Monroes, I don’t know,” Doug said.

“No idea about the scope of the charges?” Tommy asked.

“None, Carl says to relax until the arraignment, then we’ll have a better picture,” Doug answered.

“Are they going to ship him to North Carolina?” Tommy asked impatiently.

“Tommy, no one knows nothing right now. We got to wait until the arraignment,” Doug told him.

Tommy looked dejected. “I feel useless.”

“We are right now,” Doug said. “Can you focus on some business until we get word?”

No, Tommy could not, much like Doug; times of uncertainty were when their deadly anger set in. “If there’s a rat, I’ll spend every fucking penny I got to find him in their witness protection, and I swear he’ll enjoy the slowest, most fucking painful death ever in the world’s history.”

“Let’s find out what we’re dealing with first,” Doug told Tommy. “We have no idea if there’s a rat, a wire, or if it’s just fucking harassment.”

“Okay, when’s the fucking arraignment then?” Tommy asked.

“I don’t know,” Doug answered.

“What am I supposed to tell my parents?”

“Tell them the same thing you’ve told them every other time he got arrested. Shit, how many times was he arrested back in the 1990s for stupid shit?” Billy also was arrested with Doug and Tommy in 2008 on several minor tax evasion and fraud charges, which related all the way back to their purchase of their restaurant, Karma. It was more of a harassment case, and Doug pled guilty and took ten years in exchange for the charges on Tommy and Billy to be dropped. Doug used his connections in Iraq to barter the deal with the CIA to get him out of the ten years. When the trio was arrested, Doug and Billy were locked up together without bail until Billy's charges were dropped, so Billy being arrested and serving a little bit of jail time here and there was nothing new to Tommy's and Billy's parents.

"Never for no drug trafficking though. He could be looking at life," Tommy said.

"Again, we don't know nothing yet," Doug told him.

Tommy pulled out his cell phone, and it was blank. "We're out of contact in this office. I got to get out of here."

Doug sighed as Tommy got up to leave. *This was going to drive Tommy crazy,* Doug thought to himself. "Why don't you go home, grab Val and the girls, and head over to Billy's and be with Claudia and wait for word? I can have Grace meet them there," he told Tommy.

Tommy shook his head. "No, I better make sure everything's running okay at Karma."

"Tommy, listen to me," Doug said. "You're not in the right state of mind. You'll start tossing people out of there for chewing too loud. Go home, be with your family."

He nodded. "You're right. You coming?" Tommy asked.

"There's still some things I've got to do today," Doug answered. "Let me get them wrapped up and I'll meet you at the arraignment, if there's one today."

"If it's not today, then it won't be until Monday," Tommy realized. "That's why they do this shit on fucking Fridays. Rotten motherfuckers are going to keep him locked up all fucking weekend," he continued with his voice rising again.

"Calm," Doug reminded Tommy as they left the office and checked their cell phones. Both men had several messages that they had missed because of the office. "This *is* getting a little irritating with this office," Doug said as Tommy left, and Doug made his way upstairs to the restaurant.

"Sal," Doug said as he grabbed Dominic's younger brother and took him off to the side. "Billy's been arrested. Just like you did when he was in North Carolina, I need you to help keep my restaurants running well," Doug told him.

"Of course, Doug. What did they get Billy for?" Sal asked in genuine concern.

"Not sure," Doug lied. "You know the drill. It could be nothing or it could be everything. I appreciate the help, Sal."

"It's my job, no prob. Any word on when you want to start with the bread expansion?" Sal asked.

"Not now," Doug said and turned to leave. He had another stop to make.

Pulling out of the bar, he saw the tail that was on him that morning was still there. He wasn't just going to worknow; this was a stop he didn't want the feds to see. It took over an hour but Doug lost his tail and arrived at Goliath's, Dave Worowski's bar in Henderson.

Goliath's was the hottest bar in Henderson, which didn't say much. Dave bought the bar after they all had spent much of their lives over twenty-one at the bar. During the days, the bar only contained members from Dave's crew, which was considered *the* top Westside crew.

When Doug entered his old stomping ground, everyone came over to say hello to an old friend. They all asked for information on Billy and offered their best wishes. Finally, Doug got to Dave. "Somewhere we can talk?" Doug asked him.

Doug knew it was still safe to talk in the bar. He knew of the security measures that the Amicuccis used for their bar and bakery, and he knew Dave's security at Goliath's rivaled it. "I talked to my lawyer on the way here. Billy's facing some major charges," he told Dave after they took a table away from everyone else. "I doubt he's going to be free to carry on his duties, and I'm not even sure how useful Tommy's going to be while Billy's going through this. I want you to take Billy's place while he's incapacitated," Doug told him. "I'm going to have Virgil take care of everything out of state, and you take the rest," Doug told him.

"Wow, thanks, Doug," Dave said.

"Matt Young can be in charge of Henderson, and you'll be the number three until Billy's available," Doug explained. "Now I want to be clear on this. I don't want to hear nothing later on down the road. You *will* be dealing with the mob. I know you've never been fond of it, but it is what it is. You can say no. Now is the time. But if you take the job, you take *all* the responsibilities that go with it, and you see where that got Billy right now."

Dave agreed, and Doug left for downtown where Billy was going to be arraigned through a video feed to a North Carolina courtroom where the others were being arraigned. Billy Herrick was the only out of state arrest in the North Carolina raids. Kevin Monroe was at his brother Greg's house in North Carolina when the feds came for them; they searched the whole house and tore it to pieces.

"William Herrick has been a menace to society since he received his driver's license," the prosecutor told the magistrate in his bid to hold Billy without bail after he pled not guilty into the video camera. "Seven arrests in the 1990s alone, not to mention his status as the third highest ranking of the Westside crew, which I remind Your Honor is the enforcement branch for Michigan's organized crime family," the North Carolina prosecutor argued as the Michigan courtroom watched on video. "He cannot be allowed to intimidate our jurors as he has already come down here and tainted our streets with drugs."

Carl Voight got his chance next. "You can look at William Herrick's rap sheet and say, 'Wow, that's a lot of arrests in the 1990s.' But what I'd say is: what happened between that last arrest in 1997 when a twenty-three-year-old kid got arrested for being drunk or disorderly, really, just for being a twenty-three-year-old, and to now? What happened is he grew up. He got married, and his only arrest was in 2008 where the charges were dropped. In fact, he was held for ninety days without bail before those charges were dropped. What's to say that won't happen again here? Is it fair to keep holding someone without bail until the government can finally get a real case? My client should be released on his own recognizance," Carl told the judge through the camera.

The judge laughed. "Well, he's sure not being released on his own recognizance, Counselor, but I do agree with your argument. I'll release him on a $200,000 bond, and Mr. Herrick will be restricted to the confines of his home and wear a monitoring bracelet on his ankle. He will only be allowed to leave the house with the court's permissions and is subject to searches at any time that this court sees fit," the judge ordered, and the court was adjourned.

Doug returned home late that night; there was still more to do to replace Billy. Doug was feeling like he had put too much on Billy's plate, especially when tasked with having to fill all of his duties. Tommy was blaming himself for not sending his kid brother away like Doug did with Stevie Turner; both were feeling pretty down.

"You okay?" Grace asked as Doug took a seat on the couch next to her; she had waited up for him.

"Yeah, I'm fine. It just seems like everything's turning to shit," Doug told her.

"Other problems than Billy?" she asked.

"All over the place. In fact, I'm heading back to Baghdad in a couple days," Doug answered.

"How long?" Grace wanted to know; she was due to give birth in less than three months.

"I'm going there to have a conversation, then I'm coming home the next day," Doug said. "I've got problems in New York and I'm worried," Doug confessed. "Everywhere I look, there's something else."

She knew better than to ask. "Whatever it is, you'll make the right decisions for all of us, Doug. You always do," Grace told her husband.

"I might have too big a fight to fight coming," Doug said quietly.

"Then do what you do. Fight smarter than the other guy. I don't think I've ever seen you doubt yourself. Just do what you always do. Win and come home to us," Grace said simply.

On Monday, Doug returned to Baghdad while Billy adjusted to his home confinement. More details of the charges were becoming clearer, and they realized that the feds in North Carolina had a rat that was wired for sound.

In Baghdad, Doug was going to spend the night at Sami Nasser's, but he had to meet with his CIA handler first; it was the sole reason Doug was there that time. "Okay, I've kept my end of the deal. I've kept your visit a secret, even from my bosses. Now I need to know why," the agent told Doug.

"It's Colonel Cooper. There's some things I didn't tell you," Doug said. "I can't let you guys arrest him. I'm going to whack him."

"What?" the agent asked in disbelief.

"All I'm going to tell you is that I killed two people for him, for money," Doug told the agent. The story was a complete lie, but he needed something for the CIA to agree with Doug and not arrest the Colonel. What Doug didn't want anyone to know was about the weapons the colonel, who was a major back then, had sold him. Doug didn't want the public to think he was the one corrupting the military. It was Major Cooper back then who had approached Doug about buying some AK-47s, but he didn't believe the story would come out that way. "No one's going to give a pass on two murders. I'll be the bad guy and he'll be the exploited career military man that I took advantage of. You guys need to find his source so I can clip him, quickly," Doug said.

The agent was having a hard time with it. "Even if the colonel tells about the murders, he's the one who ordered it."

"Trust me on this one. If the colonel talks, our mission is over," Doug told the agent, continuing with his lie. Now that he was getting the agent to understand the severity of the situation, Doug was hoping he could get him to volunteer the hit.

"I don't know how I can spin this to my bosses," the agent said.

"So don't," Doug answered. "We can leave this between just us two. In fact, I'll be happy to pay you to do so, enough to take care of your family forever."

"I'm not that way," he told Doug.

"I know you're not. That's why I haven't asked anything of you before. But this is for the greater good. You understand that, don't you? If you tell your bosses, this becomes a mess and I'm back in jail instead of catching these bastards with you," Doug explained. "It's something that's going to happen. I'm not letting him talk, so why not get yourself a million dollars in a Swiss bank account?" Doug offered.

The agent gave in. "I'll take care of this myself while you're in the States."

The next day on his way home from the airport, Doug stopped over at Tommy's to see how he and Billy were doing. Doug had to pop in since Tommy wouldn't answer his cell phone. Val answered the door when Doug knocked. "Oh, Doug, he's not taking this well," she told him as she let him in.

He found Tommy sitting at the kitchen table with his head in his hands and his elbows on the table. "You're not answering your phone," Doug said.

"I thought you'd get the message. Guess I was wrong," Tommy answered without looking up. Doug took a seat across from Tommy, and Tommy spoke again. "You're not very good with hints today, are you?"

"What are you going to do? Shun the whole world, hoping that helps Billy?" Doug asked him.

"I'm trying to think of a way to get him out of this," Tommy answered.

"You know, Tommy, one thing that this has made me realize is that Billy can take care of himself," Doug said. "He surely doesn't want you going into some funk because of him. And I surely can't afford to have you go into a funk either, not now, my brother."

"I know, business is still business," Tommy answered sarcastically.

"I need your head right. We'll do everything we possibly can for Billy, you know that. But there's some ugly shit on the horizon for us. Billy's the start of it. We're going to lose North Carolina, and you know what that's going to cost us. We got that thing with New York, and I got something dangerous shit going on overseas. I need you, Tommy," Doug said.

"Plus, don't forget that Sal Braga fucker has a problem with us too," Tommy added, reminding Doug of the DeCarlo crime family, another New York family that could cause trouble for Doug and Tommy. "I'm here. I'm with you, but I got to be concerned about my kid brother."

"Look at me, Tommy," Doug said, and he waited to look his friend in the eyes. "No matter what happens, we're going to get Billy out. It may be years, but we *will* find a way, I swear to you. It's what we do, Tommy. We win," Doug told Tommy, repeating his wife's pep talk to him.

Tommy nodded. "Okay, if it's violence you're thinking, I'm up for it."

CHAPTER XXXVII

Politics, Real Estate, and Bloodshed

THE NEXT TASK on Doug's list of duties to fill was the election of a Lansing senator. In the Michigan legislature, Doug had financially supported two candidates. Representative Colman was one of them who Doug had backed for his first term, but Colman failed to deliver on Doug's concerns and he failed to secure a large campaign contribution for his reelection. Doug had warned him that he was giving his money to Colman's opponent; he did not, though. The election was in two weeks, and Doug didn't care one way or the other about Representative Colman.

Senator Donald O'Malley was another story though. O'Malley had another two years before his reelection, but the Westside desperately wanted Senator Victoria Cugan out of office. She had a spot on the housing committee, which they wanted for O'Malley. Before Cugan, the Westside owned that spot but failed to keep the senator in office. On that senator's defeat, Senator Cugan took his spot on the committee that decided which companies would get state contracts. Doug and Tommy were making a killing on that until Senator Cugan took over, and Billy was working on supporting her opponent, Richard Prince.

Doug met the candidate four hours away, in Traverse City, and brought Dave Worowski along. They met at one of Doug's cabins, away from any people. "So Billy has gotten you several large donations. What else can I do now that Billy's out of the picture?" Doug asked Richard Prince.

"If people listen to you, tell them to vote for me. Tell everyone," he answered.

"And my wishes do not seem too out of reach, do they? I want to get my money that's overseas over here, and I'd like legislation for drug testing high schoolers," Doug said.

"I thought Billy was kidding with me," Prince said. "Why do you want to drug test high school kids?" he asked.

"It's the first step on the real war on drugs. Our dumb government always wants to attack the supply. Trust me when I say, there will always be someone to take over for every drug dealer put in jail," Doug explained. "Just like the basic economic theory of supply and demand, if there's a demand, there will always be a supply. You've got to attack the demand. That's how you win."

"Do you have any other ideas I should be working on?" the candidate joked.

"Education reform," Doug answered. "What kind of fucking dummy ever cuts education? Isn't that just like saying 'I don't care about the future?' If the kids are the future, why would any idiot ever not invest the most money there? Our teachers should be paid like doctors, and there should be a serious commitment to make the next generation smarter than us, not ensuring they're dumber because no one knows how to spend money responsibly," Doug lectured.

"Can I use that?" Prince asked. "That's great. Health care is hot right now. You got anything for that?" the candidate half joked.

"The state spends four million dollars a year on feline leukemia research. Take that and cover four million dollars worth of uninsured people," Doug said, half in jest.

"How do you know that?"

"Are you sure you're up for this job? Don't you get briefed or do any research? Take a look at recent bills that passed and what money gets spent where. Once you start cutting out all the bullshit that the lobbyists get for their campaign donations, the state economy would be amazingly healthy and you wouldn't have to cut the education. Instead, you could invest in it and other departments that are vital for making the future better," Doug preached. "Someone just needs to do it, someone that's not owned by lobbyists."

Two weeks later it was Halloween and the night before the elections. Before it got dark and Doug took his boys trick-or-treating, he turned on the TV to get some local election info. Instead, he was watching a broadcast from Iraq. They were reporting an explosion and the death of a high-ranked military officer, believed to be as high as a colonel. "Please don't be any other deaths," Doug said to himself as Graham and Bobby came down the stairs in their costumes.

"I thought you were going to be a baseball player?" Doug asked Graham, who was dressed as a cowboy.

"I was a baseball player last year," Graham answered.

"And the year before," Grace added.

Doug leaned over and picked up little Bobby, who had recently turned two. He was dressed as a football player and had a little helmet that he wore.

"Doug, that's not a costume. He wears that every day," Grace said.

"He's Daddy's little quarterback. Of course, he wears it every day," he said, hugging his son.

"I'll be Daddy's little cowboy," Graham said.

"Who needs a cowboy?" Doug said. "Let's go." He carried Bobby out the door, while Graham tried to catch up.

"Dad, wait, I don't have my bag for the candy," Graham called out, but Doug and Bobby were gone. "Mom!"

Grace sighed and asked her father to take Graham and catch up with Doug. "My eldest and most immature child is mad that my middle child, Graham, didn't wear his baseball player outfit, so he's ignoring him," she explained to her mother.

By the time Doug returned with the boys, all was well. Graham rode home piggyback and was telling everyone all about his night as he sorted through his candy. "And then Dad stole a boy's candy," Graham told.

"You little rat," Doug exclaimed.

"Please tell me he's making that up, Doug," Grace hoped.

"He did. I tell you, he did," Graham told his mother.

"He was a bigger kid," Doug reasoned. "He put his bag down and took a leak in the bushes."

Grace stared at her son, who started giggling when Doug said leak. "So I took the bag and tiptoed away," Doug finished.

"A kid's bag of candy?" Grace asked in disbelief.

"A *bigger* kid's bag of candy," Doug reminded his wife. "Next year, I'll bet he uses the toilet in his home. I should be thanked for teaching this kid who thinks he can pee anywhere he wants that there repercussions for such behavior."

"Pee pee." Graham giggled.

Grace leaned over and took Bobby from Doug's arms, "At least he's still savable," she said as she took him upstairs to bed.

On election night, Doug enjoyed hearing of the win of Richard Prince; now he had two senators in Lansing, and one of them was about to join the development committee. It was also nice to hear of Representative Colman's defeat.

Things were starting to look a little better for Doug and his crew after Billy's arrest. Colonel Cooper was killed in an explosion, and the CIA had been able to locate his source for the military weapons, so that was a success. He could get his construction rackets back up and going soon after Senator O'Malley could start on the committee. And Vito Paganini was really trying to take the throne by peace and not by having Doug kill Bruno, yet.

Vito had spoken with Bruno and told him he was too inexperienced for the job; he told Bruno that he should be Vito's underboss. Bruno didn't step down. Vito had spoken to the other families about their opinion, and they told him to hold a vote of the captains, which he had done. The vote was to be held after Thanksgiving in Upstate New York.

At Thanksgiving dinner, Doug invited his top leadership and their families to his house. Billy Herrick, of course, could not attend.

After dinner, Doug gathered everyone in his living room for a toast. "I've got big news," Doug proclaimed.

"Hey, Doug, we know Grace is pregnant. We got eyes," Tommy joked.

"Hey," Grace yelled in jest.

"We're all moving. I've been talking it about for years, and I did it. I bought two thousand acres of wooded areas. While I get the area cleared, everyone can design their own home. We will have five acres apiece," Doug said to a shocked audience. "I'll pay for everything but furnishing it." Even Grace sat in amazement, not sure of how to act.

"Who is everybody?" Tim Lusk asked.

"You're a part of everybody, Tim. Eight houses, four side by side and four across the street. I'm going to build a mini city. Me, Tommy, Billy, and Dave on one side, and you, Tim, Matt Young, Glenn Conway, and Mike Clement for when he gets out in a couple of years," Doug told everyone.

"Um, Doug, where are these houses going to be?" Grace asked.

"Serratville," Doug answered, and everyone liked that answer. Serratville wasn't far, and it was still considered a wealthy area in that economy.

"Excellent school system, I hear," Val said.

"Excellent sports teams. They go to state championships regularly, and it's a recruiting ground for college scouts," Doug told everyone.

"Is there any limit on the cost of the houses we design?" Dave Worowski asked with a smile.

"Nope, just don't be a jerk off about it," Doug joke. Doug raised his glass. "Everybody, it's my thank you to all of you for all your sacrifice and for your friendships. Happy Thanksgiving and God bless," Doug said as everyone toasted.

"You won't furnish any of it?" Glenn Conway joked to the amusement of the crowd.

Danny sat with Nino Valenti at the airport. Nino was Vito Paganini's right-hand man, and he flew into quickly meet with Danny and then he was flying back. "The captains voted last night," Nino told Danny. "Vito won."

"He did?" Danny asked excitedly. "That's fucking great. Oh man, that saves a lot of heartache."

"If only," Nino said. "Bruno says he doesn't recognize the vote. He's been saying that all along actually. He claims he's the boss. He was named the boss in title, so there shouldn't be any vote. He says there shouldn't be a vote until *he* dies."

Danny thought about for a moment. "That's not accurate. He *has* to be confirmed by the capo regimes."

"That's what makes him so wrong, but he won't step down. It's perfect to whack him now, though. Vito's doing this totally by the book. Now he's going to talk to the other families and get an okay on the hit. They have to give their permission because of the vote, and in the meantime, Vito will continue to try and get Bruno to step down peacefully. See, Danny, now when you guys whack Bruno, if you have to, you'll be heroes instead of the villains," Nino explained. "Everything's working out."

The next night, Danny and Dominic learned that another lieutenant had died. Billy DeStefano was the crime family's liaison to all the major unions; he was a legend that went back to the mob's dominance over the Teamsters. It was a funeral that Danny and Dominic did not attend, and everyone was ordered to keep away from it. They didn't want to give the feds reasons to put their noses where they weren't already, and Billy DeStefano would need a replacement that the feds didn't know about.

While Danny and Dominic planned a replacement worthy of their precious unions, some zips headed for New York for some R & R.

Giovanni had some relatives that lived in Montreal, and he was going to meet them in New York; Benedetto and Alberto asked to go with him for the weekend getaway. They met at a bar in Upstate New York and met Giovanni's cousin and two of his friends.

Benedetto and Alberto took a liking to the other men; they laughed, they drank, and they genuinely enjoyed the men's company. The other three men excused themselves to use the bathroom at the same time, and Alberto said he'd get another round.

Alberto went to the bar and waited for a moment before wondering where the bartender had gone. He looked around the room and realized that they were the only three men in the bar. "Hey, Benedetto," Alberto called out from the bar to their table.

Just as Alberto caught Benedetto's attention, the door to the bar kicked open and all Alberto could see in the sudden surge of daylight was a silhouette in the doorway. Alberto understood what was next and jumped over the bar just as gunfire exploded from the doorway.

Benedetto dropped to the floor when he saw the silhouette pull out an Uzi. His only thought was to seek cover and crawl as fast as he humanly could to get behind the bar.

The silhouette kept firing and entered the bar with three more shooters behind him, all peppering bullets. Benedetto dove the last few feet to the end of the bar and saw that Alberto was already behind it. Alberto had his gun in his hand and was waiting for the shooting to stop so that he could return fire. For once, Benedetto was happy when someone had defied an order; he had told Alberto and Giovanni not to be armed.

He took a quick peek around the corner of the bar that had saved their lives right then; he saw Giovanni lying in a pool of his own blood. Benedetto couldn't tell where he was shot, but he appeared to be dead.

Finally the shooting stopped, and Alberto rose to his feet and fired. "They are leaving!" Alberto yelled and jumped back over the bar to chase the shooters. Bullets hitting the door pane from the outside kept Alberto inside—the desired effect of the retreaters.

Benedetto felt Giovanni's pulse; there wasn't one. He had been shot several times in the back from the initial volley. One of the shooters lay at Alberto's feet; he was the last one in the bar when Alberto returned fire and was killed by two shots in the chest from the expert marksman from Sicily.

Benedetto checked the shooter's pulse; he was dead as well. He picked up the Uzi and looked it over before they heard sirens. They ran to the back door, which they figured Giovanni's friends had taken after they had set them up. There was already a police car there with officers holding their guns in their hands. "Freeze!" one of them yelled.

Alberto drew his gun, and Benedetto stepped in front of him. With his hands in the air and his back toward the police officers, Benedetto addressed Alberto. "We cannot kill the policemen here," he told his young protégé.

"We will go to prison because someone tried to kill us," Alberto said, still trying to get aim at the cops.

"Yes, we will, Alberto. It is over for us. We cannot go down this road in this country. Drop the gun," Benedetto ordered.

Footsteps were coming from behind them then; the cops had entered the bar. "It is over, Alberto," Benedetto told him again.

Alberto dropped the gun and was tackled from behind. While Benedetto was handcuffed, he watched the other officers wrestle with Alberto, even though he wasn't resisting.

Doug sat in his office at the Four Seasons when he was interrupted by Sal Amicucci. "Doug, my brother and Danny are here."

Doug shrugged his shoulders and went back to looking at a blueprint of the house he was building. "Tell them to have a good time."

"Dominic asked if you'd see him as a favor for me, Doug. I don't know what the problem is. You don't even come over on Sundays anymore, like we're not family anymore," Sal said.

Doug nodded. "Okay, I'll see them as a personal favor to you."

Danny and Dominic took a seat across from Doug's desk. Danny spoke first, "You know we're sorry. Like I told Tommy, I take full responsibility for the whole thing."

Doug looked bored. "Is there business to discuss or is there not business to discuss?"

"Something bad has happened, Doug," Dominic told him.

That got Doug's attention. "What?" he asked.

"I talked to Vito, and he said there's a story all over the news in New York of a shootout. Three Sicilian immigrants, living in Michigan, shot up a bar in New York. There's two dead. One is one of the zips. The other is what the news are calling a DeCarlo Family associate. The other two zips are in custody," Dominic reported.

"Just for record," Danny said. "You didn't send the zips to shoot up a DeCarlo bar, right?"

Doug answered while still mulling over what had just heard, "No, not yet."

"We got to find out what happened," Danny said.

Doug got up and headed for the door. "I will, right fucking now."

"What are we supposed to tell New York?" Danny asked.

Doug turned around before he opened the door and said in an eerily calm voice, "You tell Sal Braga that if my zips shot first, I'll give him the rest of the zips on a silver platter. If he fired first, you tell him, it's his head that's going on that fucking platter." He left.

Doug met with Tommy and told him to go to Billy's house, since he was allowed there, and find out why the zips were even in New York. Billy was still handling the zips by using throwaway cell phones. Doug had no idea which zips were there; he was aware of only one. He knew that Stefano was setting up the hit on Bruno Bini, and Doug was assuming they were in New York for that reason.

When Tommy showed up at Doug's house, they talked in the backyard. "Billy says the zips were there meeting some other zips from Montreal. He says they planned the trip weeks ago."

"Was the bar a DeCarlo hangout?" Doug asked.

"Online, it says it's a known DeCarlo hangout for a gambling crew," Tommy answered. "Did Sal Braga shoot up one of his family's own bars?"

"How would he know the zips would even be there?"

"Maybe one of his people heard them talking and just called it in, sheer luck," Tommy offered.

"Who are these zips in Montreal?"

"No idea," Tommy said. "I don't think Billy knows."

"What do you think, Tommy? Are we going to war here?" Doug asked.

"It sounds like these zips met at a DeCarlo bar and didn't know it. How the hell would they?" Tommy asked. "Somehow, Sal Braga got wind and sent a hit team. The question is: what was his mentality? Did he think we were making a move or did he have no idea they were even with us?" Tommy asked as they bounced ideas off each other.

"What if the zips from Montreal set up our zips for Sal Braga, and he's had this planned for weeks?" Doug asked.

"Then that's war," Tommy answered.

"Then that's war," Doug agreed.

Over the next two days of the first week in December, Doug provided a New York lawyer for Benedetto and Alberto, who didn't even give their names to the police after their arrest. Doug received word from New York that Sal Braga didn't know they were Doug's men; he thought they were shooters from Montreal, an area where he had rackets and was having problems with. With that, he also demanded to know why Doug had armed hit men in New York.

Doug and Tommy met Danny and Dominic at Cooch's Cucina; none of them had seen any FBI tails that night, but they knew they were there in full force after the shootout in New York.

"Then you agree there'll be a sitdown?" Danny asked.

"I agree that I'll sit down," Doug answered.

"Doug, these are New York bosses. You can't sit down with them," Danny told him.

"I had plenty of drinks with Eddie Batts, and he was a hell of a lot classier than that fuck face Sal Braga," Doug told them.

"We're affiliated with the Grazzittis. That means you are too. That's why Eddie sat down with you. Bruno Bini can sit down with you, but you can't attend a meeting like this. This could have all the New York bosses," Danny said.

Doug shrugged his shoulders. "Fine, tell fuck face Sal I think he's full of shit and I'm avenging the loss of three of my men. Then tell him he can go fuck himself," Doug said with disgust.

"Is that your message?" Dominic asked. "I think it's a good idea. Let's tell them that if Doug can't sit in for himself, he's taking action."

Doug nodded to him. "Thank you, Dom, I appreciate that."

"Okay, let's tell them that. I'm sure no one really wants a war," Danny said.

Two days later, Doug was told that he would be attending a meeting with the bosses of all five families at a secret location on the day after Christmas.

CHAPTER XXXVIII

The Sitdown

"NOT GUILTY," BILLY answered the judge as he stood before the Honorable Harold Rew in his North Carolina courtroom.

"Your Honor," Carl Voight called out, "Mr. Herrick would like to utilize his right to a speedy trial, the speediest trial possible."

The prosecutor spoke up too. "The government has no problem with that, Your Honor. I'm ready to roll right now," he said boldly.

"I'll roll right now too. I'll destroy you," Carl barked at the prosecutor.

Billy stood next to Kevin Monroe and the other two defendants, whom he had never met, watching his lawyer argue with the prosecutor.

The judge banged his gavel and quieted the lawyers. "There is none of this in my courtroom. Understand that, Mr. Voight," Judge Rew told him. "Does ninety days make everyone happy?" he asked sarcastically. The judge set the court date for mid-March and adjourned the court for the day.

Doug stopped in at Goliath's, after two hours of trying to ensure he had no tail, to see Dave Worowski and Matt Young. Tommy was in North Carolina with Billy for his pretrial, so Doug came to Dave's bar himself. Like a general, Doug thought it necessary to be with his men in the days leading up to battle.

Doug walked in and made it to the bar before everyone who had got up to greet him could reach him. "Everybody, grab a shot. It's on me," Doug told the eight men who ordered their drinks. "To Henderson, the toughest motherfuckers in the world," Doug told his men as they did their shots.

"Another round," Doug ordered. "Now, this is like old times," Doug said to himself.

After a couple more rounds, Doug met with Dave and Matt. "The rat in North Carolina is Alex Groyer," Dave told Doug.

"I know. He's going to be a witness against Billy," Doug said.

"Brian Jones has been driving down to North Carolina and buying coke and pills from him and selling it up here on his own," Matt Young said.

"Brian? Really?" Doug asked. Brian Jones was a collector for the Henderson crew; he was no big loss to the organization, but he was a friend to a deceased Westsider's elder brother, and Doug and Tommy had known him since little league baseball.

"I've crossed every T and dotted every I before bringing this to you. I knew he was selling on the side, and I tracked his source. It was to the rat in North Carolina," Matt said.

"That doesn't mean he's a rat," Dave reminded everyone.

"No, but even if he's not, I want to whack for him for his side business," Matt told them.

"Matt's right," Doug said, sadly. "We've got two solid reasons to make Brian disappear. Let's make him disappear. Handle it, Matt, quietly," Doug ordered.

Claudia Herrick was waiting for her husband to return from his court hearing in North Carolina; he had been away for three days and was finally coming home. She had dinner waiting when Tommy's car pulled in to drop Billy off.

"What's all this for?" Billy asked as he entered the kitchen and saw dinner and wine on the candlelit table.

Claudia poured him a glass of wine and handed it to him. "Not going to join me?" he asked her.

"I can't, Billy," she said. "I'm pregnant!" Claudia yelled in joy.

Billy didn't respond; he was lost in thought.

"Yes, it's yours," she joked. "Come on, Billy, a baby," she said, nudging him.

"It's not that I'm not happy, but what if I go to jail?" he asked sincerely.

"This is just more pressure to make sure that doesn't happen," she said with a smile. "For one day, for one moment, Billy, this moment, enjoy it. It's a blessing, even if you go to jail. Just be happy, at least for tonight."

On the Friday before Christmas, Tommy stopped by Billy's, and they talked in the cold December air of Billy's backyard.

"How are the restaurants?" Billy asked.

Tommy laughed. "Like you don't know, you spend your days barking orders on the phone to both of them."

"What's the word on Benedetto and Alberto?"

"They're both being charged with two murders, Giovanni's and the other fucker's. Benedetto apparently picked up the Uzi that shot Giovanni and put his fingerprints on it. Cops are saying he's the one that sprayed the bar," Tommy reported. "Either way, they're gone. They'll be deported if nothing else happens to them."

"I really liked Benedetto," Billy said, and the two stood in silence for a moment.

"Look, Billy, if you don't win this thing, you got nothing to ever worry about with Claudia and your baby," Tommy told him.

"You don't even have to say it. I know, Brother," Billy said.

Doug kept Christmas smallat his house that year while Tommy celebrated at Billy's house. No one knew what the next Christmas would entail, so everyone tried to make that Christmas a little more special than others. Dominic spent his Christmas at his father's house with all the usual suspects, except for Doug Sullivan.

At midnight, Doug said good-bye to his wife and sons and left the house with his bags to join up with Danny and Dominic and make the drive to New York. They got a room at a small hotel and told Vito where they were staying. At seven o'clock, Vito arrived to drive them to their destination, a small airfield in New Jersey.

Doug wanted to get a few points across before they left for the big meeting. "I speak for myself," Doug said. "You don't speak for me and you guys don't speak for me," he said, pointing at Vito, then at Danny and Dominic. "You guys got some trust to earn back with me. Don't fuck up what's left of our relationship tonight."

They all agreed, and Doug continued. "What's the status on you and Bruno?" he asked Vito.

"We're still in a stalemate. The other bosses still have to make a statement about their opinions, but Bruno won't care what they say. The only way he's leaving office is feet first," Vito explained.

"How do you sit at a meeting with the guy you're saying isn't the boss?" Doug asked. "Aren't you giving him some clout by allowing his opinion to weigh in at this meeting? He'll be the boss and you'll be the captain, even though the other captains have voted you boss?"

"That's the stalemate we're in," Vito replied.

"You want me to tell Bruno he's not the boss anymore while we're there since no one else can? And I'm supposed to care what these people think?" Doug asked.

"You just please give these men the respect that a boss is due," Vito told him. "Sal Braga will be there with his father, Vinny. More than likely, that's who you need to hash this beef with." The men piled into Vito's car, and he drove them to the airfield.

"Smart idea, an airplane hangar for a meeting," Doug said as they approached the airfield.

"We're taking that jet over there," Vito said, pointing to a private jet waiting on the runway. "Feds can't tail us up there."

The men from Michigan climbed aboard the personal jet and were introduced to the five Mafia bosses and given a tour of the plane that was owned by Rosario Ragucci, the boss of the Ragucci Crime Family. "You own this?" Doug asked.

"I thought about getting the bigger one, but I figured this was adequate," the ninety-year-old boss told Doug.

Doug looked around the plane with his eyebrows raised. "You can buy something bigger than this?"

Rosario laughed and asked everyone to gather in the sitting area as the plane lifted off. "Dominic, do you remember the first time we met?" Rosario asked Dominic after the plane was in the air.

Dominic nodded. "I do. It was to see if there was any problem with Doug establishing some rackets in Miami."

"That's right, Dominic. That was in 2006, and I thought that was respectable of you how you handled it. Your father was on trial back then, and you didn't know what was going to happen, remember?" Rosario asked him.

"I do. You told me how you had become a boss when your father died, when you were thirty-five years old," Dominic answered.

"Thirty-one years old. It was 1952. Since then, I've been the boss, so I understand what it's like having such responsibilities at such a young age."

Danny sat in awe of the whole thing; he had never dreamt of being in such a meeting with such a man as Rosario Ragucci. The

Ragucci Family was almost mythical, the only crime family that never had a rat and never felt the wrath of the government indictments in the way the other families did.

Rosario's nephew, Antonio, pretty much ran the family for his uncle; he was present and sitting next to his uncle. "He has a lot of respect for you, Dominic," Antonio told him.

"I am the one who has respect for you, Rosario. Our whole world does," Dominic said. "Is that not why we are here, to seek your council?"

"Very well," Rosario said. "My council is that no one needs a war in the streets of New York. You yourself, Dominic, had to fight one in your streets," Rosario said, referring to Jerry Lissoni's uprising against Dominic.

"No, he didn't," Bruno Bini interrupted in disgust.

Simultaneously, Doug, Danny, and Dominic's heads all turned to look at Bruno, the man they knew they were going to kill.

"He fought it for him," Bruno said, pointing at Doug. "Jerry Lissoni never attacked a paisan."

Doug glanced at Vito, and Vito shook his head as if to say, "Don't say it, Doug."

"Brilliant in my opinion, by the Amicuccis," Antonio Ragucci told Bruno.

"None of that matters," Rosario said. He turned to the boss of the DeCarlos, Vinny Braga, who sat with his son, Sal. "Vincenzo, is there anything you'd like to say?" Rosario asked.

Vinny stood up and stood before Doug, taking his hand. Vinny was dying at a quick pace, and the man was frail. Doctors told him he had a year, two at the most to live, but he looked like he could die at any moment. "When you took over Miami, you had my blessing. My family's rackets there had dried up years before. We consider the Amicuccis an ally. Why does anyone think this incident is anything more than an unfortunate accident? I can't rest in peace if there's no peace," Vinny told Doug.

"I don't mean one ounce of disrespect, but this unfortunate incident has cost me three very skilled men," Doug told him.

Sal Braga scoffed out loud, "Yeah, very skilled at killing. What everyone's dancing around here is the question of why your three very skilled men were even in New York and in one of our bars."

"They were in New York visiting family they have in Canada, and I'm sure they had no idea it was one of your bars," Doug told Sal.

"You're supposed to let us know if someone's coming into our territories," Bruno added.

That was enough for Doug. "You got some kind of problem?" Doug asked Bruno.

Rosario cut off Bruno's answer, "Douglas, please, just as I won't let them talk to you with any disrespect, I won't let you talk to them with any either."

Doug nodded. "Okay, but it's clear there's some division in this room," Doug said.

"Be that as it may, what is that you want? Reparations?" Rosario asked him.

"I'm a simple guy. I'll take an apology with a handshake and assurances that my men are safe," Doug said.

Vinny Braga shook Doug's hand and looked him the eye. "I am sorry for this."

Doug shook his. "Again, I mean no disrespect, but it's not you that needs to apologize," Doug said and looked at Sal.

Bruno Bini spoke, "Doug, this is a tremendous amount of respect that these men have shown you. Anyone else and I imagine we'd have just told them to go fuck themselves. I think you should take Vinny's apology and consider how much these men have done for you."

"And I'm not apologizing to anyone," Sal Braga proclaimed.

All eyes were on Doug. He shrugged his shoulders. "Okay then, Vinny, I accept your apology and am humbled by it," Doug said, shaking Vinny's hand. Doug turned to Sal. "Is there a chance me and Sal can have a moment alone to talk?"

"Bathroom," Sal said and was gone before he was finished saying the word, and Doug followed him in.

"Don't say one fucking word," Sal said after Doug shut the door. The men were almost nose to nose in the tiny bathroom. "Between you and me, I'm fucking glad you lost three of your shooters. There's only nine more," Sal said, revealing his knowledge of Doug's exact number of zips. Doug didn't say a word; he continued glaring at Sal and waited for him to finish. "I don't get why these guys kiss your ass, but I'll comply with my father's orders. I'll let him rest in peace, but once he does, I'm taking Miami back and killing your whole fucking crew if you get in the way," Sal told him.

. "You got anything else you need to say?"

"Yeah, I wanted to thank you actually. I've got peace with Montreal now. They forced their men to set up his cousin. That was their peace offering to me," Sal said with a smile. "I was going to knock off your zips one by one, you know, take out your legs before my father died."

"You know, Sal, I don't say this much, but I hope and pray that I'm the guy that pulls the fucking trigger. I would really enjoy watching the life leave your eyes," Doug told him. "I am really going to enjoy this once Vinny dies."

"You can get the fuck out of here now," Sal ordered.

"Okay, Sal," Doug said and left the bathroom.

"All is well," Doug told everyone as they waited for them to return from their private meeting. "Hey, Rosario," Doug said as he sat back down at the table. "Can I get the number of where you got the plane? Unless it fell off a truck or something," Doug said as the other men laughed.

The plane actually was headed for Michigan, where they dropped off Doug, Danny, and Dominic. Vito as well was getting off the plane. "Why are you getting off?" Danny asked him.

"I thought I'd hang out with you guys," Vito said.

Danny gave him a hug and whispered in his ear, "Stay the fuck on the plane, would you? Don't let Bruno conspire with these guys." On Danny's suggestion Vito decided to fly back to New York with the other bosses.

The unexpected landing left the trio without a ride from the private airfield. "I'll call Jimmy to pick us up," Danny said.

Doug laughed. "You didn't say one fucking word on that plane."

"I was in awe," Danny told him after he got off the phone. "Rosario Ragucci has been a boss my whole life, never spent a night in jail."

"It *was* a little embarrassing, Danny," Dominic joked.

"Fuck you, guys," Danny hissed.

Doug missed the comradeship he had with Danny and Dominic. "I'm surprised they didn't think you were there to pour the drinks," Doug continued on Danny.

"Laugh it up," Danny said. "Can bygones be bygones now?"

"Just be honest with me. If Vito wants to use me as a tool, tell me. Tell me you need me to do it to keep face with Vito, I'll do it. I can take the heat. I can't take the deceit though," Doug told them. "Shit, I would've acted like a tough guy at the funeral if I knew. I could've had some real fun and you ruined that too," Doug joked. "Seriously though, please don't ever put me in a position to tell you guys to fuck off."

After everyone made up, it was back to business. "So what's your take on the meeting?" Dominic asked Doug.

"The obvious thing is that we're going to war with Sal Braga after his old man dies," Doug said. He was only going to tell Tommy of the conversation in the bathroom; to everyone else, he just said they talked. "Isn't it odd, though, how those other bosses treat me?" Doug asked. "It's almost like they're setting me up to whack me."

"It's either that or they just have some respect for you," Danny joked. "Doug, you done real well for yourself and for us, since me and Nick went to jail. Even the bosses of New York treat you like a boss."

"Danny, I know your little 'play to my ego' game you like to play with me. You make me think you're about to ask me to do something," Doug joked. "There was one other thing in that meeting though."

"Bruno, right?" Dominic asked.

"That motherfucker dies," Doug said. "I don't care if Vito gets him to step down or not, I've got the groundwork laid and I am killing that son of a bitch."

"He did sell us out up there, didn't he?" Danny asked.

"Not that you complained. You were in awe," Doug mocked.

"Fuck off, Doug, you fucking ball buster," Danny said with a laugh.

The next day, Doug met Tommy at his house in the morning, and they talked out in the back. "Billy says that Stefano told him he saw Doug get on a plane with Bruno Bini," Tommy told him. "He tailed Bruno all the way to New Jersey. He doesn't use any tail-shedding procedures, ever, Stefano says."

Doug shrugged his shoulders. "Doesn't matter. We're killing him."

Tommy nodded. "Okay, are we waiting until Vito says so?"

"I guess that depends on how long he takes and what he says," Doug answered. "But one way or another, we're killing this prick. And then we're killing Sal Braga after his father dies, two years tops, I hear. Tommy, if you would've been there, we'd have to fight our way out or bury the bodies."

"Let's not get off subject here. You want to kill two of the five New York bosses. Is that what you're saying?" Tommy asked, just to be sure. "I'm with you, but let's call what it is: two bosses of two New York families. They're both bigger than Dom's family. We're on the same page, right?"

"Yup, they want to kill us, and I don't think of Bruno as a boss of anything. He'll be the easy kill. Sal's going to cost us a big war, though," Doug said.

"It might be better for Billy to be in jail. At least, he'll be safe," Tommy said.

"I'll be honest. I wasn't feeling too bad being locked up when you were fighting Jerry Lissoni," Doug joked.

"He was a worthy opponent, I'll say that," Tommy said.

"You've got to get the apartments and all that shit that Billy had set up for him," Doug reminded Tommy.

"I will. I just feel so bad for him when I'm there. He can't leave. He can't do nothing. It's fucking winter. Claudia's breaking his heart and now there's a kid coming," Tommy complained for Billy.

"Carl says he's getting Billy acquitted," Doug said. "He ain't on no tapes. It's all hearsay when it comes to Billy and the Monroes. Carl said they blew their wad early. They pulled the plug early because we were killing too many people down there," Doug said.

"I know, he told me, but you never know," Tommy said.

On Thursday, Dominic visited his father in prison. "What the fuck is this 'sticking it day'?" Nick asked his son.

"Just something," Dominic whispered as he looked around the visiting room.

"Sixty fucking grand, Helena said she spent. Sixty fucking grand and she don't have no new car or nothing like that," Nick said.

Dominic was puzzled; he knew his stepmother had spent that kind of money at Doug's stolen goods warehouse, and he knew that she didn't use any money from a bank account. She paid with the illegal cash that was given to her every month from Nick's rackets. He was puzzled why his father would say something like that with the feds' tape recorders rolling.

Nick broke out laughing. "Oh, I was going to do this for a while, but I can't keep it in."

"I don't get what you're talking about," Dominic said.

"The guards told me there's no recording today. They think the feds are done with recording you and me, but we'll see about that next week," Nick told him. "And I got you out of the five grand you pay the guards for today as well. I told them I wanted to have some fun with you. That's why they didn't tell you when you got here."

"This means you're back in action?" Dominic asked.

"At least for today. So what's been going on?" Nick asked.

"Thank you," Dominic said and gave his father a hug, drawing the ire of the guards for touching. They needed the Amicuccis to at least give the impression that the guards had authority over them.

"Me, Danny, Doug, and Vito met with the five bosses of New York the other day, on Rosario Ragucci's personal jet," Dominic told Nick.

"What?" Nick asked in disbelief and listened as Dominic brought him up to date on his crime family.

Tommy entered his brother's house from the backyard a little after noon and found him at the kitchen table looking over some documents for the court; he was still in his robe. "Plan on dressing today?" Tommy asked when he sat down with Billy.

"What's the point?" Billy answered without looking up. "Look at this shit. It's the list of forfeitures the government wants to take if they convict me," Billy said, handing a piece of paper to Tommy.

"How can they take Karma if me and Doug own a third each?" Tommy asked Billy, who just shrugged and was looking at another sheet now. "Your house? What the fuck! You've been in this shithole since before we ever made any money," Tommy said. "How come you never bought a new house by the way?"

Billy looked up. "Because I like it here," he said simply. "Claudia's all excited about building a new house next to you guys, but I really don't want to move."

"I guess it's the new house or jail," Tommy said.

"That's not funny, Tommy," Billy told him.

"Where do they get this eight million dollars that they want to take from?" Tommy asked while reading the sheet.

"That's what I have in the bank," Billy said.

"Now, I'm not saying that that's not a lot of money, but you've made eight million dollars with me on stocks alone. Where's all your money?" Tommy asked.

"I've got another eight million in Dad's name," Billy said.

"You're hiding assets in our father's name?" Tommy asked incredulously.

"No, I would just say it was a gift from me," Billy told him.

"Yeah, the government is better than going after our parents to get to us, aren't they?" Tommy asked sarcastically. "I can't believe you. I'm so disgusted I can't even get mad."

"I thought it was a good idea. I'll take it back," Billy said.

Tommy sighed. "You got a lot going on right now and I'm not looking to make it worse, so I'm not going to throw you through that fucking kitchen window. But you tell Carl Voight about this and get his advice. I imagine he'll call you a stupid fucker and tell you not to touch it right now. I wish you would have talked to me before you guys just went ahead and did this," Tommy told him. "I'll stop back by tomorrow."

"Are you coming over Saturday for New Year's Eve?" Billy asked.

"Nope, sorry, you're spending this one with Claudia and Mom and Dad. Maybe you and Dad can come up with more stupid shit to do. I'll be at the Amicuccis with Doug. We're in the healing process with Danny and Dominic," Tommy joked. "Oh, and you get my daughters."

"I thought you'd spend what could be my last New Year's on the streets with me," Billy said softly; he really sounded hurt.

"I'll stop by before I go over there," Tommy told him. "We'll watch the bowl games Sunday together."

"Business is business, right?" Billy said.

"Yeah, Billy, business is always business. Do you understand what next year could be like? You might be lucky if you go off to jail. We got the fight of a fucking lifetime coming up once that old man in New York dies.If you get acquitted, you're going be hiding out in shitholes and peeking out of windows. We all will be. So, yeah, if I spend New Year's Eve with Danny and Dominic to keep them with us right now, then that's what I'm going to do. It ain't about you, it ain't Doug, and it ain't about me. It's about all of us and fucking survival, always," Tommy preached.

"And what about the zips in New York?" Billy demanded.

"Benedetto and Alberto? Billy, they're gone, jail, or deported, but they're gone. You got to understand that. And Sal Braga set up the whole thing. He was going to pick off the zips one by one to reduce our strength for his attack. We're taking the time that Vinny Braga's dying and planning our counterattack in New York. We're going for the head first. Hopefully, if we knock off Sal quickly the DeCarlos won't continue a war with us," Tommy explained.

"Well, 2012, and sounds like a rough one," Billy said.

CHAPTER XXXIX

New Year's Eve

BILLY HERRICK SAT alone with just one hour left before the ball dropped and the New Year began; he had his beer in his hand and watched TV. His brother, Tommy, had failed to stop by earlier as he had promised; he had errands to run all day, he had said. Both Doug and Tommy were at Nick Amicucci's house, and Tommy's wife, instead of leaving his two nieces with him and being with Tommy, had her own plans of which Tommy had no idea; she was at Doug's house, spending New Year's Eve with Grace. Billy's own wife, Claudia, was at Doug's while his parents went somewhere else as well; poor Billy was spending what could be his last New Year's as a free man alone.

At Doug's house, Grace Sullivan was hosting her best friends. Grace's parents actually hosted the party as Grace was due to give birth to Doug Jr. in less than three weeks. Billy's wife, Claudia, was pregnant as well, and that left Tommy's wife, Val, to kick back with the drinks with Grace's dad. Val had been pregnant the year before on New Year's Eve, so she didn't complain. Graham sulked because Doug didn't take him with him, and little Bobby played with Tommy's eldest daughter, Peggy, while the newbie, Caitlyn, slept. What no one knew was that neither Doug nor Tommy would be coming home that night. What no one knew, including Doug and Tommy, was when they were coming home.

"Use this number for now. We'll be changing phones every three days," Doug said, handing Dominic a slip of paper.

"Where are you guys going to stay?" Danny asked.

"It's probably better if no one knows," Doug answered.

"Not nowhere fucking warm," Tommy complained.

The men were in the backyard of Dominic's father's house; everyone else stayed inside on that freezing New Years Eve. "How much longer do you think?" Dominic asked.

In New York, Vito Paganini was meeting with Bruno Bini at the small bar he used as his headquarters. The other bosses had spoken, and they had told Bruno to step down, that Vito had the support of the family and the votes of the captains. Still, Bruno refused to step down. Vito was there to offer his final ultimatum to Bruno; if Bruno refused, a zip that was a former army sniper in the Italian Army was positioned in the building across the street as a sniper to end Bruno's reign.

The men in the Amicucci backyard were awaiting word as to the outcome of the meeting and possible hit. As Danny and Dominic continued to hold out hope that Bruno would step down, Doug and Tommy knew that the order given to the sniper was to shoot Bruno when he came out, regardless of the outcome.

"I still say that if Bruno dies tonight, the whole family will fall into line behind Vito. I wish you'd wait to go underground," Danny said.

"Once it's too late, it's too late," Tommy said.

"If this goes bad, then we're prepared. If it doesn't, we'll be home in a week," Doug told them.

"What's the scoop on North Carolina and Tommy's brother?" Dominic asked.

"Our lawyer says there's solid evidence for the other guys in the trial, but he says my brother was a throw in, something to grab a headline," Tommy explained.

"The feds released one of the Monroe brothers, Greg. He's handling North Carolina now under Virgil Boyle. You guys know Virgil? He runs Miami," Doug told them.

"Why'd they let him go?" Danny asked.

"Lack of evidence," Doug said.

"But not in Billy's case?" Danny continued.

"We grew up with the Monroes. There's no problem with Greg," Tommy told them and ended Danny's concerns of Greg being released to be an informant.

"Just keep in mind, that's all I'm saying," Danny said.

"The rat was one of three lieutenants down there," Doug explained. "The other two are going strong now, and Billy helped to get some organization down there. It's going to hold."

"Roll, millions, roll," Tommy added. Doug and Tommy didn't have a backup plan for their drug routes if they lost North Carolina; they wanted to get that done, but something else always came up.

"You guys coming in for a drink?" Dominic asked. "My whole family's inside, except Sal. His prick boss has him working on New Year's Eve," he joked.

"Your brother has been a godsend for me. You should start being a little proud of your little brother," Doug told Dominic.

"Before he goes off to jail," Tommy growled to himself.

"I am proud of him, but I still can't accept it. He's probably going to run your business into the ground," Dominic said.

"All right, we should be heading out now. I was hoping to be on the road before midnight," Doug said. "Here, this is for December," he said, handing Danny a large manila envelope. "Good month, $365,000."

"That is a real nice 25 percent," Dominic commented.

"Here's your other accounts," Tommy said, handing each Dominic and Danny a piece of paper containing their overseas bank account information. "And need I remind you about destroying those papers?"

"Do you really need to say that every time, Tommy?" Danny asked in irritation.

"Yes, I think I do," he said. "Hold down the fort, fellows," Tommy said as they said good-bye. "I still don't see why we can't go to Vegas and stay with Stevie Turner," Tommy complained as he and Doug walked to the gate.

"I told you, Tommy, I don't want to put him in the line of fire. I don't want him associated with this," Doug told him. "This isn't some vacation, Tommy." That was the last thing Danny and Dominic could hear before they were gone into the night.

"And you didn't have to fight at all against Jerry Lissoni?" Danny asked Dominic as they walked back to the house.

"No, it was all Tommy," Dominic answered. "I'm kind of hoping this all goes down that same way."

"It is nice to think we can go about our day-to-day activities and not go on the lam too," Danny said. "But even after Bruno, there's going to be Sal Braga. I don't see how we can't be involved at some point."

"Well, we could just hope or we could start getting our own apartments around town and be prepared if we do go on the lam," Dominic said.

"You're right," Danny agreed.

"Six, five, four," the countdown to the ball dropping continued. "Three, two, one!"

The men at Cooch's Corner embraced each other and sang. Paulie Bankjob gave Jackie Beans a hug and an envelope. "What's this?" Jackie asked.

"I missed the Christmas party. I was at my daughter's. This is for Christmas," Paulie answered.

Jackie thumbed through the envelope—$500.

"I know it's not much, but I don't really have much going yet," Paulie told him.

Jackie handed him back the envelope. "Take this back and go see Angelo."

Paulie did as he was told and joined Angelo, who finally had a minute to respond. Angelo's wife was furious with him for not being with her at the Amicuccis, but he still chose to spend New Year's Eve with his men, just as the crime family's five other captains did.

"What's this?" he asked as he looked at the envelope.

"For Christmas," Paulie said.

Angelo didn't even open it. "No, you've been locked up too long. Under my uncle's reign, we don't take on Christmas, we give. I brought this for you, since you missed my Christmas party. Welcome to being a made man," Angelo said as he pulled out the envelope he brought for Paulie.

Paulie looked inside and just saw hundred-dollar bill after hundred-dollar bill.

"Come here," Angelo said, wanting Paulie to lean in so he could whisper in his ear. "It's five grand. Yours is a little more than the others. A little congrats from us. Don't tell them, understand?"

Paulie said he wouldn't, and Angelo ensured he spoke with all his men that came to the bar. Fat Kenny, of course, was there, also because he had to. The crew's four made men were there—Jackie Beans, Scary Scarelli, Carlo DeMini, and obviously, Pauli Bankjob. Vince Cusamano was there for his last day; he was starting the New Year off in his soon-to-be father-in-law and lieutenant, Vinny Caselli's crew.

Gary Nussman from the bakery, Genie Evola, the crew's odds expert, Frankie Neri, and the three Gurino cousins, Nick, Bruno, and Michael, rounded out the crew that came to say so long to 2011.

Doug's bar, the Four Seasons, was packed, and Sal Amicucci came down and helped with the bar after the restaurant was closed upstairs.

It was a different atmosphere at Dave Worowski's bar in Henderson. The Westsiders that assembled at Goliath's weren't celebrating New Year's Eve; they passed out weapons and ammo. He closed the bar, missing the big sales of the holiday, and used the night to relay his orders to his men.

Dave was going underground; his crew wouldn't be in touch with him, only Matt Young would be. Dave would be the liaison to Doug and Tommy and would surface just to meet with them and Matt only. Dave told them that with everyone out of reach for any shooters from New York, they'd be coming this way and ordered them to stay armed and watch for everything.

Dave also took over control of the zips; Billy was now out of contact until Tommy Herrick returned. Dave also waited to hear the outcome of the meeting in New York. He knew the situation, that it was not guaranteed that the other crews in the Grazzitti Family would be happy about Bruno Bini being taken out by violence and would retaliate against the Westside. He knew that it could be nothing or it could be war.

"Another step, Grandma," Valentina said as she helped Helen Amicucci down the stairs. Helen had taken a nap upstairs and missed the ball dropping.

"Why did you let me sleep that long?" she asked her granddaughter irritably. "And why do you have such a god-awful bed like that in your guest room?"

"That's not a guest room. That's Dominic's room that my parents don't change," Valentina complained as they neared the bottom step.

"Just like we don't change yours," Helena reminded her daughter. Most of the family was gathered at the bottom of the stairs. Nick's brother, Daniel, was leaving, and he was driving his mother home, which wasn't far from his, and everyone wanted to say good-bye to her.

"I moved out three years ago. Dominic got married in 1995, for crying out loud," Valentina told her mother.

Vito Paganini rubbed his forehead in exasperation. "I've tried. I've tried so hard here with you, Bruno. No more nothing, I'm done. Step down and be my underboss. This is the last time I'm going to say it," Vito said.

"I don't take orders from captains. ***I'm*** not going to say it again," Bruno Bini told him.

"Then we're done here," Vito said, getting up from the table.

Bruno got up and followed Vito to the door; he wanted to get home to his family. Much to Bruno's irritation, Vito stopped in the doorway to light a cigarette before he continued on; that was the signal.

All Vito heard was a thud and then the sound of Bruno Bini's body hitting the ground. He turned around to see Bruno lying on his back with a bullet directly between his eyes. His head lay in a puddle of blood that was quickly expanding.

Vito took a drag from his cigarette, calmly got in the front seat of the car driven by his right-hand man, Nino Valenti, and sped away as the other members of the Grazzitti Family that were present ran for cover, not knowing what was going on.

The party at the Amicucci's was winding down, at least it was for most people. "Uncle Ziggy, don't you think you've had enough?" Marie Rea asked as she and Helena were cleaning up.

Ziggy flew in from Florida to spend his first Christmas without his eldest son, Charley, who died in January from cancer. "I'll decide when I've had enough," Ziggy hissed at his niece.

"Don't worry. I'll take him home," Jimmy said of his grandfather. Ziggy's wife had already gone home with Charley's wife, Lonna, and the rest of their kids. Jimmy stayed behind to be with his grandfather.

"Where'd that girl go that you brought?" Ziggy asked Jimmy.

"She left," Jimmy answered simply.

"Jimmy, how many girls do you got going?" Danny asked as he and Dominic continued drinking with Ziggy. "I never see the same one twice."

Jimmy smiled and said, "As many as I can."

"That a boy," Ziggy said, messing up Jimmy's hair by rubbing his head.

Dominic's phone rang; it was Vito. Dominic's eyes met Danny's as it rang; both still waited for the call. "Happy New Year to you to, Vito," Dominic said and ended the call. If Bruno was dead, Vito was to call and wish Dominic a Happy New Year.

"Okay, I'm heading home," Danny said. He grabbed his wife, Bianca, and said good-bye to his daughter, Sabrina, and her husband, George; they were staying there with Valentina.

Dominic walked with Danny to the backyard to talk as Danny waited for Bianca. "I think we're fine," Danny told Dominic. "How could anyone argue with whacking Bruno?" Danny asked.

"It's different there in New York. You never know which way the wind's going to blow," Dominic said. "I'm keeping a bag in my truck in case I'm taking off, if this gets ugly."

"I'm not worried about now. I'm worried about when Vinny Braga dies. You could feel the tension between Doug and Sal on the plane. We're going to get drawn in on that one," Danny said. "What happens if Doug can't win a war against a New York Family, which, let's be realistic here, he probably can't? We don't even know if we can win even if us and the Westside put everything we got into it," Danny fretted.

"You didn't see Tommy when he was at war with Jerry Lissoni. He was nuts. The day he was shot at on the road and he was in a high pursuit car chase with bullets flying, I thought he was going to shoot me when I saw him. I never saw anyone so mad, and you know my father," Dominic explained.

"So he blows up a house with an RPG. I still can't get on board with that one," Danny said.

"It kept us in power, didn't it, Danny? If Jerry Lissoni beat Tommy, I was next. I'd be dead right now, so I'm not going to complain. Without Doug and Tommy, I'd have been dead right after you guys went to jail, so do I think they can win? I think they have to because if they lose, Sal Braga's going to hold you and me accountable, more than likely with a death sentence," Dominic said. "I'm very content to sit back and let them fight this for us. They're very good at it. If someone comes after us, then we fight."

"I hope you're right," Danny said as Bianca headed their way.

"The alternative is to give Miami to the DeCarlos. Tens of millions of dollars a year we make from Miami and North Carolina, so I'd rather not give them up," Dominic said.

Danny shrugged. "Well, I know I'm not telling Doug to give Miami to Sal Braga."

"Who knows, maybe they got drunk and flew off to Las Vegas," Grace said as she and Val backed out of her garage. Neither of their husbands had come home the night before and both their phones were going to voice mail. "There're two FBI cars sitting in front of my house. I hate this crap," Grace complained as Val stopped her van. The two were going shopping, looking for New Year's Day sales.

"Grace, why is he getting out?" Val asked as both women were peering through the windows. "That doesn't look like any FBI agent I ever saw."

"Well, at least I know I'm not the one he's going to want to rape," Grace joked.

"He is kind of cute," Val said. "Oh shit, that's Matt Young."

Grace looked at Val. "Real nice, Val," she joked as she turned back to roll down the window. "Doug's not here, Matt. I don't know where he is," she told him.

"Actually, ladies," Matt said as he approached her window, "I've a message from both your husbands."

"Oh no," Val gasped.

"They're away. They're fine, but they'll be out of communication for a while. It's better for them if you don't know where they are," Matt explained.

"I could give birth tomorrow," Grace told him. "This really is unacceptable," she said as her voice cracked and she tried to hold back her tears.

"Grace, I'm sorry. You know, there's nothing I can do about it," Matt said. He pointed to the cars. "That's Sam. He's going to sit there until Doug comes home. If you need anything, just holler for him. Other than that, he'll stay out of your way. Val, there's a car at your house right now. His name is Scott. He's there if you need anything."

"And are they going to follow us when we leave?" Val asked.

"Yes, they are," Matt answered.

"Aren't wives supposed to be safe?" Grace asked.

"Of course, but you never know what evil people can really do. Why not just be safe? And some regrets are just unlivable, so please understand it that way," Matt told them. "This is my number. I am at your beck and call," Matt said as he handed them his number.

Both women knew they were powerless; they couldn't even call their husbands to yell at them. They understood that Matt Young was just following orders, and they knew how their husbands handled men who didn't complete their orders.

"Well, we're still going shopping," Grace said defiantly.

Matt smiled. "And you're welcome to go. You can even have Sam carry your bags."

"Well, that's better than Tommy," Val joked.

Matt started to walk away but turned back. "Oh, and Grace, the minute you feel like the baby's coming, call me. Doug *will* be there."

Doug and Tommy had made their hideout in one of Doug's four cabins that he had built on his sixty acres in Traverse City; the troubles of the world four hours away were no longer theirs. They shared a couple of bottles of Jim Beam while watching the Rose Bowl. They figured there was nothing they could do, so to them it was spring break.

Reality set when the phone rang; that could only be Dave Worowski, Matt Young, Danny, or Dominic. They were the only ones with the number. It was Dominic.

"I talked to Nino Valenti," he told Doug. "He said the feds picked up Vito to question him about Bruno's murder, probably be out in a few hours. The place is hot right now, Nino said. No one's talking to anyone yet. Feds are everywhere. It could be a week, maybe longer, before the captains can get together."

"Uh-huh," Doug said.

"You all right?" Dominic asked him.

"Everything all right there?" Doug slurred.

"What?"

"I got to go," Doug said and hung up to pour the next shot.

"So what's up?" Tommy asked him.

"Vito got picked up for questioning," Doug said nonchalantly.

After a moment of silence, both came to the same realization, but Tommy asked it first. "What happens if Vito goes to jail? We never considered that."

"I imagine all bets are off, and I think we might be very fucked fighting two New York families," Doug answered as he downed his shot.

Edwards Brothers, Inc.
Thorofare, NJ USA
February 2, 2012